GRAVEL ROAD

DEDICATION

M...Never forget where you come from.

GRAVEL ROAD

STEPHIE WALLS

Edited by JOSIE CRUZ EDITS
Edited by JUDY'S PROOFREADING
Cover by WICKED BY DESIGN
Photography by TODD THORP
Cover Model STEVE KALFMAN

PROLOGUE

MIRANDA

The screen door slammed behind me. Over the years, I'd grown so used to the rattling when it would bounce off the frame and settle shut that I didn't notice the footsteps approaching in the kitchen. It was an old farmhouse, and I'd long since learned to ignore the creaks and pops. As a little girl, the noises kept me up, and I had always been convinced someone lurked in the house, roaming the halls late at night.

I ducked my head into the fridge to search for orange juice. When I realized I had company, I stood, stepped back with the carton in my hand, and came face to face with my sister's scowl. Then I noticed her tapping foot. I cracked open the container, brought it to my lips—it drove her insane—and drank more than I actually wanted, simply to irritate her. I flashed my brows at her, the citrus burning my throat. And when I finally plopped it on the counter, I let out a satisfied sigh, followed by an obnoxious burp.

Sarah crossed her arms over her chest and jutted her hip out to show her disapproval. "It's amazing you have any friends at all with manners like those." We had this fight frequently, and I didn't care any more now than I had the other hundred times the topic had come up.

I shrugged, closed the OJ carton, and placed it in the fridge, in that order, hoping she'd be gone when I turned back. No such luck. Clearly, she had something on her mind; I had no idea why she didn't spit it out. We could fight about it, and then I could go on with my day. My elbows met the counter on the island between us. Had Sarah not been glaring holes in my head with her beady, blue eyes, I might have laid my entire body across the tiled top. Even at ten in the morning, the Texas sun was brutal. Leaning toward her with a grin on my face did the trick. I squeezed my breasts together with my arms for good measure— another bone of contention between the Adams girls. She was flat as a flitter.

"I got a call from your coach this morning."

Crap.

I stood, squared my shoulders, and prepared for battle. This wasn't going to go well. "Isn't that a violation of some sort of privacy law?" There had to be rules against the school sharing student information with siblings. I thought for sure they could only talk to legal guardians or parents, and my sister wasn't either one of those...regardless of what she believed her role in my life to be.

"She said you didn't show up for camp yesterday. Which is odd, since you left the house with your bag, and I specifically remember you telling me that was where you were going *and* why you wouldn't be home last night." Her nostrils flared and her cheeks flushed. The vein on her temple started to throb, and *that* was the point I was certain I was in deep.

I waved her off, hoping to defuse the situation before it reached DEFCON five. A level two or even a three I could defend, but much above that and she'd bring my daddy in—and neither of us wanted that. "It's not a big deal, Sarah."

"It's a huge deal. You made a commitment to those girls." Sarah dropped her hands and closed her fingers into tight fists at her sides. If spit started to fly out of her mouth, I was leaving. "Do you have any idea how bad it looks for the captain of the squad not to show up?"

"Previous captain." Jenna Jackson had assumed my role upon graduation. "And it's cheerleading, not the Nobel Peace Prize. There are tons of other seniors there to help." I held her gaze and refused to back down, while secretly praying her breathing didn't become any more erratic. The more her chest heaved, the greater the trouble I was in. "I'm going next week. Chill out." I dared to round the corner of the island, thinking I'd be able to shuffle by her and escape to my room. I couldn't be that lucky.

She wrapped her fingers around my bicep, and I wished I'd worn something with sleeves. The tank top I had on did nothing to ward off her claws digging into my skin. "Where *were* you?" It had to be a hundred degrees outside, yet the coolness in her tone sent chills up my spine, and goose bumps erupted across my body.

Yanking my arm from her grasp, I debated whether to lie or tell the truth. I was beyond being able to get out of this without repercussion. Now I needed to lessen the punishment...not that I'd adhere to her rules, anyhow. "The lake."

Her chest rose with the deep breath she took, and the beat in the vein on the side of her head hadn't slowed. Then she released the air along with a whistle. "All night?"

"No. There was a field party at Twin Creeks." One of the largest farms in town also happened to be owned by my boyfriend —or rather, his parents.

Sarah's shoulders relaxed, and she regained her normal color. "You were with Austin?"

That boy could do no wrong in my sister's mind. She turned a blind eye to the fact that he'd taken my virginity and had often snuck out with me in the middle of the night. The Burins were well-known and equally as beloved. Truth be told, Sarah had always had a thing for Austin's older brother, Charlie. Her desire for one Burin brother made the other angelic by default.

I fought against huffing out my irritation. "He was there. Along with two hundred of his closest friends." Sarcasm dripped from my voice. I could win points by telling her what she was dying to find out, but I had a stubborn streak a mile wide. *And* I doubted she wanted to hear that Charlie spent the evening sucking face with Sissy Tomlin.

Her lips pursed and then flattened into a straight line. "Was Charlie there?" My sister was mean as a snake when it came to dealing with me; Charlie Burin, however, melted her heart. He also didn't have a clue she existed. They'd gone to school together for twelve years, she'd headed up every social committee in Mason Belle, and we'd eaten Sunday supper with their family more times than I could count, yet he still managed to forget her name more often than he remembered it.

"Yes."

"You know he and Daddy are working on an irrigation project, right?"

I did. I just didn't care. The inner workings of a cattle farm didn't appeal to me. I did what Daddy required me to, nothing more, nothing less. Chores weren't my idea of a good time, and I loathed manual labor. I didn't mind tending to the horses his hands used to traipse all over the property, so they'd become my responsibility years ago. I was oblivious to everything else. Not even the hot guys drew my attention once they left the barn.

"So?"

"Did he mention it?" This was her way of circling a donkey's butt to get to its tail, and I didn't like the smell of crap.

"I didn't talk to him."

Sarah's eye twitched, and her nostrils flared; gone were the daydreams of Charlie. "Well, if you weren't talking to the Burins about the farm, then I can't imagine what kept you out all night." As if that even made sense.

This was precisely why Charlie didn't have a clue who she was. If she believed irrigation systems were appropriate topics for parties, she'd likely never been to one. And if her idea of socializing included mention of watering fields, it was no wonder she remained single.

She arched a perfectly sculpted brow and waited. I wondered if she could touch her hairline with them. "Your reputation is already questionable. Pulling these kinds of stunts only cements what people in town think of you."

My expression hardened, and it was my turn to cross my arms. "No one in Mason Belle gives a flip what I do. And last time I checked, you weren't my mama." I made no attempt to hide my anger, and my tone conveyed every ounce of my contempt.

Her jaw dropped like I'd slapped her and the sting of my palm pained her cheek. "I'm the closest thing you've got, and I'm ashamed of who you're becoming. This is not how you were raised."

That wasn't anything I hadn't heard from her before. The first time she had said it, it hurt. The second time, I lashed out. Then it became boring, and it no longer bothered me. Sarah hadn't asked for this role. She'd been forced into a quasi-motherly position when my own mom skipped town, leaving us alone with Daddy. He did the best he could; although, no matter how hard my sister tried, she'd never be Mama.

I ground my teeth together, biting back the words I wanted to hurl her direction. Sarah loved riding her high horse, but one day, someone would knock her right out of the saddle, and that fall would be painful.

"Are we done?"

"Not quite."

I'd neared the point of stomping my feet, regardless of the fact that it wouldn't accomplish anything. It didn't matter that I was eighteen. Even young adults were capable of full-blown temper tantrums.

"You're grounded. You can go to cheer camp. That's it. There's plenty to do around here."

My mouth hung open in shock as my sister folded her hands together in the prim-princess fashion she used to quietly claim victory. A demure, pageant smile tugged at her closed lips, and she blinked slowly, her pale-blue eyes cold and unfeeling.

"For how long?" I squawked.

With her fingers laced together and her elbows locked, she gave me a hint of a shrug. "Two weeks should make my point." A shimmer of amusement danced across her expression. And people believed she was the perfect sister.

What a load of crap.

No way. This was the summer after my senior year. Austin planned to pick me up after lunch. Legally, I was an adult. Sarah had no right—or jurisdiction, as far as I was concerned—to lecture me, much less punish me.

"Not happening." I grunted and moved around her.

My weight had shifted to the first step when she called out, "Don't test me on this, Miranda. I've already talked to Daddy." Of course she had.

"Whatever." I huffed and stomped to the second floor, making certain she—and whoever else might be near the house—heard every one of my objections. And just in case they hadn't, I slammed my bedroom door to ensure they did.

The next couple of hours, I threw things around my room in protest. And when I couldn't stand the forced captivity, I sought to make my overbearing sister's life miserable around the house. It was childish to huff and blow, and glaring at Sarah only served to further agitate me, not her. The minutes ticked by like hours, and staring at a clock didn't help pass the time.

Sarah *thought* she had the upper hand. She believed she'd won the war, although it was just an insignificant battle. I refused to *ever* wave a white flag. If she wanted to act like my mama, then she could deal with the repercussions of what would have been a teenage pregnancy, if indeed, she had given birth to me. Defiance wasn't my middle name, but now, I considered having it tattooed on my right butt cheek in her honor.

I had once again retreated to my bedroom after my antics to irritate my sister accomplished nothing. With the window open in my room, I'd created a sauna. It only added to the discomfort of living under my sister's thumb, even though it served a purpose. The second I heard it, I glanced at the clock. He was right on time. Austin's dually had an unmistakable sound of grit and brawn, much like Austin himself. It was as identifiable as a Harley or a Mustang...to anyone other than my naïve sibling who was about to be blindsided by the cavalry.

I jerked myself off the mattress, ignoring how it stuck to my sweaty back and arms, and I raced to slide my toes into my flip-flops. No sooner had I slung the door open than my sister stepped through hers ten feet down the hall. It wasn't much of a head start. My long, dark hair fanned as I twirled toward the stairs. It would only take seconds for Sarah to realize I was on the move. If she caught hold of my arm, she'd sink my battleship—fight lost, war over.

The throbbing in my chest only increased with each step I took, while a trickle of sweat ran down my spine, and despite the discomfort of attempting an escape, the satisfaction of defiance outweighed the side effects. This was one game I planned to win. I was younger. I was faster. And I wanted to leave more than Sarah wanted to stop me.

"Miranda." It was a warning—one I didn't heed.

Tennis shoes would have made for an easier escape. Neverthe-less, I had committed to a plan, and I would see it through. Once I got outside, my timing had to be perfect. Too early, and I'd have to wait for Austin to pull up before I could jump in the cab of his truck; too late, and he'd have to wait. Either would provide precious time for my sister to intervene. To be successful, my feet would need to be moving when the truck rounded the gravel circle in front of the house, so he would only have to slow down to allow Charity to help me inside.

The warnings got louder the closer my sister got. "Get back here, young lady." She had gained ground, although I didn't waste time looking over my shoulder to see how much.

Freedom dangled in front of me, only seconds away. I ripped the front door open as she hit the foyer. Two strides across the porch and I leaped from the top to the driveway as Austin's diesel engine revved. Our friends roared to life when they realized I was on the run, and I prayed Austin didn't slow down. Charity hung over the front seat toward the dash to pull on the handle; this wasn't the first time we'd executed this maneuver. The passenger-side door swung open under its own weight, and my empty spot—next to Austin—waited.

With the grace of a gazelle, I leaped into the truck. "Go. Go. Go," I yelled and waved my hand.

Austin picked up speed through the left curve, and the door closed with the motion of the vehicle. He hollered with excitement like I'd just survived the meanest bull in the rodeo for a full eight seconds. I twisted to face the house and leaned half my body out the open window, laughing. My hair whirled around my cheeks and neck with the wind at my back. Even through the strands obstructing my view, I didn't miss my sister's rant on the porch. I couldn't hear her over the truck and the people in it, but I could, however, see the fire I'd lit inside her. The fuse had been ignited, and that raging inferno was about to blow.

Thank God I wouldn't be around to witness the explosion.

I righted myself in the seat, ran my fingers through my long hair to get it out of my face, and bent across the cab to kiss Austin on the cheek. In an instant, he snaked his right arm around my lower back. Our lips met in an electric, yet brief, exchange. When he broke away to focus on the road, my gaze lingered on his profile. Austin had been the boy every girl wanted, just like his brother seven years earlier. Only *this* sister had caught *this* brother's attention early, and we'd been together since the start of our freshman year. He'd never had eyes for anyone other than me, and there wasn't another guy in Mason Belle who even piqued my interest.

It wasn't his chiseled jaw or his sandy-blond hair. It wasn't even the taut muscles or his year-round tan. Those were all bonuses. Sprinkles on top of the icing. Austin Burin was a gentle soul with the heart of a lion. And he was fiercely protective—of me. There wasn't anything that boy wouldn't do to ensure my happiness, and his parents adored me. No one within a hundred-mile radius believed there were two people more perfectly created for each other, regardless of my sister's speculations and insinuations over my reputation.

Austin pulled me close on the bench seat, and our friends clucked like chickens in the back. Half of us had been grounded for the stunt we'd pulled last night, not coming home. The other half had managed to avoid getting caught. I reached for the knob on the stereo, turning it up as loud as I could without blowing the speakers.

Country music blared through the cab and out the windows. The bass vibrated the seat, and the sound moved through me. We drove toward the lake I'd grown up swimming in, and I thought of my sister shaking her fist on the front steps of the house. Her expression was priceless and worth whatever punishment waited for me when I returned. Sarah Adams needed a hobby other than torturing me. Not that I could deny that tormenting her brought me a level of satisfaction that nothing else rivaled. Despite Sarah's attempt to calm my wild streak and end my fun, life was pretty close to perfect.

The zing of adrenaline had begun to subside by the time Austin brought his truck to a stop. He hadn't even cut the ignition, and our friends piled out of the bed in the back. A cloud of dust rose under the weight of their feet, and I coughed as it reached the open window. The same cloud followed the group on their way to the water, and we were left alone.

The music died when Austin removed the keys from the switch, yet he didn't make a move to get out. His calloused fingers caressed my jaw, and his thumb swept across my cheek. I became putty under his touch and the gentle gaze of his sweet, brown eyes. My breath hitched, and my heart skipped a beat just having his undivided attention.

"You sure you're not puttin' the final nail in your coffin?" His concern was endearing—as was his Southern drawl—even if it were misplaced.

I grabbed both of his cheeks and firmly planted my lips on his with a loud smack. I took what I wanted and gave him what he needed. Austin was confident in all areas of life, including the size of my daddy's gun collection. He'd move heaven and earth to please me, unless it meant crossing my father. I appreciated the respect Austin had for him, but this wasn't about Daddy; it was all Sarah.

I patted his cheek, the prickle of his unshaven face tickling my palms. "Sarah isn't my father. Don't worry so much."

"She looked pretty ticked." So did a rooster; it didn't mean I'd let him affect my day.

"And she wonders why Charlie isn't interested."

His forearm flexed when he reached for the handle, and heat rushed to my core. There was something about the strength in those lean lines that drove me to the edge of sexual fantasy. "Most girls would feel sorry for their sister," Austin spoke as he hopped down.

I waited for him to face me, knowing he'd extend his hand. I took it and scooted past the steering wheel. Then, instead of jumping down with his help, I spun my finger in a circle. Without hesitation, he presented me his back. I draped my arms over his shoulders and around his neck. When I secured my legs at his waist, my thighs clenched until I was confident he had balanced my weight. He shifted away from the truck and bumped the door closed with his foot.

The staggering heat was made exponentially worse by my insisting on a piggyback ride like a monkey. I loved being close to him, and Austin didn't complain. Even if he hadn't come wrapped up in a gorgeous package of Southern charm and virility, his scent alone would have claimed my virtue. My nose touched the skin below his ear, and I inhaled deeply. Only one other smell in the world carried a multitude of memories like this one did, and that was my mama's. Although at this point, I had far more memories with Austin than I did with her.

Austin's scent surrounded me with security like a blanket on a cold night. It might have been creepy to anyone else, but he knew how I felt, and he let me do it. I'd cried on his shoulder more times than I could count since we were kids, and through the years, he'd become as vital as an organ or a limb. Austin carried the key to the vault that housed all my secrets. Most guys our age would leverage that kind of power. My boyfriend coveted it, held it in the highest esteem. And regardless of the piss and vinegar I poured on Sarah, he recognized my defiance as pain that seeped through the cracks of a broken childhood. He had assumed the role of knight in my life the day my mama walked out. In a handful of words, he'd committed to me on my tenth birthday. I'd thought then that it was the worst day of my life. I realized now that it had been the best. Without one, the other wouldn't have happened.

"You two coming?" Charity bounced in the water and eagerly waved at us to join the group.

People were everywhere, primarily seniors who'd recently graduated and the juniors who would fill our spots in the fall. Football players, cheerleaders, the 4-H club members, it didn't matter—they were all here. This was a rite of passage in Mason Belle, Texas. It was the only time of the year when social status didn't exist.

By the time Austin set me down, my friends had waded into the water, and I couldn't tell who was who. We'd find them all before the sun went down. As it stood, the only thing on my mind was stripping off my tank top and shimmying out of my cutoff jean shorts.

I loved this spot. With nothing other than water and forest as far as the eye could see, it had been the place where I'd sought comfort for years. Lush-green trees surrounded the lake, and the color reflected off the water's surface. It gave the illusion of swimming inside an emerald and being drenched in jewels.

My cheeks flamed under the already sweltering day as a catcall pierced my ears from behind. I stood and stepped out of my shorts, leaving them on the ground with my shirt and flip-flops. Large, calloused hands gripped my hips, and warm lips teased the sweet spot on my shoulder. The moment Austin's teeth sank into my flesh, my knees buckled, and I forced myself to put distance between us. My cheeks ached from the smile I wore in his presence, and as soon as I spun around, my heart swelled.

"You need to quit." The weakness in which I uttered that statement left me wondering if it were a plea or a command. I was well aware that an audience wouldn't deter him.

As he took a step toward me, I took one back. Any second he'd lunge, and if I weren't prepared to take off, he'd tickle me until I peed on myself. "And if I don't?" His legs were longer than mine and closed the distance quicker.

I held up my hands, already giggling, and he hadn't so much as laid a finger on me. "I'll get Brock up here to teach you a lesson."

Austin's head fell back. His Adam's apple bobbed in his thick throat, and the muscles tightened in his abdomen, creating a six-pack that Budweiser could market. The only sweeter sound than his laughter was his voice—mellow and rich, deep and Southern. "Sweetheart, even if Brock wanted to save you, he doesn't stand a chance."

I narrowed my gaze, failing miserably at acting irritated. Austin's eyes glittered with amusement and crinkled at the sides with tiny crow's feet. With a hitched hip and attitude in spades, I lifted my free hand to wave a finger in my boyfriend's direction. Had I not been paying attention, I would have missed the quick twitch in his glance. Noticing it, however, did not prepare me for what it meant or the arms that seized my waist. Gathered up like a bale of hay, I was tossed onto a shoulder almost as broad as Austin's.

"What don't I stand a chance at?" Brock's deep baritone vibrated his entire body, jostling me.

While I struggled to get down, Austin ignored my plea for help. "Randi thinks you'll save her."

I tried to lean around his side for my words to reach Austin. "He would!" They ended up muffled by a wall of muscle.

"Hate to tell you, Randi, Austin claimed your ass long before the rest of us knew there was anything to try to mark as our own. Your fate was written in the stars years ago." A large hand came down on my butt, which remained high in the air. There was no telling whether the credit belonged to Austin or Brock, and I wasn't certain that I cared to find out. "But rest assured, if it's anyone other than him, I'll be the first to defend your honor."

The world tilted, literally. Brock hadn't put me down when he turned toward the lake. Then there was another set of feet—yucky boy feet I'd recognize anywhere—next to Brock's. Together, the two took off running in the direction of the water. My stomach bounced on Brock's shoulder, and I managed to oomph out several ignored cries for help. It didn't matter how hot it was outside; being thrown into the water would be like having ice dumped over my head. The drastic change in temperature would suck the air right out of my lungs. It was hard enough to breathe through the humidity in June; it was even harder to breathe underwater with no warning.

Dreading what was to come didn't lessen the laughter, on my part or theirs. They'd been doing this kind of thing to me for years. Had it been anyone else, I would have decked them. These two owned my heart—for different reasons—and neither could do anything wrong. I heard the cheers from my classmates, although I couldn't see beyond the muscles in Brock's back. The red dirt and patches of grass whizzed by as my captor ran, still on a path to the lake. One day, they'd get too old for this kind of thing. Today wasn't that day.

His feet slowed when he hit the shore, but not because he planned to stop. Running in water was no different than high-stepping in quicksand. It was laborious and threatened to take him under if his feet didn't land right. Brock grabbed my hips, his fingers closed around my skin, and the moment air crept between my stomach and his shoulder, I took a deep breath. Catapulted through the air, my arms and legs flailed, and the last thing I saw before breaking the surface of the lake was Austin's infectious smile.

Before I kicked my way to fresh air, Austin appeared in front of me, and the two of us swam up together. His face rippled with distortion from the water, yet through the blur, he never took his eyes off mine. Even when he and his friends played around, Austin never left my side. I gasped when we broke the surface. Remnants of the lake washed my cheeks and dripped from my jaw. It was too deep for me to stand, but Austin found his footing and circled his arm around my waist to draw me into the safety of his sculpted chest.

Instinctively, my legs held on to him to keep me from floating away, and I swatted playfully at his bicep. It was an act, one all the girls played with their boyfriends. If he'd treated me like a delicate flower, I would have bailed a long time ago.

He flinched, as if I'd actually put any force behind my punches. "Why are you hitting me?"

"You let your best friend try to kill me." It was a tad melodramatic, and the grin I couldn't erase gave me away.

He shook his head to get the water out of his hair, and I flinched to avoid the spray. "Sweetheart, there is nothing in the world that will ever hurt you as long as I'm alive."

"I love you even if you are a cheeseball." With everything in me, I adored Austin Burin.

I leaned back without waiting for his reply. Floating on my back with my legs secured around his waist, I stared at the sky and the white puffs of marshmallowy clouds that dotted the blue. The water distorted sound in my ears, yet even muffled, it wasn't hard to distinguish happiness. It was, however, difficult to understand the warning that may or may not have been issued before Justin Richert did a cannonball off the dock, landing feet from my head. The waves engulfed me, and I dropped my grip on Austin's waist to keep from drowning.

We had drifted into a depth where I didn't have to tread water, which was the only reason Austin didn't come for me versus going after Justin. "What the hell are you doing, dude?"

Austin's wrist slid through my hold when I tried to grab him. I caught his fingers and tangled mine with his, and a quick squeeze grounded him. There weren't many things in life that Austin fought over, but I'd held the number-one spot since we were kids.

"Austin..." I pleaded.

"I was just messing around, Burin. Calm down. Cheerleader

Barbie didn't drown." He dismissed Austin as quickly as he'd buried me in waves.

Justin wasn't so bad. The self-proclaimed class clown only did things to get a rise out of people. This was no different. He liked to make people smile, but sometimes, he missed the mark.

I wasn't his target, just in the way. "Hey," I cooed, tightening my grip.

By the time he faced me, Austin had cleared whatever expression he'd shown Justin. Before he could say anything, Brock waved Austin over to the group of football players and their girlfriends playing chicken.

Austin arched a brow and coupled it with a smirk that made my lady bits tingle. "You game?"

He was easily distracted, and we were reigning champions. "Of course, I'm game."

"That's my girl." Three sweeter words didn't exist. Austin claiming me held far more power over my heart than "I love you;" although, I liked that second best.

Once we joined the other couples, Austin disappeared under the water in front of me, and I climbed onto his shoulders, lacing my calves under his biceps to secure my feet against his back. He hadn't taken the first step toward engaging in the teenaged battle royal when the grind of metal on metal reverberated across the lake as if it had happened in the middle of it. My ears picked apart the breaking glass, the shriek of skidding tires, horns blaring, and a heavy thud in slow motion. Every kid stopped, and silence hung around us like a thick, black veil.

"What was that?"

"Sounded like an accident."

"Way out here?"

"I hope no one was hurt."

The random voices and offhand comments flittered by me without my brain grasping who said them or what they'd asked.

All I clung to was the absence of noise after so much commotion. Without answers to their questions, people lost interest and meandered back to whatever they had been doing. My attention hadn't wavered from the accident. I couldn't see anything, no matter how hard I tried, but there was only one road out here.

I leaned over, looking at the top of Austin's face upside down, while still perched on his shoulders. "Do you think we should make sure everyone's all right?"

He grinned and tilted his chin, puckering his lips in a silent request for a kiss. I obliged, but it was chaste. "Would that make you feel better?" His voice was smoother than honey on a warm biscuit.

I nodded, and he lowered me down. "I just want to be certain they don't need help. That sounded really bad."

"You've got a heart of gold. Come on."

My sister might disagree. I was headstrong, mouthy, and fool-heartedly carefree. I was also the girl who couldn't stand to see an animal in pain or a homeless person on the street without trying to fix it.

No sooner had we gotten to the shore than sirens rolled across the water in waves. The one fire truck in Mason Belle honked its horn and roared in the distance. I held Austin's hand, clutching it as though I were the one waiting for help to arrive. I couldn't be sure which came next, the ambulance or the police car. I wasn't quite as adept at differentiating their sounds because nothing exciting ever happened in this town. If it weren't for the parades on every major holiday, I wouldn't have recognized the fire truck, either.

I let out a breath I hadn't realized I held. My chest deflated, and my shoulders sank with relief. Simply knowing there was help set my mind at ease.

"You still think we should go?" Austin asked.

We probably wouldn't be able to get anywhere near the

wreck. And I'd be dragging Austin away from our friends for no real reason other than to be nosy. I couldn't offer any assistance or useful skill. So, I shook my head and lifted onto my toes to plant a kiss on his jaw. "Nah, let's stay here."

*A*n hour or so later, after the songs of emergency vehicles had ceased, and the accident wasn't more than a blip of a memory, we'd beaten all the other couples. It wasn't much of an honor, but in Hicksville, USA, Chicken Fighting Champion held clout. I laughed as other girls from the cheerleading squad gave me a hard time over my competitive nature.

"Miranda Adams," the voice bellowed.

With a smile on my face and words still coming from my mouth as I defended our title to Charity and Anna, I angled toward the gruff bark that caused my name to hover like a storm cloud. At the top of the path, just before the ground broke, stood Sheriff Patton. The grim expression he wore pushed me back instead of forward.

"Miranda," he repeated, as though I hadn't heard him the first time. Nobody in this town used my full name unless I was in trouble. "Darlin', I need to speak with you." He put his hands on his hips and lowered his head, his chin nearly touching his chest. I couldn't read his face when we made eye contact. Sheriff Patton shifted his sight to someone else before I identified the emotion he hid. "Austin, son, why don't you bring her up here."

"Yes, sir."

I peeked over my shoulder to see my boyfriend swim toward me. I didn't have a clue what was going on, but I wanted no part of it. "Miranda" and "darlin'" in the same sentence had only happened one other time in my life, and that was when Daddy admitted that my mom had left. When Austin reached my side, I shook my head and refused to go.

"Sweetheart, the sheriff needs to talk to you. I don't think it's open for discussion." He laced his fingers through mine. "Come on. I'll go with you." The wink that typically made me mush did nothing to calm my fear, yet I still allowed him to lead me out of the water.

I twisted, expecting to see life continue behind me, not stunned stares of pity and concern. As we climbed the path, the blue lights on top of his car circling in a dizzying pattern came into view. Nothing he had to say could be good. Cops didn't come out here, ever. And they certainly didn't do so on official business.

Sheriff Patton removed his hat with one hand and put his other on my shoulder. My gaze followed his movement, and my skin broke out in a feverish sweat. Afraid to give the officer my attention, I turned to the person who'd caught me every time I'd ever fallen. Neither of us knew what hurdled in our direction.

But Austin couldn't save me.

The man who'd watched over this town since I was little took a deep breath. "Darlin'"—I was starting to hate that term—"there's been an accident."

1

MIRANDA

SIX YEARS LATER

"*E*ason, are you ready?" I peeked my head around the door to his office, and his slate-grey eyes met mine. My heart warmed at the sight of his panty-dropping grin.

"Packing up now. Did you finish the files on the Martin case?"

I lifted the folder and proceeded across his office to drop the paperwork on his desk. "Everything you asked for is there, including a copy of the will." Real estate law was rarely exciting, but every once in a while, a case went to court, and things got juicy.

As a paralegal, I didn't get to attend many of the actual hearings, although occasionally, I did get to sit in on depositions and mediations. It never ceased to amaze me just how greedy people got after death. Brothers and sisters became mortal enemies, and long-lost relatives appeared out of nowhere—every one of them had their hand out. I'd get tickled when Eason let a case get hung up in probate because his client was an ass. "I wish I could come with you for this one. It's going to be a doozy."

The Martins—all siblings—had squabbled over their parents' estate for the better part of two years. Eason had been the deceased couple's attorney since he'd passed the bar, and out of respect for them, he'd dragged his feet. The entire thing, including Eason's agitation, had provided Garrett, another partner, and me loads of entertainment.

He stood and grabbed his leather messenger bag, slinging it over his head and across his body. Graceful and elegant, Eason was as fluid as a dancer and built like a brick house. From the hard planes of his chest to his squared shoulders and iron jaw, testosterone jumped off him in unavoidable charisma and machismo. I'd only known one other man in my life who held the attention of a room without realizing it; thankfully, that was where their similarities ended. A chill ran up my spine when Austin crossed my mind. It didn't happen often—primarily because I refused to let it, not because my brain didn't still try to linger in those memories daily—but when it did, I fought hard to shake it off.

Eason stepped in front of me and quirked his head. His perfectly styled hair had seen better days. He'd apparently had his hands in it more times than he should have. "Everything okay, Miranda?"

I forced a smile in his direction and nodded quickly. He hadn't bought it—not that I believed he would.

"It's a good thing you aren't under oath. You can't lie for shit." His chuckle echoed around us. It was hearty and warm like homemade chicken and dumplings, and it filled the soul the same way.

A shrug was all I could offer. "Last time I checked, you hadn't sworn me in, so I'm not worried about being found in contempt."

"Touché."

Without further discussion, Eason offered his elbow, which I took. Other people continued to work in the office as we left for the evening. Each one we passed extended goodbyes, and I couldn't stop the nostalgia. One tiny memory escaped from the box in my mind, and then dozens followed. Eventually, I'd capture them all and push them back into their tidy hiding place. There'd been another time in my life where I had held that coveted position in a man's life, when everyone knew my name, and I was loved by them, as well. And like Austin, Eason rewarded every person who took the time to talk to him with his attention...and me on his arm. It was a large firm, we were both well-respected, and I loved it here almost as much as I'd loved Mason Belle.

When the elevator closed in front of us, Eason turned, and I dropped my hold on him. "You want to talk about it?" He clasped his hands in front of him.

"Nothing to talk about." It would be a long ride down twenty-one floors and an even longer cab ride home.

He smirked and chuckled under his breath. "Don't forget, I remember the girl who showed up in New York in cutoff jean shorts, a tight tank top, and cowboy boots. Don't get me started on that ugly baseball hat. You thought you'd keep your secrets then, too."

The lawyer in Eason never really slept. That side of him was always present, and this silence that now lingered between us as he waited for me to respond was part of his game. Witnesses always caved.

"I'll wear you down, so you might as well tell me now and save us both the time," he gloated.

I groaned, thinking back to how out of place I'd been in a city where anything goes. There had been no plan when I'd arrived at the bus station in Laredo. All I'd had was a suitcase and a wad of cash in my bank account that my memaw had left me when she'd died. My eyes had been puffy from crying—*that* I distinctly remember—when I'd stared at the board and chosen my destination. I'd needed something different, a place where no one knew my name or my past. New York City had seemed to be perfect, and it had been across the country.

"If you love me at all, you'll never speak of that again," I deadpanned.

The elevator shook with his roaring, thunderous laugh. It was as infectious as the man beside me. I caught my reflection in the mirrored walls and took note of how different I'd become. The small-town girl without a care in the world hadn't made the trip across the country. And once I'd hooked up with Eason, who had just started at the firm we both worked at now, he'd helped me erase any remaining, outward sign of her as well.

"Aww." He smothered my face in his dress shirt, smooshing my cheek and mouth into a contorted mess, and I hoped I got makeup all over the starched cotton. "You were adorably clueless."

He'd caught me in a hug that I hadn't reciprocated, and my arms remained trapped against my sides in the awkward embrace. "Uh-huh." My muffled words were lost in his pecs, and I refused to inhale the scent of his intoxicating cologne. All my senses would be lost with one sniff, and I had a grudge to hold. "You just liked having a project."

My body expanded like a bag of smashed marshmallows when he let me breathe. He rubbed life back into the arms he'd put to sleep by cutting off their blood flow. His fingers massaged my biceps and then my shoulders before he held them firmly and leaned me back. His stone-colored eyes were now a warm grey that I only saw when he was thoroughly amused. It figured it would be at my expense. "I wouldn't have called you a project, per se. More like a work in progress. You'd started the transformation before you ever rang my bell."

Thankfully, when he had answered all those years ago, he'd maintained his poker face. I didn't have a clue how badly I stuck out.

"You were so cute with your braids and that rockin' little body—"

"Did you just use the word *rockin'*?"

He wiggled my shoulders from side to side, trying to loosen me up. "You could tilt a blind man's world with that ass. And don't get me started on your legs."

I refrained from rolling my eyes where he could see me, and instead, I closed my lids and blew a puff of air through my pursed lips. Eason appreciated the curves of the female form, although he wasn't normally so blatant about it. The ding of the elevator's arrival on the ground floor distracted us from the topic at hand. As soon as the doors parted, the downpour outside echoed in the deserted lobby.

I used to love the rain. I'd spent hours on the porch of our farmhouse in a rocking chair talking to Memaw before she had died, and then later, Daddy had taken her place. When lightning flashed across the horizon, I could have sworn I saw that girl and her grandmother sitting on a bench just across the street. I jumped when the thunder crashed, and the vision disappeared with the light. It was official; I'd lost my mind. Lack of sleep and too much caffeine had rendered me mental, and I'd begun to hallucinate.

The hand that settled on my lower back startled me. A gesture that usually calmed me now sent my heart into my throat. There, the erratic beat strummed an uncomfortable pulse until I finally swallowed past it.

"You're awfully tense. What has you so on edge?"

We were back to that. I had to find a way to distract him. Continuing to act like a loon wouldn't get it. Eason had an uncanny ability to sniff out lies like a coonhound did prey. Fabricating excuses would only intensify his hunt. A distraction was the only thing that would suffice. "I'm starving. Want to get something to eat before we go home?"

He glanced at the Rolex that adorned his wrist. It had been a gift from his parents when he had passed the bar. Eason McNabb came from a long line of money—old money, as we liked to refer to it in the South—not that anyone would know it from talking to him. "Yeah, it's late. I don't feel like cooking an elaborate meal once we get home."

I couldn't keep a straight face. "An elaborate meal, huh? Is that what you call beans and weenies now?" Eason had nearly burned down our apartment more than once when we'd first met. We'd phoned the fire department so many times, we became friends with the firefighters and often had drinks with them on the weekend.

Standing beside the exit with amusement glittering his irises, he pushed the handle on the glass, and I slipped by him. The awning that ran the length of the building kept me from getting soaked. Eason joined me, huddled under the little bit of protection we had from the wind and rain. "Ramen noodles are a delicacy in many Asian countries."

We watched the street for an oncoming cab. "Name *one*," I said.

Eason saved himself from embarrassment by darting into the rain to hail a taxi. Like a gentleman, he held the car door open. By the time I reached the inside of the cab, I was drenched. Eason's hair lay plastered to his head, and his shirt clung to his sculpted chest when he slid in, closing the door behind him.

"You look like a drowned rat," I teased.

The side of his mouth tilted in a charming grin. "Is that a synonym for devastatingly handsome?" He shook his head to rid the locks of the water dripping onto his face, sending a spray in a circle around him.

Every guy did it. I'd seen it a thousand times growing up. It wasn't a gesture unique to Austin, but memories had gotten ahold of my heart, and every minute detail of the present morphed into my past.

"Something like that." I gave my attention to the cabbie, who had started the fare when he'd stopped the car. I could practically hear the ting of a cash register as each minute ratcheted up the price while Eason and I exchanged jabs. "Pho's on Eighty-Third, please." It was my favorite restaurant in the city.

The driver acknowledged me through the rearview mirror,

although he never turned around. Eason held out a handkerchief —my daddy would have called it a hanky—and I took it. I wasn't sure how it had stayed dry while he appeared soaked to the bone, but I wouldn't look a gift horse in the mouth. After blotting my face—hopefully, without ruining my makeup—I scrubbed my hair with it like a towel. Once I'd dried it the best I could, I ran my fingers through my pageboy. It was the one great thing about shorter hair. The style still looked fantastic whether it air-dried or was blown out. It probably helped that my natural waves gave it body if I didn't straighten it.

"Are we getting takeout or going in?"

I glanced at his current condition. He'd be miserable in an air-conditioned restaurant, regardless of how shamelessly the waitresses—and waiters—flirted with him. "Takeout."

He proceeded to pull out his cell and placed an order for pick up. No sooner had he started to talk than my own phone rang in my purse. I searched my large bag for the obnoxious piece of technology, finding it on the third ring. I'd never had the need for a device in Mason Belle, and I loathed its presence in my life now. However, the firm required one, so I toted it around. The screen was lit up with my sister's name, and I groaned loud enough to get Eason's attention. What I didn't do was answer it.

When he hung up, he tilted his chin with a slight jerk. "Who was that?"

There was no point in trying to hide my feelings. "Sarah." That one word held more emotions than any other I had knowledge of in the English language, and none of them were good.

"She'll keep trying. You might as well get it out of the way. Then you won't have to hear from her again for another two weeks." Eason had all the gory details of my Texas past, and while he didn't agree with how I dealt with it in the present, he'd long ago quit arguing for me to mend the relationships.

I stared blankly at him. And blinked. "I'll call her back tomorrow morning."

"Oh yeah? Is that going to be during the car drop-off for school when you're certain she won't answer?"

I'd never been so happy to see the neon lights of our favorite pho noodle place. Saved by the car arriving at our destination and our pending takeout, I smiled sweetly and pointed toward the entrance. I refused to give him the satisfaction of being right. It would be well-timed at the precise moment she had her rugrats in the car—two nieces and a nephew I'd never met—and she'd refuse to talk on a cell phone with her kids in the car.

When Eason came back with our food, I still stared at the screen, lost in thought.

"Do you ever actually use that thing?" He then promptly turned to the driver to give him our address before allowing me to answer.

It was a dumb question. I tapped my finger on my chin and stared at the ceiling as though I had to seriously consider it. "I believe I dialed your number this morning to see if you wanted coffee. I sent you a text last night when you were at the gym. And Garrett taught me how to use FaceTime"—not that I had any need for it—"so, all in all, I'd say, yes."

"Your refusal to conform to the use of modern technology baffles me."

"I just told you I used it *three* times in the last twenty-four hours."

He shifted in the seat beside me and set the Pho's bag between his feet. "You know what I mean. Most women are as attached to their phones as they are Louis Vuitton, and they go so far as to color coordinate their cases with their pocketbooks."

"Did you say pocketbooks? Are you a hundred years old?" I snickered, not that it deterred him.

Eason's thick brows dipped until a *V* formed between them. I wondered if he'd spoken to a dermatologist about filler to correct that. Though, now wasn't the time to ask. "You only use email for work, you have zero social media accounts, and you cringe anytime that thing rings. It's a little odd."

"You're odd." That was brilliant and quite the comeback. The questioning stare wasn't going to disappear until we got home or I gave him more than two words. I sighed. "I don't see the need. If I want someone to get in touch with me, I'll give them my number, not pretend to be friends with people I haven't seen in a decade and don't care to talk to."

"What's the point? You wouldn't answer it, anyway."

The cab slowed in front of our brownstone—well, Eason's brownstone. I just lived there. I paid the driver, and Eason grabbed the bag of food. The rain had slowed to a light mist, yet we both still hurried to the door.

He stuck the key into the lock, but before he disengaged the deadbolt, he faced me. "You really should call her back."

---

*S*arah and I had played our usual round of tag for days. She tried to reach me at times she believed I was available, and I called her when I was positive she wasn't. When the phone rang on Saturday night, Eason and I were sitting on the couch watching a crappy movie. I had no reason not to answer, even though I planned to let it go to voicemail when I heard my sister's ringtone.

Eason darted off the sofa. No matter how fast I was, he remained a step ahead, grabbing my cell at the last possible second.

"Hello?" He sounded winded, and I could only imagine what Sarah thought the two of us were doing. "Hey, Sarah. How are you?" The pleasantries could be left out. They weren't friends.

They'd never even met. Yet here the two of them were, yacking it up like old pals. "I'm good. Work's keeping me busy."

I couldn't hear her side of the conversation, though I had no doubt she would regale him with her Southern charm. Sarah had a knack for wooing elderly people with her polite manners. I accidentally snorted at the notion of Eason being old. While he was six years older than me, thirty was hardly cause for canes and nursing homes. The sideways stare I got from him told me he was less than impressed.

His next sentence was all it took to get me to stop giggling. "Yeah, she's right here. It was great talking to you. We need to get you to the Big Apple. Miranda and I can show you around."

I prayed she'd turned him down.

I covered the mouthpiece with my hand when I took it from him. "What's *wrong* with you?"

Eason popped me on the ass and walked off, chiding over his shoulder, "You should have answered."

Jerk.

"Hey, Sarah." My tone correctly depicted my discomfort with the conversation.

She sighed, not bothering to mask her disappointment. "Hey, Randi." I had to give her credit. She put on a better show than I did. Her voice was as peppy as it always was during these obligatory calls. "How's it going?"

It would be easier just to get things over with by talking, yet no matter how much I wanted to let go of the past, I couldn't. Something blocked me from engaging with Sarah or Daddy. It was painful to hear about what went on in Mason Belle that I wasn't a part of. I hated that I had nieces and a nephew I'd never met. But the truth was, I'd sealed my fate that day at the lake. One foolish decision had irrevocably changed my life. And as much as I missed Texas, I could never go back to face the destruction I'd caused.

"I'm good."

"Are you and Eason still working together?" It was polite conversation. I, however, found it intrusive.

I wandered back to the couch, plopped down in the seat I'd occupied only seconds before, and covered my legs with a blanket. "Yeah. I've been there for almost six years. I like it."

"Have you thought about going to law school instead of just being a paralegal? You'd make a great lawyer."

Other than years of education that I wasn't confident I could even pass, that goal would also require gobs of money I didn't make. "I don't think law school is an option."

"Why not?" I couldn't fault her for being naïve. If I'd never left Texas, I would be as oblivious as my sister. She still resided in Mason Belle where she'd spent her entire life. If it took place outside the county lines, Sarah wasn't aware of it. And she liked it that way.

I took a deep breath to keep from snapping at her. "It's costly. Plus, I like what I do. Eason is good to me."

"I guess being under the wing of one of the partners has its perks, huh?"

"He makes sure I'm taken care of. But I really do like my job." There was no point in defending myself. Sarah didn't know what a paralegal did, and I wasn't going to explain it to her. "What about you?" Changing the subject was easier, and unlike Eason, she was easy to redirect.

"Oh, wow. Well, Kylie and Kara"—they were twins and the oldest—"started kindergarten." Obviously, she didn't remember telling me that the last three times we'd talked. "And I joined the PTA. Between that and Mason Belle's Chamber Welcome Wagon, I can hardly catch my breath. Chasing after Rand is another full-time job."

He was three and named after her husband's grandfather, Randall Charles Burin. I refused to acknowledge how closely the nickname resembled my own. From what little I knew about my nephew, he was exactly like his uncle had been growing up. The one picture I'd seen told me he looked like him, too.

"You don't have a hard time keeping up?" I winced the second it came out of my mouth.

Sarah either didn't care or chose to ignore my insensitivity. "No more than any other stay-at-home mom chasing three overly active kids whose husband leaves before the sun comes up."

I wasn't privy to how it had all happened, primarily because I hadn't asked, and I'd refused to go home for the wedding. Sarah had ended up marrying Charlie Burin about a year after I left, and the twins were born six months later against doctors' advice. There was no way to ask for details without hearing about Austin, and even years later, I couldn't bear the idea of his name passing my lips. Sarah had brought him up once, and I'd promptly hung up and refused her calls for months. She had never mentioned him again.

"I really wish you'd come home for a visit, Randi. You'd love them." Melancholy mixed with love in her tone. If only that had been the way she'd communicated with me as a teen, things might have been different now.

I gave her the same response I always did. "I can't."

"Because of work?"

"And other things." It was vague, and she always let it go at that point.

Just not today. "Like what?"

I ran my fingers through my hair, wishing for the first time that it was still long so I'd have something to pull on or play with.

"Is it Eason? Do you not want to leave him?"

"Partly." That was a lie.

I hated not being able to see her expressions when we talked. I missed the nuances that crossed her eyes, and her posture said more than the words she chose.

"Bring him, too."

"Daddy would never go for that." And not for the reasons she thought. "Plus, it would be impossible for us to get time off work together. Not to mention the cost of tickets. And there's no hotel in Mason Belle." I had to offer her something. Continually refusing her invitations got old.

"Is that it...or are there reasons *in* Mason Belle?" It was a brazen attempt at bringing up things that kept us apart. Not that we'd ever been close after Mama had left.

There was nothing there for me.

Sarah had this Mary Poppins image in her mind of a happy family reunion, when in all likelihood, it would result in more hurt feelings and cross words. Daddy had made his point the day I'd left. There was nothing else to say. "My past doesn't need to collide with my present, Sarah. You're welcome to come here anytime." She'd never come. Charlie wouldn't let her. That, I didn't have to worry about.

"Okay, Randi." Regret lingered on the line. It was the only sound I heard from home. And also the number-one reason I'd never returned. "Well, I guess I'll let you get back to Eason. Give him our love."

Somehow, I'd made it through without her detailing life at the farm, the people who worked on it, or Daddy's antics. I needed to quit while I was ahead. "Sure thing. Goodnight, Sarah."

I hung up the phone and tossed it onto the coffee table in front of me. Every call ended the same way. Every conversation left me laden with guilt. There was a reason I only did this twice a month. Miranda Adams was happy with the life and friends she'd made in the city. Randi, on the other hand, was forever homesick. Unfortunately, missing Texas would never be reason enough to return.

It was best—for everyone involved—that I stayed on this side of the Mason Dixon line.

2

AUSTIN

"Good morning, Austin." My sister-in-law beamed at me from the front porch of the Adams' house. The coo of her singsong voice welcomed me and drew me in.

"Day's nearly half over, Sarah." I strolled in her direction from the barn to give her a hug, and my nephew barreled toward me at a pace only a three-year-old could keep.

Stopping to squat, I braced myself for the force at which Rand would throw his body at me. His little frame hit my chest, and I wrapped my arms around my only nephew, though he didn't let me hold him long. The ranch wound him up into a ball of energy that couldn't be contained.

"What are we doing today, Tin Tin?" His nickname for me would have earned him a black eye had he been fifteen years older, but it was hard not to love a toddler who couldn't say "Austin." Not only had it stuck with Rand, Kylie and Kara used it, too. However, I drew the line with other family members, and Charlie had found that out the hard way.

I glanced at Sarah, not sure how long they planned to stay. She gave me nothing. "I don't know, bud. Are you guys going to be here all day?" As much as I adored my nephew, I didn't get a lot done with him around. There was far too much going on to have him tagging along today.

"Not long. I just came by to bring Daddy some honey."

Rand squinted when he peered up at me. The sun was bright overhead, and there wasn't a cloud in the sky. But over the horizon, billows of smoke rose from the treetops. "We brought bread, too. I helped make it."

He was a good kid. All of Charlie and Sarah's kids were amazing. Even at young ages, they helped their mom without complaint. "I bet your papa will love that with fresh honey."

Rand's tiny chest puffed out, and he straightened his spine. "I'm his favorite."

I didn't know about that. I ruffled his mousy-brown hair and said, "He loves your sisters, too."

He shrugged as if the twins didn't matter. "Not as much as me." Like his dad, Rand had all the confidence in the world, despite his pint-sized stature.

Sarah snickered behind her son, and I glanced up in time to see her smirk before she wiped it away. "Papa loves you all equally. Just like Mama and Daddy." She didn't include me in that statement.

I loved the girls. They were sweet as could be, but while Kara's personality was like Sarah's, Kylie had the same spunk and spark as Randi had had at her age. They weren't identical twins, and unfortunately for me, not only did Kara look like her mama, Kylie was the spitting image of her aunt.

"Papa doesn't love you and Aunt Randi the same. You're his favorite." Even spoken through a childish tone, those words struck a chord in me. A wound that had never healed.

Sarah gasped and did her best to get on Rand's level. When I reached out to help her, she swatted me away and focused on her son. "Why would you say such a thing?" Flabbergasted and embarrassed, her gaze flicked to me, and her cheeks flamed.

The little boy's eyes filled with tears when he stared at his mama, and they fell when he turned his head to me. "'Cause he made Aunt Randi go away."

I couldn't say how often my nieces and nephew heard about their aunt—or heard *from* her. The only thing I knew for sure was that her name never passed my lips, and she was never mentioned in my presence. Ever.

Sarah hesitated and looked at me. "Oh, no. Rand, sweetie..."

I was already uncomfortable. I certainly couldn't offer assistance in this.

"That's not true. Aunt Randi moved to New York."

He sobbed as he spoke, like they'd once been best friends and he missed seeing her daily. "Papa yelled at her. I heard you tell Daddy that if Papa hadn't yelled at her, she wouldn't be gone 'cause she loved Tin Tin. I heard you with my very own ears." The adamant tone only added to the sound of his frustration.

My heart broke with my nephew's. Six years hadn't eliminated the pain, and neither had two thousand miles. The truth was, thinking about her still made me angry, hence the reason no one brought her up when I was within earshot.

Sarah took her son's hand and moved toward the house. "I'm going to take him inside. I'll see you at your parents' on Sunday, right?" It didn't matter how much time passed, Sarah blamed herself for Randi leaving, and she wore that guilt like a noose.

I nodded. I no longer blamed Sarah or Jack. Randi had made a choice, and she continued to make that same decision every day she stayed gone. At this point, it was probably best she didn't come back. Her abrupt departure had caused an even bigger uproar than the accident. To this day, no one other than Jack knew what was said between him and his daughter that had caused her to pack her bags. In my mind, it didn't matter. I didn't care that she left them or Mason Belle or all of Texas.

She'd left *me*. And that wound would never heal.

"Burin, you coming?" Corey's question snapped me out of what would have twisted into a downward spiral.

I kicked at the gravel that reminded me of Randi and silently cursed her one last time. "Yeah, man."

He led two horses by the reins and waited for me outside the barn. When Jack had hired him a few weeks ago, I didn't think Corey would be able to handle the physical requirements of the job. He was older than most of the ranch hands, yet even in his forties, he worked circles around the rest of the crew.

I took the reins and rounded them over Nugget's head, stuck my boot in the stirrup, and then hoisted myself into the saddle. I leaned over to pat the horse's neck and gave him a gentle tap with my heel. I didn't own him, but he was mine. Jack and I had a silent understanding that he was off-limits to all the other hands. He'd been Randi's, and I'd taken care of him after she'd left, thinking she'd come back. That horse and I had been together ever since. And as he got older, I wanted to make sure he had a good life.

"Tommy's already got a crew out in the south pasture." Corey wasn't much on idle chitchat.

"Dogs too?"

Corey nodded, although he didn't glance my way.

We faced a lot of tough days if it didn't rain or the fires weren't contained. With close to ten thousand head of cattle and twice as many acres, driving the herd could become our full-time job. I'd been here before. South Texas wasn't a stranger to drought and fire. But I couldn't get a read on Corey or the rest of the crew. These guys were either optimistic about the threat not hitting Cross Acres, or they'd given up hope and were only going through the motions.

Wildfires did strange things that ratcheted my anxiety. The grey haze would reach us in the next couple of days, and we'd already started to see ash fall like snow that the wind had carried in. At night, the sky glowed an angry orange and hid the moon.

But it was the run of the wildlife that had bothered me, almost as much as their absence. Birds didn't chirp in the distance; field mice didn't scurry through the fields. They'd all moved north toward safety, which only left the *clip-clop* of hooves on the ground and low-flying crop dusters overhead.

I adjusted my baseball cap to block out more of the sun. No matter how many years I'd spent working on farms—my parents' and now Jack's—I'd always refused a cowboy hat. I could do the boots and even Wranglers, but I drew the line with plaid shirts and wide-brimmed Stetsons. There wouldn't be any large belt buckles in my future, either. But on days like today, when the sun was a thousand degrees, and it scorched my neck, I had second thoughts about that decision.

Corey cleared his throat, stealing my attention away from poorly planned outfits and sunburn. "Any chance I might make it to my daughter's birthday party tomorrow afternoon?"

"I didn't know you had a daughter. How old is she?" It dawned on me that I knew very little about the man beside me.

"Jessica. She'll be six." He oozed pride. "She's a handful. Smart as a whip."

I felt like a jackass. I took for granted that I'd grown up here and was well acquainted with the residents. When people moved to Mason Belle—which almost never happened—they didn't typically stay long. Other than farms, there were very few places in town to offer employment. Most of the ranches were staffed by family or close friends, so outsiders didn't stand a chance in a town this size.

"Stay home with your girl tomorrow. We'll make do." It wasn't much, but days off in the cattle business were hard to come by. Even on Sundays when we didn't "work," the animals still had to be fed and cared for.

"For real?"

I nodded. Jack wouldn't be happy, and I'd get lectured about the importance of having every hand on deck, but Corey's family was scared, just like the rest of us. "How'd you end up in Mason Belle, anyway?" It wasn't even a dot on the state map. The only way people landed here was by getting lost on their way to somewhere else.

He didn't answer right away. After several minutes, he cleared his throat. "I made some bad choices in Houston. About lost my wife and baby girl. Alexandra gave me an ultimatum: keep doing what I was doing or keep my family."

"Sounds like you made the right decision." I respected a man who could admit he'd made mistakes, and I admired anyone who chose family at all costs. It was also the reason I would endure Jack's moaning.

"You not gonna ask what I did?" He appeared surprised with his mouth slightly parted.

I shook my head. "Nah, figure if you'd wanted to tell me, you would've. Long as it doesn't affect your job, it's not really any of my business."

"What about you?"

I hadn't planned to play twenty questions, yet I had to give him the same respect he'd given me. "Grew up here."

"You got a wife? Kids?"

It was like God wanted to punish me today with reminders of the past and lost opportunities. "Nope." I didn't offer more, and thankfully, Corey didn't ask.

---

*S*unday supper was an affair at my parents' house. It had been since I was a kid, and it would be until my mom physically couldn't do it anymore. Without fail, she'd cooked for the four of us for years. As we got older, we included friends and girlfriends, and the list of guests had continued to grow. And now, every Sunday after church, Charlie, Sarah, and their three kids, Jack, and myself were regulars at the dinner table. My mom welcomed any ranch hand from their own farm and those from Jack's who cared to come, as well. In all honesty, she wouldn't have sent a stranger away. That's how Mason Belle women were.

On average, there were fifteen people seated at their dining and breakfast tables on any given Sunday. Today, that wasn't the case. Jack's truck sat in the driveway, and Sarah's SUV was behind it. It appeared no one other than family would be joining us. It didn't surprise me. Most of the men in town currently bounced between their own herds and those of their friends. Each day that passed brought the fires closer, and the town pulled together to help protect each other's livelihood. Jack and I had been up before the sun, broke off for church and lunch, and we would be back at it in a couple of hours.

I parked off to the side, close to the backyard. As soon as I opened the door, I heard the kids playing behind the house. Their laughter and little voices floated through the air.

Rand had a knack for tormenting his sisters, despite his smaller size and younger age. The girls were fits of constant giggles, while my nephew was three and a half feet of solid boy. "Poopy head."

I chuckled. His mom would have his hide if she were out back. Rounding the side of the home I'd grown up in, I stopped in my tracks. For once, Kylie and Kara had beaten Rand at his own game. Although, I'd bet my left nut that Kylie had been the one to convince Kara to hold down Rand while she secured him to a tree.

Kylie's hands were on her hips in a no-nonsense stance, and a toy gun dangled from her finger at her side. "I'm the sheriff now."

Rand struggled against the rope and tree bark. He grunted something I couldn't hear.

Kara started to waver. "Maybe we should let him go, Ky." Her blond curls bounced as she turned her head in search of witnesses. "He's gonna tell," she whined.

Kylie made no move toward releasing her prisoner. Kara started to cry. And Rand screamed at the top of his lungs. I needed to be the adult in this situation and break it up, but I wanted to see how it played out. I couldn't believe Sarah and Charlie had left the three of them outside unattended. It was a recipe for disaster.

When Kara didn't get her way and Rand didn't get parole, she did what any good girl her age would. "I'm telling Daddy."

Kylie stepped in front of her sister, daring her to take another step. "I've got another rope. You wanna be on the other side of that tree?" She narrowed her eyes to ensure Kara understood it was a promise, not an empty threat.

Kara was harps and angels, while Kylie was fire and brimstone. Even at five, Kylie could work a lasso, and Kara didn't stand a chance. She'd never make it to the house before Kylie would have her hogtied on the ground. I shouldn't find their antics as amusing as I did. No matter how hard I tried to get upset, watching was far more entertaining than tattling to their parents. And I refused to be the one to discipline them.

I crossed my arms and shifted my feet. In the process, I stepped on a twig that snapped and grabbed their attention.

"Tin Tin." It was as close to a command as a three-year-old could get, said with a stern tone and a stiff little face. "Tell Ky to let me go."

Kylie dropped the gun, the lasso, and her attention on Rand in favor of beating Kara to get to me. They swallowed me in little-girl hugs. With one in each arm, I carried them like footballs to the tree their brother was still secured to.

"Untie him." I tilted my head to indicate who I referred to in case they didn't realize it was the little boy held hostage against a tree trunk.

Kara was the first to point out she hadn't done anything wrong. Her angelic features made her easy to believe. With strawberry-blond hair, pale-blue irises, and a kiss of pink on her ivory skin, she looked like a cherub. She had yet to figure out that I had each of them pegged and knew who to blame for what.

"Ky?" I lifted my brows with expectation, and she caved.

Her caramel-colored irises peered up at me through thick, black lashes. There was another girl I'd known with those same wide-set eyes who'd owned my world with just one glance, but I'd hardened my heart to that look six years ago. And due to that, Kylie wasn't able to manipulate me the way she did other people.

With a huff, she pulled on her dark braid. "Fine." Her exasperation was worthy of an Oscar. Kylie turned her attention to Rand long enough to undo the knot. She didn't unwind the rope from the trunk, but he was able to wiggle free.

The girls took off toward the house, and Rand knocked me over when I squatted, thinking he'd want a hug. His tackle of affection caught me off guard, and he instantly forgot about his sisters.

"Tin Tin, come play with me." Rand's words burst through the air like thunder. He scrambled to his feet and dashed toward the swing set.

I followed him across the yard. Except, instead of joining him, I plucked his body off the swing and hoisted him onto my shoulders. "I can't stay long today. How about we go see what Nana and Poppy are doing first?"

Rand pressed his palms to my cheeks and wrapped his fingers around my jaw. Slowly, he leaned over the bill of my baseball hat until his nose was inches from my own, only he was upside down. "Are you gonna tell on me?"

"For what?"

"Callin' Ky a poopy head."

I struggled to keep a straight face. "Poopy head" never lost its appeal to any male. It was funny. "Nah."

"Thanks." He sat back up. However, his hands didn't move. Suddenly, he was back in my face. Excitement shimmered in his eyes, and a wicked expression of glee lifted his cheeks. "Are you gonna tell on Ky and Kara for tyin' me up?" Hope danced in his voice as he practically bounced in place.

I swayed my head from side to side to let him believe I had considered it. "Well...if I do, they'll tell your mama what *you* did. Probably best if we let it go."

His lips contorted in contemplation, then relaxed, and he disappeared again.

I tossed my keys on the table in the foyer and headed toward the kitchen. "Ma?" I called out.

Rand attempted to put my neck in a vise grip between his thighs when I tried to set him on the floor. All it took was a pinch to the side to send him into fits of giggles and loosen his hold. I swatted his butt playfully, and he raced off to torture someone else. I noted his sisters were nowhere to be found.

"We're in here, baby." My mom stepped into the living room with a dishtowel in hand. The smudge of flour on her nose was cute. It also meant fried chicken and biscuits were on today's menu. My mouth watered at the thought.

It had been roughly forty-five minutes since I'd last seen her. Even still, I leaned in to kiss her cheek as though it had been weeks. Unlike my brother and his wife, I went home after church and changed my clothes before coming here, since I had to go back to work. "Food smells good."

She patted me on the arm with a motherly grin. "Your favorite."

"Where is everybody?" I followed behind her as she returned to her conversation in the kitchen with my sister-in-law. The two of them were especially close. They gossiped, traded secrets and makeup tips, and whatever else women did together. "Hey, Sarah." I leaned down and squeezed her neck in a friendly hug from behind.

I reached into the bowl of snap peas she had cleaned and helped myself to one. I popped it into my mouth and smiled as I chewed. Sarah swatted at my hand and shook her head like she didn't know what to do with me.

"The food's almost ready; why don't you go rustle everyone up? Your daddy, Charlie, and Jack are out back watching the kids." My mom winked, and I half expected her to pinch my cheek.

"No, they're not."

My mom waved me off. "Certainly, they are."

Without taking my attention from my mother, I snagged another bean from Sarah's bowl. "Ma, I was just out there. The kids came in with me. Dad, Charlie, and Jack weren't around."

"Don't be silly. That would mean those babies had been outside unsupervised."

I cocked my head and a corresponding brow. My mom didn't engage, and Sarah didn't seem concerned. "So, you don't know where any of them are?"

There was an art to snacking before Sunday supper. It was all about kitchen position. Today, the ideal spot was leaned against the counter behind Sarah, who sat at the table. Here, I'd be able to pluck things away before she could stop me.

Kylie and Kara ran through the kitchen. Three seconds later, Rand buzzed by on the same path.

"There went the kids." It was a good thing Ma was cute and lovable, because she was clueless.

"I'm not sure how Charlie and I made it to adulthood with that kind of supervision."

Sarah came to her mother-in-law's defense with a potholder. She swung it aimlessly behind her in a vain attempt to hit me.

"Is Charlie aware of how violent you are?" I teased.

"Austin? Is that you?" My dad's voice bellowed from the back porch.

My mom spun around with "I told you so" written all over her face. I rolled my eyes. The woman was delusional. The men might have been outside, but they were *not* watching the kids. If they had been, it was unlikely Ky would have had Rand bound to a tree.

Using my foot, I pushed off the counter. If my dad yelled my name, that meant he wanted to talk to me. "Yes, sir."

I stepped through the French doors that opened onto the far side of the patio. It was really more of a wraparound porch that circled the entire house, and depending on which exit you took, my family referred to it as something different.

"Hey, Jack. Charlie."

My brother kicked a chair around and motioned for me to sit. "Jack said you've got extra hands coming to help drive the herds farther north."

I shrugged. My brother was next in line to run Twin Creeks, so he was overly involved in the farming and ranching business that took place in Mason Belle. I, on the other hand, *worked* for a cattle rancher, and I just did what I was told. "Yeah."

Before he could continue whatever interrogation was about to follow, his wife called from inside the house. "Charlie, I need your help." Sarah tried to do everything on her own, even when she shouldn't, so anytime she called for Charlie, he jumped.

Jack watched his son-in-law respond to his daughter's needs. "Your brother's a good man."

He didn't have to tell me. Jack was convinced Charlie hung the moon and named all the stars. And while Charlie might not have actually played a part in the celestial placements, I had no problem admitting what a fantastic husband and dad he was. I watched Charlie over my shoulder. When he closed the door, I turned back to Jack. "Yeah. I'm lucky to have him."

Jack's heavy hand clapped my shoulder. "You're a good man, too, Austin." His eyes seemed to lose focus as he pondered whatever lingered on the tip of his tongue. "Your time is coming. Mark my word."

There was no need to talk about it. Jack carried as much guilt as Sarah did. Jack believed he'd cost me Randi. He'd apologized once, and that had been the only time the topic of Randi had ever been discussed with me.

"Things going all right out in the fields?"

Grateful for the diversion, I would have talked about breeding cows to change the subject. "Just moving cattle." I acted as though it wasn't twice the amount of work, but Jack knew the truth.

He also didn't have to be told what kind of burden it put on our resources not to have pastures for grazing. These weren't small animals. Not only did they need space, they needed food. And the farther north we moved them to get away from the wildfire, the more cramped they all became.

The back door flew open, and three blurs zoomed by. All I could make out were smears of color and giggles.

Jack sat up and leaned his elbows on his knees. "Hopefully, the extra hands will ease a bit of the workload this afternoon."

"Yes, sir. I talked to their foreman. I know the other guys will be happy to have them on board. We have another day or two before we'll need to consider moving again."

"I trust your judgment."

Typically, Jack made these decisions, and I carried them out. I hadn't seen him Friday or Saturday before I left, and he'd been gone before I got there both mornings. And today we'd been on opposite ends of the ranch before church. So, I wasn't surprised that I'd had to wait. I *was* surprised he'd left the fate of Cross Acres up to me.

*B*y midnight, I ran on fumes, caffeine, and the grace of God. When I finally called it quits, the fires were still well over a hundred miles from our southernmost pastures. If I didn't get some sleep, I'd be worthless in the morning. At the very least, we'd moved the herds from imminent danger and bought ourselves a little more time. People were doing all they could, but land and cattle were decimated a couple of counties over. The FAA had halted all firefighting planes for several hours this afternoon because drone cameras were in the way, and it wasn't safe to fly. Thankfully, the burn rate had slowed to under four miles per hour, but firefighters hadn't contained the progression.

I dragged my aching body to my truck, and I slowed onto the gravel road that exited the Adams' property. Cross Acres had a fancy, iron gate and a ton of flowers and shrubbery at the entrance —not that I could see it in the middle of the night. And the amber haze of wildfires cast an eerie glow on the horizon and created an unnatural veil of darkness around everything else. Regardless of whether or not I could see the view, every morning and every evening for the last six years, I'd rolled down my window to listen to the crunch of my tires on rocks. It was a sweet torture, a pain I hated to love. For one mile, I'd meditate on the gritty noise.

And as quickly as it began, it ended when my truck made it to the asphalt country road outside Cross Acres. It was a straight shot from here to my house. I'd driven this stretch so many times, I'd swear I could do it blindfolded. As tired as I was, I was tempted to try. Fifteen minutes on a two-lane road with nothing other than pastures as far as I could see didn't hold my attention, even though the odd color of the sky did. It wasn't just Jack's ranch I worried about; my parents' farm was in jeopardy, too, as was every person's I knew. Our houses were all in harm's way. Mason Belle's entire way of life was currently under threat. Every abled body had a hand in helping somewhere.

Yet, there wasn't a soul on this street.

The stench of burning wood and brush crept into the cab of the truck when I cranked up the air-conditioning to keep myself awake, and I blasted the only radio station I could find that wasn't filled with news instead of music. I didn't remember much after turning down my driveway, including parking, the walk inside, or landing face-first on my mattress without changing.

It wasn't until the sound of my cell ringing tugged me from sleep that I realized where I was. I rolled over in search of my phone, only to find it buried in my pocket. Even through all that, whoever was on the other end had been relentless in reaching me. By the time I got it to my ear, the screen read three missed calls from Jack, back to back.

I shifted on the mattress and stared at the ceiling. "Hello?" My eyes burned, even behind closed lids.

"Austin, wind's picked up. The fire's moving fast. I need you to round up the guys and get as many here as you can. We've got to hurry."

It should have startled me. The words should have sent me into panic, or at least sparked motion. "How fast?" I questioned. If I'd had more sleep, it would have dawned on me that if Jack called, it was an emergency.

"Gusts up to sixty miles an hour. Steady winds of twenty."

In my weary mind, I tried to do the math. Unable to reach the answer, I got enough to understand that the fires had only been about a hundred and ten miles out when I left. Two hours later with aggressive winds, the flames would quickly lick away the land and everything in its path.

"I'm on my way."

"You'll get in touch with the guys?" he asked.

There was no easy way to break this to him, although he had

to know. "Jack." I raked my hand through my hair and located my hat on the floor. My feet were already moving faster than my mouth. "I can call. But if it's moving that fast, they're all going to be trying to save their houses or their own herds. Best hope is to get all of your own hands. If you know anyone in neighboring counties, it would be good to call them."

By the time I found my keys in the kitchen, Jack still hadn't responded.

"Jack?" I asked again and closed the door behind me.

"Do the best you can, son."

This was every rancher's worst nightmare. The devastation ran deeper than the financial implications, the loss of even part of a herd, the damage to the land, the potential danger, it all ate a man's soul because his heart was in every piece of that farm.

After I had disconnected with Jack, I started a group text with every man's name that I had a phone number for in Mason Belle. It was a good thing the road from my house to Jack's was straight, since my attention was everywhere other than on it. My mass SOS didn't go unheard. There simply wasn't much available manpower. We would be doing good to have half of Jack's hired hands show up. When I passed the intersection of Route 14, I stared down the dark street and prayed my parents were safe. The fire chased me from behind, the winds were strong, and I wondered if we'd be better off to save ourselves, but that wasn't a rancher's way of life.

My tires screeched when they left the pavement and spun when they hit the gravel. The back end of the truck fishtailed, narrowly missing the iron gate outside Cross Acres. I slammed the truck into park next to Corey's vehicle and threw open my door. Every light in the house was on, and the barn was lit up like Fourth of July. The fire no longer teased us from beyond the horizon, I could see it dancing its way into the heart of Mason Belle. I fought against the wind and soot to get inside the barn.

Corey, along with a stunning woman and a young girl, waited beyond the doors. I assumed this was Alexandra and Jessica, though there weren't any introductions made. Corey pointed to a corner out of the way, and the two went without question.

He leaned into me so they couldn't hear him. "I couldn't leave them at home."

"No explanation needed." They didn't have any family here. He needed to know they were safe so he could do his job. "Where's Jack?"

Corey shook his head and shrugged. Fear widened his eyes, and the vein on his neck thumped a visible pulse. "I haven't seen anybody since I pulled up."

Tommy and Brock were here, or at least their trucks were. And Jack's was parked where it always was. "Check the stalls. See how many horses are missing. I'm going to check the house."

I started moving, while Corey kept talking. Even experienced ranchers shouldn't go out without a game plan. Anything could happen, and they'd be miles away from help. Cell phone signals weren't reliable, and if no one was aware of their location or destination, they also didn't know where to look. I couldn't imagine why Jack would have gone before I had gotten here.

"I'm sure it's fine." My bark wasn't as settling as I'd hoped. "Saddle up Nugget for me. I'll be right back."

Corey didn't make another peep, except to turn on his feet. His footsteps got faster, as did my own. Before I rode all the way out to the far end of the property with an inexperienced ranch hand, I needed to make certain the old man hadn't snuck inside without being seen. It wasn't like him, yet neither was not waiting for me to arrive.

I called out his name like a song stuck on repeat. "Jack?" Pushing open each door in the house, I checked every room. The stairs passed under my feet two at a time. He wasn't on the first or the second floor. "Jack!" My voice reverberated off the walls, but I didn't get a reply. The place was empty.

The screen door bounced wildly against the frame under the unnecessary force I'd pushed it with. It clanged behind me when it finally shut. By then, I was halfway to the barn.

"Corey? You got Nugget ready?" Hell, it'd only been about three minutes since I'd asked him to saddle the horse. If I hadn't been in a race against time, my jaw might have gaped when Corey appeared from within Nugget's stall, reins in hand.

"Good to go." He handed me the strips of leather. "There are six horses gone. You want me to ride with you?"

I didn't. However, refusing him would make me as foolish as the man I chased. Corey understood my curt nod, and he took off through the stables. Thankfully, he'd had a horse geared up. I hoped it wasn't one that had worked all day. Wasting time wasn't in my plan.

If Corey sensed my irritation, he didn't let on. He kept up as the horse I rode galloped in front of his. My stomach rumbled with a reminder that I hadn't eaten in hours, and I wished I'd grabbed something inside the house. Once we got out here, I didn't have a clue what we'd face, and hungry or not, I'd have to wait it out.

Corey and I rode as far south as we could manage. A dense layer of smoke ate up all the breathable air. My eyes stung, soot settled on my arms and legs, and every step we took closer to the fire only amplified the coughs between Corey and me.

We slowed the horses to look around. Any other day, the fields went on forever. Tonight, it was difficult to see a quarter of a mile in the direction of the wildfire and not much better away from it. "Do you see anyone?" I questioned over the wind.

Corey studied our surroundings and finally pointed south-west. "There!"

In the distance, barely even a speck, were five mounted horses pushing a small herd. Corey didn't wait for an invitation. When I clicked my command for Nugget to move, he followed. I dug my heels into the horse's haunches, urging him to pick up speed. As his pace increased, I sank down to his neck and held the reins. My body flowed with the rhythm of the animal, and with each stride, my heart banged harder beneath my sternum. The air whipped through Nugget's mane and whistled past my ears, drowning out the crackle of the fire, the rush of wind, and the stampede of hooves driving forward.

Staying lower in the saddle helped to avoid some of the smoke, but it was dangerous for Nugget to be using that polluted air to fuel my race. We needed to get the horses and the cattle as far east as possible if we had any hope of saving them. The flames might as well have been a locomotive, as fast as they came. The wind gave them drive, and every minute that passed left me wondering if we could outrun them.

Once we were in earshot, I called out to Tommy. "Where's Jack?" There were only four guys with him, and Jack wasn't one of them.

"He went back for stragglers." He didn't linger to talk. All the guys were pushing the cattle hard.

Jack had always had the herd mentality. It shouldn't shock me that he went after a few head that couldn't keep up, and under any other circumstances, it would have made sense. Today, saving their lives could mean losing his.

"Tommy, how far back were they?" I had to yell to be heard.

"A couple hundred yards when he went after them." He halted his horse and turned him toward me.

I didn't need any more information. Tommy had faced me to keep from saying what he thought. His expression might as well have been Jack's death certificate.

At that point, I wasn't sure who was the bigger fool, Jack or me. "Corey, go with Tommy. I'm going to see if I can find him." I knew better than to go alone. Jack knew better than to take off after a few measly head. Nevertheless, he'd done it, and I was about to, as well.

Corey gave me a curt nod, and Tommy shook his head. The others were none the wiser. Time was a precious commodity we didn't have much of, and I burned through more of it with every second I sat there. Before I took off, Corey tossed me a bandana that I tied around my neck and then lifted over my mouth and nose. I didn't bother to check behind me when I pulled the reins to the left and headed toward the glowing inferno that lit up the night sky.

All the landmarks were now gone, the smoke obstructed any view of things in the distance that might have proved useful in tracking, and the fire seemed to burn in a circle that surrounded me from every angle. It snaked its way along the ground, shadowing everything around it. It was the first time in years that I thanked my lucky stars for knowing these pastures like they were my own. I'd spent most of my life out here. Anyone else would have been lost.

With no hope of finding Jack, I almost turned around to save myself and Nugget—until the silhouette of Midnight rearing in the distance caught my attention. If I'd had a camera, the picture could have won awards. He was a beast, massive yet graceful. The flames were too close, and the stallion was unhappy, even though he was steadfast and diligently working at Jack's command.

Nugget went where I told him at a pace that wasn't fair to him, given the conditions. I counted the cows Jack risked his life for, and I could have wrung the old man's neck. Twelve. Twelve head. He'd put his life on the line, mine, and two horses for twelve damn head.

"Jack!" No man could wrangle a frightened herd on one horse, no matter how small. "Jack! We've got to get out of here." I coughed and tried to shield my face with my arm; unfortunately, the only clean air to be found hovered close to the ground.

Jack hadn't moved, and neither had two of the cattle closest to him. When I neared, I realized why. The stench was horrid—it was more than burned hay and singed wood. Jack hadn't gotten all the stragglers out, and the pair of heifers at Midnight's hooves needed to be put down. I'd left the house in such a hurry, I hadn't thought to grab a gun. Jack had.

There wasn't time to debate it. He would either shoot them, or we would have to leave them to suffer. They weren't pets. None of them even had names. But to Jack Adams, they were part of his ranch, and the ranch meant everything to him.

"You need me to do it?" I spoke loudly enough to be heard without yelling. If Jack detected the fear in my voice, he didn't let on.

With the shotgun in hand, he tossed his leg over the saddle and slid down. Jesus, he was going to get us both killed. My attention darted between him and the fire crawling toward us. The *boom* of the first one went quick, reverberating through the thick night air. I held my breath for the echoed blast of the second. The shot rang out, and Jack slumped to his knees. I'd seen it play out in movies a hundred times before. There, in front of me, he dropped the gun, his arms fell to his sides, and he went face-first into the dirt as though he'd taken the bullet rather than the animal.

Fuck. In seconds, I was off my horse and at his side. My best guess was smoke inhalation, worst-case scenario, heart attack. I didn't have an MD or a clue. Nor did I have time to assess the situation. Nugget and Midnight were anxious. It wouldn't take much for either to bolt. If they did, the cows wouldn't be the only things to succumb to the forces of nature.

In a split second, I made a decision. I grabbed Jack around the waist, and when he didn't help himself to his feet, I put all my energy into my thighs to lift his dead weight. I had never struggled with the physical requirements of the job, and I doubted I could ever recreate the adrenaline needed to hoist Jack onto Midnight's back. I unbridled the horse and used the reins in a pitiful attempt to secure Jack to the saddle. We'd barely be able to trot out of here without him slipping, and if Midnight got spooked, it would spell disaster. I could only hope Midnight would follow Nugget out. I couldn't save the other ten head. And I couldn't let them suffer, either. I did what I had to do as quickly as possible and mounted my horse.

The evidence of the massacre would be obliterated soon enough.

3

MIRANDA

*E*ason followed me into the elevator. I noticed his snicker and then tracked his line of sight down my legs. Seeing nothing to gawk at, I glowered. "What are you giggling about?"

"You have something under your stockings."

Alone with Eason, I craned my neck and contorted my body. Finally, I found the pair of red panties bunched behind my thigh, beneath my pantyhose. My cheeks flamed. Quickly, I tried to figure out the best way to remove the offending lingerie before the doors opened. I wasn't even sure how he'd seen it. There was only the slightest bit of fabric showing past the hem of my skirt.

"Here, hold this." I shoved my bag at him.

Eason clutched my purse against his chest. His laughter increased with every second that passed. "Did you just pluck a pair off the floor?"

A pointed scowl in his direction did nothing to deter him. "I was in a hurry. Hush." Right as I was about to hike up my skirt to reach beneath the fabric and grab my misplaced thong, I noticed he hadn't stopped staring. "Do you mind?"

"Not at all. Do what you need to do."

"How about turn around?"

His boisterous laugh died down to a half-hearted chuckle. "You realize you're surrounded by mirrors, right? Plus, it's not like I haven't seen your legs or your ass before."

Ignoring him, I prayed to God no one got on between here and our floor, or they would be in for quite the show. The fabric slid up my legs with ease, and once I had my skirt bunched at the waist, I stuck my hand down the length of my thigh. No sooner had I nabbed my panties and freed them than the elevator dinged. Eason shifted in front of me, effectively blocking the view so I could straighten my clothing before moving into the office.

Together, we stepped onto our floor, and he stopped to hand me my bag. I slid the strap onto my shoulder, still clutching the red satin in my fist. Eason caught my eyes and held them long enough for me to realize he was waiting for something. His palm was outstretched, and I darted my gaze back and forth between it and his stormy irises.

There was no way in hell I'd give Eason McNabb my panties. "Are you insane?" I whispered, appalled by the thought.

He leaned down and placed his mouth next to my ear. The warmth of his breath on my skin nearly caused me to forget my name. "You don't have any pockets." Like that somehow changed anything.

I stared at him as though he'd lost his mind. "I'll put them in my purse."

The grey in his eyes danced with hints of blue, and he fought to hold back the smile that played on his lips. The spell between us was broken when the receptionist interrupted. "Good morning, Mr. McNabb. Ms. Adams." She was new, and I couldn't remember her name, but I needed to figure it out so I could ask her about the intoxicating perfume she had on. It was sinful in the best way.

Eason reached out, gently touching her elbow to accompany his greeting. "How are you, Rachel?" *Rachel!*

Her lids drooped in a lust-filled daze, and a hint of a glossy luster washed over her seductive, brown eyes. When her dark lashes fluttered, I managed to stifle my amusement, although not by much. Anticipating it, Eason elbowed me in the side when he removed his fingers from Rachel's arm.

"Ow," I muttered while he flirted shamelessly with the newest member of the staff.

Rachel squared her shoulders, and I noticed the handful of pink slips folded between her fingers. "Ms. Adams, I have several messages for you." Nervous jitters caused her voice to shake.

There was nothing for her to be apprehensive about. Then I realized, she was staring at Eason and talking to me. If it weren't unprofessional, I would roll my eyes and tell her not to bother. However, I didn't need to come off as catty, jealous, or possessive.

"Thank you, Rachel." I was no longer interested in her perfume, just escaping the possibility of drool dribbling down her chin if she didn't close her mouth and stop gawking at Eason.

I took the messages without glancing at them and left Eason to deal with his latest office crush. No sooner had I taken a step around Eason and Rachel than I was tackled by the office courier, Rhett. My hands flailed in an attempt to keep myself upright, and without missing a beat or even stalling his conversation with the receptionist, Eason's arm snaked out and wrapped around my waist. He managed to keep me from falling. Embarrassingly, my panties and bag went flying. In my attempt to get Eason to release me so I could scurry across the floor, not only had I drawn attention to my thong, but Rhett had picked up the panties and my purse.

With his finger holding out the satin, my underwear dangled in mid-air for everyone in the office to see. I could only imagine what ran through their heads about Eason and me on the elevator and why I didn't have panties on...even though I did. I reached out to retrieve them from Rhett, but Eason was faster. He snatched them away without once glancing at Rhett, stuffed them into his pocket, and kept talking to Rachel.

Demanding that he give them back would only cause more of a scene than the one that had already played out, so instead, I took my remaining things from Rhett. And before I left, I offered Eason a snide smirk, smoothed out my clothing, and then walked back to my office.

It wasn't until I sat down that I let my body relax. My bag slid down my arm to the floor, and I slouched into the leather chair. There was nothing ladylike about my posture, but sometimes, a girl simply needed to shake off the morning and start over.

In my current state, I hadn't heard the door open. "Do you always sit like that when your door's closed?" The rumble of Eason's voice jolted me upright and alert.

"You know I don't."

He crossed the threshold and took the only chair in front of my desk. My office wasn't large to begin with; there was barely enough room for the furniture. Add Eason McNabb's enormous body and larger-than-life personality, and it suddenly dwarfed the space. Most people were suffocated by his presence; I was comforted. Nothing about Eason intimidated me, although my co-workers all attributed that to my relationship with him. I couldn't argue against it, since I'd known him prior to working for him.

When he didn't bother returning my panties voluntarily, I leaned across the desk and held out my palm. Eason stared at my wiggling fingers, seemingly oblivious to what I wanted.

"Give them back, Eason."

His hand slinked into the pocket of his suit jacket with graceful ease. In what seemed like slow motion, he seductively dragged out the blood-red satin and lace. I was mesmerized by his movements. Eason exuded sexuality and masculinity. If I weren't careful, I'd get swept up in the façade and forget what I was doing.

And right now, I needed my underwear back. I grabbed them right before he used them as a slingshot.

I shook my head in disbelief at his childish antics. "Seriously? Do men ever grow up?"

He shrugged. "Not if we're lucky."

"You have an uncanny ability to make people believe you're all kinds of put together. When in reality, you're no more mature than a five-year-old in a sandbox sticking his tongue out at a grody girl."

"Girls are still grody. I'm convinced they all have cooties."

His tone was playful, and his eyes danced with amusement. The man before me was an anomaly. At work and in the courtroom, he was no nonsense and all business. There was never a hair out of place on his head, his suits cost more than most people's monthly mortgage, and no one had fingernails *that* perfect. Yet at home, or when it was just the two of us, Eason had a boyish charm, youthful banter, and could make the Grinch laugh.

"Who are all the messages from?" He also had the attention span of a gnat if he wasn't focused on a case.

I glanced down at the stack I'd dropped onto my desk when I came in. "No clue. I haven't looked."

His brow dipped into a *V*, and three prominent, vertical lines formed between them. "Miranda, we left here late last night. You shouldn't have *any* messages at nine o'clock on Tuesday morning." As quickly as he'd prevented my fall, and as fast as he'd stolen my thong, he retrieved the papers in question. One by one, he thumbed through them.

I wouldn't have been able to read them upside down even if he had shown them to me, which he didn't. "Anything important?" I'd lost interest and directed my attention toward starting the day and my computer.

"They're all from Sarah."

"My sister?" I practically shrieked.

"Do you know any other Sarahs?" He had gone from playful to annoyed. "Yes, your sister."

I couldn't fathom what she needed on a Tuesday morning. I'd just talked to her last week. "It's too early."

"Even with the time difference, I'm sure she's been awake for a couple of hours with the kids."

I stopped, turned to face Eason, and blinked. Three times. "Not too early to be up. Too early to call. She's like seven days ahead of schedule."

He tossed the slips of paper onto the desk. "Maybe it's important."

"You think every call she places is important. Typically, all she wants to tell me is what flavor pie she made, or what color macaroni necklace one of the girls brought home." It wasn't that I didn't care about my sister, regardless of how blasé I sounded. I refused to allow myself to get invested in Sarah, the kids, or anything else in Mason Belle. I couldn't have them, and my heart ached whenever I allowed myself to remember everything I had lost.

Eason leaned back in the chair in front of my desk—it wasn't anywhere near as nice as the ones in his office—and crossed his arms over his chest. That didn't bode well for me. Anytime he took that posture, I lost. It didn't matter what the subject was; if Eason took a stance, I caved.

"Fine. I'll call her back at lunch."

His modelesque smirk made an appearance, though I knew he'd never give in that quickly. "You could call her now."

"I have work to do, Eason. Lunchtime will be fine."

He unfolded his arms, leaned forward, and then picked up the receiver on my phone. "I'm pretty tight with your boss. I'll make sure he understands."

Sticking my tongue out at him wasn't any more mature than him playing with my panties. I didn't care; I did it anyhow. Then I grabbed the handset from him and pressed it to my ear while I dialed my sister's number.

Sarah answered on the second ring, and Eason sat in front of me, waiting. "Randi?" The way she said my name had me holding my breath. Any second now, she would knock the wind out of me. She'd managed to make two syllables into one, and panic lined her heavy breathing.

Despite not wanting to find out the reason for her urgency, I exhaled and said, "Yeah."

"You need to come home." Her voice cracked, and it wasn't difficult to make out the muffled crying. "There's been an accident."

The last time I'd heard those words, everything in my life changed in the course of a few weeks. But this time, today, this very moment, I didn't have Austin to catch me or hold my hand through it. I wanted to stick my head in the sand and pretend I hadn't heard the words she'd uttered.

"Randi? Did you hear me?"

I didn't have the courage to ask who. There were only two people she would have called me for—Austin and Daddy. And I couldn't handle either one. My chest rose in rapid succession, and shallow breaths left me in a dizzy fog.

"Randi! Say something."

I couldn't. Whatever lay on the other side of my response would decimate me. My eyes pooled with unshed tears, and then they flitted to Eason. The moment our gazes met, his juvenile demeanor morphed into the man made for the courtroom.

"Miranda, what's wrong?"

The lump in my throat kept me from speaking, and I struggled to swallow. An intense pain lined my jaw and slithered down my neck. All I could do was shake my head. When the first tear fell, I managed to find my voice and croaked, "Who?" I wasn't prepared for the answer, and in the split second I had to contemplate it, I didn't know which one I'd rather it be.

"Daddy." Sarah had as hard of a time stringing together sentences as I did. "The wildfires..."

"When?" I was nothing if not eloquent. I needed to slap myself. This wasn't who I was. *Randi* was ill-prepared. *Randi* fell apart in emergencies. *Randi* couldn't handle bad news. *Miranda* was not that girl.

"Austin found him late Sunday night out in the south pasture."

I was oh for two. I didn't have a clue why Austin would have been on my daddy's ranch, much less that far out in his fields. Now wasn't the time to ask. "What happened?" It was like listening to someone else talk. I'd heard of people feeling as though they'd drifted outside their bodies and watched themselves; I'd just never experienced it...until now.

Her sobs had eased enough that I was able to understand her broken speech and cracked words. "He tried to save some cows that fell behind when they moved them to another pasture. He went alone." My daddy knew better than that. It wasn't safe. There had to be another explanation. "When Austin found him, he was still conscious. He's not now."

I shouldn't still be stuck on the fact that Austin was involved, yet my mind couldn't let go. That thought was easier to handle than the image of Daddy alone in a pasture in pain. "Why was Austin there?"

"Seriously?" Gone were the tears. They'd been replaced by sass and grunts. "That's what you're worried about? What about Daddy's condition?" She huffed into the receiver. "Great day in the morning, Randi. You need to get your head on straight and get home."

Great day in the morning? She'd turned into one of those old women in Mason Belle who did nothing other than get into people's business. They called it concern; the rest of the world called it gossip.

I felt like I was eighteen again, and she was daring me to cross her. The last time I'd done that, things hadn't ended well for any of us. Tamping my irritation at her tone and the fear crawling up my neck, I tried to focus. "Is he..." I wasn't sure I could get the words out of my mouth. "Is he going to make it?"

Sarah sighed on the other end, and Eason stood abruptly. "I don't know, Randi. You need to get home."

There was no fighting this. I didn't care what Daddy had said or done that caused me to leave Texas. It didn't matter why Austin had been at Cross Acres. The only thing that mattered was getting back to Mason Belle.

I'd tried to stay at work yesterday, but after talking to Sarah, I was pretty much useless. Eason had brought me home about an hour after we'd gotten to the office, and he hadn't let me out of his sight since. I drew the line when he followed me into the bathroom. I wasn't suicidal. I was just a basket case. Worried about my daddy, dreading stepping foot in Mason Belle, fearful of what the next twenty-four hours would bring—it made for an emotional mess that Eason wasn't accustomed to seeing.

The sound of the zipper on my suitcase echoed around me. There was finality around that noise. I wasn't in the same room, nor were these the same circumstances, yet the low-frequency zing of metal combining with metal brought on the same anxiety as it had the day I'd left Texas. But Eason didn't let me linger in it.

He grabbed the handle of my luggage and pulled it off the mattress. "Are you ready?"

I nodded, uncertain of what I had said yes to. With my

inability to function, Eason had taken care of getting a taxi to pick us up, the flights to Texas, and transportation to Mason Belle once we got to Laredo. All I'd managed to accomplish were a few measly texts to my sister, a shower, and packing.

Eason took my hand and led me down the stairs. I wasn't sure how he navigated the narrow steps with a suitcase on one side and me on the other, yet like everything else, he did it with refinement. I followed him out the front door, which he locked behind us. The driver appeared to have already loaded Eason's luggage, and now, he waited at the back of the black Lincoln Town Car to take mine.

The large hand that had comforted and protected me for the last six years grazed my lower back to guide me into the vehicle. Once I was settled inside, Eason followed silently. He wrapped his arm around my shoulders, and my head rested in the nook of his neck.

Curled into his side, I murmured into the collar of his shirt. "You know you don't have to go, right?"

His chest rumbled with forced laughter. "Of course, I do. You're convinced the wolves are coming for you. I'd never forgive myself if anything happened."

I pulled back to see that he understood. "I have no idea what kind of landmines I'm walking into, Eason. It's not going to be pretty."

"Hospitals don't scare me, Miranda."

I half snorted, and I could only imagine the heinous expression that lingered on my face. "It's not the hospital I'm worried about." With a humph, I threw my weary body against the seat.

He took my hand in his and stroked the top with his thumb. Any other time that would calm my worries. "If they didn't love you, they wouldn't have begged you to come home."

"It's not Sarah that bothers me."

He puffed up and squared his shoulders, right before he let out a *pfft*. "Is it this Austin character?"

If I could glare holes into anyone, Eason would have two the size of quarters going straight through his forehead. As many years as we'd been friends, Austin's name had only come up a handful of times—just often enough for Eason to recognize how potent it was.

"You realize I'm not exactly a small guy, right?"

It was the first time in twenty-four hours that I'd cracked a smile. "Last time I checked, neither was Austin." I flattened the lapel of his sports coat. "And I can assure you, he won't be in a suit if things come to blows." The wink I sent Eason only served to rile him.

"You think a jacket will prevent me from taking care of you?" He shook his head. "My, my, Miranda. How little you've noticed over the years. Nothing, not even Austin, is going to hurt you on my watch."

The weak grin that parted my lips didn't make Eason happy. Those words were all too familiar. I dreaded the two men coming head to head and hoped I could prevent them from ever meeting. There was no reason either of us had to see Austin. I was going back to Texas for my sister and my dad. But if we happened to run into my old flame, I'd take whatever he dished out—I deserved anything he could give and more. And I wouldn't let Eason interfere in whatever way Austin chose to deliver his message.

It hadn't taken long to get through the airport, and once we were settled on the plane, I fell asleep on Eason's arm, nestled in the comfort of first class. There were some benefits to traveling with a McNabb...other than beautiful man candy.

He didn't even make a big deal out of the puddle of drool I left on his shoulder when we landed. Eason simply pulled his monogrammed handkerchief from his pocket and wiped it away before offering it to me to blot my mouth. By that time, I was already mid-swipe with my sleeve.

The chuckle next to me calmed my fears. It didn't eliminate

them, but at least I knew I wasn't entering the lion's den without a loaded gun. "I guess it's a good thing you didn't have on any lipstick."

I pulled a compact from my purse to check my face. "Oh God, were you planning to tell me I looked like death warmed over?"

"I thought I just did."

Glancing away from my mirror, I scowled at him. It had been years since I'd stepped foot in Texas. I didn't want to even remotely resemble the girl I'd left behind when I got on that bus. Warpaint was a necessity.

While I reapplied my face, the plane taxied to the gate. And once we unbuckled, Eason stood to get his bag out of the overhead compartment. Where I'd expected time to crawl as I approached impending doom, it raced at the speed of light. The two of us had walked through the airport with our hands clasped together until we reached baggage claim. There, at the bottom of the escalator, stood a man in a nice, black suit holding an iPad with Eason's name on it.

"Overkill much?" I asked and swatted at his arm.

He didn't respond. He was too busy talking to the driver and moving us toward the conveyor. My eyes roamed wildly over the crowd. Laredo was a large city. The likelihood I would run into anyone I knew was almost none, yet my anxiety had kicked into overdrive. I was drowning in a sea of unfamiliar faces. Their anonymity suffocated me.

My pits began to perspire, and I worried the sweat would show through my white blouse. I tried to lift my arms casually to air them out, and in the process, I ended up with my hand wrapped around the nape of my neck. Suddenly, the anxiety ratcheted into a sensation akin to bugs crawling over my skin, and I wondered what would come next, hallucinations or passing out.

When fingers secured my elbow, I jumped, startled by the unexpected visitor. Had my hair been long, it would have whipped Eason in the face when I jerked to see who had touched me.

His brow rose, and he stared at me for a moment longer than necessary. "Miranda?"

I dropped the death grip on my esophagus and waved my hand in the air. My face scrunched into an expression that indicated my current state was nothing to be alarmed over, when in fact, Eason might need to locate a strong sedative and a straitjacket. I was losing my marbles, and I hadn't stepped foot into Mason Belle.

"You don't look so good. Let's get you some fresh air."

My shoulders shook, and an overly dramatic rumble started in my chest, then bubbled up through my throat, and finally burst out of my mouth. Confused by my laughter, Eason's eyes narrowed, while his lips pursed in thought. I grabbed his hand and pulled him toward the door with the driver leading the way. The instant the automatic doors opened and a wave of heat and humidity waffled us, he finally understood.

"Jesus. It's like breathing water. How the hell do people survive here?" His handkerchief appeared out of nowhere, and now, he was the one blotting his face. Perspiration peppered his forehead and lingered under his nose.

"Wait for it." Funny how so much changes when so many things stay the same.

He craned his neck to peer down at me, and his eyes flitted between the man we followed and me. "Wait for what?"

Three. Two. One—

"Hell no." He quit blotting his face and started pulling off his jacket and then his dress shirt out of the waist of his slacks. "Sweat ran between my—" He stopped himself from spitting out the words. "You could have warned me."

I shrugged. "I thought I just did." Turnabout was fair play. "Around these parts, they call that swamp ass." I laid on a thick

Southern accent to illustrate my point and gave him a wink for good measure. I didn't think he appreciated my humor.

Eason pushed his jacket toward me to hold and pawed at his skin under his shirt. And the moment we reached the vehicle, he started to undo the buttons. A striptease from a man who looked like this one would do nothing other than attract onlookers. Especially next to a *limo*.

"You ordered a limo?" I practically shrieked under my breath.

He merely nodded and kept working to free himself from the confines of wet, sticky cotton.

I stomped my foot. It hadn't taken thirty minutes of being back in Texas for me to start acting like the brat I'd left here six years ago. "Are you *trying* to draw attention?"

"I'm not going to take off my shirt until we're in the car. Calm down."

At this point, the world seeing Eason's bare chest was the least of my concerns. "I'm talking about the car, Eason!" Rock-hard abs, biceps of steel, and back muscles that would make Adonis jealous were a dime a dozen compared to the likes of this vehicle.

He slid into the back and talked to me through the open door. "There wasn't a lot to choose from on short notice."

Just to illustrate how absurd I believed this to be, I jutted my hip out and jammed my hand onto it in a show of defiance. "Somehow, I don't believe there was nothing available in Laredo besides a Hummer that seats twelve."

Eason leaned toward me, grabbed the hand on my cocked hip, and then pulled me in next to him. And as soon as my feet left the ground, the driver sealed us inside. I continued to gape at him, and he proceeded to strip like this was completely normal. He removed the last stitch of fabric from his body and then faced me. "What's the big deal?"

Blink. Blink. Blink. Breathe. Blink. Deep breath.

"I had hoped to arrive with as little fanfare as possible. This"—I circled my hands in the air between us—"screams *look at me!*"

"I'm sure the residents of your hometown have seen a limo before, Miranda. You're making something out of nothing."

"Nope. People in Mason Belle don't do limos. They wear cowboy boots and Wranglers. They drive huge trucks and ride fast horses. They do not rent over-the-top cars with drivers in suits to traipse down to the Piggly Wiggly for groceries."

He tilted his head to the side, considering what I'd said. "What's a Piggly Wiggly?"

I closed my eyes and slumped against the seat. This was pointless. It didn't matter what I said. Depending on traffic, we'd roll through town in roughly an hour, and every head would turn. Gossip would start. And within ten minutes—if I were lucky—the entire town would know someone from "the city" had arrived. "Never mind."

"Um, all right. Well, if we're done discussing our transportation, can you give the driver the address?"

My lids lifted slowly to find the chauffeur facing us from the front, waiting for instructions. I gave him the location, settled back, and tried to quiet the voices that screamed in my head.

Eason wasn't having any of it. "You weren't kidding when you said you lived in the middle of nowhere."

I peeked out the window, still trying to pretend he wasn't talking.

"Are we going to come to civilization before we get wherever we're going?"

My chest dropped with my exhalation, and I gave in. "You didn't have to come." My temples throbbed. I just wanted to go home...to New York. I didn't want to do this any more than Eason did—probably less, actually. By the time I faced him, he'd managed to pull a T-shirt from the bag he had taken on the plane and drew it over his head. That was one less thing for me to worry about.

He rubbed my thigh like a father would a child who was cold. "Don't take it like that. This is all so...desolate." Suddenly, the ground went from green to black. Lush grass to grey ash. "And burned."

Eason scanned the acres and acres of pastures destroyed by fire.

"It's remote. But surely, you've been to small towns before. You travel all the time." I chose to ignore the charred remains. I wasn't ready to face that aspect of this trip.

"Yeah, somehow, I don't think this experience is going to be quite like going to a tiny island near Fiji."

I snorted. I couldn't help it. I snapped my hand to cover my nose and mouth and the smile I tried to hide. Through my giggles, I confirmed, "You're right. It's nothing like blue lagoons and island princes."

"One time, and you're never going to let that go, are you? You weren't even there. I never should have told you."

"About the lagoon or the prince?"

He tossed his sweaty dress shirt at my head. "Both."

Even if I'd wanted to—which I didn't—I couldn't have stopped myself. "Maybe you'll fall for a lake and a cowboy. Or possibly a horse and water trough." The stern expression that marred his gorgeous face only spurred me on. "A pig and slop. Cow and field?"

"You were a lot cuter when you were broody."

"Was it the cow that tipped you over?" That was only funny to me. Eason McNabb had never been cow tipping. I'd bet money he'd never even heard of the pastime.

The driver agreed it was humorous. Even from this distance, I caught the twinkle in his eyes through the rearview mirror.

Thankfully, Eason had missed it. Unfortunately, he missed it when he'd zeroed in on something far more sobering.

"That sign can't be right."

Mason Belle. Population 1809. After the natural disaster that had blown through here in the last few days, he was probably right. The number might be lower today than it was last week.

I only knew of three new people who'd been born and one who left. That meant seventeen other kids had joined the community in six years. "They've had a baby boom. They're up nineteen. It was seventeen ninety."

Eason craned his head, keeping his focus on the city limit sign as we passed it. "Wow." That one word held so much wonder. Like a child at an aquarium or an amusement park, his jaw hung slightly ajar as he stared in amazement. Or it might have been the acres of blackened fields that stunned him.

"Don't blink. You might miss it."

I cracked the window enough to let the smell of Texas in. It was more than that, though. Hay and livestock. The purest scent a small-town girl could ever inhale. Everything about it was perfection, except none of that floated into the car. Instead, we were assaulted by death and ashes...and then, the people came into view.

"What's everyone staring at?"

I rolled my eyes, grateful he couldn't see them and chastise me. "The parade rolling through town." Sarcasm dripped from my lips.

Eason mashed the button on the door, and the window crept down.

"Are you insane?" I pulled on his arm. Leaning over him, I sent the glass in the opposite direction. "Now is not the time to stick your head out like a dog."

He scoffed and again dropped the window. I died a thousand deaths when he stuck his hand out. While he smiled and waved at the gossip-hungry onlookers, I crouched as low in the seat as possible, hoping no one saw me. I didn't have to endure it long. The entire town wasn't more than five blocks. A feed and seed store and a tractor supply place were the only things left to ogle before the driver would enter Cross Acres. Everything on the left side of the road was charcoal. The right, beautiful Mason Belle.

And I held my breath the entire way.

The cast-iron gates were still as ornate, as was the landscaping at the entrance to Daddy's ranch. The limo slowed to make the turn, and that's when I rolled my window down completely. The smells, the sounds—my brain flooded with memories. Growing up, I had never imagined I'd leave this place. A week ago, I never thought I'd come back.

"Damn, Miranda. This is gorgeous. I had no idea it was so big."

Seeing it through Eason's perspective made it even more spectacular than I'd remembered. It wasn't *Dallas*, and we didn't have the Ewing mansion, but we had a ranch that had been in the family for generations. The farmhouse was nothing short of *Gone With the Wind*, and every blade of grass and stalk of hay from here as far as the eye could see belonged to Jack Adams. My daddy's land was the envy of cattle ranchers for miles, and there was a time it had been my paradise. The house and surrounding area seemed untouched, and for that, I was grateful, although, I knew devastation didn't lie too far off.

"You can pull into the circle," I said to the driver, who responded with a quick nod.

I didn't recognize any of the trucks parked by the barn, and I hadn't seen anyone near the house as we'd pulled in. It was late in the afternoon, and the likelihood that any of Daddy's hands were still here was slim, especially without him around to guide the troops. I had to wonder how Sarah kept this place running with Daddy gone. I didn't know how many acres had burned, but there could be a massive herd in a space way too small to contain and feed them.

The Hummer came to a stop. The driver opened my door first. Eason didn't wait for him to come to the other side. He hopped out when I placed a precarious heel onto the gravel. I cursed myself for wearing such inappropriate footwear. Hell, my entire outfit screamed New York, not Mason Belle. I didn't own anything that would even remotely fit in here anymore.

I dropped my sunglasses onto my nose to shield my eyes from the afternoon sun and took a step away from the car to face the house I'd grown up in. Someone had painted it since I'd last been here, although it was still the same pale yellow.

There was a new porch.

My rocking chairs were gone.

In their place sat benches that looked miserably uncomfortable. No woman in her right mind would care to sip tea and watch the sunset on those things. Then I remembered, there hadn't been a woman living here since I'd left. The truth was, I wasn't even certain how often Sarah came by. I bit my lip, letting my teeth sink in, to fight off the emotion that threatened to overtake me. I'd caused those changes. I had no right to cry over them.

The sound of boots on the gravel driveway should have alarmed me or, at the very least, gotten my attention. Instead, I watched Eason's interest shift from talking to the driver unloading our bags to the person approaching.

"You folks lost?" Even though it was deeper, more mature, I'd recognize that voice anywhere.

I couldn't bring myself to move. Suspended in time, my heels remained firmly planted right where I stood. My mind screamed for me to stop Eason. My heart let him go.

"Hey, man. I'm Eason McNabb."

The sound of palms clasping together in what I could only assume was a friendly handshake made me jump...and I nearly fell over when my ankle rolled in my stilettos. As fast as it always was, Eason's arm snaked around me. In one swift move, he spun me into his side to keep me from busting my tail in front of Austin Burin.

Mother Nature decided to give our reunion a moment of silence while I took in the boy I once knew and had always loved.

Except now, he was a man.

His sandy-blond hair hid beneath his ballcap, but even the bill couldn't conceal the brown eyes I'd memorized as a child. His neck was thicker, as were his chest and arms; nevertheless, it was clearly Austin. My heart stalled, then sputtered, and finally returned to a rapid rhythm that flushed my skin with heat...or maybe that was just the Texas sun.

"Randi," Austin deadpanned. Not quite the greeting I'd hoped for, yet better than the one I'd expected.

Swallowing proved especially tricky around the cotton in my mouth and the lump in my throat. Speaking was even worse. "It's Miranda."

"Of course, it is." He didn't hide his appraisal of Eason or the sneer that lifted the corner of his lip when his sight landed on Eason's arm still cradling my waist.

All it took was four words from Austin, and I felt Eason tense. He was oblivious to who stood in front of us. He didn't care. Gone was carefree Eason McNabb. The grip he had on my side indicated the vengeance he quietly threatened to unleash.

I didn't have a clue what to say or how to start any type of exchange. I'd convinced myself I could avoid Austin whether I was here for two days or two months. Clearly, I was wrong. "I wasn't expecting you here." *Well, duh.*

Austin stuck his hands in his pockets, although he didn't relax. "That makes two of us." It was a warning, as if he had more right to be standing on my family's property than I did. "What are you doing here?"

"Sarah called me."

Eason's talons hadn't let loose. Taking his aggression out on me wasn't fair, but if it kept him from lashing out at Austin, I'd take one for the team.

Austin scoffed. "From what I understand, she does that a lot. It hasn't brought you running back. Why now?"

That was it. It wouldn't have mattered if a herd of buffalo came charging down the driveway at eighty-four miles an hour. Eason McNabb wouldn't let Jesus Christ himself talk to me in the manner that Austin Burin currently did. It wasn't so much the actual words as the tone and sheer hatred that lined each snarly sentence.

"I'm sure you've heard about Miranda's father." Eason still didn't have a clue this was Austin in front of us. If he had, he would know that Austin was the one who'd found Daddy. So when Austin pulled his hands from his pockets, crossed his arms over his chest, and rocked back on his feet, Eason took it as a challenge and finally let go to shield me.

"Eason—"

He glanced at me over his shoulder. "Miranda. Why don't you go inside?"

"Don't do this." I managed to get the sentence out without my voice cracking, and I hoped he saw the plea in my eyes. "Please."

"Does Sarah know you're here?" Austin directed his question to me.

This was my battle to fight. I'd just hoped I'd have a little more time to prepare for it. As I stepped to Eason's side and moved forward, I lifted my sunglasses to the top of my head. With one hand, I took Eason's, and my other found his forearm. "Why don't you take our bags inside, and let the driver go. There's no need for everyone to witness this."

Eason glanced between Austin and me several times. "You sure?"

It was a weak smile, but I managed it all the same. Eason kissed my temple and did as I asked. Even though I heard the door open and close, I was confident he wasn't out of earshot. He'd figured out who this was, just not why the man was here.

I plucked the sunglasses from my head and folded the stems. Austin watched as I reached into my Gucci bag for the case and tucked them neatly inside. Once I returned the purse strap to my shoulder, I straightened my spine and dared to ask, "Why are you here, Austin? Why are you on my daddy's ranch? And why were you in the pasture that night?" There was more bite in my tone than I had any right to unleash.

He was like a concrete wall. Not one word I said unnerved him or even caused him to flinch. Austin stood stoically. Then he licked his lips, drawing the bottom one between his teeth before releasing it. I'd seen him do it a thousand times to calm himself. The only difference was, every time I'd ever witnessed it, it had happened when he'd been protecting me. Something told me that wasn't what was about to take place.

"You can't really be that clueless."

It was offensive, yet sadly, I was. I didn't have any idea why he was here. "Apparently, I am."

"Guess you changed more than your hair and your clothes since you've been gone." He sneered as his gaze traveled from the top of my head to my toes. "It seems you've also forgotten where you came from."

I pulled back, not certain what kind of insult he had thrown at me. "Pardon?"

"When things get tough in Mason Belle, the town comes together. They don't run. I've been *here*"—he pointed to the ground—"for six years. Every morning at five. Working the ranch when no one else could. The real question, *Miranda*, is why *weren't* you here?"

Breaking down, confessing what had happened, none of that

would do any good. Austin had formed his opinion a long time ago, and I hadn't been around to shape those thoughts. Anger, resentment, and hurt were written all over the lines in his face and the tight purse of his lips. I'd bet every penny I had that if I got close enough, I'd see all the flecks of gold and strands of honey were gone from his irises, and his pupils would be mere pinpricks. When his nostrils flared a hint, I sealed my armor. "I'll make sure to stay out of your way. We won't be here long."

Austin shook his head slowly. "Imagine that."

4

AUSTIN

*R*andi didn't argue. She didn't fight back. Any other time, she would have put me in my place. Reminded me of whose property I currently stood on. It wouldn't have surprised me if she'd gotten in my face and barked at me. Instead, she let some man speak for her and then cowered.

I'd watched her sulk into the house, while I stood in the same spot, staring at the front door that she'd closed behind her. Nothing about her was right. Everything was wrong. Off. I could have dealt with that awful haircut and the uppity clothes. Hell, even I had to admit, the heels were hot. That was where the heat ended. The fire that had lit her up like the sun in high school had burned out. Her eyes were sad and lifeless, and it wasn't just because of her dad. I didn't have a clue where the girl I loved had gone, but she sure wasn't the person who had walked inside that house.

A part of me wanted to march up the steps, fling the door open, and demand answers...right after I tossed that preppy, suit-wearing asshat out. I could admit he was a good-looking guy if a girl liked that type—Randi didn't. I didn't give a rat's ass what she did to change her appearance or the reasons behind why she had done it—although, all fingers pointed to Eason. His name grated on me. It was too soft. Maybe if he added a *T* in the middle, it would toughen it up. Randi didn't need soft. She'd never needed soft.

The longer I stood there, and the more I pondered it, the angrier I got. Yet, I couldn't figure out who I was madder at, Sarah, Randi, or myself. Sarah could have given me a heads-up. Randi could have picked up a damn telephone once in six years. And I should have moved the hell on when I had realized she wasn't coming home. None of those things had happened. Once again, Randi Adams wreaked havoc in Mason Belle, and she'd been here all of ten minutes.

"Austin?" Tommy called from the barn.

I finally dragged my stare away from the house. "Yeah?"

He brushed the dust off his jeans as he approached. "You need anything else?"

I needed a beer, or maybe even a shot of SoCo. "Nah. I'll see you in the morning."

"Have a good night, man."

Tipping my head in a quick gesture, I wished him the same without speaking. I wasn't in the mood to be cordial, but my mama would hogtie and dangle me from a tree by my toes if I were rude unnecessarily.

Tommy clicked the alarm on his truck, and I shook my head, wondering who he imagined would break into it. Before he got in, he stopped. "Hey. Who was in that limo? Is Jack thinking of selling the place?"

Shit. It hadn't occurred to me how Randi's arrival would appear to the guys who hadn't met her. I wasn't certain which of the hired help were even aware Jack had another daughter. "No one important. And no, he's not selling." Hundreds of singed acres wouldn't draw a terribly high bidder, anyhow.

Suddenly, Tommy removed his hat and waved his hand at something behind me. "Ma'am."

I dropped my head, my chin nearly hitting my chest, and I prayed she hadn't heard me say she wasn't important. Not that I cared whether she believed I thought she was insignificant to the ranch because she was. It had run just fine in her absence. What I couldn't handle would be her crying.

"I'll see you tomorrow, Tommy. Have a good night."

Thankfully, he didn't question me or try to interact further with Randi. He took the cue and got in his truck without another word. I, on the other hand, could feel her stare. Eighteen-year-old *Randi* would have stomped down those steps, sashayed right past me, and straight up to Tommy with her hand out to introduce herself. If *Miranda* had moved, she hadn't made a sound.

I didn't glance back. Instead, I marched to the barn, removed the saddle and reins from Nugget, and then spent the next hour brushing him out. He was a better listener than any human I knew. I also needed to prepare him. Unlike the people in my life who hadn't bothered to let me in on the secret of her arrival, I couldn't do that to Nugget. She'd come for him, and he needed to be ready. It was silly, and all I was doing was wasting time. The horse wasn't going on a date. He wasn't about to be showcased in a parade. Somehow, in my mind, the way I'd cared for her horse was as significant as how I would have cared for her...had she bothered to stick around.

By the time I exited the stall and then the barn, the sun had long since set. I hadn't seen the house so lit up in years. There weren't all that many lights on, yet somehow, it still seemed bright. Until a shadow moved on the porch. The man descending the steps of Jack's house was shrouded in darkness, yet I didn't have any difficulty identifying him.

I took a deep breath and let it out through my nose. It was

probably better this happened now versus another time when other hands might see it.

"Hi." The friendly tone I'd heard when he introduced himself was long gone. "Got a minute?"

I didn't have the energy for whatever this was, so I leaned against the back of my truck and let Eason come to me. "Yeah." If he wanted to talk, he could do the walking. He could scream across the driveway for all I cared.

He ran his hand through his hair, and I watched as it went right back to where it had been before he'd touched it. Clearly, he had something to say. However, I was struck by how pained he appeared to actually have to spit out the words. His entire demeanor was different than it had been with Randi around. Maybe it was the fact that he'd put on jeans and a T-shirt or perhaps not having her at his side weakened him—it sure as hell had me.

"I know you and Miranda have a past—"

"Randi."

He wrinkled his brow and stared at me for a fraction of a second. "What?"

Crossing my ankles and my arms, I explained, "I don't know Miranda. I have a history with Randi. They aren't the same person."

"Seriously?"

I wasn't sure what had confused him. It seemed crystal clear to me. All I knew was that if this was going to turn into an all-night cockfight, I needed to eat first. My stomach growled, but I was fairly certain her boytoy thought it was me. "We don't know the same person. That's all I'm saying." I kept my tone free of irritation and contempt. The faster I could get out of here, the better.

Eason cleared his throat and suddenly appeared uneasy, like he expected an argument. "This is really difficult for her." He swiveled his head, looking around. At what, I wasn't sure. It was dark as Egypt beyond the house. "She just wants to see her dad and try to get out unscathed."

I pushed off the truck with one foot. "Look, I don't know what she's told you. Hell, you may have more insight than I do. Regardless, if she believed she could stroll into town and the Mason Belle Welcome Wagon would pull up with a basket of freshly baked cookies and bread, she's got another thing coming. I'm not interested in making her time here difficult. In fact, I want to make it as easy as possible so she'll leave sooner."

"You don't have to be like that, Austin."

"No, I don't have to be, but by God, I have every right to be. There's a reason she hasn't come home. Maybe you should ask her what it is." I wasn't interested in his reply, so I didn't wait for it.

I hadn't gotten three strides away when I felt him grab my bicep. "I get that you're hurt, man. Can't you let bygones be bygones?"

I lowered my head, and subsequently my stare, to his fingers wrapped around my arm. When he released his hold, I didn't answer his question. I warned him. "If you love her, I'd advise you to get her out as fast as you can. This town is going to eat her for lunch."

*A*ttempting to sleep was pointless. Every time my lids drifted shut, images of Randi popped into my head. Memories from years ago. Except it was the version of her I'd seen today, not the one who'd actually created the stories my mind held onto. No matter how hard I tried to push her from my thoughts, my resentment prevented me from letting her go.

A lack of rest on a cattle ranch was never a good thing, much less after the week we'd had. The work was physical, and the days were long. Add to that an ache of resentment that settled into my gut the second I pulled into Cross Acres, and I had been less than pleasant to the other guys all day. For the most part, they'd all given me a wide girth and let me be. They'd been around long enough to know not to ask questions. There was plenty to do without making conversation, so I kept my hands busy with it. I'd also managed to stay as far away from the farmhouse as possible since the first light had come on.

Maybe it was immature, and I should quite possibly figure out a way to make amends. However, the last thing I had any desire to do was extend an olive branch to the girl who'd broken my heart and ruined me without so much as looking back. Never in a million years had I imagined Randi would leave Mason Belle, much less under the cover of night without a word to anyone. But that one choice opened my eyes to what she was capable of. And so had her absence since. The best thing the two of us could do was stay far away from the other. It was clear she no longer belonged in Texas, and I would never belong anywhere else.

I'd been tortured by my thoughts all day. Luckily for me, Corey wasn't much of a talker. It never bothered me, even though it made it difficult to bring him into the fold. Today, I was grateful he didn't have a need to fill empty space with words. He tossed me a bottle of water as we both took a much-needed break. It had to be in the nineties, and there wasn't a cloud in the sky, although the lingering smoke hadn't burned off yet. After taking a long drink, I lifted my hat and poured the rest over my head. My shirt was already drenched in sweat. In this heat, the fabric under my arms stayed damp all afternoon. My sides were chaffed, which only added to my discomfort and irritation.

Corey had remained quiet, other than to ask questions about the irrigation we worked on. I'd specifically picked him to ride out with me for that reason. As the sun tipped toward evening, we finished up and headed back toward the barn. The low thud of the horses' hooves on the ground and an occasional squawk of a bird were the only sounds around us. I hadn't heard the rustle of wildlife in days.

Until Corey decided he'd been quiet long enough. "Ain't none of my business," he started without looking at me.

My chest expanded as I took in a deep breath. "Probably not."

"That limo, and what it brought with it, what's bothering you?"

I could have lied. I could have told him I didn't want to talk about it. Yet something told me Corey wasn't asking to gossip or share with the other guys. So, I nodded.

"She mean something to you?"

I didn't realize he'd even been around when Randi and her boyfriend had appeared on Jack's doorstep. Tommy was the only one I saw, but Corey had been with me since he pulled in this morning. And I knew he and Tommy didn't talk outside of work.

"Used to."

His head bobbed in my periphery. Corey was a soft-spoken man. Kept to himself. I believed that was due to the reasons he was in Mason Belle and what he was trying to accomplish. He wasn't here to make friends. It was all about his wife and daughter —that was it. "Who is she?"

"Jack's daughter." If it had been anyone else, they would have given up with my clipped answers.

"I didn't realize he had two. I thought Sarah was it."

I scoffed. "Might as well be."

"She stayin' long?"

I wished I had an answer to that question for my own sanity. "Knowing her, not likely. Not really sure why she came to begin with."

He didn't say anything for a long time, and when he finally spoke again, there was emotion in his voice I couldn't identify. "You're a good man, Austin. I don't pretend to know what she did or why she left. But I'm guessin' if she meant something to you, she's pretty special."

I clenched my jaw and ground my teeth together. Corey wasn't the person to lash out at. He didn't know our history. He didn't know *any* of the history in Mason Belle. Although, I'd bet if he were to make a trip into town, he'd get an earful.

"People make mistakes. I'm livin' proof of that, Austin." He was right, but that didn't change anything for me. "Lovin' them means findin' a way to forgive 'em."

"Forgiving and forgetting are two different things, Corey."

"Don't sound to me like you've done either."

My nostrils flared as I kept my temper under control. Corey didn't wait for a response. The farmhouse and barn were in sight, and with a tap of his heels into his horse's haunches, the animal picked up the pace, leaving Nugget and me behind. I didn't chase after him. In fact, I pulled back on the reins to slow the palomino beneath me.

Just as I had hoped, by the time I got back to the barn, the other guys had left. Alone in the barn, I unsaddled Nugget and brushed him out. When I glanced at my watch, it neared five o'clock. I'd tried to time my day to avoid Randi. She wasn't up at the crack of dawn, and I made myself scarce around the property at the first sign of life in the house until I was certain she'd be heading back from the hospital by the time I got up there.

I closed the barn door behind me and glanced at the house. Not seeing anyone there or a car out front, I hopped in my truck. With a quick shower, a layer of baby powder on my sides that were indeed raw, and a fresh set of clothes, I took off to the hospital. It wasn't exactly close, which made all of this even more difficult.

Jack had been airlifted to the nearest facility after I'd found him and gotten close enough to the house to get a signal on my cell. It wasn't quite in Laredo, though it might as well have been.

Thankfully, it was outside the city limits, and therefore, not nestled in the heart of traffic. A couple of miles farther and it would have added another half an hour to the already thirty-minute drive.

As I made the trek, I wondered what kind of toll this was taking on Sarah. I hadn't had the time to check on her since it had all happened. She had Charlie. Charlie had my dad's backing at the farm. I was Jack's only line of defense at Cross Acres. With three kids who adored their papa, I couldn't imagine how her heart broke. Add to it the physical strain of chasing that horde around, and it would quickly take its toll. Sarah was a strong woman, but everyone had a breaking point. And her daddy was the apple of her eye—she loved that man. No one, not even an adult, ever wants to be orphaned. If she lost Jack, that was precisely what she'd become. I doubted she'd recover.

By the time I arrived at the hospital, it was a little after six, leaving me about two hours with Jack to myself. The parking lot was relatively empty. I didn't see Sarah's SUV or Charlie's truck. And thankfully, there wasn't a limo in sight. Thinking about Randi having the audacity to traipse through town in that show-boat did nothing other than irritate me.

"Good evening, Mr. Burin," the receptionist greeted. That was the great thing about small towns. It didn't take long for the locals to learn your name.

I tipped my head and gave her a bit of a smile without saying anything. She was young and cute, and there was no need for me to encourage anything beyond being polite. A few strides later and I was in the elevator, on my way to the third floor. Jack's door was down the hall on the right past the nurses' station.

Rapping my knuckles on the door didn't get a response from the other side. I breathed out a heavy sigh of relief when I realized Jack was alone. He was also asleep. That was fine with me. I was perfectly happy to take a seat next to his bed and hang out. I hadn't ever been hospitalized; although, if I ever were, I thought it would be awful to wake up and not have anyone there. I couldn't stay all night—they wouldn't let me—but I could put some time in. Jack was family, and not just because my brother was married to his daughter. I'd known the man my entire life. He was close to my parents. My connection to him ran deeper than Randi or Sarah. I had worked day in and day out with him for years. I'd been around for every significant event in his life since the day I was born. It just bonded people.

He didn't look good, although I guessed that was relative. Jack appeared a helluva lot better than he had lying with his nose planted in a cow pasture. However, his face remained ashen. Even his lips were nearly white, and they were so severely chapped that I wondered how they hadn't cracked and bled. His color wasn't the worst part, though. It was the wires, the machines he was connected to. The bandages, the bruises.

I sucked in a fast, deep breath, trying to calm my heart. Regardless of what had happened with his wife and then later with Randi, Jack was a good man. He believed in God, treated people right, and worked hard. Seeing him so broken in that bed could have only been worse had it been my own father. Leaning forward, I scooted the chair I'd sat in so I could hold his hand. I didn't care if it wasn't manly. There were times I still felt like a child, and this was one of my childhood mentors. I carefully wrapped my fingers around his and tucked them into his palm, making sure to avoid the IV. And then, I dropped my head to the mattress and prayed.

When I finally sat up, I found two sets of eyes concentrated on me. She was like a damned ninja. She was also the last person I cared to see.

Randi's chest deflated, and her shoulders slumped when our sights met. "What are you doing here?" There was no accusation in her tone, only confusion.

"I'm not going to dignify that with a response." Yet, I didn't move. I held her attention with her father's hand in mine.

Her boyfriend shifted awkwardly next to her. I didn't know him, but he didn't seem to be the type to get unnerved around strangers, which made me wonder what exactly he knew about me. His movement caught my attention, and I dropped her stare for his.

"You want some coffee, man?" He pointed his thumb over his shoulder. "I could go get us all some."

I didn't have a clue how to answer that. There was no way in hell he should leave his girlfriend alone with me. This was the same man who'd asked me to give her a break last night. Now he trusted me in the same room with her without him around. Things must be done way different up north than they were in the South.

"Nah. I'm good." I could use a cup of coffee. Desperately. I did not, however, need any time alone with the woman at his side. "Thanks."

"Why are you here, Austin?" It was like she was a CD stuck on repeat and someone needed to nudge her to get her to move on.

I let go of Jack's hand and leaned back. "Checking on Jack."

"How long have you been here?" Neither she nor Easy-E moved from the spot they'd stood. It wasn't like I had leprosy. They weren't going to catch anything sitting near me, yet they kept their distance.

No part of me felt as if I owed her any explanation nor that she deserved one. Yet for whatever reason, I answered her, although there wasn't a hint of warmth in my tone. "Not long. I came after I left Cross Acres. I assumed you'd be on your way back by the time I got here." I could only assume by the look on her face that my expression was just as cold as my voice.

"Sarah and I are taking shifts. I didn't get here until lunch. She's got mornings after she drops off the girls."

The girls. Unless she'd met my nieces this morning, she had no right to present any type of familiarity to them.

"Hmm." It was all I could muster without being snippy or rude.

Randi was uncomfortable. I doubted the guy at her side even realized it. If he had, certainly he would have shielded her from it. She tucked her hair behind her ear, and my sight drifted from her chin-length cut down her slender neck to the teal, silk tank top hanging from her shoulders. It did nothing to flatter her, even if it looked like it cost a fortune. She was too skinny, and it only accentuated her bony shoulders. The black slacks didn't do anything, either. Add the black-patent leather heels, and her legs looked like pencils attached to her waist. Oddly, she was exactly what I would have expected him to have on his arm, and they were the picture of society—high society.

"Has he been awake?"

"Not since I've been here. Not today, I mean." I shouldn't care, but I asked anyhow. "You talked to him?"

Instantly, her attention met the floor, and the dress-shirt-covered arm slid around her waist the way it had yesterday. I couldn't bring myself to attach it to the man moving it. In my mind, that appendage needed to stay an inanimate object to prevent me from ripping it from the socket. Randi's hair moved with the shake of her head. That was a demon I didn't have any desire to witness her facing.

I huffed out through my nose, and a snide smirk rose on one side of my mouth. "Good luck with that, Randi."

"Miranda," *GQ* corrected me.

I got to my feet and made a mental note to visit in the morning when Sarah was on duty. "Whatever you choose to call her. You won't be able to protect her from that fall."

She turned into his side without lifting her face. The shake of her shoulders indicated her emotional state. If I'd actually seen the tears fall, it would have shredded me. Since she had spared me that visual, my heart hardened, and a chill filled my chest.

"No boyfriend can fix it. She's going to have to face it on her own. And crying on your shoulder won't change that." I had to leave before this got out of hand. The last thing I needed was to be banned from visiting.

McDreamy opened his mouth and simultaneously took a deep breath, expanding his chest. Clearly, Randi felt it because she pulled back as he started speaking. "I'm not—"

She caught his attention, but I couldn't see her expression, so I didn't witness the warning she'd issued. Whatever it was had halted him mid-sentence. Her hand on his pecs, the distance between her face and his—I'd been in his shoes more times than I could count. I couldn't watch it with another man.

"If Jack wakes up, let him know I stopped by, and the ranch is in good hands. I'll come back another time when Sarah's here."

And like our meeting the day before, she didn't step up or speak out. Her gaze never left him. I'd been that white knight when neither of us knew what it meant—her armor, her shield. Now, every encounter with her was like another slap in the face. Each time I saw Randi go to him and him step up, I wanted to throw him on the ground and beat the ever-loving horseshit out of him right before I demanded answers from her. Neither would solve anything.

So again, I stepped around the two of them and walked out.

5

AUSTIN

PAST

"*A*ustin, son, don't forget Miranda's present," my mother called out to me when I was halfway up the Adams' front steps.

It wasn't like she couldn't grab it from the back seat, but I knew better than to make that statement with my father rounding the bed of the truck. He'd backhand me into next week for sassin' my mom.

"Yes, ma'am." My shoulders slumped as I gave in and went to retrieve the bag.

Staring at the mounds of pink tissue that spilled out of the top, and the sparkly polka dots on the paper, I groaned as I took hold of the strings. Sure, Randi was a girl, but there was enough pink on this bag to make Pepto puke. And I wasn't terribly interested in being seen carrying it into my best friend's birthday party. It was bad enough my mom made me get her a doll that she would never play with. I ran as fast as I could back up the steps and into the house to find the first place I could to dump the stupid thing.

Luckily, the gift table was right inside the front door. I promptly left the offending bag with all the others as if I might somehow be contaminated with cooties if I didn't drop it fast enough. My feet carried me as quickly as possible through the house to find my friends out back. Rounding a corner to my destination, I ran smack-dab into an Adams wall. Mr. Adams to be exact. "Oomph." I was on my rear end before I realized what'd hit me.

Randi's dad extended his hand to help me up. He'd always scared me—he was gigantic and hardly ever talked—today, he terrified me.

"Slow down, Austin. You ain't gonna miss out on nothin'." The words weren't unusual. It was the look in his eyes and the fact that there wasn't a shred of happiness on his face or in his voice.

I searched for my parents, praying they were close by and wouldn't let him spank me. Not finding them, I returned my gaze to the brooding giant. "Yes, sir."

He didn't say anything else, just stepped aside and let me pass. I straightened my shoulders and eased by him as casually as I could. I didn't let out the breath I held until I heard the screen door slam behind me.

It was a circus beyond the kitchen. I'd only seen stuff like this at the fair, and I wondered how on earth Randi had gotten her parents to spring for rides and bouncy houses that would have all had to be brought in from another town. Mason Belle didn't have things like this. Scanning the property, I searched for my best friend amongst every kid in the entire county. Mrs. Adams always went all out, but this was over the top, even for her.

Near the white tent, where most of the parents hung out, I finally found Randi swinging in circles, hand in hand with Charity. Her mama was going to be ticked when she saw Randi's hair and dress. At one point, she'd had a fancy, curled ponytail on top of her head. Now, it was loose and hanging near her neck in a tousled mess. There was no way Mrs. Adams would ever be able to get the dirt stains off the bottom of the white lace. I shook my head and chuckled to myself. I'd known Randi my entire life.

Surely her mama knew her better. No one in their right mind would ever give that girl a white dress to play outside when she could have ruined it in Sunday school.

I hopped off the porch, my gangly legs strolling across the grass toward the birthday girl. A couple of people grabbed me along the way, and I had to be polite not knowing where my own mom was in the crowd. When I finally had Randi's attention, her face lit up like a neon sign, except it didn't blink. It continued to glow.

She stopped short and dropped Charity's hands, nearly sending the other girl to the ground with the loss of support. I didn't hear what Charity yelled when she stumbled. All I saw was the flush of Randi's cheeks from being in the sun and her wild hair blowing with the gentle breeze. I continued moving toward the two, and Randi left her friend to run to me. In true Randi fashion, she threw her arms around my neck and squeezed. She was the only girl who hugged me other than my mom. Even at ten years old, I was aware that she didn't show anyone else the same affection—well, other than her girlfriends.

Every time she did it, my heart sped up a little, and my chest felt bigger. I was tall and scrawny, so anything that made me feel like I could conquer the world was something special, even if I didn't understand it.

She pulled back to look me in the eyes, although she didn't let go of my neck. I felt awkward holding onto her waist, so I dropped my hands to my sides and grinned at her like a possum eating persimmons. "You came!"

I laughed and shook my head. "Of course."

Randi released her hold only to take my hand in hers. "Did you see the Ferris wheel?" Even if her excitement hadn't been painted across her face, it was evident in her tone.

The ride was hard not to notice. It towered above everything else in sight. Not that it was huge, because it wasn't. There were only ten carts on it. Still, Miranda Adams was the only girl I'd ever known who had a Ferris wheel at a party. "Yeah. Have you been on it?"

She shook her head, and more of hair fell from her ponytail. "Uh-huh. I've been waiting for you."

I'd never noticed a smile before hers. Every time she graced me with it, I couldn't help but return it with one of my own. Her teeth were perfectly straight and bright white, yet that wasn't what made it so spectacular. She had high cheekbones, and when she grinned really big, her cheeks pushed against the bottoms of her lashes. It was like her eyes smiled, too. It was uniquely Randi, and so were the sparkles that danced in her irises like ballerinas.

We took off running, without letting go of each other. I'd catch crap about it from Brock later—or any of the other kids in our class. I didn't care. They were either jealous or confused. Having Randi Adams's attention was nothing short of spectacular. The two of us stood at the front of a line forming while we waited for the ride.

I glanced down and noticed she wasn't wearing shoes. "Your mom's gonna be crazy mad when she sees you barefoot."

She shrugged with indifference. "I'll put them back on before she gets here." Randi tilted her head and shielded her brow from the sun to watch the metal wheel spin.

"She's not here?" Even *I* knew that was odd.

The ballerinas had quit twirling when Randi locked her gaze with mine. She shook her head quickly and then stared over my shoulder at something in the distance.

I couldn't think of any reason her mom would miss a party she had planned. "Where is she?"

She dropped her head, and my attention shifted to her feet. Her toes kicked at the grass nervously. "I don't know." It was barely a whisper.

Had I not been listening for an answer, I would have missed it over the chatter of people around us and the rides running. The bouncy house to our right provided all kinds of white noise to keep it inflated. It didn't take a rocket scientist to recognize she was upset. Even realizing that, I didn't have a clue how to fix it. Thankfully, the ride stopped, and we were seated in the empty cart. There wasn't a word exchanged between the two of us. She stared over the side and clung to my hand. Our fingers wound together, and I wondered if that was the only thing keeping her grounded. Her thoughts were a million miles away. She could have easily floated off with them.

I didn't know much about girls and even less about women, but I had an older brother who was an expert. Charlie always told me that if a woman was quiet, and I was positive that I wasn't the cause, then keep my mouth shut. That's what I did through all ten circles we took. And when the guy running the ride let us off, I decided she'd had enough time in her head. The bouncy house was the first thing we came to, so I pushed her inside and climbed in after her.

It only took a few bounces before I had her moving like a jumping bean. Her dress flipped up over her face, and I was grateful she'd had the forethought to put shorts on under it. No matter how hard she tried to scramble to her feet to retaliate, I kept her flopping around on her back with the help of some other kids from our class. Her laughter overtook the air like she needed it all.

When I finally saw her eyes again, the ballerinas were back, as was the glitter. I was lightheaded, and my chest felt big. Gasping for a breath, I jumped high, and then when I landed, I promptly flopped to my back next to her. Everyone else moved on to another part of the bouncy house or out the front flap when they saw the show was over. Randi and I lay there for as long as I could stand the heat. That thing was like a sweat box.

"Come on. I smell barbecue. Let's get something to eat." I

could always eat, but anytime the scent of meat on a smoker hit my nose, I was like a hound hunting prey. I had to have it.

She scooted out on her bottom, and I tried my best to keep my balance in front of her on my feet. "Do you ever get full?"

"Nope. My mom says between Charlie and me, we're going to eat her out of house and home." I helped her between the flaps and steady her feet on the grass. "I don't really get that saying."

Randi tossed her head back, laughing. "I think it means you eat a lot."

Well, duh. I just thought a house and a home were the same thing. "Charlie eats way more than I do."

She didn't care about our refrigerator or what was in our pantry. "There's jalapeño poppers."

"With sausage and cream cheese?"

Her eyes rolled. "Is there any other kind?"

Not worth having. I followed her to the huge, white tent lined with more smokers than I could count and even more men manning them. I didn't have a clue what was under each of those lids. Randi didn't hesitate to meander through the crowd to one in particular. She chattered on as we waited our turn, and I glanced around. I hadn't noticed the lights strung from all four corners of the tent. They went down the sides, through the middle, and up to the top. It was like her very own circus tent without the red stripes. The only people I'd ever seen with this kind of thing were having a wedding. Randi Adams had one for her tenth birthday.

We loaded up on enough poppers to put us both in a food coma and found a seat. Every adult within earshot decided that was the time to tell her happy birthday, keeping her from eating.

During a brief intermission of good wishes, I asked, "You want a drink?"

Before she could answer, her dad sat next to her. Randi nodded to me, and I took that as my indication to grab us both something. Drinks were located in troughs of ice at the far end of the smokers. It wasn't that it was all that far, there were just that many people there. And in small-town Texas, you didn't pass a neighbor—young or old—without speaking. Not unless you wanted to have your hide tanned with a strap or twig when your parents got wind of it. Personally, I wasn't interested in a blistered bottom, so I talked as I moved.

By the time I made it back to Randi, it felt like I'd been gone for an hour, although it was probably only minutes since the ice in the cups hadn't melted and the cans stung my hands they were so cold. However long I'd been gone had been too long.

Randi's dad still sat at her side, and somehow, he'd brought gloom that had settled in alongside him. My brow furrowed in confusion and irritation. Whatever he said to Randi had produced a scowl in response. In all the years I'd been friends with her, I hadn't ever seen that look on her face, and I had witnessed some real doozies.

I didn't know what to do. I didn't dare be disrespectful and interrupt. I also refused to let him continue to ruin my best friend's birthday, which he was clearly doing. Right here in front of nearly every person that lived in Mason Belle, he continued to deliver news that I couldn't hear. He spoke close to Randi's ear. The instant I saw Randi's chin dimple and her lip quiver, I didn't care if I couldn't sit for a week or how many lashings I got...and it would be a lot.

"Randi, are you all right?"

Slowly, she turned away from her dad and toward me. Her tongue slipped out and across her lips to capture the tears that fell. She shook her head. Had I not been watching, I wouldn't have noticed it. Bloodshot, brown eyes stared back, pleading with me to save her. And for the first time in my life, I felt the opposite of my chest getting big. It shrunk, constricting painfully at the sight of her emotion running down her cheeks. It physically hurt to breathe, and I could tell she was in more agony than I was.

Without thought, I dropped the cups I still held, stood on the chair, stepped onto the table, and then took her hand. I jumped off the other side, pulling Randi with me. Her dad hesitated long enough for us to get away before he called after the two of us, but we ignored his requests. I wasn't sure what reaction I had expected since my mind hadn't processed what I was doing. It just responded. My feet moved faster. Randi kept up beside me, even without shoes on. The bad thing about cattle ranches and farms, in general, was that there were very few places to hide in fields made for hay and cows. But Randi knew this property better than I did, so when she took the lead, I followed. We ran until our thighs burned and neither of us could run anymore. And together, still holding hands, we fell into the tall, uncut hay.

A sob ripped through the air around us. It took me a minute to realize she hadn't injured herself when we fell to our backs. This was worse. Far worse. There wasn't a cut or a scrape. There was no open wound. A Band-Aid wasn't going to cover this hurt, and I doubted whatever scar that lingered would ever heal. Prior to that moment, I didn't realize words could be so painful—life-changing.

All I could do was pull on her hand and try to hug her until the tears stopped and she could talk. She covered her eyes, yet she came without a fight and tucked herself into my side. Lying in the hay where no one could see us through the tall stalks, I held on for dear life while she soaked my shirt.

I didn't have the foggiest idea how long we had stayed in the fields. It had to have been hours with just nature and a lone cow who came to say hello, briefly. The sun had dropped from its highest place in the sky, and the heat had started to fade. Even through hearing our names called, we never moved. Punishment was inevitable, so at this point, leaving before Randi was ready wouldn't lessen whatever I faced. There hadn't been any sirens, and no one turned out the dogs, so they believed we were safe, just avoiding them. *Them* being whoever looked for us, most likely her parents and mine.

As if she'd heard my thoughts, she pushed up, breaking free of my hold. Righting herself, she folded her legs Indian style underneath the skirt of her dirty dress, and I followed her lead. With each hand, she swiped at the moisture on the opposite side of her face, leaving streaks worse than makeup would have caused. Her eyes were rimmed red and puffy, and the fury of her emotions fanned out in raw color. The pattern reminded me of a raccoon, although I was smart enough not to share that.

I was captivated by how her features had changed with her bout of tears. The tip of her normally thin, straight nose was prickled pink and swollen. If I hadn't been with her, I would assume she'd blown it over and over, irritating it with tissues. And her lips were an ashy shade of grey and puffy. I wasn't dumb enough to believe she didn't hurt inside; nevertheless, staring at her, she looked like she was in pain on the outside.

And at some point, I would have to ask, or we would have to go back to the house. Neither appealed to me. We couldn't stay out here after dark. It wasn't that I was scared. It wasn't safe. Nighttime on a cattle ranch brought predators in search of prey. Randi and I didn't need to be dinner for any four-legged creature with sharp teeth.

Unable to face her, I cast my eyes toward the ground and played with a weed. "What did your dad say?" My voice was meek and could barely be heard over the rustle of the wind through the field. "He didn't look happy."

Her eyes focused on something in the distance. I didn't try to make out what it was. There was no doubt it wasn't important because she hadn't reacted. If I had to guess, she was lost in remembering the conversation at the table. The one I'd missed by going to get soda. The same one that caused us to miss out on poppers. And the one I had no misconceptions would leave my rear end so raw that putting on jeans would hurt for several days. My dad would make an example out of me for the rest of the town to see. And he wouldn't go easy. There was no "sparing the rod" in the Burin house.

Lost in the scripture my dad used to justify harsh discipline, I missed Randi shift her gaze from the horizon to the ground. The world was eerily quiet. It wasn't that birds weren't chirping or that I couldn't hear cows in the distance—it was that none of it mattered. The wind crept through the acres of hay that surrounded us like a low rustle of crumpling paper. Even through the muted natural noises, somehow, I heard Randi swallow. It was followed by a guttural sound I couldn't identify, but years later, I would realize it had been her heart breaking.

"My mama's not coming back."

If Mrs. Adams had been traveling, Randi never mentioned it. People around here didn't go anywhere other than Laredo or to auctions, and those were day trips.

"From where?" The moment those two words left my mouth, I remembered she wasn't at the party.

She wouldn't miss her daughter's birthday. Not to mention, someone put this event together. There was no way it was *Mr.* Adams—there was too much pink.

Randi shrugged. My mind warred with whether she truly didn't know where her mom was or if she simply didn't care to tell me. If it was the latter, that was fine. Pushing her wasn't on my agenda.

"Daddy said she needed a break."

"From what?" I scoffed and scowled. The woman didn't do anything that I had ever seen. "She doesn't have a job." My mom would have slapped me across the face for that last sentence.

Women on ranches—well, the ones I was familiar with—were

typically the first ones up and the last to bed. Even if they didn't feed their ranch hands, they fed their families and days started early. They took care of homes and kids and often anything near the house, too. My own mom wasn't a stranger to the fields, either.

I'd never seen Randi's mom step foot off the porch except to get into the truck to leave, and I certainly hadn't ever caught her breaking a sweat. She was unique in Mason Belle…a princess of sorts. I'd never tell Randi that, although I was sure she'd heard the hens in town clucking about how her mama had it made.

Her shoulders shook, and her chest heaved. I hadn't been prepared for the wail that ripped through her throat and out her mouth. That agony hung in the air like a bird not flapping its wings—suspended, defying gravity, waiting to fall. This time, the tears didn't come. Nothing followed for a long beat.

"I don't know," she screamed. Her tiny hands balled into fists and pounded the dirt on the ground next to her hips.

"Did your dad say?"

Randi's head moved side to side, rapidly. She shook so hard I worried she'd hurt herself or induce a seizure. And right there, in that field, her entire face boiled crimson red. "She's *never* coming back, Austin!"

I couldn't fathom a woman leaving her husband, much less her children. Sarah was a parent's dream, and Miranda was everything her sister wasn't. Their mom loved the girls. She wouldn't leave them.

"But why?"

She stood, stomping her feet and banging her fists against her thighs. "I guess she doesn't love us." Her chin met the sky, and her hair finally gave up the ghost. The tie that had held on for dear life all day let go of the last strand and fell into the dirt. Like a drop of water hitting the surface of a lake, a tiny cloud of dust rose around it.

There was something significant in the finality of that dust settling, but I was too young to realize what it was. I just knew.

"Maybe he was wrong."

"He isn't wrong."

"How do you know?"

Randi shifted her eyes back to me and quit screaming at the sky. Her expression stilled and softened—not in happiness, rather defeat. The odd colors dotting her skin hadn't disappeared, although the pink had returned to her lips. They were slick and shiny where she'd licked them. I studied her mouth, waiting for her response.

"She asked Daddy for a divorce."

Those words didn't register, or their significance didn't. Until they did. And once they had, I stumbled over my thoughts and bumbled up all attempts at speaking. The only thing I knew to do was put my arms around her shoulders and press her to my chest until she stopped moving.

"It's my fault, Austin." Her words were muttered into my shirt.

With firm fingers, I grasped her shoulders and pushed her back. There wasn't much I could believe with absolute truth at my age. This I knew with complete certainty. "Her leaving is her fault, not yours. She loves you." I believed that with everything in me. Mamas love their babies. Always.

Her sad, brown eyes met mine. "If she loved me, she wouldn't have gone without saying goodbye."

And that would forever be the reality that Mrs. Adams left her youngest daughter with. "Why today?"

Randi pulled her bottom lip between her teeth and chewed on it for a second. "She knew if she missed my birthday that Daddy would know she was serious."

That was crap; even I knew it. "Did your dad tell you that?" My voice strained as I tried to keep from yelling. My anger nearly got the best of me. The only thing that kept it in check was that Randi didn't deserve to be on the receiving end of it.

My eyes searched her face as her expression changed from deep sadness to sorrow. "I've been asking him all week when she was coming home. And I bugged him a lot this morning. I didn't want her to miss my party."

"So, he decided to tell you in the middle of it?" I didn't claim to understand adults; however, this went above and beyond anything I could have ever anticipated one doing.

She shrugged. "I asked when he sat down."

"He didn't come over to tell you that?" *Please let her say no. Please let her say no.*

The shake of her head confirmed that, at the very least, he wasn't a total monster. "I kept pushing."

That didn't surprise me. Randi was used to getting what she wanted. Not that she was spoiled because she wasn't, but she did spend considerable time swaying opinions. In the end, she was rewarded with the satisfaction of having people change their minds. It was an artform she'd perfected at a very young age.

I rubbed my hands up and down her arms without a clue of what to say or do in this situation. "Maybe she needs a little time. Once she sees how tough it is on her own, she'll realize what she left behind."

Her chest rose and fell. "I don't think so."

This was one of those times my mom would tell someone she'd pray for them or offer to meet them at the diner for coffee if they needed to talk. If it were really bad, she'd ask them over for supper with their kids. Randi didn't need prayer; she needed her mom. Neither of us drank coffee. And while I didn't believe my mom would care if I invited Randi over for dinner, I probably shouldn't do it before I found out how long I wouldn't be able to wear pants and how long I would be grounded. There was little I could do to comfort her. Some wounds could only be healed by time, which we didn't have in this field.

It was time to start reasoning with her. Dusk was fast approaching, and we had quite a hike back to the farmhouse. "It's gonna get dark soon. We can't stay out here."

I expected the danger to register. Either it didn't, or she didn't care. I wasn't sure which.

My audible sigh got her attention. "They *will* come looking for us. We're ten. It's not like we can hide forever." Truthfully, I was shocked they'd given us this much leeway. It wouldn't be long before the dogs would be searching the fields and the horses would be brought out. If we reached that point, there would be no hope for our futures.

"I'm scared." Her voice shook with uncertainty. This wasn't a girl I'd ever seen before. Randi was fierce, faced everything head-on like a bull.

She needed reassurance, and I aimed to give it to her. I had been blindsided by this. There wasn't a piece of me that had seen it coming when I got up this morning. Right there, I made her a promise I'd die trying to keep. "As long as I'm breathing, nothing will ever hurt you again."

I waited for a response; instead, she lifted each arm, one at a time, and wiped her tear-streaked, dirty face on each one. Then she wound her fingers through mine. Nothing in me wanted to pull away. If I could have kept her there in that moment, where I knew she was safe and people couldn't hurt her, I would have.

Her eyes searched mine, and the corners of her mouth lifted ever so slightly. Then, she lifted onto her tiptoes and leaned in to peck my lips in the softest of kisses. If any other girl in all of Mason Belle had planted their sloppy mouth on mine, I would have gagged right before I spat and wiped their slobber away. That day, as the afternoon drifted into evening, my chest filled again, and heat stirred throughout my body. It was something akin to pride, although not the same.

"Thank you, Austin."

It didn't matter what we faced when we got back to the Adams' house. Those three words made it all worthwhile.

*T*he first two days Eason and I had been in Mason Belle were spent at the hospital, for the most part. I had no idea how exhausting it could be to sit next to a bed all day. The drive back and forth didn't help, and I wished now that we'd gotten a hotel room. I'd done a fairly good job avoiding Sarah and only coming a few minutes before she had to leave. So much remained unresolved between us. We'd managed to meander around it on the phone; yet somehow, in person, it was like dragging an iron ball on a chain by my ankle. The weight was crippling.

Eason and I sat on the couch in Daddy's room. The tick of the clock kept me engrossed, wondering when Sarah would leave. At twelve past the hour, I finally asked, not so eloquently. "Don't you need to go?"

She snickered from across the room and shook her head. It was the same thing she used to do when I was younger and she thought I'd said something stupid. "The kids are out of school today, so I left them with Charlie's mom this morning. I don't have anywhere to be."

Oh. Well, great. "How long are they out of school?"

"All next week."

I didn't know what that meant for our shifts at the hospital. "Are they going to stay at the Burins' house all week?"

"That's the plan. It works out well. Daddy will need help with his physical therapy."

My eyes darted between my sister in her chair and my dad lying in bed. I wasn't sure what she believed the doctors were going to do to rehabilitate lung damage. Sarah was naïve, but even she wasn't that daft. "Umm, Sarah. I think maybe you've missed something."

She had returned her eyes to the magazine in her lap. "Like what?" she asked, continuing to flip the pages.

I looked at Eason, and he shrugged. "I don't think there's anything they can do for his lungs. They'll have to heal with time, right? Same with the burns."

That same chuckle, which indicated how ignorant I was, blew past her lips. "He's in his sixties, Randi. If he's in that bed much longer, someone is going to have to get him up and walking. I don't see you helping him dress, bathe, change bandages, walk…"

I decided to ignore the cheap shot. Maybe I was an idiot. None of that had entered into any equation I'd calculated. In my ignorant world, Daddy would be released in a couple of days and sent home, and he'd go back to life on the ranch. Lord knew there was enough damage to keep him busy for eons.

Sarah closed the magazine and then placed her folded hands on top of it. I'd seen the expression on her face more times than I could count. A lecture loomed. Apparently, six years hadn't proved to her that she wasn't my mother or that I was an adult. "It'll give you some time to get reacquainted at home. I can handle the stuff here. The ranch needs attention."

"How are you going to help with physical therapy?" I ground my teeth at the reality of how callous I could be.

"I'll do fine." Sarah didn't make any mention of my inference, and I was grateful.

Eason cringed at my side; although, he kept his opinion to himself as well.

Even with my blunder, I didn't bother to mask my irritation at her suggestion. "So, you want me to hang out at Cross Acres and stare at burnt fields and cramped cows?"

"No, Randi. I'd like for you to put on something other than four-inch heels and silk and help out."

"I'm not slinging slop, Sarah."

A smug grin tugged at her lips. "That's good. Daddy doesn't have hogs."

Eason stifled a laugh next to me, and I elbowed him in the side, reminding him of whose team he should be on. "You're well aware of what I meant." It was hard enough to face my sister and my dad. "I didn't come here to work on a cattle ranch."

Her brows lifted, and her eyes flickered with what appeared to be humor. "Oh? What *did* you come here for?"

To see my dad in case he died. I couldn't say *that* out loud. "For Daddy." It wasn't what she wanted to hear.

Sarah needed me to confess my desperation for resolution. I couldn't give her that. Every time I saw her, there was another reminder of why I'd left and the damage I'd caused. If we settled things, that would mean I'd made reparations, and we both knew I could never do that. There was no absolution for this guilt.

"Daddy needs your help at the ranch."

As far as I was aware, Daddy had only had a few minutes of lucidity since the fire. He'd spent his time doped up on pain meds to allow his lungs a chance to heal and to give the nurses the ability to deal with the burns on his arms and face. "Oh yeah? Did he tell you that?" It was a crappy retort aimed below the belt—his and hers.

"As a matter of fact, he did."

My jaw dropped, and I gaped at my sister. Maybe she'd been the one heavily doped up on narcotics the last couple of days. "When?"

"This morning. He was awake for a bit and said he needed someone at the house."

I rolled my eyes, knowing how insipid she believed the gesture to be. "That's a far cry from him saying *I* needed to work at the ranch." In my mind, that equated to him not caring for me to be here, not him needing me to bail hay or tag cows. I didn't have the first clue what to do after a fire. "If he doesn't want me here, you can tell me that. It's not like I haven't heard it from him before."

My sister's eyes went soft, and she cocked her head in sympathy. "Randi..."

I held up my hand to stop her. "It's fine, Sarah. If you'd prefer I stay at the house, I will." I'd hate every moment of it, but it wasn't like I hadn't done it for years and didn't know my way around. I'd be lost in this place, and the awkwardness between Daddy and me when he woke up would be far more painful than the muscles I'd overwork doing manual labor.

"You took that the wrong way."

"There's only one way to take it, Sarah. It's fine. If it means more to Daddy for me to be at the ranch, then that's what I'll do until I go back to New York."

Eason's arm circled my waist. He was no stranger to the discomfort this situation brought me, even if he hadn't been involved first-hand. He took the hint when I leaned into his side. "You ready to go?"

I nodded and then stood. Without thought, I took his hand and let him lead me to the door.

Sarah called out when I opened it. "When he's up and moving, I'll call you so you can come see him."

I didn't know how long I'd be in Mason Belle, but once my daddy was up and walking, once I was certain he was out of the danger zone, I would be out. I wasn't a ranch hand. I wasn't a rancher's wife. I hadn't even been a rancher's daughter in years. This wasn't my home. My family no longer lived here. I needed to get back to New York—quickly.

"Of course, Sarah," I said.

The door closed behind us with a loud, metal click. I expected to fall apart at her dismissal, yet I surprised myself. A couple of deep breaths and I was determined to do what she'd asked, despite how dismally she believed I'd fail.

Eason gently squeezed my hand once we were in the elevator. "You okay?"

My head bobbed. "Yep. I need to run by the mall on the way back to Mason Belle."

"There's a mall around here?"

I sucked on my teeth and dropped his fingers to swat him on the arm with little force. "Yes. People do have to buy clothes...even in the middle of nowhere."

He flinched and held the spot I'd hit. "I figured they made them."

"It isn't *Little House on the Prairie*, Eason."

"Might as well be," he muttered.

No sooner had we stepped out the front door than the limo arrived at the curb. "You find a lot of limos and drivers out in the fields?" I rolled my eyes, having forgotten how perfectly that gesture suited so many situations since I'd quit doing it.

Eason didn't wait for the driver to arrive at the passenger door. He pulled on the handle and waved me inside. "Enough money, and you can make anything happen."

"Good. I need a mall. Make it happen."

He gave the driver instructions and made my goal a reality. I still deplored shopping and would much prefer to do it online, but desperate times called for desperate measures. If I were going to help out at the house, I wasn't going to do it in any of the clothes I'd brought.

As soon as I saw it, I forgot about the mall and frantically got the driver's attention to get him to pull into the Walmart parking lot.

"You're kidding, right?"

I'd never thought of Eason as a snob, not even when I first met him. Yes, he was high class and had the best of everything, but he never made me feel like less for not having more. "No. Why would I want to spend a lot of money on jeans and T-shirts that I'll never wear again."

He turned back toward the superstore only to face me again. "My treat."

"Don't be silly. It's only for a couple of days. I can get what I need here and not break the bank on stuff I'll toss in the trash the moment we get home."

He let out a sigh. "At least you aren't contemplating giving that crap to a charity."

"Oh my God, you're ridiculous." I pushed the door open and stepped out. I stuck my head inside when he didn't follow. "Are you coming?"

"Do I have to?"

"Yep. That's what friends do."

He said something under his breath that I didn't hear, and then he scooted across the leather seat and out the door. "No, friends treat their friends to Egyptian cotton and luxury wardrobes, not polyester and welfare."

No one in Mason Belle would think any differently about Wranglers and T-shirts. They would, however, mock suits, skirts, and heels. It was funny how different things could be with some miles between them. "Just for that, I'm going to buy you a pair of jeans and a hat."

"I'm not wearing a cowboy hat, Miranda."

"Keep complaining and see how fast your pretty-boy clothes disappear." I winked, but he wasn't certain whether I was playing or not, and if he kept this up, he'd find out I wasn't.

I tried to make the experience as painless as possible for both of us. He acted like he might be infected by a brand of cotton he wasn't familiar with, and I was terrified he'd embarrass me. In less than an hour, I'd picked up two pairs of fitted, dark wash jeans, a pack of cotton panties, two sports bras, three T-shirts, athletic socks, and a pair of work boots.

"I'm not sure which is more hideous, the jeans or the boots. Thank God you won't be trying to pick up men with that pitiful excuse for lingerie." He waved his hand over the garments as they slinked down the belt toward the cashier.

It was easier to ignore him than deal with responding. The cashier wasn't impressed by his commentary, either. Typically, women melted at the sight of Eason, but this proved his uppity condemnation of a lifestyle other than his own was a turn-off to people who lived it. I'd never been ashamed of Eason before. I didn't want to be now, although I struggled to remind myself that this had never been his reality.

I paid the cashier and thanked her. And I burst out laughing when she said she hoped my day got better. The smile it brought to her face was radiant, and I realized her grim expression had been a reaction to the asshat at my side.

***

The blare of my alarm at four thirty was as unwelcomed today as it had been during my childhood. As I fumbled to silence the offending noise on my phone, I wondered what I'd been thinking when I agreed to this charade. I hadn't been fit for the part growing up, and I wasn't any better suited for it today.

Moving through the house that once was as familiar to me as

the back of my hand, I tried to remain quiet so I didn't wake Eason. I didn't flip on the lights until I was safely inside the bathroom. My disheveled appearance was a sight to behold. There wasn't much point in doing anything with it, either, so I washed away the remnants of makeup from the day before and ran a brush through my mop. It wasn't much of an improvement, but at least I no longer looked like I had stepped out of *Night of the Living Dead*. After I brushed my teeth, I moved back to my room. The Walmart bags were on the floor next to my suitcase, and I didn't bother to look at what I pulled out. I wasn't here to impress anyone. It took me roughly three minutes to shed my pajamas and put on clean clothes. Sitting on the bed, I slid each boot over fresh socks and then tied the laces. When I stood, I vaguely recognized the girl in the mirror.

I didn't dwell on the changes in my appearance. Each one had been a conscious decision upon arriving in New York, and I didn't regret them...at least not when I was there. Here I felt like an imposter. I was grateful I'd been spared the embarrassment of seeing anyone I knew other than Austin. Most wouldn't be so dismissive; they would ask questions and cast judgment.

It was nostalgic in an uncomfortable way to walk into the kitchen this early in the morning. When I was a kid, Daddy would have been up long before me. The aroma of coffee would have lingered in the air from the moment my eyes opened until I walked out the screen door. And Sarah always had a massive spread of food on the counter for the three of us and any of the hands who liked to eat. None of that was present today. Although, the percolator my parents got as a wedding present still sat on the stove, and the fridge had plenty of makings for a hearty breakfast.

I'd regret not eating more later, but all I could stomach was some toast and several cups of black coffee. Daddy used to say it would put hair on my chest. I had hated the taste when I was younger. The bitter bite didn't appeal to me, even if the caffeine did. I had learned to drink it, hoping I never saw a single, strange hair appear where it shouldn't be, and now I couldn't consume it any other way.

The other hands would start showing up a little before five. If I wanted to be included in the day's labor, I needed to be in the barn before they got there. I hoped Austin wasn't the first to arrive. If one of the other guys showed first, then I wouldn't be the focus of his attention.

I rinsed my coffee cup and set it in the sink. My stomach felt like dragons battled inside it, and the war only got more brutal with each step I took toward the barn. I hadn't made it down the front steps when I saw the truck parked across the driveway. It hadn't been there last night when I went to bed. I also hadn't heard it pull up this morning. I was fairly certain it belonged to Austin. Those dragons didn't just beat their wings and thrash about; now they breathed fire and threatened to take flight up through my esophagus. Swallowing hard, I forced the discomfort down and straightened my spine.

The crunch of gravel under my boots echoed through the darkness. There was nothing to distract from the noise, and it amplified as I approached the open doors. The lights were on, but I couldn't hear anyone inside. Unless something had changed in the years I'd been gone, this was where everyone would gather before they dispersed.

While the barn wasn't any different, just about everything inside it was. The tack, saddles, none of it was where it used to be. I did recognize most of it. The stalls were unchanged even though many of the horses occupying them were. In front of the first I'd come to, I had a view of four from where I stood, and there wasn't a familiar animal amongst them.

The silky, black mare came to me without much coaxing. When I stuck out my hand, she nudged it gently. The laugh that I followed it up with was as unexpected as the smile on my lips. I petted her head and stroked the part of her mane I could reach without opening the door. Since I didn't know the horse, I wasn't about to enter, even though she seemed gentle.

"Hey, darlin'. You lost?" A husky voice came from the driveway, and I jumped at the intrusion.

I snatched my hand from the horse and faced the man who'd spoken to me. "Um, no." I wiped my palms on my jeans and moved forward to extend my hand in greeting. "I'm Miranda Adams. Just thought I'd come help out while I'm in town."

He eyed me with suspicion and returned my handshake. "You related to Jack?"

It shouldn't have felt like a slap to the face. I hadn't ever seen this guy. He didn't know who I was. Somewhere in my mind, I had assumed Daddy or Sarah or maybe even Austin would have at least mentioned Jack had two daughters, not just one. Apparently, that wasn't the case.

"His daughter." The recognition I hoped for never crossed his face. "And you are?"

"Tommy Campbell. Second in command." He stuffed his hands into the pockets of his well-fitted jeans. "Sorry to say I didn't realize Sarah had a sibling."

There wasn't a response to that statement that wouldn't make us both uncomfortable, so I chose to bypass it. "So you work closely with Daddy?" I needed to keep this lighthearted and try my best to find a few allies in this pack if I were going to survive.

His mouth contorted into an expression of confusion, and his brows followed. "Uh, not really. I work alongside Austin for the most part."

"Oh." I wiped away the bewilderment written all over my face. "When you said second in command, I assumed you meant to Jack."

A stall slammed behind me. I was certain my body had

responded visibly even if Tommy hadn't reacted or acknowledged it. "Nah, he's pretty much handed Austin the reins."

My eyes went wide, and my surprise nearly choked me. "Austin...Burin?"

"One and only, sweetheart." His voice made me cringe, but I didn't acknowledge him.

Instead, I smiled brightly at Tommy. "It was nice to meet you."

Tommy tipped his hat. I wasn't sure if it was to me or the man who approached from behind, and I didn't look.

"What are you doing here, Randi?" Austin didn't have the decency to extend me the same courtesy.

At the gruff tone, Tommy raised his brows, thinned his lips, and silently excused himself.

My shoulders slumped; Austin couldn't make things any more difficult if he tried. "Sarah asked me to help out. Get reacquainted with the ranch." I used air quotes to ensure he understood that was verbatim.

He put his hands on my biceps and used them to direct me toward the driveway. "Not on my watch." Then he gently gave me a little push. When I stopped, he was right behind me and slapped me on the ass. "Go on. Get going." There was no room for argument in the way he had dismissed me.

If that wouldn't have been mortifying enough without an audience, a handful of men watched in silence. It seemed Austin's goal was to humiliate me and guarantee I stayed out of his way. And his crew didn't bother hiding their amusement. In less than five minutes, he'd destroyed any confidence I had in being here—not that it had been much to begin with. I had a split second to make a decision: stand my ground or walk away with my tail between my legs.

As much as I wanted out of Mason Belle, I refused to be the butt of jokes amongst these men, least of all Austin. My back remained to the man who tried to make my life hell, so I plastered the brightest Randi Adams smile I could across my lips and lifted my hand to my hip. I didn't miss the air leaving Austin's lungs when I spun around because it hit me in the face. He was close enough that I could smell the coffee on his breath and see the humor dying in his eyes when he realized he was about to be challenged. He hadn't expected it, and catching him off guard was priceless.

"Daddy wants me to help out. I've done it for years. You can either include me or answer to Jack. Up to you."

My heart skipped a beat, then raced, then tripped over another, and again sprinted. I tried to take in all the nuances that made up Austin. The way his eyes narrowed ever so slightly, the almost imperceptible flair of his nostrils, and the whiskey-and-honey blend of browns swirling in his irises. God, he was beautiful. He was also on edge. He didn't know whether to strike or retreat. I struggled just as much. The pull of everything that was *him* was nearly impossible to resist. I forced my feet to stay level. My fingers clutched at my sides to prevent me from throwing my arms around his neck. And my lips held that forced smile to keep from planting themselves on his.

"Fine." He grunted, and his gaze dashed beyond my shoulder before returning to me. I noticed he didn't step back. He also didn't grin or touch me. "You want to help?"

I nodded. There wasn't a single fiber of Austin's being that believed that. He knew how much I hated working outside. As kids, we always joked about how I'd been born into the wrong family.

He tipped his head to one of the guys behind me, somehow silently communicating a command. I flinched as he stretched his arm out and something whizzed past me. Seconds later, another flyby took place, and he caught it with his empty hand. Austin dipped his sight to mine, and a shit-eating grin lifted the corners of his full lips. "Here ya go."

I took the gloves he forced on me and then grabbed the shovel. "What's this for?"

Austin stepped back and pointed toward a wheelbarrow that had seen better days. "The twenty stalls that need to be cleaned."

My jaw dropped. He couldn't seriously expect me to shovel manure.

"Problem, sweetheart?"

I praised God the men behind me hadn't seen my shock. If I wanted to be taken seriously, I had to do the same crap jobs they all did. And I was certain none of them complained when tasks were assigned. "Not at all," I said through clenched teeth, "*baby*."

Two of us could play this game. He might have the upper hand now, but I aimed to reclaim it. Austin Burin had forgotten who he was dealing with.

He slapped me on the ass one more time before he walked past me to the other guys. They all chuckled at my expense; giving them satisfaction by turning around to acknowledge it wouldn't help my cause. Instead, I tossed the gloves and shovel into the wheelbarrow and moved to the nearest stall on the left.

I tried to eavesdrop. Nothing would please me more than to melt into the tone of his voice and let it lull me to a safe, happy place the way it had so many times in my youth. He didn't give me the chance.

In no time, he had everyone out of the barn and off doing whatever it was he'd told them. What little I was able to hear, I clung to. It didn't surprise me that Austin was authoritative or that the other guys appeared to respect and like him. He'd always had the natural ability to command a group. And he'd never done it as a dictator. People simply flocked to him and his charisma.

It didn't take long to remind me of why I'd hated doing this stuff most of my life. The flies drove me insane, and even in the early morning hours, the heat was oppressive. The stench of the wildfire's destruction produced a headache less than thirty minutes after I walked out the kitchen door. The only decent part of the tasks were the animals. They'd always been the bright spot in the chores around here. Daddy had always been fond of paint horses. He swore they were the best for working cattle. Personally, I'd never cared what breed they were. I loved them all. But I didn't know the names of any of the ones I'd seen. Daddy hadn't had them when I was here last, which seemed odd. Everything was different in a town so small that nothing ever actually changed.

Voices lured my attention, and I peered out from the stall to find Austin with another worker at the front of the barn. His tone was low, so I couldn't hear him; I wasn't interested in his conversation, though. Since I'd been home, I hadn't so much as ventured into the barn before this morning. Seeing all these new faces made me wonder about the old ones. It was stupid; they were just horses. Still, they'd been friends growing up, and I was curious which ones were still with us. Austin couldn't hang out forever. At some point, he'd have to leave to do whatever he was now responsible for. I had yet to figure out why he was here to begin with, and finding out my daddy entrusted him with the foreman position had me scratching my head.

Every time I believed I had an opening to check out the stalls I hadn't yet reached, someone else came plodding through the barn. I was slow and thorough. If I were a paid hand, I wouldn't have survived a day, and Austin likely would have fired me before lunch. Any of the other guys could have had all the stalls cleaned in a lot less time. I didn't care. Sarah had asked me to get reacquainted with the ranch, and in my mind, part of that included the horses. They were critical to everything done here. They needed their own type of attention. Attention I doubted they'd received since I'd left. None of them showed any signs of neglect by any means. I just knew that guys who worked on a ranch didn't invest the love that a kid who lived on it did.

I finished the seventh stall and closed the heavy, wood door, making sure the latch secured before I stepped away. My shoulders burned from the workout, and my biceps were already like jelly. It didn't matter how much it hurt, there was no way I'd wave a white flag for Austin to see. I was free labor, so anything they got out of me enabled the person who usually did it to use their skills somewhere else on the ranch.

"Hey, boy." I made a mental note to find out the names of the horses. Calling them boy and girl simply wouldn't suffice. I greeted the beast in front of me and waited for him to give me the okay to enter his stall.

"This job would be a lot easier if you turned the horses out." Tommy came strolling through the open doors of the barn. "You got any idea what you're doin' in here?"

I stared at him without answering. I couldn't hear any condemnation coming from him. Nevertheless, I didn't trust anyone, especially not friends of Austin. "I've spent my fair share of time with horses." Not that it showed. "I didn't know why they were stabled. The last thing I needed to do was set them out and have Austin crawl my butt for it." It sounded like a good excuse, even though it was total hogwash. It simply hadn't occurred to me when I'd been handed a shovel.

Tommy eyed me like he planned to contradict my rationale, and I waited for it to come. Instead, I got more of the one person I didn't have any desire to see.

"Tommy, saddling horses doesn't include making small talk with the help." Austin's growl rumbled through the barn and bounced off the walls. If he weren't careful, he'd spook the horses.

The two men glanced at me. My attention darted between them both. I'd be more than happy to get a couple of horses ready for them. "Need my help?" The sneer in my top lip must have tipped Austin off to what I had in mind.

Austin scoffed at the same time Tommy winked. Unfortunately for Tommy, Austin caught the flirtatious gesture, and what had sounded like a growl before was merely a whimper in comparison to the vibrations that rumbled from his chest now.

Interesting.

None of these guys had a clue who I was in relation to my dad or Austin. Yet even with Austin's casual dismissal, the possessive streak was a mile wide. He'd likely say he was protecting his crew, not me, but I'd seen that gleam in his eyes more than once. His fist clenched at his side, and his lip curled when his nostrils flared.

I couldn't help myself. Austin Burin hadn't changed one bit, not where I was concerned—except for the chip the size of Texas on his shoulder. Even when his pupils surged, and his irises darkened into something akin to espresso, I hadn't stopped giggling. It only served to tick him off further. Tommy wasn't sure what to do. The dopey look on his face indicated how clueless he was.

"That's enough, Randi." Austin turned to Tommy. "Get the horses ready...on your own."

I cleared my throat and stilled my giggles. "It's Miranda." Might as well make him see red if I aimed to antagonize him.

He shook his head. "Pretend to be whatever you want in New York or when your boyfriend is nearby, but *sweetheart*, around here, you'll always be Randi." There wasn't a single bit of playfulness in his expression or his tone.

"Can't you make the best of this?"

His gaze dove to his feet, and his hands landed on his hips. His fingers moved to settle, and each twitch made his pecs jump. Even with a shirt on, it was easy to see just how much he'd matured in recent years. His biceps tried to tear the seam on his T-shirt, and I could only speculate about what else desperately craved to be set free.

His chest heaved, and I prayed he wouldn't explode with people around. I knew better than to push his buttons. Whatever his reason was for being here, the workers clearly respected him, and I threatened that every time I crossed him or questioned him in front of them. In the end, I'd get on a plane and go back to my life, and he'd be left cleaning up another mess I had made.

"For once, how about doing what you're told? You should be able to clean stalls blindfolded. It's virtually impossible for you to start trouble or get into any in here."

I sucked my lips between my teeth and rubbed them together to keep from saying the things that hovered on the tip of my tongue.

"Brock, Huck, and Corey are on their way in to help with the horses. Please keep your head down and mouth shut until they're all gone."

In all fairness, I hadn't said anything to anyone that should have put him on edge like this. I'd actually said very little in retrospect.

"You're the worst kind of distraction." Austin didn't have to tell me what that meant. He'd said it a thousand times before. The only difference now was his hands weren't on me, and his voice was a million miles away.

I let most of what he didn't say go in one ear and out the other and, instead, focused on the word that stuck out like a sore thumb. "Brock?"

Austin shook his head and dropped his chin.

"Brock Pierson?" My exuberance shocked us both. It wasn't until I'd heard his name that I realized how much I'd missed some of the people in this town—besides the obvious ones.

"Let him be, Randi."

I folded my arms across my chest and lifted my brows. "Maybe we should let him decide."

"It's your death wish that'll be granted, not mine. Suit yourself."

I hadn't left on the best terms, but there was no reason Brock would want me dead. He'd always loved me like a sister—well, maybe that wasn't such a great comparison, seeing as how I'd treated my own sibling. The point was that we were tight. "Why would he want to kill me?"

He laughed and finally dropped his hands from his hips. "Oh, it won't be him that isn't thrilled to see you. However, his wife might prefer to gouge your eyes out."

My jaw dropped. It was overly dramatic, and it got the point across. "Brock's married? To who?" Shrieking was another way to illustrate my surprise.

"Charity."

"Phillips?"

"The one and only."

I closed my mouth and stared at the man who'd once been my everything. I hadn't had any misconceptions that life stood still after I left Mason Belle. I guess I assumed that if my best friends got married that someone would have mentioned it or sent an invitation to the wedding.

Another one of the ranch hands that I hadn't been introduced to grabbed Austin's attention, leaving me to stare into space. If Brock and Charity had gotten married, I couldn't imagine what else had changed. And instead of wanting to find out, instead of wanting to throw myself into small-town life, I wanted to run—fast.

When Austin turned, the hits kept coming. We hadn't been talking that long. I scrunched my nose. At least I hadn't thought so. However, it had been long enough for Tommy to come waltzing back from the tail end of the barn—the end I'd been trying to work my way toward—with reins in each hand and two horses following behind.

To his left was a quarter horse I hadn't met. To his right was the most beautiful palomino I'd ever seen. Tommy wasn't aware of my connection to that horse. Austin was. When Tommy handed Austin the reins, Austin didn't just look at me. He stared holes through me. My eyes filled with tears when Austin slid his foot into the stirrup and hoisted himself into the saddle on my horse.

"Nugget," I whispered. I hadn't thought it was loud enough for anyone else to hear, yet I'd managed to catch Tommy's attention.

I wasn't sure which bothered him more, the tears dangling from my jaw or the fact that I obviously had an affinity and an acquaintance with the animal he'd given over to his boss. "You know him?"

I reached out to touch his blond coat. "He's my horse," I croaked my admission.

My fingers barely grazed Nugget's neck when Austin commanded the horse to move. "Was."

7

MIRANDA

PAST

The high of winning homecoming was wild throughout the town. There wasn't much that went on here, outside of cows and farms, so winning at football drew a crowd. Truth be told, losing attracted the same crowd; they were just in better moods following a victory. And there were two people the town coveted after a win—or maybe only one. Since we came as a package, I'd always believe it was two.

The quarterback and the captain of the cheerleading squad.

Austin and I were like royalty, and a win only served to cement that notion. It wasn't a secret to anyone who had ever stepped foot in Mason Belle, Texas. There were lots of unknowns in life; however, Austin Burin and Randi Adams weren't one of them. It was a given, like pancakes and syrup or gravy and biscuits, that the two of us would end up together. And the town's people salivated when we were together. It was a high I wished every kid my age could experience. Then again, it probably wouldn't be all that fantastic if it were ordinary.

It had taken nearly an hour for the football team to get back to the locker room after the fans stormed the field. I'd jumped into the girls' shower to rinse away the scum brought on by extreme heat and exercise. Cheering was queen to the king of football, and I loved my place on the throne, but I didn't enjoy the after effects. Once I'd put on some shorts and a tank top, I waited for Austin on the benches outside the school. Whoever said women took forever to get ready had never spent any time with football players in Texas.

Charity plopped her bottom down on the bench next to me. Her hair was done up, and her makeup was flawless. "You sure you guys won't change your minds and come to the dance?" Like most of the other students, Charity had dressed for a formal evening in the school gym.

I hadn't even bought a dress, so that wasn't going to happen. "We're going back to my house."

Her eyes went wide. I watched with amusement as she folded her hands in her lap and crossed her legs at the ankle. A lecture was forthcoming, and I'd heard it before. "Tonight?" She practically gasped the word.

It was way more fun to play with her and concede to whatever fantasy she had in her head than to set her straight. "Yep. It's time to toss the *V* card. I've held onto it for almost seventeen years."

I had no intention of getting jiggy with Austin. Daddy would be home, and since Sarah had no life, I was sure she'd be there, as well. Even if I wanted to take the plunge into life without a hymen, it wouldn't be with an audience, and it certainly wouldn't happen tonight.

Charity's entire face pinched. "You don't have to do that. If he loves you, he'll wait." She paused, possibly anticipating my rebuttal. "True love waits."

I went all goofy-eyed to play the part Charity was determined to lead me away from. "This will just make our union that much stronger. I'd hate to lose him by being a prude." If she were even remotely listening to the sound of my voice, she'd know I was full of it and messing with her.

"This is a gift you can only give to one person, Miranda." Oh hell, she'd used my real name. She was about to go off the deep end. "Don't be so flippant. Why buy the cow when you can get the milk for free?"

I shrugged. "I don't think anyone in this town needs to buy cows for free milk, Charity." The grin I fought to hide broke through, and I burst out laughing.

She was on the verge of tears, thinking I was going to throw my virginity into the wind and hope someone caught it. I loved the girl, but her newfound, devout religious beliefs would land her in a lonely life of solitude like my sister's. Charity swatted at my thigh as Austin and the rest of the team poured out of the locker room. "I'll be praying for your soul, Miranda Adams."

I missed half of that sentence when the most gorgeous boy in town grabbed my hand, pulled me from my bench seat, and melded me flush against his chest. If he'd heard Charity, he hadn't cared. In one swift motion, he had me in his embrace, and then his arms secured my lower back, and his mouth pressed to mine. I didn't think twice about indulging in a celebratory kiss or who witnessed it. I didn't care. The world knew Austin and I were together, and most were happy for us, evident by the clapping and cheers that erupted at our display.

I was short of breath by the time he broke free. He tilted his forehead to mine and pressed another quick kiss to my smile.

"You ready to get out of here?" he murmured against my lips.

"Yep."

Charity stood and made sure to get between us. "You guys still have time to change your minds and come to the dance with everyone else." She reached into her purse and pulled something from inside. "I just happen to have two extra tickets," she sang and waved them under our noses, like she'd somehow entice us with the scent of paper.

Austin shook his head. "We're going to have to sit this one out,

Char." He slapped my rear end and ran the tip of his nose up the side of my face.

Her shoulders slumped with defeat. I'd told her over and over she wasn't responsible for anyone else's sins, but she still took it to heart as if she had committed them herself.

I decided not to ruin her evening by forcing her into a candlelit, prayer vigil. When I went in to hug her neck, I whispered into her ear, "We're going to sit with Lacey tonight. It's not a big deal or even remotely scandalous. I promise."

Charity pulled back to look me square in the eyes. "You're missing homecoming to babysit a horse?"

It was far more amusing when I saw the look on her face than when my dad had first brought it up. "You know how the old man feels about me putting in my time."

"Couldn't you do it another day?" she squealed.

Austin's arms surrounded me from behind, and his voice bellowed next to my ear. "Randi wanted to be responsible for the horses." We'd argued about this so many times I'd lost count. "That means birthin' babies, Charity." God, he sounded just like Daddy. "If we're lucky, we'll be up to our arms in placenta by sunrise."

I squirmed in his grasp. He had accomplished his goal. Charity was back to giggles, and I was right where he needed me.

"Gross."

"Damn straight it is. Thank God you didn't tell him you wanted to impregnate cows. I might have had to draw a line in the sand."

I rolled my eyes. I loved the horses. I loved all the animals. What I hated were the chores that went along with them. I didn't mind them near as much during the winter, but summer, spring, and fall, I'd rather be anywhere on earth than Cross Acres.

*T*here were some pluses to having grown up in the same small town where everyone knew each other, and all my friends' parents were well acquainted. It wasn't unusual for ranchers to spend time helping each other, and they often came from other counties. It was even less rare to find kids hanging out at all hours of the night with each other tending to animals. Or maybe that was just in Mason Belle. Either way, it was a regular occurrence for other kids in the county, just not one I'd experienced before tonight.

Daddy loved the Burins and their sons, and he trusted Austin with my life. He didn't have any reason not to, although I wasn't sure Daddy remembered what life was like as a seventeen-year-old boy with raging hormones. If he had, I couldn't be certain he would have allowed Austin to spend the night in the barn with me while the two of us monitored Lacey...alone.

Daddy could have easily made Sarah sit out here, which would have been far less entertaining for me, but Austin had been around for the delivery of other horses and calves. Daddy thought it would be good for the two of us to do this together. Austin's parents had agreed. Sarah joked about the two of us—Austin and me—having an arranged marriage, and at times like these, I could see her point.

Nothing had happened last night, and we'd missed the dance unnecessarily. This morning, when I dragged my exhausted body into the farmhouse, I'd made mention of that to Daddy, who was getting ready to start another long day.

"Welcome to life on a cattle ranch, Randi. It's hard work and even longer days."

I didn't bother to acknowledge him, and I waited until I was confident he couldn't see me before sticking out my tongue. He should have had that painted on the walls in the house. It was like his mantra, and I knew better than to argue or point out that I'd been up all day and all night while he'd gotten a solid night's sleep. He'd only remind me that he'd been doing it for years and rarely with any company. Instead, I shuffled through the kitchen and up the stairs. Once in my bedroom, I didn't even bother to close the door. I fell face-first onto the mattress and was out before I could kick off my shoes.

I woke to a gentle kiss pressed against my forehead. My lids fluttered open to blinding light blocked by an enormous head. I would have giggled had I not been so tired. Instead, I yawned in Austin's face. "What are you doing here?"

He lifted his hand to move a chunk of hair from my cheek, and then he grazed his knuckles along my jaw. "Came to see if we could grab something to eat before our shift starts."

I wanted something to eat, but it wasn't going to be found at a hole-in-the-wall in Mason Belle. It currently sat right in front of me, looking perfectly edible. An easy grin rose on my lips, and my lids hung lazily, only allowing a slit of sight, and every bit of it zeroed in on Austin's mouth. He focused on my tongue as it slid between my lips and then from one side to the other. He craved the same things I did. He was just too much of a gentleman to push for it—not that it would have taken much encouragement.

I wasn't sure what we were waiting on. We'd been together for years, and neither of us had any interest in ever changing that. It was unspoken, but a given all the same. At some point, I would take Austin's last name. As though he could read my mind, his eyes glazed over, and the left side of his mouth quirked in a way that made my insides warm and my lady bits tingle.

When he sealed our connection with a kiss, I rolled to my back, taking him with me. My fingers were laced in his hair when he settled half on top of me and half at my side. His weight did nothing to ease the sexual tension coursing through my veins. And when he lifted his thigh that was nestled between my legs, I broke away with an audible gasp. He took the opportunity to lavish my neck with attention.

And as quickly as it started, it ended with the thud of my daddy's boots climbing the steps to the second floor. Austin moved back to his knees at the side of the bed, and I remained on my back, staring at the ceiling. I didn't flick my eyes to my father as he strolled by my door, even though I was certain his timing was strategic. He might not have poked his head in or said hello, but he saw everything—even things he wasn't actually a witness to. It was one of those freaky parenting things that he had honed after Mama left.

I still hadn't moved, and neither had Austin when he meandered back down the hall, down the stairs, and out the front door. I probably should have been irritated, yet somehow, I found it oddly amusing. Austin was revered in our house. He was also terrified of my dad. It was a healthy fear.

"You think that's funny?" He poked me in the side, breaking the silence and tension my dad had produced without even speaking to us.

I shrugged. "A little."

He stood, and I let my head roll toward him. There, in front of me, stood all six feet of broad shoulders and thick muscles. He leaned down, grabbed my hand, and with it, he cupped his junk. I didn't even try to stop myself from squeezing just a bit. "You think that's funny?" When I rubbed the heel of my palm with a little more pressure against his length, he jerked back. "You're playing with fire, Randi."

"Maybe I want to get burned."

"Don't be coy."

I didn't have a clue what that meant. I assumed he believed I was joking. "If you think I'm kidding, then put your money where your mouth is. Or better yet, let me put *my* mouth where your money is." I wagged my brows suggestively.

Austin removed my hand from his crotch and held it in his. "That isn't going to happen on a dare, and you know it."

There was no point in discussing this. We'd gone around and around. I wasn't the one holding out. Austin was. He'd never given me a viable reason to wait. I mean, we both went to church and believed in God. Premarital sex was a sin. Teenage pregnancy would be awful. Blah, blah, blah. But he never cited any of those as reasons for not doing the deed. The only thing he'd ever said was it would happen naturally. He didn't force it or fight it.

He was absolutely fighting it.

I rolled off the bed in the opposite direction of where he stood. Cooling off wouldn't happen with his hands on me, and they would be if I were within reach. "So, what did you have in mind?" I asked as I pulled off my clothes.

He spoke to my back while I put on a clean T-shirt. "Greta's?"

Then I shimmied out of the shorts I'd worn last night. The shirt I'd just put on covered my rear end and allowed me to drop my panties, as well. "Or we could swing by the hot dog stand."

I'd donned the shortest pair of cutoff jeans I could get past Daddy and slid my feet into a pair of cowboy boots. Cheering had sculpted well-toned, lean legs, and the sun had colored them into a healthy bronze.

"Nope."

I flinched in misunderstanding. "Nope?"

"You are not going into town wearing shorts with pockets longer than the legs."

I situated myself in front of the mirror on my dresser and lifted onto my tiptoes. At that angle, I could see the tops of my thighs and the bottom of the shorts. I smiled and made eye contact with my boyfriend in the mirror. "Most guys would appreciate that their girlfriend could rock this outfit."

He came up behind me, never dropping his stare from the mirror. His hands landed on my hips, and the two of us burned holes into each other through the glass. Seconds later, the heat of his fingers slid down my sides to find the bare skin of my thigh. When they circled under my butt and grazed the spot where the frayed hem hung, I leaned my head against his chest. God, I wanted more. More of his touch, his lips, his attention. I wanted it all. All over me.

"This"—he created a trail of goose bumps from the backs of my legs, under my rear, and to my inner thighs—"is not for anyone else." He kissed the spot beneath my ear that was almost as sensitive as the place his fingers danced. There was a hint of tongue and a nip of teeth that nearly had me jumping out of my skin with anticipation. "It's mine." Leaving one hand between my thighs, he brought the other to my hair. He wove his fingers into my long locks, then he curled them into a fist and tilted my mouth for him to take.

I wasn't sure how I managed to get my front to his or why his hand had left my thigh, but if kissing Austin was all I could have, then I'd make the most of it. Our tongues delved into the other, each swipe fueled the desire that burned between my legs. It was probably best he had moved his hand. I feared I was embarrassingly wet, despite his obvious arousal pressed against my stomach.

He bent at the knees, and his erection ran the length of my sex when he stood upright. Austin knew exactly what he was doing. I just couldn't figure out why he aimed to drive me to the point of certifiable insanity. Fully clothed or completely naked, all it would take was a word from his mouth strategically breathed next to my ear, and I'd shatter in his arms.

The word I longed to hear wasn't the one he uttered. "Change." He popped a chaste kiss on my cheek and smacked my rear end.

I glared at him—death rays—and he rumbled with an explosive laugh. I was starting to think he was a masochist. "Fine." Two could play at this game.

Instead of trying to be discreet, I lifted the bottom of my shirt and held it between my teeth, leaving my flat, toned, and tanned tummy on display. In no hurry, I unfastened the shorts he'd insisted I remove, slid the zipper down—it was so tense and quiet, the metal teeth could be heard unhooking as it went—and then I stuck my thumbs in the belt loops on each side. Rocking my hips, the shorts finally broke free. Austin's pupils and nostrils pulsed, and I had to hide my grin. The denim fell to my ankles, and I stepped out of them to face my dresser. Austin hadn't expected the show, but he was completely caught off guard by the black, lace thong that was now fully visible.

"I'll wait downstairs." And he was out the door.

Austin's face was tomato red when I reached the kitchen, and it didn't take long to see why. Daddy stood at the island with a stern expression marking his brow. My eyes widened until Austin shook his head, assuring me he wasn't in trouble for my stunt upstairs. It was then I noticed how tired my father appeared. I took my place at Austin's side without interrupting.

"I turned the other horses out, so Lacey is the only one in the barn. She's pretty restless but nothing uncommon. I'm sure you've seen mares bitin' at their flanks."

With a grunt, Austin confirmed he had. He'd done this several times on his own farm.

Daddy was merely prepping him for the shift change, and it didn't sound like food was in our future. "It's no different than any other woman trying to get comfortable. It's just an uncomfortable process."

Austin listened intently without reminding my dad that he knew what he was doing. That's something I would have done, not one of the Burin boys.

"Ben's out with her now. I'm gonna grab a bite to eat. Why don't you two go keep him company? If she breaks water, you come get me, ya hear?"

"Yes, sir."

I reached across the counter and laid my hand on top of my dad's. His skin was calloused from working a ranch his entire life, yet it was still incredibly soft and comforting. "You want me to fix you something to eat real quick?"

He patted the top of my hand with his other. "No, darlin'. No need to spend the rest of the afternoon in the john when we got a foal comin'." He winked.

Austin chuckled. I did not.

I might not be the best cook in the world, but I could heat up leftovers and make sandwiches without anyone becoming physically ill. "Suit yourself."

Austin tried to take my hand on our way out.

I wasn't having any of it and crossed my arms over my chest. "Don't try to warm up to me now, you brownnoser."

He continued to smirk as we walked side by side to the barn, and I kicked at the gravel beneath my boots, scattering it in waves in front of us. "I'm not kissin' your dad's ass. I was listening. Last thing I need is for him to lose the foal and Lacey because I was too busy checkin' out his daughter's tits."

"You shouldn't cuss. It's ugly," I chided playfully.

Since I had refused him my hand, he slung his arm over my shoulders and pulled me to his side. "Love you, Randi. Even if you are a pain in the butt."

I leaned up, careful not to trip over our still-moving feet, and kissed his jaw. "Love you back."

We untangled from each other once we were inside the barn. Austin went into business mode, and I sat on a bale of hay and swung my legs while we waited. Ben had stepped out of the stall, and I whispered—in case he was still close by—"Why are you acting all serious?" He hadn't cracked a smile or made any small talk since we'd come in.

Austin pushed off the wall he'd been leaning against and

settled his Wrangler-clad legs between my thighs. The gold was missing from his irises. Whiskey became chocolate and hovered in a pool around his pupils. "This isn't a joke, Randi. This is our future." He had taken this to the extreme.

"Lacey's foal is our future?"

His eyelids closed, and he exhaled. When he opened them again, the light returned, and honey swirled in the sea of warm brown. "No, Cross Acres is. And your daddy needs to know I can handle whatever he throws at me. I'm playin' for keeps here."

Austin was seventeen and had his sights set on forever. That eternity included me. And I came with Cross Acres. I didn't have any brothers, and my sister didn't have any suitors. I hadn't thought about it, but Austin was right. If we got married, it made sense that he would come work for Daddy. His brother, Charlie, would be first in line to take over the Burins' farm, and Cross Acres couldn't run itself.

The enormity of what had crossed my mind and how it all strung together was somewhat mindboggling. What was even more perplexing was that Austin had figured it out long before I had. Typically, women were the ones looking for ways to draw a man into a commitment—Cross Acres was quite the dowry—but Austin had searched for it on his own. I still wasn't brave enough to ask if he'd discussed this with Daddy. That was a topic for another day. For now, I was content to know where Austin's heart lay.

Austin's back was still to the mare, now on her side with her head on the ground. The weight of the foal on Lacey's bladder brought new meaning to the saying, "Pissing like a racehorse." The poor girl couldn't stop urinating. This, however, wasn't the same sound.

I pointed, grabbing Austin's attention. "Is that normal?" I cringed a little at the sight of the greyish-white bubble poking out of my favorite horse, along with the stream of what I could only assume was amniotic fluid. I shouldn't be a stranger to this sort of thing, but I'd kept my distance throughout the years. Had this not been my horse, I would have tried to get out of it this time, too.

Austin turned to see what I was talking about. "Yep. Run, get Jack."

It was on the tip of my tongue to argue with him and tell him to go get Daddy himself. Then it occurred to me that if something happened in the amount of time Austin was gone, I wouldn't have a clue how to handle it. I shut my mouth and took off running.

Two hours later, we had a beautiful, palomino colt. Daddy and Austin made sure I left the little guy alone while we waited for the placenta to pass and then gave Lacey and her boy time to get acquainted. My attention wasn't on the guys searching the placenta—once it was expelled—to make certain it was whole. I focused on the wonder of the tiny life in front of me.

It was as though he were my own miracle. I grinned when the little horse shook his head, and I rooted for him when he tried to stand on wobbly legs. And when he suckled Lacey for the first time, it was my personal victory. Each thing Daddy told me to look for was there, right on time, and what I hadn't seen, Ben pointed out. I couldn't believe how fast the colt was up and walking, much less how quickly Lacey seemed to recover. Animals were far more resilient than people. There were women in town who'd used childbirth as a reason not to get out of bed for a month.

"What's it gonna be, Randi?" My daddy jarred my thoughts.

I shifted my gaze from the blond beauty before me to the warm, blue eyes above me. "Huh?"

He jerked his head toward our new four-legged friend. "His name. What is it?" Daddy chuckled at the shock he clearly read in my expression. "Your horse. You name him."

"Nugget." He kind of looked like a chicken nugget. His coat was a muted tan, and he was more body than anything, with legs like sticks.

I loved seeing my daddy look at me with pride. All I'd done was watch, so there wasn't anything to boast over. I hadn't even been the one to break the sack so Nugget could breathe.

"You're on Nugget duty," Daddy said.

A smile spread across my lips and lifted my cheeks so far my eyes scrunched. It wasn't clear how long baby duty would last, and I hoped I didn't have to do it alone. Not being able to touch him or play with him would make this difficult.

Daddy turned to my boyfriend. "Austin, you stayin' with her for a bit?" I loved that he knew I wanted company without my having to ask.

"I'm here for the duration, sir."

"All right then. I'm going to try to grab some shuteye." His eyelids drooped, and his shoulders slumped with exhaustion. "You need anything, don't hesitate to holler." Daddy disappeared without waiting for confirmation.

Ben tipped his hat and followed. He was an odd bird who hadn't said more than a handful of words throughout the entire birth. Daddy cared a lot about him, though. He was older and had been around since I was little. There was a lot he could no longer physically do. Daddy didn't care. Ben had been a devoted hand, and Daddy would be a loyal employer until Ben no longer had a desire to work.

Austin wandered past the other stalls, closed the barn doors, and then came back with several blankets. "Hop up for a second," he said.

Together, we spread the blankets over the bales of hay I'd occupied for the last couple of hours, and then we took a seat.

"Your dad's a good man."

"Did you know I'd get to name the horse?"

He snickered. Clearly, we hadn't been talking about the same thing. "It didn't surprise me, but I was referring to how he is with Ben." Austin leaned back against the wall of the barn. Neither of us took our eyes off the mare or the colt. "Lots of people woulda cut him loose when he couldn't keep up. Jack didn't do that. He makes sure Ben has an honest day's work, and everyone on this ranch respects both of them for it."

"Hmm..." I hummed my acknowledgment, yet my heart was wound up in the little colt I got to call my own. I curled into Austin's side and admired the blond from a distance.

The sun had long since set, and I didn't have a clue what time it was. The only light I could see before Austin closed the doors had been coming from the porch. The rest of the world seemed to have gone to sleep. If I weren't wired from all I'd seen in the last few hours, I wouldn't be far behind them. As it stood, I was content to relax in Austin's arms, mesmerized by my new horse.

He kissed the top of my head, and I pulled back to meet his eyes. They were liquid with love, and I nearly panted with desire. Hesitantly, I eased toward him. I didn't want to mistake what I saw for hunger if it were merely exhaustion. When he slid down and took me with him, it was evident I hadn't misread the intent in his gaze.

A mewl escaped my mouth when he cupped his hands around my jaw. And I struggled to catch my breath when our tongues tangled. Goose bumps erupted on my arms when my shirt came over my head, and chills ran down my legs when he tugged off my shorts and panties. I wasn't sure when it had happened, yet there we both lay, naked as the day was long. Wrapped in each other, fused together.

Our souls had long since formed a union, but that night in the barn, our bodies became one. Together, we exchanged the greatest gift either of us could ever give, and we lost a piece of ourselves neither of us could ever get back.

I didn't have one ounce of regret.

8

AUSTIN

*J*ack needed to worry about getting better, not about the problems at the ranch. Unfortunately, there were decisions to be made, and I didn't feel right making them on my own. Thus far, Sarah and I had managed to keep the details of the fire damage from Jack. We had reached a point where that was no longer an option.

The wooden door to his hospital room seemed to weigh a thousand pounds when I pushed it open, although that might have just been the burden I carried. Sarah glanced over her shoulder from beside Jack's bed and gave me a soft smile. She'd never been my type, nor had she been Charlie's, yet seeing her here, it was obvious how she had managed to steal my brother's heart. The role she'd played in Randi's life in high school trained her for the role she played as an adult, and she was perfectly suited to be a farmer's wife.

Once I reached her side, I leaned down and kissed the top of her head. "Hey, girl," I said with a gentle squeeze to her bicep. "How's the patient?"

Jack appeared better than I'd seen him in days. Pink tinged his cheeks, and the dark bags under his eyes had faded. "On the mend. It's good to see you, Austin." Jack's voice wavered. The strength behind it had yet to return.

"You too. You look like you feel better." I searched the room for a chair. Without another one to drag next to the bed, Sarah gave me her seat and moved to the sofa. I used that term lightly. Foam blocks stacked on top of each other did not make it furniture, in my opinion.

Jack pushed up and situated himself against the pillows. His expression stiffened, and he squared his shoulders to prepare for the conversation he knew I had come to have. I imagined, based on his demeanor, that Sarah had given him a heads-up.

I leaned forward in the plastic chair and rested my elbows on my knees. There, I searched for words to make this less difficult.

"Quit pussy-footing around, Austin. Just spit it out, son."

I grabbed the ballcap from my head, ran my fingers through my hair, and then fiddled with the bill to keep from meeting Jack's eyes. "I brought in a vet from Oklahoma. He's been at the ranch all week."

The movement from the hospital bed drew my attention. Jack shifted and crossed his arms. "And?"

"We've got some issues."

I hoped he'd ask questions, or that Sarah might help me out. Jack remained stoic, and Sarah didn't make a peep. The only option left was to lay it on the table.

"We lost nearly twenty percent of the pastures and a tenth of the herd. We have hundreds of head suffering from smoke inhalation, calves without mothers, some with burns, and Dr. Thomas—he's the vet who came down—is worried about latent hoof damage."

Jack stared at me as if I spoke a foreign language, even though the recognition showed in his eyes.

"We need to bring in hands from out of state, since none are available locally, to deal with the fences and irrigation systems. The ranch needs the vet at our disposal for at least another couple of days, maybe longer. And I'm not sure where we're going to get the antibiotics needed for the head with respiratory issues."

His head bobbed slowly. "That it?"

I shrugged. "Well, that's the short list with the highest priority."

Jack raised a hand to his scruffy face, and the scratch of his whiskers on his palm was audible even from a few feet away. The same eyes that had seemed alert when I arrived were now weary, and the bags under them became more prominent. It was the first time in my life that I could remember Jack appearing defeated, haggard.

He took a deep breath in and then let it out. "Well, that's what we have insurance for. I hate that I'm not there to help you deal with all of it, but do what you need to do to keep the place running."

That was the nail I didn't want to drive into the coffin, the final blow that might send him over the hill. There was one more problem I hadn't mentioned. "The insurance lapsed, Jack."

I hadn't even told Sarah. I'd hoped there was something I could do. I'd been fighting all week to get the policy reinstated with no luck. It probably wouldn't have been an issue had we not had significant damage or loss. As it stood, every rancher in town had a claim.

Sarah gasped from the other side of the room.

Jack sat up straight. That look of exhaustion quickly transformed into one of rage. "What do ya mean?"

"I called in the claim to get an adjuster out. They said the premiums weren't paid when the policy renewed in February." I didn't go on to tell Jack, or Sarah, that multiple letters had been sent to Cross Acres that went unanswered or that calls had been ignored. It wouldn't do any good, not now. There was no point in adding insult to injury.

Jack shook his head, and Sarah stood to take her dad's side. They talked on top of each other, essentially stating the same things: there must be a mistake, and that can't be possible.

I let them go. They both needed to say whatever was on their mind. And I listened, patiently. There wasn't anything they could throw at me that I hadn't already tossed at someone else...and had it shot down.

A lull presented itself, and I took it. "Unless you can provide a voided check or proof of a bank draft, there is no coverage."

That summed it up.

Sarah angled toward Jack and took his hand in hers. "Daddy, you paid the bill, right?" The concern in her tone would be evident to a deaf person. It wasn't just her voice, her body language screamed worry. Slumped shoulders, pinched facial features, mouth slightly ajar, all the classic signs were there.

"Of course, I paid. This is utter nonsense. Nothin' but some huge corporation where the left hand don't know what the right hand's doin'. Cross Acres ain't never gone a day without insurance."

Until February first. And it hadn't had any since. I couldn't sort any of that out, though.

"Austin, you need to get on the phone and ask for a supervisor." Sarah's attempt at being helpful was noted; it was also useless.

I jerked my head toward the door while maintaining eye contact with Sarah. "Can I talk to you in the hall?"

Jack latched onto my forearm faster than a snake struck. "You two might think I'm old and feeble, but last time I checked, my name was on the deed to that ranch."

I sucked on my teeth and willed lightning to strike or some

other deadly force to take me out in the next two-point-five seconds. When neither happened, and I hadn't vaporized, I did my job.

"We need cash, Jack. And we need a lot of it. The vet has dozens of ranches vying for his attention, and we need him full time. The animals need medication—that takes money. And we need extra help to get fences rebuilt and to haul hay to feed the herd, who can't be sustained on the property we currently have them on. That doesn't even begin to address the ongoing issues about those acres not producing, the irrigation systems, or the fact that several of our own hands lost their houses to the fires and are displaced."

"We have guys who lost their houses?"

I nodded. "Several."

The county was in a bad way. Fires didn't just take out empty fields; they ate anything in their paths from animals to homes. Cross Acres had lucked out; the ranch saw far less devastation than many others the fire hit first. Jack would have lost everything had the wind not shifted again and taken the flames east. The damage was bad, but it would have been catastrophic.

"Open the house. I've got a couple extra bedrooms, the couches, the barn. Anything you need, use it."

My chuckle didn't gain a favorable response.

"There a problem?" The grit in Jack's tone rubbed me with uneasy frustration.

This entire conversation was emotionally equivalent to navigating landmines. I didn't have a clue what would set Jack off, although I presumed just about all of it. So maybe it was more like dodging bullets from an automatic weapon in a hail of gunfire. "You're going to need your room when they release you."

"Okay, that still leaves three others. We can't accommodate everyone in town, but we can certainly take care of our own."

I scratched my head and then put on my hat. The damn thing

acted as a security blanket these days. "Except that Miranda and her boyfriend are there."

I'd never understood the expression, "he looked like he'd seen a ghost," until that moment. "Randi's in Mason Belle?"

Sarah came to the aid of her father. "Daddy, I told you she came home. Don't you remember?"

Jack shook his head and then turned evil eyes on me. "You're shackin' up with my little girl? In *my* house? And why hasn't she come to see me?"

"What?" I was confused as the day was long.

Sarah patted her dad's forearm. "She's been here several times, but I thought it was better for her to help Austin at the ranch than to get you worked up."

"Some help," I muttered.

Jack's face went from stark white to beet red. "What's wrong with you, boy?"

Before I could respond, Sarah intervened. "Daddy, she came home from New York, and she brought her boyfriend, Eason, with her. You've heard me talk about him." She spoke to her father the way I'd heard her explain something to her kids.

He bobbed his head, yet the slight squint and vacant look in his eyes told me he didn't follow. "I need to meet this boy."

Sarah giggled. "He's hardly a boy. He's in his thirties and a lawyer."

I stifled a laugh when Jack puffed up his chest.

"I don't care how old he is or what he does for a livin'. I wanna meet him. And I wanna see my daughter."

The pieces weren't falling into place for Jack. He didn't give any indication that he'd been estranged from his youngest child for over six years. There was no hesitation in his demands.

Sarah gave him her pity smile, the one I hated to receive. "Eason is leaving this afternoon."

I sat back and watched this unfold.

Jack grimaced. "*Eason*? That's the boy's name?"

"Yes, sir. Eason McNabb," I confirmed with snark.

He shook his head. "That's a sissy name."

Sarah didn't fall into the pit of name calling, and oddly enough, she came to the guy's defense. "Actually, it's a family name."

Jack lifted his nose and scoffed. "Oh, so he's never done an honest day's work?"

Over the last few days, I'd felt everything Jack actually had the nerve to say. I just hadn't voiced it. Eason's hands had never seen a callus, and I thought his name was somewhat soft myself. There wasn't a rough edge to the guy.

"He's a nice man, Daddy. And he brought Randi home. We should be grateful."

"I'll be grateful once I meet him and see her. Call her." Accustomed to issuing orders, Jack seemed to have forgotten that Randi had quit listening to him the day she left Mason Belle.

It was hard to tell if Jack had turned a blind eye to the past or didn't remember it. He'd been on large doses of narcotics in recent days, so maybe this was temporary. Or perhaps it was a way to forget whatever happened and move on.

Sarah left the room; I presumed to call her sister. And Jack gave me the third degree.

"How could you let this happen?" His words were crisp and clear.

I flinched. "Me? What did I do?"

His nostrils flared, and I readied myself for the finger of blame. "You didn't chase her." He accentuated each word with his pointer aimed at me.

"I was *eighteen*. What was I supposed to do? I didn't even know why she'd left. Hell, I still don't." I couldn't figure out the angle he played.

Seconds earlier, he had acted as though nothing had ever gone down between the two of them. Now, he wanted to pretend it was my fault she'd never come home.

Before he could answer, Sarah came back.

"That was short," I pointed out.

Sarah ignored me and went to her father. "Randi's on her way to the airport with Eason now."

It was just like her to run off when things got tough. Honestly, I'd expected more from Daddy Warbucks than I had Randi. Even if he'd logged more manicures than hours of physical labor, Eason appeared to be a stand-up guy. He just came wrapped in a suit instead of Wranglers.

With Jack's eyes downcast, he said to no one in particular, "Maybe I'll see her next time." Although, he had to doubt whether there would actually be a next time.

Sarah waved her hand in the air, dismissing her father's down-trodden words. "Nonsense. She'll be here in about thirty minutes. She has to get a rental car." And then she resumed her spot on the foam couch.

That was my cue to leave. I stood and stuck my hands in my pockets.

Sarah picked up a magazine and flipped it open. As she thumbed through it, staring directly at the page, she challenged me to take a step toward the door. "Sit down, Austin. We have things to figure out, and you are at the center of making it happen."

---

*T*he hair on the back of my neck stood before she had even entered the room. Other than the occasional encounter at the ranch, which I made certain were painful for her, I'd avoided her like the plague. If I could have gotten out of this room without having Sarah attack me, I wouldn't be sitting here now. This was a family matter. They needed to decide what they wanted to do, how they intended to do it, and how they planned to pay for it. I was merely a hired hand in the scheme of things.

Yet when she knocked on the door and then entered, it wasn't me who played the part of the outsider. We were all on edge, and none of us knew what to expect. I assumed Jack would have some sort of reunion with the daughter he hadn't seen in six years, but he didn't so much as make a fuss over her. They didn't hug. They didn't even shake hands.

"Randi." Jack's icy demeanor left me uncomfortable when only half an hour ago he'd demanded to see her.

My attention shifted back and forth between them and then to Sarah, who hadn't lifted her nose from the magazine to make any of this go smoother.

Randi swallowed hard. "Miranda."

My jaw dropped. I couldn't believe she had corrected her own father. The father she hadn't seen or spoken to in years. It was a statement. One that made no bones about the distance between them.

"I know your name; I gave it to you." This wasn't going well. "Sit."

Eighteen-year-old *Randi* would have argued. Twenty-four-year-old *Miranda* did not. She assumed the seat next to her sister, folded her hands in her lap, and crossed her ankles. Randi held her father's stare, yet she didn't cross him.

Once Jack had our attention, he commanded the room, and I traveled back in time to a place in my youth where I revered and feared the man before me. It was like old times. Sarah sat on her high horse, and Randi and I prepared to do the bidding.

"We've got some problems at the ranch," he started. "Together, we need to figure out how best to handle them."

Sarah closed the magazine and set it on the side table. Randi, Miranda, or whatever the hell her name was these days, cocked her head. I leaned back and crossed my arms over my chest. I could take direction from Jack without a problem. It wouldn't be an issue for Sarah to lead the way. But Randi didn't have a stake in this game. She needed to sit there and keep her mouth shut.

When Jack looked at me, I didn't try to hide the smug expression that crossed my face. "Austin, how long can we survive on what we're currently doing?"

And all the joy I'd had when he turned to me first died a quick death. "A few days at most."

Randi leaned forward and opened her mouth, then closed it. Open, close. Open, close. Like a fish. "I-I don't understand. What exactly are we discussing here? I've definitely missed something."

Jack addressed his daughter like he would a hand, not like his offspring. "In case you missed the fire damage, the entire herd is in distress. We have a vet who needs to be paid to keep him around, medicine that needs to be purchased, land that's been destroyed—"

"Yes, I can look out my window every morning and see that. When is the adjuster coming out? Surely the vet has dealt with insurance companies before. And the guys don't get paid until after they've worked."

This wasn't my goat rodeo, but Jack and Sarah sat silent, so I spoke up. "It appears the insurance lapsed."

Jack immediately denied that accusation, yet all I could focus on was the fire those words lit in Randi's eyes. The vein in her forehead—the one that made an appearance when she was angry —throbbed, and she stared me down like I'd been the one to cancel the policy. If I didn't detest her, and if we didn't have an audience, I might have stomped over to her, yanked her from that pile of foam she sat on, and forced my mouth to hers in the most aggressive display of ownership I could muster.

Her lips curled in a snarl. "What do you mean the insurance lapsed?"

It might have been the way she said it, or maybe how she glared at me. Either way, that momentary lapse of judgment disappeared when I bit back, "Did I stutter?"

"How are we going to pay for all that needs to be done if the ranch isn't insured?"

I stood when she stood. The rest of the room fell away, and all that remained was Randi Adams and Austin Burin. I'd waited six years to go toe-to-toe with her. This wasn't the topic I had planned to argue, although I'd take whatever I could get. Having the ability to unleash over something I was passionate about would serve the same purpose. I loved Cross Acres almost as much as I'd once loved her.

I took a step toward her. She challenged me with one of her own in my direction. "The ranch has assets, *Miranda*."

"Are you suggesting we sell them, *Austin*?"

Another step.

My hands fit nicely in my pockets where I kept them to prevent her from seeing my balled fists. "Unless you have another suggestion," I ground out. I'd started to talk through my teeth instead of actually opening my mouth.

Step.

Randi didn't bother to conceal her agitation. Her left hand was firmly planted on her hip, and she used her right index finger to stab my chest. "Let me tell you something." *This should be good.* "That ranch has been in our family for generations. Not one acre has ever been sold off to pay a debt. And we aren't starting today." She gave me one final push, and I held my ground.

"Correct me if I'm wrong, but I didn't say anything about selling off the land. I said the ranch held assets, some of which currently double as liabilities. So, the way I see it, we have two options that—"

She threw her head back and laughed. It was short-lived and clearly done for dramatic effect. "*We?*"

I ignored her and kept talking. "Jack can either put a mortgage on the house, or he can sell off some of the herd."

"Who asked you?" she quipped.

My chest heaved as I tried to contain my growing anger. I jerked my hand from my jeans and pointed at her father. "Your dad did!"

She raised her brows, took a deep breath, and folded her thin arms under her breasts. "Last time I checked, this was a family matter. And unless you've been adopted since I left, your last name isn't Adams."

"It might not be written on my birth certificate, but I'm a helluva lot closer to being family than you've proven to be. You think you can waltz in here after six—"

"Enough!" Jack bellowed.

Miranda flinched, and I took a step back when I realized that we stood so close I could feel her breath on my skin.

The door opened, and a nurse peeked her head in. I hadn't considered the commotion our argument caused beyond the scope of this room. The nurse's glare warned us without saying a word.

Sarah materialized out of thin air and gently pushed Miranda and me apart. "Why don't you both sit down and stop yelling before we all get thrown out?"

We both backed away, holding the other's stare. I never took my attention off the anger that radiated from Miranda. It oozed from every pore in her body, and it had gone from sexy as hell to downright ugly. She didn't have a clue what Cross Acres was up against. None of them did. Jack hadn't seen it, Sarah had never concerned herself with the financial piece, and Miranda had been gone her entire adult life. Come to think of it, I didn't understand the need for either sister to even be in the room.

"Jack," I said as I broke the stronghold I had on his daughter,

"I really think this is a matter for the two of us to discuss. Why don't I come back another time?"

Miranda couldn't stay quiet. "Because of me? Is that why you want to leave?"

Sarah attempted to soothe her sister. "No, Miranda. Of course not. It's just a difficult time for everyone."

"Yes. It's absolutely because of you," I retorted. I refused to coddle her. "You don't know the first thing about cattle ranching, much less what needs to be done. If you're so concerned with your family's estate, then pull your head out of your ass and recognize that your dad is in deep shit. We either liquidate in the very near future, or you won't have to worry about the ranch since the bank will own it."

Sarah's eyes brimmed with unshed tears. As if time had slowed, she shifted her attention to her father, no longer caring about keeping Miranda and me from wringing each other's necks. "Is that true, Daddy?" Fear laced her voice, and when she practically limped to his bedside, I could have slapped myself for losing my cool.

Jack scratched at the beard covering his face. There was more grey than brown, and once again, he appeared older than his age. "If there's a problem with the insurance like Austin says, then yeah."

My chest constricted at the pain I'd imparted on everyone in this room. I came here to talk to Jack because he needed to make some decisions. I hadn't intended for Sarah or Miranda to be part of the discussion. They both had an emotional tie to that land, but they were out of their minds if they didn't think I did, as well.

Miranda helped Sarah back to the couch, and I took my seat in the plastic chair. The room was silent except for the occasional sniffle from my sister-in-law. My brother would kick my ass later for upsetting her.

Jack cleared his throat, and all eyes shifted to him. It was like he sat on a throne in the hospital bed above us. I'd do whatever he told me to do. I just hoped he understood how dire the situation would become and how soon it would happen.

"Austin?" he said.

"Yes, sir?"

If words could get lodged in his throat, Jack was choking on them. "What do we need to do?"

"We need to sell off at least a thousand head to have viable pastures for the cows you keep."

Randi couldn't stop herself from interjecting. "We still have the land." Like somehow, I'd missed that the fire hadn't actually devoured the land. What she'd missed was that the land no longer offered grazing for its occupants, nor did it have a fence surrounding it to contain anything we put in it.

Instead of lashing out, I tried to explain that. I did not linger on that topic since it wasn't open for discussion. "If it were me, I'd sell two thousand. One to make up for the food deficit and one to buy us some breathing room for medical needs. You won't be able to sell off any of the animals that potentially face health issues."

If Jack took my advice, in what amounted to the blink of an eye, he would have lost a third of his herd. And if we could have this discussion anywhere else with any other company, I would tell him I wasn't sure that was enough. It was just a starting point.

"Or I can mortgage the farmhouse?" he asked. The innocence in his tone not only concerned me, it obviously took his daughters by surprise, too.

I tilted my head to consider his expression. "I wouldn't do that, Jack. You can rebuild the herd. It will take some time, but you can. It's the best solution. It solves the manpower issues by not forcing us to haul hay or bring in tons of additional help from around the state—help that is scarce at this point, mind you. Also, we won't have to rebuild fences immediately, the irrigation in the south pastures can hold off, and it would fund the medical treatment."

He nodded his consent. And I confirmed my understanding. The lack of verbal acknowledgment told me how hard this decision was for their father. And I could only imagine how difficult it would be to allow someone my age to make the choice and agree with it.

Miranda refused to let it go that easily, or what she perceived to be easily. "That's *it*? You're going to let *Austin* dictate what happens to Cross Acres without so much as a fight? You have insurance, Daddy. You don't need to sell off any of the herd, and you certainly don't need a loan from the bank." Her head swung between the three of us, trying to get someone to agree with her.

Cross Acres should have a surplus of funds. The insurance should have been in place. None of this should have been an issue. But I'd tried to use the credit card Jack gave me for the ranch this week, and it had been denied. I'd spoken to no less than twelve people at the insurance company, and the premiums weren't paid. The cash dried up, and only Jack knew when. Just like whatever had happened with Miranda the night she left Mason Belle, I'd bet Jack would take that secret to the grave, too.

Jack ignored Miranda's outburst and addressed me. "Austin, do what you have to do. I trust your judgment."

Miranda shot up from the sofa and lunged across the room. I assumed an attack was imminent, so I got up to prepare myself. Instead, she brushed past me, not the least bit gracefully, tore open the door, and stomped out.

When I turned back, still unsure of what had just happened, Jack and Sarah both stared at me as if I held the answers, or maybe the key. "Not quite the reunion you envisioned, huh, Jack?" I huffed, exasperated by Miranda's reappearance in my life.

To my surprise, he didn't agree with me. "She's home. Let's figure out how to keep her here."

It was official. The man was bat-shit crazy. Certifiably insane. If either he or Sarah believed I'd aid in that attempt, they'd both lost their ever-loving minds. Miranda Adams needed to go back to where she came from, and if necessary, I'd help her pack and drive her to the airport.

9

MIRANDA

"Are you sure you're going to be okay with him?" I asked Sarah after the two of us had struggled to get Daddy situated upstairs.

She scowled. "Why wouldn't I be?"

I pursed my lips, glanced at the steps, and then back to my sister. I held up my hands in surrender. Far be it from me to question her judgment. She'd been here. I had to trust that she knew what she was capable of and what was too much.

"It's not like there aren't people all over the place, Randi." She caught herself. "Sorry, Miranda. If I need help, I'll get one of the guys. What is it that you think is going to happen?"

I couldn't answer that question without upsetting her, so I shrugged. I was making too big a deal out of this. Daddy wasn't an invalid; he just had a hard time breathing and got winded easily. Sarah was one of those people who needed to be needed, and this provided her with that outlet. The girls had gone back to school today, and Rand was running around the ranch, leaving her with mounds of time on her hands. She defaulted to playing nurse to Daddy to fill that void.

"Where are you going to be?" She considered me quizzically.

Avoiding her son probably wasn't an answer she cared to hear, and I doubted replacing Rand's name with Austin's in that sentiment would endear me to her, either. "Helping out wherever I can." Meaning, I'd find Corey, Tommy, or Brock and beg them to shove their crap work my way to keep myself away from their foreman.

Sarah leaned her hip against the banister in the foyer. "You can't avoid him forever."

I played dumb. "Avoid who?" I didn't have to be a genius to figure out exactly who she meant.

And then she gave me a look that said just that.

"Ugh. I'm not avoiding him. I'm just not interested in talking to him." I glanced over my shoulder and out the glass in the front door to ensure no one might walk in. "Look, Sarah, I want to do whatever you and Daddy expect me to and then go home."

"You mean back to New York?"

Unless she knew something I didn't, that was where I lived. "Well, yeah."

Her eyes narrowed with mischief. "Okay."

"Okay? What's that supposed to mean?"

She offered me a nonchalant shake of the head. "Nothing."

I waited.

"You may live there, Miranda, but it's not your home. You're going to end up hurting a great guy when you finally admit that to yourself."

She needed to get over this whole Austin bit. "I hurt Austin six years ago. He'll probably throw me a thank-God-you're-leaving party and shove me toward the plane. Plus, my entire life is in New York."

Sarah smirked, pushed off the stairs, and strolled toward the kitchen. "Your entire life *used* to be in Mason Belle." She walked and talked. She also effectively dismissed me and ended the conversation.

Before I could spend too much time pondering what kind of drug addiction my sister must have developed or what program I should check her into in order to get her help for her delusions, I caught sight of Brock. I spun on the ball of my foot, took off out the door, and raced down the steps.

"Brock," I called across the driveway.

He stopped, and his shoulders sank. It wasn't the response I'd hoped for, although probably the one I should have expected. He covered his discomfort with a bright smile that didn't quite reach his eyes. It was forced, but at least he tried. "Hey, Randi."

I didn't correct him. I hated to hear that nickname pass anyone's lips, but right now, I needed a friend more than I needed to let go of my past.

Brock searched the vicinity for onlookers and spoke when he found none. "How's your dad?"

Small talk. I could handle this. "He's good. Glad to be home, I think." We stood there and stared in uncomfortable silence. Things shouldn't be like this. Not with Brock. Austin, fine. My dad, I got it. However, I didn't do anything to Brock. "So, umm, Austin said you and Charity got married."

"Yep."

He couldn't keep this up. Brock was too outgoing. We'd been too close. It wasn't possible for him to hold a grudge this long.

"I bet the wedding was gorgeous. Charity would make a beautiful bride."

Brock dropped his head and put his hands on his hips. When he lifted his chin, a flash of regret crossed his eyes. "Woulda been better if her best friend had been at her side."

I wanted to tell him I would have, had I been aware the event had taken place, but that was a lie. "Brock..."

"Save it, Randi." Gone was the mellow baritone he'd had since puberty, and in its place came an abrasive scratch I hoped never to hear again. "I ain't gonna pretend to know what caused you to bail, 'cause it don't matter. What matters is, we ain't heard from you since. And that ain't how things are done here."

I bit my lip and chewed on it for a minute before releasing it. "I didn't handle things the right way. I should—"

"That's the understatement of the century." Austin cut off my attempt at an apology. "Brock, don't you have better things to do than stand around chitchatting? Last time I checked, you got paid to work."

Brock tipped his hat in my direction. I wished I thought it was a kind gesture. The truth was, Brock was merely raised to be polite. It had nothing to do with me and everything to do with the manners his mama gave him.

The moment I was satisfied Brock had moved from earshot, I hit Austin in the arm. "Seriously? You couldn't let me have that?"

"Apologize on your own time."

"My own time? My own time."

"Are you a parrot? Yes, your own time."

"Newsflash, Austin. This *is* my time. I'm not being paid to work. As a matter of fact, I'm not even being paid at my *actual* job while I'm here doing yours."

He jerked off his hat and started messing with the bill, bending and flattening it out. "First of all, you aren't doing *my* job. This ranch ran just fine without you for years, and it will run just fine when you hightail it back to the big city with your hoity-toity friends."

I didn't attempt to stifle my laughter. "Just fine? Nearly a quarter of it was lost to fire, and even more is going to be lost because no one bothered to pay the insurance. Not sure what your definition of fine is, but that doesn't qualify in my dictionary."

"One was an act of nature; the other wasn't within my control." Spit flew from his mouth when he hurled his excuses my direction. "Cross Acres will survive, just like it always has...without you here." If he weren't careful, he would have a stroke. I could only guess at what his blood pressure had risen to, based on the color of his face. And if that vein in the side of his neck throbbed any harder, it might explode.

I'd tried to avoid this at all costs. I'd been foolish enough to believe that I could. Had I known Austin Burin managed my daddy's ranch, I can't say that I would have returned regardless of my father's condition. With every fiber of my being, I wished I had gone back to New York with Eason. Austin was right. I didn't have any business being here. It was a joke, and so was my presence.

Crying wouldn't help, and I refused to give Austin the joy of witnessing my pain. The only way I could fight off tears was through anger. And I lashed out. "What's your problem, Austin?" Heat rose in my cheeks, and my heart pounded beneath my sternum. Nerves, anxiety, fear—they all fueled whatever explosion brewed.

"My problem?" he screamed. He had his back to the barn, so he didn't see the group of men who'd gathered behind him.

Since I didn't know any of them well, I couldn't be certain whether they were there to collect gossip or to guarantee Austin didn't do something he'd regret.

Austin threw his hands in the air. "*You*, Miranda. *You* are my problem."

I shook my head and clenched my hands so tightly that my nails broke the skin on my palms. "It's been *six years*, Austin. And guess what, you won. You got it all." I spun in a circle with my arms outstretched to indicate the vastness of his rich world. The same world that I'd left behind. "Every last bit of it. You got it." I should have been embarrassed by the scene I caused.

This wasn't the time or the place. Yet even though I was aware that I'd lost control, I couldn't bring myself back. My brain screamed at me to quit, not to engage. Yet the longer we held each other's gaze, the more entrenched I became in the battle with little regard for who won the war.

The bill of his hat would be ruined by the time this ended. "You think I won? What world do you live in, Miranda?"

I gasped for breath. "Of course, you won. You have my daddy's love and his ranch, my sister's admiration, all our friends, life in Mason Belle, and—"

He leaned in and narrowed what little gap remained between us. "And I lost the *only* thing that mattered," he hollered, inches from my face. "You didn't even leave a damn note. I didn't get an email, not a phone call—hell, you didn't even mail me a Dear John letter. You just vanished. I didn't win a damn thing other than a life without you in it."

Austin stopped hollering. He expected me to retaliate. And I wanted to. I just couldn't argue with the truth, and without more explanation than I was prepared to give, I couldn't justify anything that had happened.

"We were supposed to make it, Miranda. You and me. Anyone who'd ever come in contact with us believed that as much as they trusted the sun would rise and set." Austin ran his hand through his hair and then clamped it down on the back of his neck. He let out a huff and shook his head. "You were my forever. You were supposed to be my wife. And you left...without me." His tone had softened, even if his expression hadn't.

I didn't have a response that would fix that hurt. For either of us. My voice was barely a whisper when I uttered his name. "Austin." I reached out to touch his forearm, and he swatted my hand away.

"No." He stepped back and shook his head. "You don't get to waltz back into my world with your live-in and rub your happiness in my face. I may not have known any better then, but I sure as hell do now." Austin scanned me from head to toe before hurling another insult at me. "You're toxic, Miranda. You didn't just obliterate *me*, there was a long line of people you left in the wake of your departure. I don't have a clue what Jack said to you that made you leave...although I'd wager that every word was spot on."

I lost the battle against tears right about the time that Tommy approached. The first one fell when Tommy put his hand on Austin's shoulder.

"Hey, man. Why don't you step away and calm down?"

Austin was out of breath from his emotional unloading, and his chest heaved as he gasped for air. His brown eyes held mine for a painful beat, and his Adam's apple bobbed when he swallowed. And when his lips parted, I was certain his words would hurt. "You need to go, Miranda."

Austin didn't give me the chance to respond. He retreated with Tommy, who glanced back. If expressions could speak, his apologized profusely. By the time someone intervened, it appeared everyone on Daddy's staff had witnessed it, along with a little boy I'd never met but definitely recognized. With tears running down my cheeks, I stared at my sister's son. He was the spitting image of Austin at his age, and he'd just witnessed his uncle tear apart the aunt he'd never met.

He held my stare, and he didn't turn away. Even as young as he was, he regarded me with sympathy, not condemnation, as if maybe he understood me, even though we didn't know each other at all. Rand flicked his attention to Austin, and when he confirmed no one watched him, he raised his tiny hand and waved. I didn't have a chance to wave back before he took off around the side of the barn and out of sight.

*T*he front door creaked behind me, and the stilted sound of footsteps approached. I swiped at my cheeks to remove the visible signs of my distress. Before I turned around, I took a deep breath and straightened my shoulders.

My sister waited at the top of the steps. "Wanna come inside?"

I didn't. Hiding sounded like a much better option. Or packing. That would be an excellent precursor to a flight back to New York. It had been stupid to come here and even more foolish to believe I could escape without harm.

Sarah waved her hand to encourage me to take the first step. Somehow, it seemed more significant than simply dodging my embarrassment. The men behind me had dispersed, yet the trail into the house still felt like a walk of shame. If this was anything like the talks Sarah and I'd had in the past, or better yet, lectures, I couldn't handle that on the backside of Austin humiliating me.

When I reached the top of the steps, I pleaded with Sarah. "Please don't make this any worse than it already is."

She smiled, and it reminded me of my mom. The way I remembered her when she still loved us. It was gentle and kind. And most importantly, it reached her eyes. When I was in high school, I'd always sensed anger or resentment. Sarah hadn't wanted the role she'd been dumped into any more than I wanted her to be in it. Yes, she could have handled it with a bit more finesse...so could I. A piece of the wall I'd erected when I left Mason Belle crumbled with that admission.

"Come on. I'll get you some tea, and we can talk."

I accepted her peace offering and followed her into the kitchen. It seemed as good a place as any to chat about whatever Sarah had on her mind. The stools had been replaced since I'd left. I couldn't say that I was a fan of the new ones. Saddles were made for horses, not sitting at a bar.

"Lemon?"

I stopped appraising the seat and stared at my sister. "Huh?"

She set a pitcher on the island, along with two glasses filled with ice. "Would you like lemon for your tea?"

"Sure." I couldn't remember the last time I'd had sweet tea. I quit asking for it shortly after I got to New York. A packet of sugar and a glass of cold tea did not equate to what I was accustomed to. I tried to explain to a waitress that it needed to be mixed before adding ice. She didn't care, or she didn't understand. Either way, I had quit drinking it.

Sarah went to the fridge, and a wave of nostalgia hit me. With age, she'd become more and more like Mama. Her grin, her mannerisms, the way she played hostess even when she wasn't supposed to. "Are you hungry? I can whip up something for you."

I wasn't. "No. I feel like puking." The scene in front of the house didn't just knock the wind out of my sails; it ripped them from the masts and sent them flying out to sea.

The hum of the refrigerator almost drowned out the low sigh that passed her lips. "Miranda, he's hurt."

"That makes two of us," I mumbled.

She quit rummaging for food, poured us both glasses of tea, and took the stool next to me. Her fingers were warm when she gave my forearm a gentle squeeze. It should have been comforting; instead, it reminded me of all the things I missed. I'd never get them here again, and I just wanted to go home, back to the life I'd made in New York with Eason. Even though our relationship wasn't conventional, it worked for both of us.

"I don't have a clue why you left. I assume it had to do with the accident, but I was afraid to ask Daddy, and you barely talk when I call, so I haven't asked you, either. The only thing I *can* tell you is what happened here once you were gone."

I had a hard time believing she didn't know what Daddy said. They were thick as thieves, and according to him, my departure had been her request.

She traced the trail of condensation down her glass while she stared at it. "Austin had a tough time."

"So did I," I quipped.

Sarah shook her head. "I don't doubt that. I just think you should be aware of his side since I would be shocked if he ever tells you himself."

Fair enough. I could keep my mouth shut and listen. Or I could try.

"He came here every morning before the sun came up and did all your chores."

My mouth dropped, but since she wasn't looking at me, she didn't see the shock.

"Austin took care of Nugget like he was his." She paused as if she were remembering the days after I had first left. "There wasn't a single day that boy wasn't in that barn, taking care of things for you. He believed you needed time. That you'd come back. And he wanted you to know he hadn't forgotten you. He loved the things you loved the way you would have loved them." She paused long enough to glance at me and absorb my reaction.

I didn't have one to offer. I understood the words she said; they just didn't make sense.

"I would hear him talk to Nugget out in the barn. He made promises to him about not leaving him and waiting for you."

"That was a long time ago."

She pulled back and held her position to stare at me. "You don't understand. He never quit, Miranda. Every day. For six years. He has shown up and done your chores and taken care of your horse."

I rolled my eyes. "Yeah, because he gets paid to. He's Daddy's foreman," I scoffed. I refused to accept guilt that didn't belong to me. I had enough of my own to handle without added pressure.

"Daddy only hired him because he was always here. Don't be

so daft. He could be working at the Burins' farm. And let's not forget, that was the summer after his senior year of high school. He didn't spend it playing at the lake with his buddies. He waited...for *you*."

That summer had been awful. I'd met Eason minutes after I'd arrived in New York. Looking back, I should be amazed he didn't give me the boot. I was a sloppy, teary-eyed mess until he made me get off my tail or get out. Without anywhere else to go, I opted to get up. I can't imagine what it would have been like for Austin here. There was something new around every corner in New York. And once I had started school and began to work for Eason, life fell into a comfortable stasis. Austin had no way to escape *us*. Although, he didn't have to torture himself at Cross Acres daily.

"He should have moved on." It was a callous thing for me to say in light of what she'd shared.

Her head bobbed in agreement. "Probably. But that's not who he is."

"You mean who he was," I corrected.

"No, *is*."

The implication that Austin's anger remained firmly rooted because he continued to wait wasn't one I would willingly accept. "Meaning what exactly?"

She lifted the glass to her lips and consumed half of the liquid before setting it down. "I don't believe he's ever moved on."

I'd always considered my sister rather level-headed, even if I hated that she was a stick in the mud. This made twice since I'd been home that I had questioned her sanity. "It's been six years, Sarah. Austin Burin is not still carrying a flame for me. You heard what he said in the driveway." I crossed my arms in defiance. I would have leaned back to further illustrate my position, except the new barstools didn't allow for that.

Sarah snickered and shook her head. "And clearly, you didn't.

He believed he would marry you, Miranda. That only happens once in a lifetime."

"There has to have been other girls. He'll find the right one." As soon as it flowed out of my mouth, I realized the words were for me. They made *me* feel better. In some odd way, it justified my silence, the way I'd left town, the fact I'd stayed away, regardless of whether they were rooted in any truth.

She finished her tea, got up to put the glass in the sink, and faced me. Sarah leaned back against the counter and held her hands in front of her. I'd hated that stance when I was in high school. It always showed up just before I got schooled or punished. "Not one."

Not one. "Not one girl?"

"Nope." She popped the *P*, yet it wasn't followed by a smug I-told-you-so expression. If I didn't know better, I'd think hope glittered in her expression. "Not one."

That I refused to believe. "You just don't know about it, then. No way Austin Burin has been celibate for six years." My eyes went wide to illustrate my point when I continued. "Trust me."

Her right shoulder lifted in a weak shrug. "Believe what you choose, Miranda. I was here. You weren't."

"Has he told you that?"

That question seemed to dash the hopeful gleam I'd just witnessed and replaced it with something akin to sorrow. "No." She pulled her lips between her teeth and chewed on them, briefly. When she released them, she took a deep breath before she spoke. "It's kind of unspoken that we don't talk about you in front of him...or Daddy."

Figured. Austin I got. Daddy, that was unjustified. "Of course." Sarcasm dripped from my response.

"That's not fair. You can't blame Austin for not wanting to talk about you. You decimated him. Obliterated his heart. He never recovered from you leaving. Don't you see that?"

"Clearly, I don't." I tried to keep my anger under wraps. I struggled, and Sarah knew me well enough to see it, even if she couldn't hear it. "He's done nothing other than yell at me and embarrass me since I stepped foot in Mason Belle."

She picked up the tea pitcher and slid it into the fridge. "Then maybe you need to swallow your pride and have a conversation with him about what actually happened. Why you left. And most importantly, why you haven't been back. He needs the closure as much as you do."

I hated that she'd gotten so wise. It probably came with being a mom. Regardless, I wasn't willing to tell her she was right. She knew it, and that would have to be enough. For now.

"Based on how things went down in the driveway, I don't think it's the best idea." That wasn't true, but I'd cling to it.

"Don't you have any desire to be able to come home again?" Well, that took an unexpected twist. "Be able to bring Eason with you to see your family? Spend time with your nieces and nephew...without the animosity and lingering resentment."

"Sarah, Eason isn't—"

She waved me off. "He doesn't have to come."

This was so much bigger than Austin. I wished my sister recognized the situation for what it was. Yet before I could explain any of that, the screen door flew open and banged against the frame as a flash of boy raced through the kitchen.

My sister tried to grab her son. She couldn't move as quickly as he did, and her left arm slinking out to catch him did little other than slow him down a tad. "Rand."

I'd hated that tone when I got it from her in high school. Sarah could take one syllable and draw it into two, starting with a low pitch, then to high, and back to low.

Rand slid to a stop on the opposite side of the kitchen. He stood stock-still, and I giggled when he didn't face his mother. "Yes, ma'am?" His little voice made my heart jump.

I'd never been a fan of kids, but there was something about my sister's only son that tugged on my heart, and I didn't even know him. I'd only caught a glimpse of him outside the barn, and staring at his back certainly wasn't what I'd call an introduction.

"Turn…" Sarah once again morphed one syllable into two.

The poor kid was about to get the wrath of Sarah Adams—or I guess it was Sarah Burin now. If only someone could save him, swoop in and whisk him away. In another life, I might have been that person. Every fiber of my being wanted to run by her, tuck him under my arm, and race out the front door.

Rand did as his mother instructed.

"Randall Burin, what do you have all over you?" She reached for paper towels.

He could have gotten away. There was no way Sarah would ever catch him. He fidgeted, clearly thinking about taking off. Instead, he held his ground, planted his feet, and stood tall. "Poop."

Good thing I had held off on that impromptu rescue. *Gross.*

Sarah flinched. "What do you mean?" Surely, she could smell it. It was hard to miss now that he'd stopped moving.

His big, brown eyes peered up with an innocence I didn't believe he possessed. "I was jus' tryin' ta help." Okay, so maybe he was as pure as he appeared…or I'd become a sucker for the cutest kid in the world.

My sister took hold of the counter and tried her best to lower herself to his level. When I moved to help her, she glared at me, daring me to take one more step in her direction. She settled on her knees, less than gracefully, and folded her hands in her lap. That was a move I'd never seen as a kid.

"Who were you trying to help?" She even sounded like Mama—the understanding Mama, not the one who got mad when I did stupid things.

In some ways, it hurt to hear and see her maturing into the

woman who'd left us, and in others, it made me happy to know her kids had a woman like the one I'd adored until I was ten. Only, Sarah would never abandon her kids—not for anything in the world.

"Tin Tin." Rand's eyes welled with crocodile tears.

I didn't know who Tin Tin was, but I had half a mind to knock my sister over to get to her son. Poop washed off, hurt didn't, and Rand was upset.

Sarah rubbed his arm—the part without manure on it. "What happened?"

The screen door banged for the second time in two minutes, and in walked Austin. Damn, this day couldn't end soon enough. "He tried to put a bit in Nugget's mouth."

"Oh sweetie, you shouldn't do that kind of thing without help. Nugget's a very finicky horse."

I flinched. Nugget had been one of the most docile creatures I'd ever encountered. I couldn't imagine he'd be any different.

Austin maintained the scowl he'd stomped in with. "I've told you to stay away from that horse, Rand. You could have gotten hurt." Maybe his anger was born from fear; I didn't know. I was still stuck on my horse being anything other than friendly.

Rand hung his head in shame. Tears dropped to the floor, yet he made no attempt to wipe them away. "I thought"—he stammered—"I-I...he could make Aunt Randi smile."

Sarah shook her head, and my brow arched. "Why would you think the horse would make Aunt Miranda smile?"

He didn't answer right off.

"Or that she needed to?" she continued.

"Tin Tin said she loved Nugget." He looked up and stared straight into my eyes the way he'd done next to the barn—without fear or reservation. "And she was sad."

My sister and her brother-in-law shifted to me with accusing glares.

I let out a long breath I hadn't realized I'd been holding. Instead of giving one of them my attention, I held Rand's. "He heard us argue in the driveway. When Austin walked way, he was at the corner of the barn. I don't know what all he heard."

The little boy lost control of his emotions. Hiccups and jerky sobs accompanied the tears. "You're just like Papa, Tin Tin. You teld me how much you loved her..." He balled his fists at his sides and tried not to yell, but he lost the struggle. "You said she was your Spiderman. You lies."

I could only assume Spiderman held significance in Rand's life. He didn't skip a beat to allow me to interject and ask that question, and I certainly wasn't about to interrupt.

"You were mean and screamed. She gonna leave." He gasped for breath, and his little shoulder shook. "And this time, it won't be Papa's fault." Then, he raised his right hand and pointed at his uncle. "It's yours!"

10

AUSTIN

PAST

"*Miranda*," Sheriff Patton repeated. "Darlin', I need to speak with you."

My attention flicked between the sheriff and my girlfriend. Something was terribly wrong. Everything about his posture, his demeanor, it all put me on edge. His hands on his hips and his lowered head made me uneasy. With his chin down, I couldn't see the sheriff's face, and then he turned his attention to me.

"Austin, son, why don't you bring her up here."

"Yes, sir."

Nervous energy pumped through my veins and drove me across the lake as I swam toward Randi. I was lost as to what his agenda might be; nevertheless, I wasn't brave enough to disobey. I popped up at Randi's side and motioned for us to get out of the water. She shook her head, adamantly refusing to go.

"Sweetheart, the sheriff needs to talk to you. I don't think it's open for discussion." I couldn't tell which of us was more terrified, so I pretended it wasn't me and took her hand. "Come on. I'll go with you." I tried to wink, although it came off more like an awkward twitch and did nothing to soothe her.

Randi glanced back at our friends. I didn't bother. I could

sense their stares. I didn't need confirmation that they all had the same sick feeling I did.

We neared the top of the trail, and the patrol car came into view, as did the flashing lights on top of it. Time sped forward yet crept at a snail's pace. It seemed like only seconds since the sheriff had called Randi's name, but every step we took was labored and slow. I had the time to take in the details of Sheriff Patton's dirty shoes and worn uniform—it had seen better days. And once we stood in front of him, I'd memorized every wrinkle and crevice in his leathery skin, trying to determine why he was here.

He removed his hat and held it to his chest. His bald head glistened with sweat in the summer sun, and I forced myself to stay focused on his face. But my gaze moved with his hand that landed squarely on Randi's shoulder. The sheriff quickly found my eyes, and in that split second, I saw that whatever he planned to say would decimate Randi. I braced myself to catch her.

Sheriff Patton met Randi's stare and inhaled. His chest expanded, and then he appeared to hold his breath. "Darlin', there's been an accident."

In my gut, I knew he referred to the one we'd heard, the one Randi had wanted to check on. And if he'd come to find her, someone she was close to had been involved.

Randi shook her head. "I-I don't understand."

Again, Sheriff Patton grabbed my attention without uttering a word and then faced Randi. "You need to come with me."

Her head jerked back, and she steeled her expression. "I'm not going anywhere until you tell me what's going on." Randi's sharp tongue only spoke to her fear, and the sheriff recognized that as quickly as I did. She folded her arms and cocked her hip out in confidence. Unfortunately, I noticed her hands shaking, even if she tried to hide them.

"We need to get you to the hospital." Sheriff Patton struggled to maintain his composure. He'd known Randi all her life. The quiver in his chin worried me more than the words he spoke.

I hovered between reality and what had to be a nightmare. My mind raced as I considered whether her sister or her dad had been out by the lake and why. We'd laughed at how angry Sarah was when Randi left the house. Now, I wondered what we'd done. Randi might not have put the pieces together, and I hoped she never did, but they hit me like a freight train at full speed.

"Who?" she asked.

I hated to hear the answer. Now was the perfect moment for time to stop altogether. I'd give anything to go back to an hour earlier and change everything.

"Sarah," he choked out, and then promptly lost control of his emotions.

I couldn't remember ever seeing a grown man cry.

Sheriff Patton covered his mouth and swallowed hard. "If you want to say goodbye, we need to go *now*, Miranda."

The freight train that had hit me seconds earlier plowed past me and took Randi out with that sentence. I caught her when her knees buckled. It was a reflex, not forethought.

"Austin!"

My name registered in my ears, the person shouting it did not. I did my best to turn, yet with Randi in my arms, it took everything I had not to drop her. She'd become dead weight. I couldn't tell if she'd passed out or just lost the ability to hold herself together.

"Austin!" Brock.

I didn't have time to answer questions. Instead, I put my arm under Randi's knees and lifted her to my chest. Somehow, I'd missed her moaning, and the tears that normally tore me to shreds didn't hit me, either. Time no longer stood still, we weren't hovering in a dream state—we'd entered hell at warp speed, and the fire lapped at my feet. I couldn't decipher cries from footsteps or directions.

All I could process were the sheriff's words. If Randi wanted to say goodbye to her sister, we had to go. Now. Brock got to the passenger door of my truck before I did and opened it. I slid my girlfriend into the seat and managed to buckle in her crumpled body. When I rounded the hood, Brock had beaten me to that side, too.

He held out his hand. "Keys?"

I stared at him. At first, I didn't understand what he meant, but then it registered. "In the ignition." My voice sounded a million miles away.

"Scoot in. I'm driving," he announced.

Following instructions proved to be easier than making decisions, so I did what he told me. There wasn't a seatbelt in the center, but somehow, I doubted Sheriff Patton would make an issue out of it. Randi curled into me, and I put my arm around her. I didn't have a clue what we would find when we got to the hospital, or if we'd even make it in time. What I did know was that I needed to pull myself together. I'd promised her a long time ago that I'd protect her, and now, it was time to step up and make good on that.

The road we used to get to the lake had never been paved, and it was littered with potholes that made the ride down bumpy. Brock followed behind Sheriff Patton, who seemed to have thrown caution to the wind as he flew over the old country road. At last, we hit the paved street, and the ride evened out.

Randi sat up and pulled out of my embrace. "It's my fault, Austin."

Brock leaned forward to face her while he continued to check the road in front of him. "How is it *your* fault?"

He must have gotten information from the sheriff since

neither Randi nor I had told him anything, and he hadn't been up there when we'd received the news.

She rubbed her snotty nose on her bare arm. I reached into the glove box and prayed there was a napkin or something in there to give her.

"I left when I wasn't supposed to. If that accident we heard was my sister, then the only reason she had to be anywhere near the lake was to chase me."

I handed Randi a wadded-up tissue that I hoped was clean, although I wouldn't bet my life on it or where it had come from. And Brock returned his focus to the road without commenting on her proclamation one way or the other. I didn't need to question Brock—neither Brock nor I agreed with her.

The blue lights held me in a trance as we rode the rest of the way in silence. I'd always thought it would be cool to have a police escort with flashing lights and sirens, yet following the cop car didn't fill me with anything other than dread.

*M*r. Adams's hard glare met us at the entrance to the emergency room. "Where the hell you been?"

Pointing out that the two of us were damp, barefoot, and wearing nothing other than swimsuits wouldn't prove to be a wise move on my part. I chose to remain quiet and let Randi handle her father until he directed his questions at me. Which was about two seconds after he'd asked Randi, who hadn't answered.

Mr. Adams practically growled in my face. "Well?" His presence hadn't been this intimidating in years, yet suddenly, he was larger than life and angry as hell.

I cleared my throat and prepared to be the man I'd promised Randi she'd always have at her side. "We got here as quickly as we could, sir." It would have been nice to have backup in the form of my best friend at my side, but Brock had gone to park the truck.

Jack cracked his knuckles and posed the question a different way. "And where were you comin' *from?*" The last word became a hum that hung in the air, daring me to answer.

There had never been a time I believed Jack Adams would physically hurt me. Until that moment. I'd always had a healthy dose of fear, but in the South that was called respect. I ground my teeth together and prepared for whatever lashing he dealt. "The lake."

"The lake," he repeated in a dry monotone. Then he angled his head toward Randi. "That where you were supposed to be, li'l girl?"

I'd heard the voice of an irate Mr. Adams in the past. More than once, Randi and I had been scolded for stupid things kids did. This level of rage hit a whole new dimension. I didn't recognize the man talking to his daughter. His face contorted into a menacing expression, and his tone had dropped two octaves, while the volume rose. It was the equivalent of a spoken sonic boom.

"No, sir."

I glanced at Randi. She hadn't crumpled into a sobbing mess. There were no more tears. Her shoulders weren't slumped, and her head wasn't hung in shame.

Mr. Adams raised his hand in the blink of an eye, and Randi remained stoic. Her demeanor was the complete opposite of what it had been in the truck, like she'd accepted her role in this mess and planned to take whatever lashing she got without flinching.

Not on my watch.

He swung, and I stepped between Randi and her father, catching his wrist in my hand. If Jack Adams had an urge to beat on someone, it could be me. It sure as hell wouldn't be Randi.

"She needs to see Sarah." I didn't regret intervening. I might later, but right now, my only concern was my girlfriend saying goodbye to her sister and making whatever amends she needed. Jack would be around tomorrow; Sarah might not.

Jack jerked free from my grasp and stepped back. Something passed between us when he held my stare. For the rest of my life, I'd believe that moment defined who I'd become to Randi. It also signified the moment her dad lost her. She was no longer his little girl. I wanted to sympathize with him. I could only imagine how he must have felt to lose both of his children in one day, even if neither were physically gone yet. The pain would be excruciating.

"Sarah's in surgery. If she makes it out, Miranda *won't* be the first to see her. That I can assure you."

I opened my mouth to tell him I understood his grief, although I didn't really, but Randi beat me to a response.

"I understand." She kept her voice low enough for the other people around not to hear. Then she took a seat in the corner of the waiting room.

Her expression remained blank. I imagined it was how a corpse looked before it was made up by the funeral home. She appeared to be made of wax instead of flesh. The beautiful girl I loved more than life itself was vacant and lifeless. If her chest hadn't continued to rise and fall, or if I hadn't seen her blink every once in a while, I could have been convinced she'd died with her sister.

I took a step toward the nurses' station when Jack stopped me.

"Where you goin', boy?"

I flicked my sight toward his hand on my bicep and then looked at his face. It was the first time that I noticed I now stood taller than Jack and had about twenty pounds on him. I was no longer a kid that any adult could push around. He must have recognized the same thing, because he dropped my arm.

"To see about getting Randi some clothes." I sneered. It took every ounce of control I could muster not to spit in the man's face. "In case you missed it, your daughter is sitting in a cold waiting room in a wet bikini. Not only do I think that's bad for her health, I don't like people staring at my girlfriend's body." As if I'd made up her current state and attire, he took note of her in the corner. "If you'd kindly step aside, *sir*, I'd like to get something to cover her."

My heart throttled my sternum. I'd never talked back to another adult in my life. There'd only been a handful of times that I'd been brazen enough to do it to my own father, and he was required to love me. The adrenaline didn't slow until Jack actually moved to let me pass. Even then, my hands shook, and my pulse throbbed in my neck.

Thankfully, the nurse at the desk was sympathetic. She didn't even act as though it were an unusual request. She simply stood, peered around me to the corner Randi sat in, and nodded. I waited for her to return a couple of minutes later.

I took the hospital-green scrubs and thanked her. Randi hadn't moved since she'd sat down. She hadn't blinked since I took the chair next to her, either.

"Sweetheart?" I spoke to her in the tone that usually made her purr. "Why don't you put these on?" When she didn't move, I got concerned that she'd gone into shock. "Randi?"

Her dark eyelashes fluttered, and she faced me. "Okay."

There wasn't much point in her finding a bathroom, since she wasn't changing. I squatted in front of her to help with the pants and then slid the top over her head. I didn't know what to do to reach her. It terrified me to think I'd lost her. If Sarah didn't pull through, I wasn't sure Randi would ever come back.

"Adams?" A man with a surgical mask dangling from his neck called out into the waiting room. The grim expression he wore didn't bode well for Sarah's condition.

Randi and I jumped at the sound of her last name called, as did Jack. The three of us swarmed the doctor and waited with bated breath for answers. Of which, he didn't provide many.

Jack pummeled the surgeon with questions without allowing him to actually answer any. "How is she? Is she stable? Can we see her?"

"She's in recovery right now. If she makes it out, she will be moved to ICU. We believe we have the internal bleeding stopped, but there's a lot of damage." He talked about broken bones I'd never heard of, much less their location in the body, spinal cord damage, paralysis if she lived. It went on and on with dismal chances for recovery. He ended by telling us that the next twenty-four hours were critical.

Randi didn't make a peep. When the doctor exited, Jack turned to the two of us, and he snarled at Randi. My flexing bicep caught his attention, and I imagined her dad thought better of whatever he'd planned to say. He dragged his hands down his face as if he might be able to wipe the day away.

"You two should go home. There's no point in you being here." It wasn't a suggestion so much as a command.

Randi flinched. "What if she wakes up?"

"Then I'll be here." Her dad left no room for arguments, nor did he offer to call Randi to update her. He didn't throw her any bone at all. "Go."

She nodded her acceptance.

I refused to give up that easily. Sarah was Randi's sister. The accident was unfortunate; nevertheless, it was just that—an accident. Randi hadn't driven the semi into Sarah's car. She also hadn't told Sarah to chase her down the street. Randi might have disobeyed, but in all fairness, her dad should have doled out the punishment, not his twenty-four-year-old daughter. Had he done his job as a parent, things might be entirely different, because Randi wouldn't have crossed her daddy. "With all due respect, sir—"

"I'd say we're pretty well beyond that, Austin. Go home."

*T*he days that followed Sarah's accident were awful. She'd defied the odds and made it past each milestone the doctors said she would never reach, although it happened at an unbelievably slow pace. She'd been kept in a medically induced coma while her organs and bones heal. Even that hadn't been without complications. Sarah had spontaneous internal bleeding that required additional surgery; her appendix burst, which the physicians swore had nothing to do with the accident— I didn't believe it. And the list went on so long, I'd lost track.

Jack had spent every waking moment at the hospital with Sarah, leaving Randi home by herself. I'd been apprehensive about staying there without his permission, and then I realized he'd left her to the wolves. It wasn't in Randi's best interest to be isolated. She'd been despondent at best, and each day that passed, it only got worse.

Her dad had done everything he could to keep Randi from Sarah, even against the advice of her physicians.

"She's going to wake up, Randi. And she'll want to see you." I tried to reason with her. "You'll have the chance to tell her that you love her."

She peered up at me through thick lashes. "I just need to apologize, Austin."

I was desperate to take her into my arms and promise her she'd get that chance. I'd seen more tears from my girlfriend in the last couple of weeks than I had in all the years we'd been friends. Each one wrecked me in a different way, mainly because I couldn't do anything to ease her heartache. There was nothing I could do to make any of this easier.

We'd snuck into the hospital a few times when Jack wasn't there, although those moments had been few and far between. And when we'd end up running into her dad, Randi would leave without a word, only to spend two more hours sitting on a bench outside the hospital. She wouldn't talk. Randi just stared out into the parking lot, like she waited for someone to show up and tell her it had all been a joke.

That person never came, and neither did her reprieve. If Sarah didn't wake up soon, there would be permanent damage in Randi that no amount of counseling could cure.

"Come on, let me take you home." I nudged her with my shoulder. When she didn't move, I wrapped my arm around her lower back and kissed the side of her head. "Please, sweetheart."

It never failed. That one word always brought Randi back to me.

She leaned into my side and wrapped her arms around my waist. The warmth of her breath on my chest was a sign of life I was desperate to feel. Then, for the first time since the accident, she tilted her head and placed her lips behind my jaw and under my ear. It was her spot, the one no one else would ever touch. Typically, it drove me wild; today, it just felt good.

"Will you stay with me?"

I rolled my eyes, mocking her. "Like you even have to ask."

She laced her fingers with mine, and together, we walked to my truck. The spark of hope her kiss had lit died in the cab as we drove back to Cross Acres in silence. It was a long ride, although one I'd grown accustomed to making, sometimes more than once in a day.

It was after dusk when I pulled onto the gravel drive that led to her house. I rolled the window down to listen to the crunch of the rocks under my tires. Everything about that gritty noise reminded me of the girl who sat next to me, or the *her* she was before all this had started. She was still in there; I just had to help her find her way out.

I parked in the circle and set the emergency brake. "I need to call my parents when we get inside, so they don't worry." At this point, I didn't think they cared. They knew exactly where I was and where I'd been every day since Sarah's accident.

My dad believed I was helping Jack on the ranch, and I did to some degree. Randi wasn't up to doing much, so I pitched in to get her chores done. Other than that, Jack had a crew in place that worked like a well-oiled machine with a foreman who kept the gears greased in Jack's absence. My mom was aware of the truth. She'd also promised not to breathe a word of it to my dad. Neither had said much about what had happened, but they were the ones who kept me in the loop about Sarah's prognosis. I, in turn, relayed it to Randi. Without those updates, Randi and I would be in the dark.

Her dad hadn't said more than a handful of words to her since I'd stepped between them in the emergency room. She could blame me later. I'd do it again if I had to choose. I didn't understand how Jack could call my dad and talk to him in great detail about Sarah's recovery and purposely outcast Randi. It was cruel.

Together, we climbed the stairs in front of the house, and she opened the door. I went right to the kitchen to call my mom, while Randi went upstairs. I listened for her steps to cross the house followed by the sound of her bedroom door closing. Then I dialed my parents' number.

"Hello?" My mom's voice gave me so much comfort that there were days, especially in recent weeks, that I wished I could turn back time and crawl into her lap.

"Hey, Mom."

"Austin, sweetie, how's Randi?" Her upbeat tone surprised me. "Does she know?"

I prayed whatever my mom was about to tell me would bring a smile to my girlfriend's face. "Know what?"

"Sarah's awake."

I shook my head, not that my mom could see it. "What? We just left there." While that was true, we hadn't just left Sarah's room. We'd left the bench outside. In all actuality, it had been hours since we'd been in the hospital itself.

"Your dad just got off the phone with Jack right before you called. I thought for sure Jack would call Randi." She trailed off in disbelief that Jack's first call hadn't been to his other daughter.

"I'm not surprised, Mom. How's she doing? Sarah, I mean."

"Confused. In a lot of pain. Jack said she wasn't awake long. You know how these things go." Actually, I didn't. "Hurry up and wait. There'll be a lot of that."

As much as I wanted to listen to my mom talk, I needed to pass the news on to Randi. "Will you call if you hear anything else? I'm going to stay here tonight."

"Of course. Tell Randi we love her. God answered one prayer today. He'll answer more."

God was as big a part of the lives in this town as the cattle and farms. "I'll tell her. Love you."

"Love you, too. Goodnight."

I hung up and took the stairs two at a time until I reached the top. With a couple of long strides, I reached Randi's door and swung it open. She had let down her hair and changed into cotton shorts and a matching tank top. When I burst into the room, she met my stare, and I couldn't bother to find a way to ease into my mom's news. "Sarah's awake."

Randi's eyes sparkled with the light I thought had gone out permanently, a perfect glimmer of hope mixed with happiness. She stood at the same time I moved toward her. I caught her against my chest when she threw herself into my arms.

Her hands cradled my jaw, and she dragged my face down. Our mouths greeted each other with passion and love. She hadn't admitted it, but she'd denied herself any type of comfort or pleasure. It had been a self-induced punishment, and she'd just let herself off restrictions.

One swipe of her tongue and my lips parted to welcome her.

The warmth of her hands roamed down my neck, leaving a trail of goose bumps in their wake. Her featherlight touch traced a path down my chest, igniting every nerve ending she crossed, and onto the hem of my shirt. She wasted no time lifting it over my head, even at the expense of breaking our kiss. Her desperation, the need for intimacy, a connection—it was all wild. Frantic yet controlled. The bite of her nails into my skin, the nip of her teeth, her frenzied attempt to have all of me at once commanded her. And I let her take what she needed. I'd give her all of me, freely.

We stood next to her bed, naked. Everything had happened at a fervent pace, and I expected it to continue that way until I took her over the edge, gave her the release she desired. I needed to be inside of her with as much urgency as she needed to make us one. I'd missed her touch and craved the caress of her skin.

Randi stopped. Our chests heaved in tandem when she took my hands in hers and peered up. Her features appeared softer than normal, and she radiated love. "Thank you."

It was an odd thing to say at this point, considering we hadn't done anything tonight other than some heavy petting, certainly nothing to be grateful for.

She lifted our twined hands and kissed my knuckles. "I've always known you were my knight in shining armor, but I never expected you to have to prove that you're my fairy tale."

Randi wasn't one for sentimental displays or mushy exchanges. She made no bones about loving me; however, she wasn't that girl who needed, or even wanted, flowers and poetry. We merely lived the way we loved, passionately.

"And one day, I'll make you my wife." It wasn't a secret. I'd marry her tomorrow if I thought she'd let me claim her with a ring.

Her lips tilted into the most gorgeous smile I'd ever seen. "Make love to me." Those four words weren't quite a request, nor were they a demand. They just *were*.

Like the two of us.

And two became one.

An unspoken covenant was signed under the sheets. Our bodies committed to each other again in a way they'd never spoken to anyone else. And never would.

I didn't know when or where, but that night, with Miranda wrapped in my arms peacefully sleeping, I made a vow to God to give her my last name.

11

AUSTIN

*M*iranda had slinked out during Rand's meltdown in the kitchen. I stuck around to calm the little guy. Once he'd quit crying, he made me promise to find his aunt to apologize. Sarah didn't find humor in her son's outburst, but I fully believed she was perfectly content to let him send me on a wild goose chase to locate Miranda.

After an hour of searching around the house and the barn, noting none of the horses were missing and none of the guys had seen her, I got concerned. Sarah hadn't heard from her, and I couldn't find her.

"Did she rent a car?" I asked Sarah as I threw open the screen door. It creaked and then banged closed behind me. After a decade, I'd think *someone* would have oiled that damn thing.

She stopped whatever she'd been doing to question me. "Miranda?"

I let out a sharp exhale through my nose and counted to five so I didn't come unglued on my brother's wife. "Who else, Sarah? Yes, Randi. I can't find her."

Sarah wiped her hands on a kitchen towel and leaned on the counter. She was overdoing it. I could see the exhaustion in her eyes, and her leg shook from being on it too long. "Yes. She got it when she was at the airport, but it's parked next to the barn."

"Well, she isn't here."

"She has to be."

"She's not." We were going in circles. "Any idea where she might have gone?"

Sarah shook her head. "She hasn't left the ranch except to go to the hospital. Oh, and to ride with Eason to the airport."

Right. Eason. He'd left his girlfriend in Texas, and somehow, I'd become responsible for finding her because of a promise I'd made to a three-year-old. "Call *him*. Let him search for her."

Her brow furrowed, and genuine concern lined every wrinkle her sister had put on her face over the years. "Wait right there." She pulled her cell out of her pocket and touched the screen.

I wasn't interested in listening to her conversation with Miranda's bed buddy, so I busied myself with pouring a glass of tea and making as much noise as possible, rattling ice cubes.

"He hasn't talked to her since he left." That was quick.

I swallowed several large gulps while I considered what she'd said. "At all?"

She shook her head.

What an ass. The guy left his girlfriend in another state, hadn't heard from her in a week, and he hadn't bothered to check on her. "He didn't think that was at all odd?"

Sarah shrugged. "Well, he does now. I guess things are different up north." She pressed the phone to her chest, and her eyes roamed the room aimlessly. "She had to have set off on foot."

Only Miranda Adams would take off with no destination in mind or mode of transportation to reach it. "Where exactly would you suggest I look, Sarah?"

"You tell me. Where did she run off to when you guys were younger? You should have more ideas than I do." Sarah seemed to have a misguided opinion of what Randi and I did as teenagers.

"She never ran off. That didn't start until Jack pushed her out the door." It was a low blow, and one I shouldn't have taken, but I was agitated and not sure how any of this was my problem.

"Don't get sassy." She wagged her finger. "You have to know where she'd go. It's not a big town."

That was just it. It wasn't a big town. There weren't many options. In high school, we'd always hung out with friends, went to field parties, spent days at the lake. There was no searching for Miranda because we were always together. "Not a clue. The lake. The diner, maybe?"

She shooed me out of the door with her hands. "What are you waiting for?"

If I didn't dread listening to my brother's mouth about his wife being upset, I'd get in my truck and go home. But the moment Sarah walked in their door and told him that I hadn't helped, he'd either call or come by, which would ruin my night, anyhow.

It didn't do me any good to be irritated; there was no one to take it out on. I stomped out to the truck simply to make myself feel better. It dawned on me as I put the keys in the ignition that this must have been what Sarah felt like when we were teens. I cranked the engine, rolled down my window, and backed out.

I didn't think Miranda would go to the lake. It wasn't hard to get there if you were familiar with where you were going; however, our spot was several miles from the Adams' ranch. I hadn't seen her in a single pair of shoes that she could make that hike in. She was smart enough not to thumb a ride to somewhere that desolate...or at least I hoped she was. Nevertheless, I went, anyhow. She'd always loved that place; we both had. I hadn't been back since Sarah had her accident, though. Until that day, the lake had held everything good.

I could flip through memories of every trip Randi and I had made there. Every detail was crystal clear from the way her hair blew around her face with the windows down in the truck, to the swimsuits she wore, to her laugh as she'd jump into the water to splash me. Years of trips all as vivid as if they'd happened yesterday, including the crash.

Everything had changed with the screech of tires and the crunch of metal. The smoke. The sheriff. The hospital. That was the day I lost her. And this was why I never came back. Nostalgia started with a smile and ended in heartache.

I pulled as close to the edge of the makeshift parking area as I could get without going over the side, and I turned on my high beams. The headlights reflected off the dark water and cast deeper shadows around the streams of light. The dock sat empty and rickety. Nothing could ever be easy with Miranda Adams. I put the truck in park and left it running when I hopped out.

"Miranda?" I hollered, not that I expected a response. I moved down the overgrown path and wondered if anyone ever came out here anymore. "Miranda?" God, I hated using her full name. It was as stuffy as her clothes and hair.

I nearly busted my ass when my boot got stuck under a tree root. I managed to break my fall with my hands and dusted them off on my jeans. It only served to skyrocket my anger. I'd been sent on a wild goose chase to find a woman who obviously preferred to be left alone. Yet, here I was, walking down a dock not sturdy enough to safely hold a small child, much less a two-hundred-pound man.

I'd gone as far as I could. At the end of the wooden walkway, I closed my eyes. Her laughter played in my head; the splashing, the goofing off, it all still existed in the recesses of my memories. The sun shone bright, and the heat was horrific. A smile danced on the corners of my mouth when I glanced over the water to see her floating on her back. Randi's flat stomach dipped under the surface, and she wiggled her toes. It was all there as though I could touch her if I jumped in.

"Austin? Son, is that you out there?"

Lost in the last day I remembered being whole, I hadn't heard Sheriff Patton pull up. The lights on the patrol car spun, yet the siren didn't ring. "Yes, sir." And just like that, the memory vanished.

"What are you doing out there?"

I started toward him, careful to watch my step. "Looking for Miranda Adams."

He belted out a hearty laugh, one that came from the gut. "You been drinking?"

I climbed the path, wondering if *he'd* been drinking. "No, sir." By the time I answered, I stood in front of him.

He'd gained weight over the years, and his face showed the wear and tear of decades on a small-town police force. Mason Belle didn't have a high crime rate, but the sheriff's job in this county went beyond just arresting criminals. He played counselor to misguided youth, peacekeeper to squabbling spouses, and charity organizer to families in need. "What are you doing out here after dark?"

I was tired and not the least bit interested in having a conversation, but Sheriff Patton wouldn't think twice about getting in his cruiser and calling my dad to rat me out. "Like I said, looking for Miranda Adams." I sounded like a broken record.

He clapped my shoulder with a firm grip and chuckled. "Son, she ain't been in these parts for years."

There was zero chance word hadn't spread about her arrival. Mason Belle lived for gossip, and her return was the perfect thing for women to chatter about over coffee. "Hate to tell you...she showed up a couple of days after Jack landed in the hospital. Been here since."

"Randi?"

I nodded. "Yes, sir."

He stared at me, waiting for more information. I didn't have anything else to share.

"And you thought she'd be out here in the dark?" He looked around. "Without a car?"

"Truth is, I don't have a clue where she went. Rand got upset because he heard us fighting."

He jutted his chin out. "Charlie's boy? I didn't think he'd ever met her."

I wasn't going to get into this with him. Family business stayed within the family. "I promised my nephew I'd find her."

Sheriff Patton quirked his brow in anticipation of something far juicier than anything I had to share.

I widened my stance and crossed my arms. "It's not like that. At all." I hadn't convinced him, but I didn't need to. I needed to find Randi, take her home, and let Sarah deal with her. "I gotta go. If you see her, will you take her back to Cross Acres? Sarah's worried."

"That girl's got a heart as pure as snow. Not sure I coulda forgiven her if it'd been me."

If I were a dog, the cockles on my back would have risen. Since I was a man, the hair on my neck stood on end, my heart hammered, and I clenched my fists under folded arms. Regardless of how much time had passed, Randi wasn't responsible for what happened to her sister. I didn't care what anyone said. In my eyes, Jack had as much blame, if not more, for putting his oldest daughter in the position to play mom to his youngest. Randi didn't make Sarah get in that car to follow us. She didn't T-bone the car with a semi. She hadn't been the one to consume enough tequila to put a small army on their ass before getting behind the wheel of a tractor trailer. None of that was on Randi, but Mason Belle—and Jack Adams—let her shoulder the blame for the last six years.

"It was a tough situation for everyone involved." I tipped my hat to the sheriff. "I hate to cut it short, but I have a nephew depending on me."

"Yeah, yeah. Of course."

I started moving as soon as he accepted my departure. I needed to find Miranda before someone else in Mason Belle did. His opinion was mild compared to the other residents of this town. They'd eat Miranda up and spit her out. And based on how she'd taken my lashings, I doubted she'd fight off any of them, either. Regardless of whether or not I liked the girl, I couldn't allow anyone to face a lynch mob. Not even Miranda Adams—the one person in my life who deserved it.

I slowed the truck when I hit the edge of town. There weren't many people on the sidewalks after dark, so the likelihood that I'd miss Miranda, if I saw her, was slim. Most of the shops closed at five, along with the tiny post office. I hadn't stopped at the feed store when I passed. I couldn't imagine any reason she'd have gone in there. Clancy, the owner, was a hundred years old if he was a day, and crotchety as all get-out. I had no desire to interact with him unless I had to.

There were a couple of cars at the filling station, so I pulled in and inched my way down the glass front. Unless Miranda had taken a seat on the floor, she wasn't strolling the aisles of the Pump & Go. I wondered how long it would take someone to flag me down to question what in tarnation I was doing, and at the rate my truck moved, they could jump in front of it and not risk being mowed over. With only two places left—other than Clancy's—that remained open, I pulled into the diner parking lot. It was either here or the Piggly Wiggly.

I parked behind the building. There wasn't much of a crowd. In fact, the two other cars in the lot belonged to the cook and the waitress. I hesitated. The truck door remained open, and I turned to hop down; I just hadn't actually let my feet hit the ground. I didn't have a choice. Nevertheless, I dreaded stepping inside the diner. Charity was there. I'd have to answer questions I wasn't prepared for. The moment anyone in Mason Belle got wind of me out looking for Miranda Adams, I'd face the onslaught I had six years ago. A replay of that didn't appeal to me.

My phone rang in my pocket, giving me an excuse to prolong my exit. I shook my head when I saw Sarah's name on the screen. Either she had someone following me, or she had ESP.

"Yeah?" It wasn't friendly, but it would do.

"Any luck?"

I hadn't deposited her sister on her father's doorstep, so I'd say it was a safe assumption I hadn't had any. "Not yet." I was a man of few words.

"Call me when you find her."

There had to be a reason I took orders from my brother's wife; although, I'd be damned if I knew what it was. "Will do." I hung up without a goodbye and slid out of the driver's seat.

The heavy door slammed behind me, and I wondered if it foreshadowed what I'd find inside. My high school English teacher would be proud I had even remembered that word. Mrs. Gault had always hated me.

I rounded the corner of the building, took a deep breath, and exhaled when I put my fingers around the handle and opened the door. Charity leaned against the counter next to the register. The moment she caught my eye, I was certain she'd either seen Miranda or Miranda was still here. Charity exaggerated the chomp of her gum in annoyance. I lifted my head in question, and thankfully, she just tilted hers to indicate the direction I needed to go. For once, Charity kept her thoughts to herself and her mouth shut—well, except for the grotesque display with the gum.

Miranda sat in the far corner with her back to the entrance. With her hair cut short, no one would recognize her. Not that the diner currently had any patrons. From behind, she could have been any number of women in Mason Belle.

I slid into the booth opposite her and got Charity's attention with the lift of my chin. She raised a pot of coffee, and I nodded. If they had something stronger, I'd have taken a double shot straight. Since caffeine was the most potent thing I'd find, it would have to do. For now.

Her lifeless eyes met mine. She had clearly spent a good bit of time crying. A part of me wanted to switch sides, move next to her, wrap my arm around her, and fix whatever was broken. The rational part of me remembered that wasn't my job. Miranda Adams wasn't mine anymore. She belonged to another man, and I'd never cross that line.

"What are you doing here, Austin?"

If I hadn't been listening when Miranda's mouth opened, I would have missed her question.

Charity showed up with an empty cup and a fresh pot of coffee. She filled a mug for me, topped Miranda's off, and then left without a word. I took a sip, noting she still drank hers black, too. Every other woman I'd ever met treated coffee like dessert.

"Looking for you."

She leaned back and put her hands in her lap. "You found me."

I had, and now, sitting here in front of her, the last thing I had any desire to do was haul her to my truck, drive her down the road, and dump her off at her daddy's. I'd spent too many years angry. The opportunity presented itself to clear the air. I'd blown my top earlier and released most of the pent-up aggression or hurt, whatever it had been.

Miranda lifted her hand to tuck her hair behind her ear. Like a movie, a flashback of the past, a vision of eighteen-year-old Randi, blinked before me. I'd always found that habit seductive, primarily because she wasn't conscious of the fact that she did it when she was nervous. I loved the innocence in her expression and the way her eyes almost cowered behind her lashes. It was pure and as close to angelic as Randi ever got.

It took effort to soften my tone. I ignored the bell that rang over the door. She was on the defensive. If I wanted to have a discussion, I'd have to make her believe she was safe. "Can we talk?"

Her pupils narrowed, though her expression remained flat. "About?"

I'd thought about this conversation more times than I could count, yet when the chance to have it arose, my mind went blank. I shrugged. "What have you been up to?"

She shook her head in disbelief. "Really? You have me alone in a corner, and *that's* the question you want an answer to?"

No. It wasn't even the tip of the iceberg. "It's a good place to start."

Miranda shifted in the seat, uncrossing her legs and crossing them again. She was thinner than she had been in high school. I hadn't noticed it so much on the ranch, yet sitting across from her, it was quite obvious. "Okay... I moved to New York. I met Eason the day I got off the bus. He helped me get into school for paralegal work and hired me in his law firm. We've lived together since, and I still work at the practice."

She'd summed up six years in a handful of meaningless sentences that told me nothing other than stats I could have found on Facebook *if* she used social media.

"Are you happy?" It came out before I realized what I'd said.

The question appeared to surprise her as much as it had me. "Sure. New York's a great place to live." There was no smile in her voice, nothing that indicated she loved life.

That wasn't a ringing endorsement. Warning bells, sirens, whistles, they all went off in my head. For a girl who'd been with a man as long as Miranda had Eason, I expected more. He obviously defined her life if she lived with him and worked for him.

"Is Eason good to you?"

Her features scrunched, and that look was all Randi. The Randi *I'd* loved. The one who died the day that car crashed. "Of course." She appeared offended, yet she didn't defend him.

Miranda watched me intently, although she remained quiet. I hadn't realized until that moment how desperate I was to hear the sound of her voice, to engage in a normal conversation. I wanted to forget the last six years and pretend like there'd never been an accident. I'd kill to see her tilt her head back in laughter or witness one genuine smile.

"I'm not going to bite you, Miranda. You can talk. We can catch up. That's what friends do." *Friends.* I hated that word. She'd never be a friend. We may never be anything more again, but I'd never place her in that category in my life.

"I don't know what to say, Austin. You've made it pretty clear how you feel about me since I arrived at the ranch."

I needed something to do with my hands. They shook beneath the table, and if I didn't get my nerves under control, I'd start babbling. "I'm sorry." I paused, and her facial muscles relaxed. "I wasn't expecting to see you." It was an excuse. "Not that anyone had to warn me." And that sounded awful. "I didn't recognize you." That was the painful truth.

She wrapped her hands around her mug, yet she didn't lift it. Her thumb traced circles on the ceramic. "I don't look all that different." It wasn't just her appearance. "So, what was it then?"

"You cut your hair." There were days I marveled at my conversational brilliance.

She grazed her fingertips over the ends self-consciously. "You don't like it?"

I wasn't sure why it mattered if I did or didn't. "You always loved your hair. I'm just surprised."

"Is that it?"

I couldn't figure out how to get away from this. "I don't

know. You don't sound like you, anymore. And you showed up in a limo for Christ's sake. You looked like you stepped off the runway, not an airplane." I didn't mean to be harsh. "It caught me off guard."

A tear trickled down her cheek. "If anyone had told me you worked at the ranch, I wouldn't have come."

My chest constricted painfully. All these years, I'd believed she hid from Jack. Now I had to wonder if it was me.

She swallowed hard and closed her eyes. When she opened them, any emotion that had surfaced had cleared. They were empty again, soulless. "I didn't mean it the way you took it."

"How'd you mean it?"

Charity came around with the coffee at the perfect moment for Miranda and the wrong one for me. It didn't escape my attention, or Miranda's for that matter, that Charity refused to look at her and only spoke to me. People in Mason Belle hurt for a long time over Miranda's disappearance. And if they continued to treat her the way Charity and I had, they wouldn't have to worry about her ever returning.

She waited for Charity to leave before she responded. "I owe you an explanation. You more than anyone." There was a pause, and I was afraid if I filled the silence then she'd quit talking. "I never meant to hurt you."

I ached, seeing her this way. Nothing about her had healed in New York. She'd withered into something unrecognizable. "What did he do?" I whispered.

"It doesn't matter."

But it did. Without regard for my actions, I reached out and placed my hand on top of hers. "You can always come home." I didn't have a clue where that had come from. Mason Belle would not open its arms to the princess who'd shunned them, not without a lot of explanation.

She snickered, and her shoulders dropped. She did not,

however, remove her hand from underneath mine, and I took the chance to give her fingers a gentle squeeze.

"It's not that easy, Austin."

I kept my voice low. "Why not?"

"Sometimes you can't come home."

That was bullshit. It might be uncomfortable. People might expect apologies. Even still, she absolutely could make that choice, just like she'd made one to leave.

"Why? Because of some guy? Some job? A fancy town? You can leave every bit of that behind."

She stared at me with wonder instead of gall.

"If you want to come back, you can. But it would take the gumption of the girl I knew, not the one who showed up in a Hummer with a man in a suit."

As if I'd slapped her, the mention of Eason had her withdrawing her hand. "And just walk away from my life?"

"You've done it before."

She flattened her lips and nodded defensively...slowly. "And there it is."

"Damn, Randi. Come on. What do you expect?"

"Nothing. That's why I've tried to keep my distance. *You* came looking for *me*, remember?"

"Your sister sent me."

She reached into her pocket and pulled out a wad of cash. "Of course, she did. I should have known you'd never come on your own. God knows you never made any attempt to find me before, but Sarah waves her hand, and you're on a mission." She tossed a few dollars on the table and slid across the bench.

Shit. I pulled my wallet out and tossed a couple of bucks down. Miranda had made it to the front door and grasped the handle when Charity decided *now* was the time to chime in.

"You're wastin' your time, Austin. Let her go. She's not worth it." Disgust lifted her lip in a snarl, and I'd never hated the sound of a Southern twang until that moment.

"Ah, shut up, Charity." I'd have to apologize for that later. Hopefully before Brock found me to turn my face into a punching bag for speaking to his wife that way.

Miranda had heard her and pushed open the door with all the strength she could muster. The bell rang wildly, and I took off after her.

"Miranda!"

The last thing either of us needed was another scene, especially in the middle of town. "What?" She spun and then screamed, "What do you *want*, Austin? To humiliate me? Are you out for blood? Tell me what you need so I can make it happen. I'll do anything you ask. I just need this to end." Tears ran down her cheeks, her shoulders shook, but she held her ground.

I didn't have an answer, because I didn't know.

"That's what I thought," she murmured in defeat.

The light on Main Street flickered overhead, and I was at a loss for words. She was beautiful under the yellow hue, despite all the changes I hated. Before I could beg her to go somewhere we wouldn't be disturbed, a place we could yell or cry or hug or laugh, Sheriff Patton's car pulled up to the curb next to her. He said something I couldn't hear. She glanced at me, then back at him, and nodded.

In a split second, she was in the cruiser and gone. And once again, I was left in her wake, alone on the streets of Mason Belle, drowning in Miranda Adams's monsoon.

12

MIRANDA

I hated that he'd gotten the best of me, that he'd made me cry. The cruiser idled a few feet away, and I dropped my shoulders when Sheriff Patton leaned over the passenger seat.

"Miranda, darlin'"—I still hated that term and every memory that came with it—"you need a ride home?"

At first, I didn't answer and instead, I glanced at Austin. I'd begged him to tell me what he wanted me to do, what punishment would suffice, and in return, he'd stared at me, bewildered. Without a response, without an end to this insipid feud, I chose what I believed to be an out that had presented itself unexpectedly.

It wasn't exactly home, but Cross Acres would have to do for tonight. So, I nodded and took the ride he had offered. Yet sitting alongside the man who'd delivered the news that had brought my world crashing to the ground, I wondered if I would have fared better with Austin.

"Gotta say, I'm surprised to see you back in these parts." He shifted his attention from the road to me, I assumed, expecting a reaction. "What with all that happened, I mean."

Yes, I knew exactly what he meant. I just refused to discuss it with him. "Yes, sir." It wasn't an answer.

"Kinda like ol' times seein' you and Austin together again." He chuckled, as if the tears he'd witnessed had been part of a fond homecoming or a great trip down memory lane.

I didn't bother to hide my confusion, but the sheriff kept his eyes on the road and missed my disdain. He kept talking. I only listened enough to nod or grunt at appropriate times. I just had to make it ten miles. And when he turned into Cross Acres, I thanked God I'd made it back without engaging in any discussion about where I'd been or why I was back.

That was until my daddy and Sarah came into view. It was late, and he should have been in bed. I had no idea why my sister was still here. When I grabbed the handle, I questioned which fate was worse: the sheriff or my family. "Thank you for the ride."

He patted my shoulder from behind. "Anytime. Don't be a stranger, now. Ya hear?"

"Yes, sir." The effort it took to remain polite when all I wanted to do was cry—or sleep, I'd take either—was monumental. "Have a nice night."

Thankfully, he didn't stop to chitchat with my dad and sister. If he'd gotten out of the car, I might have lost my mind right there in the driveway. As it stood, sanity remained questionable.

I dragged myself up the stairs and onto the front porch. With only a few remaining steps until I reached the door, my sister foiled my escape.

"Miranda, come talk to us." Her usual cheer rang into the night. "I've got an extra glass of tea." She held up the cup to entice me to join them, and I wondered how she knew I'd be home. There wasn't even any condensation on the outside.

Refusing to talk or to take the drink would only prolong the evening. I just wanted to go to bed and pretend Austin hadn't shown up at the diner and that I hadn't begged him to free me from the slavery of my mistakes. So, I took the glass she offered but not the seat. Instead, I leaned with my lower back against the rail and faced them. "How'd you know I'd be here?"

My dad chimed in. "Austin called your sister." *Of course, he did.*

That just confirmed they weren't on the porch shooting the breeze. They were on the porch waiting. "It was nice of Sheriff Patton to bring me back."

The ceiling fan swirled shadows along the side of the house and moved warm air. I wished the rocking chairs were still beside the door. No matter how far I got from here, there was nothing that compared to rocking under the stars and the quiet of the country. New York didn't have a view that even came close, and the city never slept. I sipped the tea and thought of the women I'd shared this porch with and how much I'd missed them over the years. Nothing would ever bring Memaw or Mama back, or—

"Randi?" My father's voice jerked me from my thoughts.

I wished he'd call me Miranda. I wasn't that girl anymore, but I'd corrected him once, and he'd chosen to continue with the hillbilly nickname instead. "Yes, sir?"

"You look a million miles away." Just like his voice sounded.

There was a time when my father had held the world at his fingertips just waiting for me to take hold. Now, he seemed to have as much interest in me and my whereabouts as he did my mama's.

"Just thinking."

Sarah leaned forward, and her long hair fell over her shoulder in a sea of curls. We'd both been blessed with gorgeous locks. "Penny for your thoughts."

"I miss the rocking chairs."

My dad's eyes sprang up in surprise. He straightened his spine and squared his shoulders. I couldn't imagine why he'd be shocked that his removal of my memories bothered me.

"And Mama." I thought for a second and realized there was something else missing. "And the sounds of frogs and crickets. Where'd they go?" Nature's nighttime music seemed to have taken a permanent vacation.

Daddy crossed his legs and relaxed against the bench back. The rustle of his breath reminded me of how close we'd come to losing him and how, despite everything that had changed, it was all still the same. "Fires. What they didn't kill, they ran off. It'll take a bit for things to return to normal."

The irony in that statement wasn't lost on me. I wondered if wildlife felt the same loss of home that I had when they were displaced, or if that was an emotion only humans carried. "I suppose that's the cycle of life. The landscape is forever changing." I stared out over the open fields—not that I could see anything other than what the moon highlighted.

The silence between us was stifling. I doubted it would ever be normal again. Maybe this was the new normal. Uncomfortable conversations that led nowhere, ill-timed visits we all wanted to avoid, and relationships that could never be mended. While nothing had been said, my mind was too heavy. I didn't have the energy for Mason Belle.

"Sarah, thanks for the tea." I set the glass down on the table. "I think I'm going to head upstairs. Be careful driving home." I turned to my father and wished like hell things were different. "Goodnight, Daddy."

My sister stood abruptly. "Wait." Indecision clung to her cheeks and pity lingered in her eyes. "We wanted to talk to you." Or maybe I'd seen regret.

I didn't have a clue what time it was; regardless, it was too late for any discussion they could want to have as a family. I might not provide the level of support around the ranch that the hired hands did, but four thirty still came early, and I wasn't great at manual labor. There was no disguising the exhausted sigh I released or the way my shoulders slumped. "Okay..."

"Maybe you should get a chair," she suggested.

If the rockers were still there, I wouldn't have to. "It's fine. I can stand. What did you want to talk about?" I leaned against the doorframe, hoping they'd see how tired I was and not keep me from bed much longer.

My father uncrossed his legs and put his hands on his knees. When he took a deep breath, his lungs rattled, and he coughed several times. He swatted Sarah's hands away when she rubbed his back like a child. "I wanna talk about the ranch."

I pursed my lips and chewed on the bottom one. Since I didn't know what in particular they wanted to discuss, I couldn't help propel the conversation to a faster end.

"Daddy is meeting with his lawyer tomorrow and—"

"I can speak for myself. I may be fallin' apart, but my mouth still works." My dad didn't normally cut Sarah off.

I raised my brow at my sister, who rolled her eyes behind my father's back. Never, in all the years I'd been alive, had I witnessed that gesture from Sarah Adams. She hated it when I did it, and she'd told me how stupid it made me appear. A bit of a giggle passed my lips when she sat back in her seat and made goofy faces at the back of Daddy's head. She wasn't even aware she did it, which made it that much more humorous...until it registered that she'd said something about a lawyer.

Daddy stared me straight in the eye when he spoke. "Sarah's takin' me into Laredo tomorrow to have some paperwork taken care of."

I pushed off the door and stuck my hands in my back pockets to keep myself from balling them into fists. "Are you selling land to pay for the damage?" There was no way on God's green earth one acre of this land was leaving my family. "That's crazy. I don't have a lot, but I'll give you my savings until Austin can sell some of the cattle." It sounded stupid, even to me. The few thousand I had in the bank wouldn't put a dent in the resources needed.

He shook his head to quiet my argument. "I'm not selling the land."

"Then I don't understand." My gaze darted between my sister and my father for an answer.

Pity could be defined by the blue color of Sarah's eyes, and determination marked my daddy's brow.

Sarah stood, her leg stiff. It took a couple of steps before it loosened up enough for her to walk without a noticeable gait. "Miranda, why don't you sit down. The two of you need to talk." She squeezed my arm as she ambled by me.

"Where are you going?" I practically cried the words.

If I'd never known Mama, the expression on Sarah's face would have been foreign. Since I had, I remembered it from my childhood, and not fondly. Whatever was coming wouldn't be fun, but she believed it was best in the long run. Which meant, I'd hate it.

Sarah opened the door as she answered. "To get my purse. And then I'm going home. I'll be back in the morning to pick up Daddy. You're welcome to ride with us." She glanced at our father, tapped her fingers on the wood, and then disappeared inside.

I hadn't been alone with my father since I'd gotten here. Any time I'd been at the hospital, Eason had been there, and Daddy wasn't awake. A chill slid up my spine like a snake slithering through grass, and it coiled around my neck, threatening to choke me.

"Sit down, Miranda. I ain't gonna bite." There was a softness to his gruff tenor.

The porch creaked beneath my weight as I moved to take the seat Sarah had vacated moments earlier. No sooner had I sat down than my sister strolled out the door and waved over her shoulder.

I tried to focus on my father and ignore the gravel as Sarah walked to her SUV. I hated how old and tired he looked. His hair had greyed entirely since I'd left, and wrinkles hung where crow's feet used to stand. Even his neck had aged, and the skin dangled beneath his chin like a turkey.

"What did you want to talk about, Daddy?" Even though I was exhausted, I tried to keep my tone inviting.

He scrunched the side of his face and then scratched his temple as if he were pondering what to say or how to say it. "Ain't no way to say this that ain't gonna fire you up."

"Then just say it."

He swallowed and bobbed his head. "I'm turnin' the ranch over to Austin."

The force of that blow couldn't have hit me any harder if it had been delivered with a rock upside the head. My dad searched my face, likely for some sign of emotion, but I doubted he saw anything other than shock.

"Burin?" As if there were another Austin roaming the pastures.

"Now, before you go gettin' all worked up, you need to hear me out."

But I didn't. That was just it. This entire trip, everything about it, just brought clarity and confirmation to what I'd believed to be true for years. "You don't have to explain anything." There was no point.

Nothing he could say would justify giving the Adams' family farm to someone who wasn't an Adams. Generations of heritage and lineage roamed these fields, and that's the way it should stay. But I didn't get a vote in that decision, and apparently, my sister agreed with our father, regardless.

"Humor an ol' man then, huh?" He waited for me to connect with him—meet him eye to eye—before he continued. "Austin's spent a lot of years here. He works hard."

So did lots of men who'd worked at Cross Acres in the past. It didn't mean they should own an acre, much less the whole dang thing.

"He's a good man. He loves ranchin', and he loves Cross Acres." My father stopped speaking when I dropped my focus to the porch beneath my feet. "Randi." Again, he waited for me. "I can't do it anymore. Don't you see that?"

I didn't see it. "I don't guess so, Daddy. You've been sick the whole time I've been here. Nobody expects you to work in your condition." Admitting my father couldn't handle the workload equated to accepting his mortality. I wasn't prepared for either, despite the discontent between us.

He reached over and patted my knee. His hand didn't linger or give me a reassuring squeeze. It was probably for the best. "I made poor decisions that night. It coulda cost me a lot more than the cows. If Austin hadn't found me, I'd have died in the field with 'em."

"That's still not a reason to *give* him a ranch that's worth millions." I wouldn't budge on that stance, even if I tried to remain calm about it. "None of this makes any sense." I'd tried to hold back. I hadn't wanted to release any of this because I would just come off bitter, and that wasn't the case. But I lost that struggle. "I don't understand where the money went. I don't understand why you didn't have insurance. I don't understand why you're selling cattle and—"

"The money's gone, Randi!" His voice echoed across the porch and got lost in the night. "It's been gone. I was doing fine until the droughts, and I thought I'd recover...then this happened." He flipped his hand toward the pastures.

"But...where did it go?" I whispered. "You should have been set. There should have been plenty for generations. That's how Memaw left things." At that point, I talked more to myself than my father.

The sigh he let out when he sat back against the bench caught my attention. "Sarah's medical bills mostly. We didn't have no insurance, and I couldn't burden her with that debt when she needed to focus on gettin' better. I just been payin' what I could. We had a tough winter, and I forgot the property insurance. But it wouldn't a mattered. There wasn't nothin' left to pay it, no how."

He almost sounded relieved to give me that information, yet it wasn't possible that he'd spent that much money after her accident. I didn't have a response, so I sat in silence. Eventually, he kept explaining.

"She was in the hospital a long time, Randi. Lots of physical therapy once she got out. The car insurance company took care of most of that part." He raked his hand through his hair. "But then she got pregnant." He was as lost in his thoughts as I'd been in mine. "I love those younguns, but she wasn't ready for any of them. Doctors warned her. And it cost a fortune to get 'em into the world safe. The twins were preemies. Bills just kept pilin' up."

"So you bailed them out..."

He pressed his lips together. I couldn't tell if he regretted that decision or had resigned himself to the choice he'd made.

"I'm surprised she let you do it." And pissed at her, too.

Sarah had never been that selfish. I hadn't been to her house, but I could tell by her SUV that she and Charlie weren't hurting for cash. And while I'd never asked, I was confident she'd gotten a settlement from the accident. There was no reason why they shouldn't have paid their own bills.

"She don't know."

My mouth gaped. Sarah couldn't possibly have believed childbirth and a stay for two in the NICU had been free. I didn't understand any of it. My guilt of my own indiscretions turned into anger. It was hard to face the series of events—the domino effect that I'd started by running out that door. One decision, one mistake, and six years later, everyone paid for it.

"And I don't aim for her to." It was noble, although incredibly dumb. He should have protected his assets and worried about his debts later. But that wasn't how a Southern man was raised. You paid people what you owed, you worked hard, and the good Lord provided.

"This is insane. You spent all your money paying Sarah's medical bills? And now you're going to give away everything you have left, so the Burins have it all?" There had to be more to the story. "What am I missing?" Regardless of my part in this situation, I couldn't let go of the hurt I felt—about everything.

He shook his head slowly. "I'd hoped you'd understand."

"Clearly, I don't."

"Austin's the closest thing I got to family to pass it on to."

I'd just thought the blow I'd felt earlier had been damaging. But this one took me out. "I see."

Defeated.

I surrendered.

13

AUSTIN

"*W*hat are you doing here, Austin?" Charity must have forgiven my outburst at the diner earlier this week. She raced up to me the moment she saw me standing at the bar.

We didn't have a lot of indoor places to hang out in Mason Belle. Well, actually, we had one. The Hut. It wasn't much to write home about. A handful of local, retired vets had gotten together and started the bar. They only opened on Friday and Saturday nights, and they only sold beer and a handful of liquors. Anyone who cared to call a label from the shelf needed to ride into Laredo, because they couldn't do it here.

It didn't bother me. I wasn't much of a drinker, and when I did drink, it was Southern Comfort, which they stocked, or an occasional beer. I rarely came into town, and I spent even less time at The Hut. I'd become a bit of a loner since high school, and I preferred my own company to that of others. I saw enough of Brock on the ranch, and I socialized with everyone else in town at church every Sunday. However, today had been especially trying, and I needed to unwind. I hoped a couple of shots and a few games of pool might help.

Charity wrapped her arms around my waist in an overly affectionate embrace. I circled her shoulder with one arm and downed a shot using the other. I slammed the glass on the bar and looked over Charity's head for my best friend. If she was here, Brock was, too.

She tilted her chin toward the back of the bar. "He's in the corner. Come on."

I let her go and followed along through the haze of smoke to a group of people I'd known my entire life.

Brock pulled me in for a brotherly hug and clapped me on the arm. "Good to see you out and about. I wondered how long it'd take."

I didn't have to ask what he referred to. Apparently, Justin Richert did. He'd been a pain in my ass since high school when he had designated himself the class clown. "You mean Randi being back in town?"

"Have you seen her?" Charity turned her nose up as though, somehow, Miranda had grown an extra arm or lost an eye. "New York has not been good to that girl." She was hurt, and apparently, being a bitch was her way of avoiding the pain.

Brock didn't want to admit it, and I guessed he never would in front of his wife, but he still had a soft spot for Miranda. They'd been close when she left. He'd always believed she would call him, even if she didn't reach out to me. When it didn't happen, it cut him pretty deep. Regardless, I saw how he looked at her in the driveway when I caught them talking. I heard his voice. That wound was raw, but it could heal.

"Don't be like that, Char," Brock pleaded with his wife, although she missed the memo.

While they debated the changes in a girl none of us knew anything about anymore, I grabbed one of the two waitresses who roamed the place and ordered a drink. I'd nurse it until I left, which wouldn't be long if this crap continued. "Can you guys stop?" My voice carried farther than I'd intended.

"You hittin' that again, Burin?" Justin's smart mouth might look better with my fist between his teeth.

Brock pushed against his chest with one hand and scowled. "Grow up, Justin."

He laughed as though something was actually funny. And Brock tossed me a cue stick. The waitress brought me a longneck, and Brock racked the balls. He didn't try to talk, which I appreciated. If I wanted to have a discussion, I'd bring the subject up. I came here for a distraction, and Brock respected that. He'd also carry my ass home if I got knee-walking drunk and couldn't drive. Then he'd pick me up in the morning on his way to the ranch and laugh at me for having to spend Saturday hung over. That's what friends did.

Once the group around us lost interest, I finally opened the floor for conversation. He was kicking my ass at pool; I might as well get some counseling out of this beating. "Jack's turning the ranch over to me."

He spat beer all over the table. "Are you shittin' me?" Brock wiped his mouth with the back of his hand.

"Nope. I just left him." I sunk the two into the corner pocket and lined up another shot. "He met with his lawyer Tuesday morning, and the lawyer drew up the paperwork."

Brock's hand suddenly appeared in my line of vision, shielding my target. I stood with the stick in hand and faced him.

"Do Sarah and Randi know?"

I leaned down to take the shot he'd prevented seconds earlier, and he blocked it again. "What the hell, man? I can talk and play."

"You can't walk and chew gum at the same time. This is huge. And I take it by your attitude that one of the Adams girls didn't take the news well. Since Sarah is already legally family, I'm going to assume it was Randi."

I grabbed my beer off the rail and took a long pull. "Yep."

"I'm not knocking Jack's decision. To be honest, it doesn't really surprise me. But you had to know that would cut Randi deep."

If we were going to do this, I had to tell him all of it. He was my best friend and the only person I'd ever talk to about anything personal in this town. There wasn't a doubt in my mind that he'd never repeat a word I said. And if someone asked him, he'd lie—even to his wife.

He came around the table, and I leaned against the edge without actually sitting on it. "I don't think he planned to do it this early."

Brock bobbed his head. "I imagine the hospitalization and the problems at the ranch sped that up. Dude, he's getting up there in age. That place is huge, and it takes a ton of work."

"It wasn't the fire that sped it up."

He tossed his empty bottle into the trash can a couple of feet away and waved to the waitress for another. "Then what was it?"

"Miranda."

If anyone else were telling this story and I'd just watched Brock's face fall flat, I would have laughed. Currently, that wasn't an option, and I didn't find it the least bit humorous. "He did it to spite her?"

I finished my own bottle and tossed it in the same can he'd thrown his. "Nuh-huh. To get her to stay."

"I don't claim to be the brightest man on the planet, but in what universe does that make sense?"

Pool balls cracked at the table next to us, and people mulled about. Conversations happened all over the place. No one paid us any attention, but I still worried about gossip in Mason Belle. "Jack thinks it will bring her home for good."

"Let me get this straight. He's giving you the ranch that's been in their family for generations, including the house he currently lives in and that his daughters were raised in, and he believes that will bring Randi back from New York? In what? A legal battle?" He faced me, and his eyes went wide. "Holy shit. Do you think her fancy-pants boyfriend is going to represent her?"

I pulled back and stared at him like he'd lost his damn mind. "What the hell would she sue her dad for?"

"Not him. You!"

"Me? What did I do?"

"I've heard about family members suing beneficiaries because they say the person wasn't of sound mind to make changes to their will."

I waited for it to dawn on him that number one, Jack wasn't that old; number two, he didn't make any changes to his will; and number three, Miranda didn't have any interest in Mason Belle. It didn't come. "Brock, she's not going to sue anyone. She is, however, mad as an old red hen."

The waitress dropped off Brock's beer. He snickered, shook his head, and took a drink. "I'm sure Jack explained to you whatever delusional thoughts he had about how this would play out."

"He did. And I argued with him. He couldn't be swayed." God, I'd tried.

"Give it to me."

Brock didn't need all the gory details, only the gist of what Jack believed. "He doesn't think she'll go back to New York now that she's been home. And he doesn't believe she'll ever marry anyone other than me."

"He's trying to blackmail her?" He sounded like a hog in slop when he squealed.

I turned quickly, checking to see if anyone had been alerted to our conversation. When I didn't find a soul who'd even heard him over the music and chatter, I said, "Basically."

"I'm not sure if you should be insulted or flattered. Either way, I reckon it works in your favor."

"If she decides to stay, it needs to be because she wants to be here, not because of who's running Cross Acres or how desperate she is to keep it in the family."

He pushed off the table and stood in front of me. With his beer in one hand, he crossed his arms over his barrel of a chest and loomed over me. "You don't believe that shit."

I didn't know what I believed anymore. My life had twisted into a pretzel since she'd waltzed back into town, and my heart had gone with it. Depending on the time of day and which way the wind blew, my feelings toward Miranda Adams swayed between strong dislike and bitter indifference—not that any such thing existed—and every once in a while, my brain threw in a hint of uncontrollable lust to balance things out.

"Maybe you should talk to her?"

"Miranda?"

"Why the hell do you keep calling her that? You sound like an idiot."

"She insisted that was her name. More than once."

His belly shook as the laughter rumbled in his chest, up through his throat, and out of his loud mouth. "You're still jumping for her."

"Whatever."

"It's nothing to be ashamed of, Austin. You loved her. The question is, what are you going to do about it? You bitched for months after she left. Held a grudge for years after that. Now she's home, and you've been at her throat every chance she's dared to breathe the same air you did."

He didn't get it. He and Charity didn't date until after high school. Neither of them was the other's first, much less their only. Once they'd hooked up, they had gotten hitched a few months later.

"I've moved on."

"You haven't moved on to shit. So, quit being an ass and go

talk to the girl." He tilted his bottle toward the bar where the devil herself sat perched on a stool with two fingers of liquor in her hand.

Randi spun the ice with a tilt of the glass, and I stood mesmerized. I didn't have anything to say. I'd tried to talk to her; it was her turn. I hardened myself to her presence and resumed the game of pool that had been halted by this conversation.

I kept watch over her from the corner of my eye. She didn't talk to anyone other than the bartender to order a drink. The amber liquid never appeared to diminish, but I'd kept count of how many glasses she'd ordered...and consumed. I assumed it was whiskey, although that was nothing more than a random guess. It didn't matter if it was whiskey, tequila, bourbon, or rum. Unless she'd taken up drinking in New York, the moment she stood from that stool, she'd fall flat on her ass.

I wasn't here to keep her from embarrassing herself, but I'd be damned if I would have to face Jack Adams after another one of his daughters nearly killed herself in a fatal car accident. If that meant I had to stay here until last call to ensure she didn't become a smear on the highway, then so be it.

Brock kept me occupied with several crappy games of pool, a few rounds of darts, and water in a glass that made it look like vodka without the regret of alcohol. Twenty-four years of friendship and the man could read me like a book. And when she finally moved, my back was turned. He lifted his chin in her direction without calling attention to her.

Charity bounced around behind him with several of her friends. I didn't want to fight her off again, and I didn't want to put Brock in the position to do it, either.

Miranda left her empty glass on the bar and wobbled a bit

before she put her arms out to steady herself. Once she had her footing—I didn't have a clue how she walked in those damn heels—she dropped her hands to her sides and practically floated the few feet to the makeshift dance floor. The song on the jukebox moved at a beat she could dance to alone, so I eased toward the wall and took a seat on a stool to watch.

A couple of times since she'd been home, I'd caught glimpses, however fleeting, of the girl I'd known all my life. As soon as I had recognized them, they disappeared. Right now, I could watch her from the corner of the bar, undisturbed, and it was like the last six years had never happened—except for her being drunk. She moved with the music, and I'd swear it was Randi, not the Miranda chick she tried to be. If her hair were longer, she'd be a vision I'd seen a thousand times. Her smile was bright, and she was free. The ability of liquor to wash away the pain had proven itself again.

I caught the grin on my lips and forced it back. Miranda might look like the girl I once loved, but that was where it ended. Nothing about her remained the same. Nostalgia be damned. That girl had ruined me. She'd taken the most vital piece of me when she'd left Texas—her.

That one thought flipped my happy disposition to resentment. My jaw ticced, and I ground my teeth together to fight back the desire to let her cards fall wherever they might. Her sister or her boyfriend should be here babysitting her, not me. And just when I'd reached my limit, the song ended, and someone played a ballad on the jukebox. Couples took the floor, Brock and Charity included.

Miranda swayed by herself in a sea of brides and grooms. There weren't any single guys here who didn't know her and what happened, so she wasn't in danger of someone taking advantage of her. I decided to bow out undetected. Brock wouldn't care that I hadn't said goodbye, so I made a pitstop at the bar.

I knocked on the wooden top to get the bartender's attention. "Hey, Louis."

He faced me with three opened beer bottles in each hand, passed them off to the waitress who waited on them, and then he smacked his hands down. "Burin, my man. You heading out?"

"Yeah, I've got to be at the ranch in the morning."

Louis glanced at the clock on the register. "That's in like five hours, man."

I hadn't realized it was already midnight. I felt every minute of it in every muscle in my body, even if my brain hadn't gotten the message. "Can you do me a favor?"

He nodded. "Of course, what's up?"

"Can you make sure someone takes Miranda home tonight?" I peered over my shoulder to point her out. "Shit—never mind."

Charity stood inches from Miranda's face, and by the animation in her expression, they weren't talking about getting together for breakfast. Charity did all the communicating while Miranda remained stock still...the way she'd done when I went after her in the driveway. I couldn't hear anything over the music, but Brock tried to intervene, only to have his wife push him out of the way.

If I'd left five minutes sooner, if I hadn't stayed to watch her dance, then I wouldn't feel any sense of obligation to get her out of here, away from Charity's wrath, and home safely. I wished I could go back in time and beat the crap out of ten-year-old-me, bind and gag him, anything to prevent him from following Randi into that field and making a promise he couldn't keep.

"You can't leave her to the wolves," Louis spoke from behind me.

I didn't have to turn around. He was talking to me. Louis had been around since the dawn of time and was one of the owners of The Hut. Damn, people needed to mind their own business. "I know."

When I pushed off the bar, I told myself this wasn't for Miranda. It was for Jack, and for Brock, who pleaded with me from across the room to do something so he wasn't forced to pick between Charity and Miranda. I was reasonably confident of which one he'd choose, and it might not bode well for his marriage if Brock defended the girl who'd trashed my heart and crushed his wife.

I didn't care to play peacemaker any more than Brock did, but I could get away with it. When I reached Miranda's side, it blew me away that I hadn't overheard every word Charity screamed. I stepped between the two women with my back to Charity. She attempted to move me aside, but she didn't stand a chance in hell at budging two hundred pounds of dead weight. She could nag Brock all she wanted, but I didn't sleep with her at night, so she had nothing to use against me.

"Miranda, why don't you let me take you home?" It took every ounce of self-control I had to remain pleasant. There were a bunch of people in this town who wanted a shot at her, and I wanted to let them take it. But at the end of the day, I just couldn't do it.

She cut her eyes over my shoulder and stumbled when she looked back at me. I caught her by the elbow to steady her, and her hands landed on my chest. Miranda tilted her chin, and her eyes met mine. The heat of her breath warmed my skin, and the scent of liquor filled my nostrils. The corners of her mouth rose in what I assumed would be a smile, but at the last second, she parted her lips. "Dance with me." Those three words were crystal clear, without a hint of a slur.

The rest of the world faded away the same as it always had with Randi around. I shouldn't have conceded. I should have told her that I needed to go. But I'd never been able to tell her no, and tonight wasn't any different. I held up my left hand, she placed her palm to mine, and my other went to her hip. I needed to look

222 | STEPHIE WALLS

away, because getting trapped in her gaze wouldn't end well for me.

Just when my eyes flicked away, she rocked my world without a hint of a warning. "Eason's not my boyfriend." She shrugged when I stared down my nose at her. She'd pulled the pin, and the bomb was about to explode. "He's not. Never has been." The little sigh that followed wasn't exasperation; it almost came off amused.

My brow furrowed, and I was certain she saw my confusion.

"I don't have the equipment he requires."

I quit dancing, although I didn't move my hands. I pondered what she'd just confessed. There was no way that man liked men. "No."

Her head bobbed. "Yup."

"So why does Sarah think you guys are a couple? Why have you let *everyone* think you were a couple?"

"No one ever asked." She had to be kidding.

Of course no one asked. Sarah was terrified she'd upset Miranda and lose what little contact she'd regained over the years, and no one else had any right. Even if I hadn't known they lived together, the man had brought her home. Friends didn't leave their jobs for an undetermined amount of time to fly across the country together for moral support. Although, it now made more sense why he hadn't kept close tabs on her while she was here.

Miranda leaned into me and rested her head on my chest. We no longer moved with the music, we just stood together. I dropped her hand and wound my arms around her waist. It was dangerous, but I couldn't stop myself. The smell of mint tickled my nose when I tucked my head next to her ear to whisper, "Let me take you home."

She nodded against my chest, yet she didn't break away. For a bit longer, we lingered in a moment I had thought would never come. The grudge I'd held for six painful years no longer seemed relevant. There were questions I needed answers to, but as drunk as Miranda was, tonight wasn't the time to ask.

*G*etting Miranda to the truck hadn't taken much effort. She had followed willingly, and I didn't hesitate to take advantage of her fingers laced with mine when I pulled her out to the parking lot of The Hut. It was hard not to acknowledge how it felt to have her back in my arms on the dance floor, or how much I'd missed holding her hand. And when she climbed into the cab of my truck, it took effort not to focus on the sway of her hips or her tight ass. There had never been another woman who did for me what Miranda Adams did, and that clearly hadn't changed. If it hadn't changed in six years, it wasn't going to in sixty.

The ride back to Cross Acres proved uneventful. Country music played on a low volume, and Miranda stared out the window. I snuck glances at her and noticed she didn't even mouth the words. "Do you not listen to country anymore?"

"Hmm?" Not only did she not appear to listen to country music, she wasn't listening to me, either.

I pointed toward the radio. "You can change the station if you want."

But she was a million miles away. I wondered what she thought about and if she were reminiscing as we drove down Main Street or past fields we'd played in as kids. She didn't give any indication, so I let her be.

I turned off the county road and rolled down my window as the truck tires hit the gravel.

Miranda leaned back and angled her body toward me. "What'd you do that for?" It was the first time since she'd been home that I had heard any hint of a Southern drawl, and it made my heart race to realize she hadn't completely washed away her Mason Belle roots.

"Do what?" I asked.

Her eyelids were parted in nothing more than slits, and she appeared half asleep. "Roll down the window."

The likelihood she'd remember anything I said tonight when she woke up tomorrow was slim, so I chose to be honest. "To hear you."

"To hear me?" She giggled, and the sound was magical. "What does that mean?"

I shrugged and kept my hand on the steering wheel. Without glancing at her, I answered—not that I believed she'd ever under-stand. "I spent my life loving the sound of tires on this driveway, because it meant you were less than a mile away."

The laughter died, and while I knew she hadn't, she appeared to have sobered. "How long have you been doing that?"

"Since I was a kid." I didn't remember the first time I'd done it or when I associated that noise with seeing her. It had just happened, and now I couldn't undo it if I tried.

Thankfully, I pulled into the circle in front of the house before she could pry any further. I put the truck in park, tossed the driver's door open, and then rounded the front of the vehicle to help her. The last thing I needed was for her to bust her ass on the steps and wake Jack. Miranda had the door open on her side, and she'd turned to hop down when I stopped in front of her. She took the hand I offered and slid off the seat and to the ground.

There wasn't an inch of space between our chests, and every time she breathed in, her taut nipples teased my pecs. She hadn't let go of my hand when she stood on her own, and I couldn't look away. The gleam in her eyes awakened parts of me that hadn't been roused in years. A lot of men would have used it to their advantage, especially one who hadn't touched a woman in as long as I had. My fingers craved the heat of her bare skin, and my lips were desperate to taste hers. I couldn't even acknowledge the stiff pull below my waist. Randi Adams was just as intoxicating today as she had been in high school.

"Let's get you inside. I need to get home." Before I did something stupid. "I have to be back here at five." I wrapped my arm around her waist and eased her away from the truck to close the door.

She let me lead her up the stairs, and she used my side to steady her path toward the porch. "You could stay here."

I couldn't tell if she was flirting or offering me the couch. Both were tempting, neither would happen. "My house isn't far from here."

"Do you live alone?"

I took the hidden key out of the light fixture on the porch. "Yep." I would never understand why people locked their doors around Mason Belle. The last time I'd checked, coyotes didn't have opposable thumbs, and cows didn't steal.

"So, no one would notice if you didn't come home?" Her innuendo and coy grin could no longer be passed off as anything other than lust.

"No."

She kicked off her shoes in the foyer, all while keeping a tight grip on me. Her foot slipped on the hardwoods and almost took us both to the ground. It wasn't funny, but she couldn't quit laughing, and I couldn't stop the smile that spread across my face while I watched her.

Her eyes flicked to mine, and her rich-brown irises hid beneath hooded lids. The air became thick, and time slowed. I needed to get her to her room, and then I needed to leave before the art of seduction became an act. My resolve waned, and I refused to be *that* guy. I slipped my arm behind her knees, shifted the one around her waist to cradle her weight, and lifted her into my arms. Miranda was piss drunk, and I doubted she'd remember anything that happened tonight, but I would. And I'd be damn sure she never questioned if I'd changed, not in that regard.

She wrapped her arms around my neck and lay her head on my shoulder. I focused on each step in front of me and wished I'd switched on a light before climbing to the second floor. Miranda hadn't so much as shuddered since I picked her up, and I thought she might have passed out. Even when I pushed open her bedroom door, she didn't budge.

The light from the moon that came through the window illuminated the room enough to see that her bed remained unmade from where she'd gotten out of it this morning. I didn't bother with the lamp and gently put her down on the mattress. When I brought the comforter to her chin, she fisted my shirt in her tiny hand and drew me close.

Her eyes were obscured by the shadows, and darkness blinded my view, but every nuance, every detail, every *thing* about Randi Adams remained etched into my brain. And when her nostrils flared, I pulled back before our mouths met. I stood, and she lost her grip, at least the physical one she'd had on my T-shirt. I'd tried for six years to break the hold she had on my heart, and it was a battle I'd never won.

"I still love you, Austin," she whimpered.

My chest ached to repeat those words, but I couldn't do it. If they passed my lips, I'd end up stripping the clothes from her body, removing my own, and then crawling on top of her to reclaim her. That couldn't happen. Her dad was down the hall. She was drunk. And I was sober.

I did the only thing a Southern gentleman could. I bent down, kissed her forehead, and then I left. Miranda didn't call after me. She didn't beg me to stay. And that was for the best, at least for tonight. God knew, there was no way I could have said no had she asked.

My heart, my brain, and my dick all fought a mental and physical war inside me. Each stair I descended put more distance between where I wanted to be and where I should be. The last thing I needed was for her to wake up with regret.

If she still loved me, then we'd do things the right way, and that didn't include me sleeping with her tonight. I took a deep breath when I reached the kitchen. The fixture above the sink provided enough light for me to rummage around in the drawer to find a pen and a piece of paper. I stared at it for an eternity, or maybe it seemed that way because I was exhausted and had to be back here in a handful of hours. There was so much I wanted to say, but all I needed to say could be summed up in three words.

I refused to give those to her on a piece of paper with my phone number after six years.

So, I scrawled my name in black ink and left a way for her to reach me. I crept back up the stairs, slid the paper under her door, and walked out, hoping to God tonight hadn't been a drunken mistake...on her part.

14

MIRANDA

The sun that came through the slats in the blinds might as well have been a wrecking ball. The light hit my eyes with a blinding blow that amplified my hangover. I jerked the blankets over my head in search of darkness, but it didn't help. Last night was nothing more than a fuzzy memory at the moment —well, other than the whiskey—and then it all started to come back, bit by painful bit. Each scene that played out in my mind sent a zing of agony to my temples, and the moment I remembered telling Austin that I still loved him, my stomach lurched. Then it rolled.

With one hand over my mouth and the other flinging the quilt back, I then took off toward the bathroom. My foot slipped, and I found myself scurrying across the floor like a monkey. I fell to my knees in front of the toilet and lifted the lid to purge. I didn't need a reminder of how much alcohol I'd consumed while I sat at The Hut, but in case I'd forgotten, I now had a visual.

Even after I had flushed the toilet, the vile stench remained. I didn't have the energy to get up from the cool tile floor, and instead, I pressed my heated cheek to the surface and closed my eyes. I'd never been so hung over that the room spun the next day, but here was living proof that it could happen. I propped one foot flat on the floor in hopes of stopping the virtual merry-go-round; unfortunately, unless my eyes were open, it didn't do any good. And if I could see light of any kind, my head throbbed instead of the dull ache in darkness.

Another wave of nausea had me clutching the porcelain bowl. I didn't care that my face hovered inches from the water or that my hands were covered in germs from the rim. I desperately wanted the comfort of the bed. I just didn't have the strength or the confidence in my ability to keep from retching to actually move. The toilet seemed an appropriate place to reflect on the current state of affairs in Mason Belle, or rather, *my* state of affairs here.

Last night was a culmination of my time here: lonely at the bar, screamed at by an old friend, rejection from an old love...it couldn't get any worse. Until it dawned on me that I'd practically begged Austin to spend the night. My groan echoed off the sterile tiles with nowhere to land. There wasn't a soul alive who cared about my well-being—other than Eason. Gah, Eason. I hadn't talked to him in almost a week. I'd add that to my list of things to atone for. It was too bad I wasn't Catholic; confession and some Hail Marys would do me good, even if they wouldn't fix anything.

When I was confident my stomach was empty, I crawled across the bathroom to my bedroom. It was there I came across the paper I'd slipped on, and I almost cried when I recognized the handwriting. I'd told him I loved him, and he'd left me his phone number. Great. He hadn't even acknowledged that he heard a word I said, he hadn't stayed with me, and I was quite certain he hadn't taken me up on my implied offer and then gotten up before the rooster crowed.

The only other man I knew who could resist a woman

throwing herself at him with zero expectation for anything further was Eason. Somehow, that didn't make me feel any better. I missed my best friend. I missed New York. And I needed to get out of Mason Belle before I made an even bigger fool of myself. Charity had made it clear last night that I wasn't welcome here. Austin reminded me he'd given up on me long ago. And with Daddy turning over the ranch, there was nothing left. Not even hope. I didn't know my nieces and nephew, I hadn't even seen my brother-in-law, and my sister didn't need my help.

Some small part of me had hoped this would be a reckoning, even if I had refused to admit it. And although I'd anticipated every reaction I'd received since I arrived, it still hurt to actually experience them instead of just worry over it. It was time to move on from Mason Belle once and for all.

I clutched the slip of paper and used the handles on the dresser drawers to pull myself upright long enough to slap the phone number on the top, and then I used the top for leverage to stand. It was a gutsy move, considering how volatile my stomach and head were, but it made progress back to the mattress easier—and it wasn't so hard on my knees.

Once I tucked myself in, I reached for my phone on the night-stand and sent Eason a message. I could only hope that he would book a flight and not ask for details. But, I could never be that lucky. The continuous ding of my cell promised a litany of questions that I didn't have the energy to deal with. The last thing I wanted to do was discuss my embarrassment with my best friend.

I cringed when I picked up the phone. The light from the screen was almost as damning as the sunshine. I found Eason's name on my favorites list, tapped it, then touched the speaker icon and turned down the volume. Once he answered, I pulled the blankets over my head and closed my eyes.

"Hey, stranger." Any other time, his voice soothed even the worst ache. Today, it amplified it.

I winced and pushed the phone farther away. "Shh. You don't have to talk so loud," I whispered in hopes that he'd get the hint of what an acceptable decibel level was.

"Why are we whispering?" he cooed into the phone.

If I'd been in a better frame of mind, then I would have recognized I had given myself away. Had I merely told him that I wanted to come home, Eason would have booked the flight. My desperate text threw up red flags, and then my perceived secrecy raised more.

"It's a long story that I prefer to rehash from the comfort of our couch when I'm not hung over and praying for death."

Silence held the line. "I'm afraid to ask."

It proved easier to give him a brief overview and gain his sympathy than resist and be stuck here until I came clean. I talked. Eason listened. And when I finished, he didn't throw open his arms for me to rush into.

"Maybe you should give it a little more time, Miranda."

More time. "What else do I need? My childhood best friend called me every name she could think of last night, the love of my life rejected me, and my dad gave our family ranch to someone *not in our family*. It's the start of every horrible country song." Each word only served to increase the pounding in my head. "Should I wait for them to escort me out of town? I'd like to have some semblance of dignity remaining when I get on a plane."

"Have you talked to your sister?"

Ugh. "About leaving?"

"No, about why you left to begin with."

I would never understand Eason's need for my reconciliation with people who, up until recently, he hadn't met. "Sarah and I are fine." Fine was relative. We were status quo.

He made no attempt to hide his frustrated sigh. "Okay. I'll see what I can do about getting your return flight booked."

I should have figured out how to do it myself and shown up at the brownstone. In my current condition, Eason seemed an easier route to the end result I craved. In hindsight, a nap would have cured the hangover, and then I could have called the airline to get it taken care of. Now, guilt weighed my conscience down into slumber. And when I woke, I'd have no other choice than to come to peace with my sister before I left.

*I*t didn't take long to pack my bag. I'd bought more at Walmart than I'd actually brought, and none of that needed to go back to New York. I folded it all and neatly put it into the drawers in my old dresser. It seemed silly since I doubted I'd ever be back to claim any of it, but it belonged here; I didn't.

With my suitcase in tow, I glanced back one final time at the bedroom I'd grown up in. It was bittersweet, but at least now I wouldn't have regrets. I had come back. I'd tried to face the demons, even if I hadn't righted any of the wrongs. There was no sense in lingering. Nothing would change, regardless of how long I stood there.

And for the second time in my life, I walked away. There were some decisions in life that couldn't be undone. I couldn't make reparations in this town for a choice I'd made years earlier. Teens everywhere disobeyed without the consequences my actions had brought. That wasn't my fate; this was.

Daddy sat in the kitchen with Sarah when I reached the bottom of the stairs.

"Where are you going?" Sarah tried to jump up and had to brace herself on the counter. She wasn't agile the way a thirty-one-year-old mother of three should be, and I was responsible for that.

I glanced down at my bag and scrunched my nose when I faced her again. "I think it's time for me to go." This didn't need to get heavy. "Daddy's home and on the mend. You're here. Austin's got the ranch under control."

Daddy swiveled the stool my direction to keep from having to look over his shoulder. "Sugar, you don't need to rush off."

If only I believed that. I wanted to. "You guys have it covered. I need to get back to work." Part of that was true. Eason didn't care when I came back to the firm; he'd hold my job for a year if I asked.

"Miranda, come on." She eased between the two stools to come toward me. "You haven't been here that long."

Two and a half weeks seemed like an eternity to those of us who didn't fit in. "Eason's already booked a flight." I hated to ask her for a favor, but taxis didn't exist in Mason Belle. Calling one from Laredo would cost a small fortune just to take me to the bar to get my rental. "Would you mind running me up to The Hut to get the car?"

Sarah glanced back toward our father. His expression was soft, and his eyes warmed when he gazed at my sister. They now had the relationship that Daddy and I had growing up. A twinge of jealousy stabbed me right in the heart. I missed that relationship. Truth be told, I missed my sister, too.

"I've got to pick up the kids from Charlie's mom. Are you in a hurry?"

My flight didn't leave until nearly ten tonight. I had plenty of time to return the rental car to the airport and check in. I just didn't want to spend any of those hours lingering here, and I certainly didn't want to risk running into Austin the moment I stepped out the front door. "No. I have time."

She leaned down and gave Daddy a kiss on the cheek. I tried to give him a soft smile, even though it fell just short of awkward and odd. Sarah grabbed her keys from the counter, and I lifted my hand to wave. Daddy didn't stand to hug me, and I didn't move to him to initiate one, either.

"Bye, Daddy," I half whispered as I followed my sister out the door.

"Bye, Randi." Hearing that nickname pass his lips squeezed my heart.

I almost turned around. I almost ran back and threw my arms around him. I almost cried and begged him to love me again. Instead, I bit my tongue and beelined for Sarah's SUV. I couldn't get inside fast enough. She rounded the car with a slow gait. Sarah had never regained a hundred percent mobility in her legs. I wondered if it ever bothered her or if she'd simply become accustomed to her awkward walk.

She struggled a bit with the weight of the door and released a huff once she'd finally settled into the driver's seat. "The gravel gets me every time," she explained with a grin. There wasn't an ounce of anger in her tone.

Sarah pressed the ignition button and put the car in drive. When we passed the barn, I noticed Austin. With his back to the house, he hadn't seen us leave. The pain of pulling away without a goodbye for the second time wasn't any easier than the first. I squeezed my eyes closed to fight the sting of tears until I was certain that when I opened them, he wouldn't be there. My heart constricted painfully, and I wondered if the agony would ever go away.

"I'm sorry, Sarah." It needed to be said. I'd never really apologized, and my sister deserved that. I couldn't fix her legs. I couldn't change the problems she'd deal with for the rest of her life. I could, however, let her know that I'd take it all back if I could. "I never should have left that day."

Her fingers squeezed the steering wheel hard enough that her knuckles turned white before she responded. "I'm grateful you did." Her grip relaxed, and she stopped at the end of the driveway. "You see my accident as something to regret. I see it as the catalyst for everything I got after."

She looked both ways to ensure there wasn't an oncoming car and pulled out onto the country road. I never quit staring at her. Dumbfounded. That accident wasn't a blessing, unless she referred to it sending me out of the state. I didn't want to hear that, though. So I remained quiet.

Sarah placed her hand on mine without taking her attention off the road. "Do you know what happened after you left? To me, I mean."

"No. I didn't talk to anyone from Mason Belle until you found me." And that had been nearly a year later. Without a cell phone, locating me had taken effort on her part.

A smile played at the corner of her mouth. I wished I could see her eyes and her expression instead of just her profile. "Well, you know Austin came to the ranch every day."

"Yeah."

"So he helped Daddy take care of Cross Acres. And the rest of the town pitched in everywhere they could, as well. Other ranchers sent extra hands so Daddy could be at the hospital. Women brought food to him and to me—the stuff at the hospital was gross." She glanced at me long enough to make a horrible face to indicate just how bad. "The townspeople really pulled together. You know how they do."

I did. I'd seen it time and time again growing up. If the citizens of Mason Belle could prevent a neighbor from experiencing pain or help make their burden lighter, they did whatever it took. And women loved to dote on Daddy. He'd been single for a lot of years, and older, unattached men didn't exist in our little town, especially ones as handsome as my father. I snickered, thinking about who might have tried to make a play for my dad's heart while he focused on Sarah.

"Do you remember that irrigation project he was working on with Charlie?"

It was a long time ago, but it vaguely rang a bell. "I think so."

Although, I hadn't been interested then, and I didn't know the details now.

"Well, Charlie got several guys around town together to make sure they got it done so Daddy could take care of me." That sounded like something a Burin boy would do. "Charlie couldn't ever catch Daddy at home, so he started coming to the hospital." She squeezed my hand. "One afternoon, he showed up, and Daddy had already left. I had just finished physical therapy. When he came into the room, I was sitting on the edge of the mattress in tears."

I pulled my hand away and leaned back to angle my body toward her. "Why?"

She huffed as if to say, duh. "I wasn't in a great place mentally. Anger, pity, shame...they all played with my head regularly. That particular day had been especially hard in therapy, and I'd about given up the hope of ever walking again."

Here it was. This was the point Sarah would get to release the years of blame. And I couldn't escape—not that I would have tried.

"Charlie sat next to me and patted my knee." She shook her head, clearly thinking back to the day she spoke of. "Remember, he didn't even know my name back then. And here was this boy I'd been infatuated with for years, seeing me at my worst. I begged him to leave. Of course, he refused." Of course, he did. That's how the Burins had been raised. She sighed, and it was a sigh of adoration. "He took my face in his hands, and it was still pretty beaten up at that point. My hair hadn't grown back in where they had to shave it to put in stitches. I was a mess. But Charlie saw past all of it. He brushed the tears off my cheeks, looked me in the eyes, and said, 'You can't give up, Sarah.'"

I couldn't clearly see my sister's face, but I could see enough of it to imagine the dreamy expression she likely had and the dopey look of love that animated her eyes.

"It was the first time Charlie ever *saw* me. It was also the first time he'd remembered my name. I know, that's a dumb thing to realize when you're in the hospital with a spinal injury and lucky to be alive. But *that's* what I remember most."

That couldn't be the end of the story, because somehow, between that moment and now, they'd gotten married and had three kids. I desperately wanted to hear how she got there. But we'd turned into the entrance to Twin Creeks, and in a matter of seconds, we'd be sitting in front of the Burins' house.

She pulled the SUV onto the side of the driveway before the bend in the road to hide our arrival. A tingle ran through my blood when she put the SUV in park and situated herself in the seat to face me.

"He stayed until they kicked him out that night. The next day, he came back before my physical therapy session, and he went with me. While we were there, he asked the therapist to teach him how to help me do the exercises. From that point forward, Charlie showed up every day." She closed her eyes, and I wanted to capture the smile that lifted her lips. It was as beautiful as she was. When she parted her lids, her blue irises sparkled with joy. "The guy who'd never noticed me became my champion, Miranda. When I didn't think I could push any harder, he had the strength I couldn't find."

At a loss for words, I stared at my sister and waited for more. That wasn't the end of their story. Technically, they didn't have one, and I hoped they never would.

"Even after I left the hospital, he took me to every therapy appointment. He came to the house to get me and drove me to Laredo three or four times a week. I never asked. Charlie never offered. The first time he ever hugged me was the day I took my first unassisted step. It was only one, but he was right there waiting and caught me. That was also the first time he told me he loved me."

Only my sister could turn tragedy into the start of a romance novel. No one deserved it more, either. My lips parted to say something, yet words didn't come. Tears did. I blinked, and they slid down my cheeks.

Sarah smacked my leg. "Don't cry, silly. That was the beginning of a really hot love story." She shook her head as if she were still in disbelief that it had ever happened.

My sister and I had never had this sort of relationship. She didn't date when I was in my teens, and I didn't confide in her about the things I'd done with Austin. Not that she hadn't known I loved him—everyone was aware of that. We'd just never shared secrets. Sarah had been too busy playing the role of mom, and I'd been too insistent on not letting her.

She rolled her eyes playfully, and I couldn't stop the laugh that followed. "Did you just roll your eyes?" That was twice I'd caught that gesture.

"Girl, I had no idea what I'd been missing." There was that goofy grin I'd expected to see when she spoke earlier. "The doctors had been pretty insistent that I not engage in sexual activity. I'd blown them off, because I was a virgin, and I hadn't paid the least bit of attention to anything they said. In my mind, none of it would come into play. Until it did."

I slapped the console with excitement. "Shut up! You had sex with Charlie while you were still in therapy?" The Southern accent I'd spent years hiding resurfaced with my exclamation.

"A lot." She nodded while she spoke. "Doctors should incorporate that into every patient's recovery." Sarah laughed, and it was deep, straight from the soul. "It certainly improved my outlook."

These were the things we should have shared as kids. It didn't matter that Sarah was six years older than I was; she was my sister, and this was what sisters did. But Mama had stolen that from both of us.

"I can only imagine." I thought back to the first time I'd had sex with Austin, and what an addict I'd become afterward. It wasn't just how good it felt, although that had been mind-blowing. Those were the only times since my mom had left that I ever felt connected. Nothing else in the world existed when we were intimate.

"Unfortunately, I was pretty naïve. I'd been on birth control for years, but I took it to regulate periods. No one ever bothered to tell me what every other teenage girl in America knew from puberty on."

"What's that?"

"Antibiotics alter their effectiveness. I'd been on some form of them since the accident, and I got put on another round after every surgery. Charlie and I never used protection because I thought I was covered."

And that's how the twins got here. "But you weren't…"

A bit of a grimace replaced the grin for just a minute. Then it cleared as quickly as it had appeared. "The doctors wanted me to abort the pregnancy. Every medical professional I came into contact with encouraged me to terminate. They didn't think my spine could hold up to the additional weight, and if I survived the pregnancy, they weren't sure I'd make it through delivery. Or if I did, they believed I'd be paralyzed after."

I clasped my hand over my mouth when I gasped. I hadn't learned about any of this until after the twins were born, and even though I'd known the doctors didn't want her to have the babies, I never understood why. Nor had I asked. "What about Charlie?" I said through my hand.

"He begged me to listen to the physicians. And I nearly broke when he told me he loved me too much to let me go. Then, when he promised me he'd buy me a baby if he had to in order to keep me safe, I made the appointment."

"Oh God, Sarah. I…" I didn't know what I wanted to say. She

hadn't had the abortion. There were two girls right down the driveway to prove that. Yet, she'd faced that decision. No woman should ever be asked to choose between themselves and their children. It was an impossible choice.

She waved me off. "I didn't go. In my mind, that was no different than what Mama did to us. And I refused to pick myself over the welfare of my kids, even if I'd never met them."

"How did Charlie take it?"

Her exasperated laugh likely didn't do the situation justice. "Not well. He didn't talk to me for almost two weeks."

"What changed?" I begged for an answer. This was better than reality TV.

Sarah raised her brows to heighten my anticipation. "Austin."

Charlie's little brother shouldn't have come into play in their decision to keep a child. "Austin? How so?"

"I wasn't there for the conversation, so I can only paraphrase what Charlie later told me."

I circled my wrist, turning my hand, desperate for her to give me the information.

"He told Charlie that it was a piece of both of us, and neither of us was guaranteed tomorrow." This would hurt by the time she finished her next sentence. "And he would have killed to have a piece of you still with him after you'd left."

I bit my lip and nodded. Sarah's story wasn't about me, or Austin. But this had happened months after I'd left, and he saved his nieces' lives by wishing for a piece of me to still be in his. I swallowed hard to keep from losing my composure. There wasn't anything I could say, so I sat there and stared at my sister. Her strawberry-blond curls hung by her cheeks, and her blue eyes radiated with happiness that I didn't remember seeing as a child.

She shrugged. "Anyway, there is a point in me telling you all this. Miranda, if you had stayed home that day and done what you were told, the accident never would have happened. If it hadn't,

Charlie never would have found me, and I wouldn't have married him. None of my kids would have names or even exist." Sarah reached out and took my hand again. This time, she held it in both of hers and stroked the top with her thumb. She stared at them for a moment before making eye contact with me again. "Sometimes we have to endure the worst pain of our lives to find the greatest happiness. And you did that for me, Miranda. Intentional or not, you started the chain of events that led to my destiny. For that, I can never say thank you enough. I love you."

I lost my ability to stave off the tears. My throat lurched in a loud hiccup of emotion. I tightened my hold on her fingers, wishing I could verbalize how grateful I was for her forgiveness.

"You're my sister. And whether you're in Mason Belle or New York City, that will never change."

Sarah hadn't even brought up her limp, her disfigured fingers, or the scars all over her body, much less dwelled on them. For the first time in my life, I recognized the beauty of Sarah's soul, and I hated that it had taken me so many years to see it. I'd let her take the blame for Mama leaving because she'd stepped up to fill that role the best she could. Everyone else saw what she sacrificed, and I'd missed it because I'd been blinded by my mom's departure.

"I'm glad you're happy, Sarah." I choked back another sob. "You deserve it. Charlie is a very lucky man."

She reached out and stroked my hair, then let her hand linger on my jaw. "So is Eason, Miranda. Don't ever forget your worth."

It wasn't funny. Sarah had tried to make this meaningful. She had no idea why I laughed or what I found so amusing. There was no point in keeping up the charade. I'd admitted it to Austin last night, so it was only a matter of time before he'd spill my secret. I'd rather be the one to tell her. I took a deep breath, and on the release, I confessed, "Eason and I aren't together, Sarah. We never have been."

If she'd pulled away any harder, she would have hit her head on the window behind her. "What?"

I shook my head, and my eyes fluttered with my stupidity. "He's gay."

"Then why did you tell me you were a couple?"

"Technically, I didn't. You assumed it when you found out I lived with him. I just never corrected you." I tucked my hair behind my ear while I tried to find the words to explain. "It was easier for you to believe he was the reason I didn't come back to Texas. I didn't want to fight, and I couldn't face this place."

She crossed her arms like she used to do right before she scolded me. "Then why did he come home with you?" I didn't miss the accusation in her tone.

"He's my best friend." It was that simple.

Sarah dropped her hands to her lap, and the hard lines that had formed on her forehead softened until they disappeared. "You couldn't face Austin alone."

My throat hurt it was so tight. If I tried to swallow, I'd choke. Even the glands under my jaw screamed in pain. "Eason was a layer of protection. He has been since the day I left Mason Belle." My words were barely a whisper, and I wasn't certain Sarah had even heard them.

Then I recognized the pity in her eyes, and I knew she'd caught every word. "Has there been anyone else?"

I turned my head back and forth. "No one."

Her hands flew to her chest and covered her heart. "You have to tell Austin."

That was the real kicker. "I did." And here we were on our way to the airport. I hoped my sister picked up on that detail without making me draw her a picture.

"Oh." She got it. And if it were possible for another person to hurt for you, my sister did right now. She hurt for me. "So, because of you, I got my happy ending, and because of me, you lost yours."

"Everything happens for a reason. I'll be okay. I just need to get home." Thankfully, God had given me the strength to execute that lie well enough that my sister nodded and let it go. I didn't believe it as much as it sounded like I did.

---

*S*arah and I had taken a couple of minutes to compose ourselves before she pulled back onto the driveway and parked in front of the Burins' house. Just like my own, nothing about this one had changed since I'd been gone. There were so many memories here and around their property. I'd spent as much of my youth roaming the pastures of Twin Creeks as those of Cross Acres. I fought a mental battle against letting the happiness of my youth shadow the reality of my life. I doubted I would be any more welcome here than I had anywhere else in Mason Belle, probably less.

I'd hurt their son as much as I had myself and my sister. Parents weren't likely to forgive that type of indiscretion. Not that I blamed them, or anyone else. I didn't. They all had every right to hate me, to hold a grudge.

I reached for the seatbelt, still unsure whether I should sit tight or accompany Sarah to get her kids. When she didn't stop me, I pushed the button, released the belt, and then got out of the car. Austin's mom must have been watching out the window. As soon as my feet hit the pavement, the front door opened. She hadn't aged a bit. Just as elegant as the day was long. I could only hope to look that good in twenty or thirty years. Jessica Burin had the class of Jackie O and the grace of Audrey Hepburn.

Her eyes held mine for an extended length of time. Even though I was aware the kids had pushed past her and through the open door, it hadn't registered to me that they'd flown off the porch and ran toward us. Rand hit my legs at full force, yanking my attention from the woman I had thought would be my mother-in-law to his body pressed against my knees. His little arms wrapped themselves around my thighs, and he chattered a hundred miles a minute.

"Auntie Randi. You came to see me."

I patted his head and stroked his hair. I didn't have a clue what to do with kids, especially this one. He got me better than people I'd known my entire life, and I'd spent less than ten minutes with him. "Hey, Rand. Did you have fun with your grandma?" It seemed like a good thing to ask.

He let go and stepped back, shrugged, and stared up through the height difference that separated us. "I guess."

"You guess?" I kept my tone light in hopes that he'd start to fill the conversation before he realized I had nothing to talk about.

He quirked his lips to the side and bobbed his head. "Yeah, I got in trouble." Somehow, I didn't believe that was unusual.

I squatted so he didn't have to look into the sun. "Oh, no. What did you do?"

Just over his shoulder, movement caught my eye. I hadn't been prepared for what stood before me. It was like looking through a mirror and back in time.

"Rand pushed me into the horses' trough." One of the twins' wet hair hung down her back, and her glare burned with agitation.

I couldn't get over how tan she was in comparison to her fair-haired sister. My eyes shot between the two. It was uncanny to see how much one looked like me and the other like Sarah, although I didn't know which was which. And I refused to ask.

Instead, I focused on the kid whose name I knew. "Rand, why would you do that?"

He shook his little head and lifted his brows. His look was so serious, it was difficult not to laugh. "You have no idea how mean Kylie is. Trust me, she had it comin'."

Kylie! Which meant the blonde was Kara. "You should be nice to your sisters." Do as I say and not as I do probably wasn't the best parenting approach. It was a good thing I didn't have children.

"Yeah, Rand," Kylie taunted.

I stood and huffed a bit of humor under my breath. Everything about her reminded me of myself. And then my attention drifted to the silent beauty at her side. If angels took human form, Kara was one. I could see all her soft edges in the way she held herself, the gentle way she observed me, and the fact that she hadn't lashed out or gotten involved. Sarah's luck apparently ended with her. She was the oldest of the girls, and evidently, just like my sister. Kylie and Rand likely tried her patience...daily. At least she'd gotten practice with Austin and me over the years. That thought should have stung; however, it brought a sense of pride to believe I might have helped her parent, even though I hadn't been around.

Sarah stood next to Kara, and Kylie had her hands on her hips, still glaring at Rand. I chanced a peek at the porch, and Jessica lifted her hand. Her smile grew when she wiggled her fingers. Maybe she didn't hold as much hate for me as I believed she did. I'd never get the chance to ask her because she turned and closed the door.

"Who is that?" Kara's whisper wasn't quite as soft as she probably meant it to be.

Before I found my sister, I knew her daughter would be addressing Sarah with the question, and I had no idea how she'd respond.

"That's Aunt Randi, you dope." Yep, Kylie was just like me.

Sarah detected my discomfort. "Come on, y'all. We need to get Aunt Miranda to her car so she can get to the airport."

Rand grabbed my hand and pulled. "You're leaving already? We haven't even had time to play. You can't go *now*," he whined.

I needed a lifeline. I couldn't tell this kid I'd see him soon. I wouldn't. I refused to make him a promise I had no intention of keeping. Sarah did not come to my aid. I ruffled his hair. "I have to catch my plane."

"Tin Tin told you she wouldn't stay, dummy. Maybe if you listened, you wouldn't need to cry like a baby." Kylie's words hurt, so did her resolute tone. There was no denying she'd been prepped by her uncle to keep her distance—they all had.

Rand's eyes were indeed filled with tears. Sarah motioned for the girls to come to her side of the SUV, which they did without question. I squatted, scooped up Rand, and did the only thing I could. I held him against my chest, and when he tucked his head into my neck and threw his arms around me, I hated to let him go. "Maybe we can talk your mama into letting you come stay with me for a couple of days in New York."

Sarah would kill me for that suggestion, but I didn't care. I'd take him home with me if I thought she'd let me. He was the closest thing I'd ever have to Austin again. It might be selfish to love him for the reminder of someone else, but I didn't care. I would never admit that to another living soul. They could all just assume I had a favorite...because I did. Rand.

"Promise?" He sniffled.

I nodded and helped him into his car seat.

It didn't take long once we left Twin Creeks to reach The Hut. The rental car sat where I'd parked it the night before. I leaned over and squeezed the life out of my sister. Goodbyes weren't my thing. Then I looked between the seats to the back and told the kids I'd see them later. Rand was on the verge of tears. As much as I wanted to stay just to spend time with him, it was better for everyone if I left. Rand held my eyes, and the same understanding lingered that had passed between us when he'd heard me arguing with Austin in front of the house.

"Bye, Aunt Randi."

I blew him a kiss and got out of the SUV. A bolt of lightning didn't strike as fast as I moved. This time, I'd leave Mason Belle, Texas, without looking back.

15

MIRANDA

PAST

*T*he pounding that came from the hall startled me. Disoriented and unsure of what was happening, I sat up straight. My sudden movement jostled Austin. How he continued to sleep through the clamor was beyond me. My heart raced, although I couldn't say whether it was from fear or irritation. When the fog cleared, I realized that it was unlikely an intruder had bothered to knock, much less a knock as angry as the one that continued to rattle the wood.

"Miranda," Daddy bellowed. "I know you're in there. Open this door, right now."

Crap, crap, crap. Any other day since my sister's accident, if my dad had come to my door, I could have let him in without hesitation. Not only had I always been fully clothed, so had Austin. Now, I sat on my knees in the middle of my mattress buck naked and paralyzed.

Austin scurried out of bed the instant he recognized the voice. There was no way out. Nevertheless, Austin looked for places to either escape or hide while he gathered his clothes.

"Girl, I will tear it off the frame if you don't let me in."

Austin had managed to get boxers and his jeans on. I, on the other hand, remained naked as a jaybird with my sights fixated on the locked knob.

Something hit me smack-dab in the face. "Randi, put that on. Hurry up." Austin tried to keep his voice low enough that Daddy wouldn't hear.

The beating stopped. That scared me more than knowing he was on the other side. Silence with Jack Adams didn't mean he'd given up. Usually the opposite. I slipped on a pair of panties and cheer shorts before the loud thump landed in the center of the door, it rattled, and the frame cracked. I climbed off the bed, now afraid to get anywhere near the door to actually open it.

The second blow caused a high-pitched yip to echo in the room, and I recognized it as my own. Austin stepped in front of me like a shield when the third impact swung the splintered wood into the room.

His eyes narrowed into beady, little slits focused on Austin. Daddy's nostrils flared, yet his chest didn't heave like he'd just kicked down a door, and his face wasn't red with exertion. It was evident he was mad, but in a calm, eerie way for someone who'd demolished part of his house less than sixty seconds earlier.

Austin stood his ground, and I hid behind him.

"You been here all night, boy?" He already knew the answer. I hated when adults asked questions to bait kids into trouble.

Just as I tried to step forward, Austin either sensed my movement or saw me from the corner of his eye. He blocked my attempt to face my father. "Yes, sir." He owned it.

"Go home, Austin." It was a direct order from Daddy.

I couldn't be certain whether I wanted Austin to follow my dad's instructions or stand up to him. He hesitated long enough for Daddy to get in his face.

"I'm not going to tell you again to get the hell out of my house. There ain't a cop in this town that'd believe anything other than I thought there was an intruder in my daughter's bedroom." He was right. Daddy had grown up in Mason Belle just like we had. He and Sheriff Patton were friends, and no one who'd ever met Daddy would believe him capable of hurting Austin Burin.

This time, I didn't allow Austin to keep me back. "Daddy. Why are you so mad?"

Austin hadn't said another word. He hadn't moved, either. "Mr. Adams—"

"Austin, I ain't gonna tell you again to get the hell outta my house. Now."

I turned back and put my hand on Austin's chest. "It's okay. I'll call you later."

Austin glanced from me to my dad and back. "I don't feel good about leaving you here." He looked down his nose, and I saw dread in Austin's eyes.

"He won't hurt me," I whispered. Then I lifted onto my tiptoes to kiss his cheek. "Promise."

Austin kissed my forehead, but before he pulled his lips back, he pressed the words "I love you" onto my skin with his mouth.

I gave him a weak smile and then faced my father when Austin walked by him and through the busted doorway. Daddy waited. The longer the silence went on, the worse it would be. I knew my dad well enough to realize that he counted Austin's steps down the stairs. Then he listened for the front door, which could easily be heard from my room. His stare jerked to the window where he could watch the truck pull out.

When his attention returned to me, there was no doubt in my mind that whatever was about to come at me would be bad. I'd always known when I was little that the longer Daddy waited once he told me to go to my room, the worse the spanking would be. If he had to calm down before he could be in the same room with me, then I'd get a blistering. He hadn't spanked me since Mama had left.

"This what you been doin' while Sarah's been laid up in the hospital?" He jerked his head toward my bed.

"Sleeping?"

His arm lashed out, although not at me, and his fist went through the drywall next to the other hole he'd created. "Actin' like a damn Jezebel." Spittle flew from his cracked lips. "It ain't good enough that you've ruined my life and your sister's, now you wanna take Austin out with you?"

I didn't understand what he was talking about. "Daddy, I don't—"

"You tryin' to get knocked up?"

"God, no." I flinched at the thought. "Why would you think that?"

I'd never seen my dad so furious. He'd maintained his cool until Austin pulled out of the driveway. Now, his chest heaved, and a web of saliva clung to the sides of his mouth when he yelled.

"I'd heard rumors you two were shackin' up in my house, but I couldn't believe you'd use your sister's accident to spread your legs."

That wasn't true. It wasn't true at all. "That's not fair."

He stopped surging toward me and pulled back in surprise. "Which part? Because you damn sure sent your mama running. Sarah ain't never gonna walk again. And I ain't dumb enough to believe you're a virgin." His fury was irrational, and I didn't have any idea what had set him off, much less how to slow him down.

I searched his face for some sign of the man I'd loved my entire life, the one who'd kissed my cuts, who stood in the bleachers at cheer competitions. The same man who'd never let me go a day without feeling completely adored—until Sarah's accident. There wasn't even a hint of him.

"You're home gettin' your rocks off while your sister's gettin' the most devastatin' news of her life."

Too shocked to say anything, I gawked at my father. Sarah

woke up last night; that had to be a good sign. But I hadn't had a chance to ask about that because I wasn't allowed to be there, and my father hadn't so much as picked up the phone to tell me.

"Goddammit, Miranda, say something!" He slung his arm along my dresser and swept everything I'd ever worked for onto the floor—every trophy, every medal, every award. It all crashed onto the hardwood with the crunch of glass. "Your selfishness never ends." And his rage didn't, either.

I stood in the same spot Austin had left me in as my dad stormed around my room. There wasn't a thing he had left untouched. Including me. At first, it was my heart that he slaughtered, then he reared back and slapped me across the face so hard I thought my eye would explode.

Tears ran down Daddy's cheeks, and my own pooled. I thought better of letting them fall or clutching the searing pain in my jaw. "Sarah ain't ever gonna walk again thanks to you." He threw his hands into the air. "Why couldn't you just do what you were told?"

I didn't have an answer for that, although he didn't actually want one. Daddy wasn't after excuses. He needed me to take what he had to let go of. And I owed him that.

He gasped for air. His voice appeared stuck in his throat, or maybe that was his heart. If I didn't know better, I'd think he'd been on a two-day bender as bloodshot as his eyes were and as bad as he slurred his words. But they ran together in frustration. A drop of alcohol had never passed my daddy's lips.

I winced when he grabbed hold of my arm. The harder he shook, the tighter his grip became. He jerked me with such force, I thought my shoulder had popped out of the socket. "Daddy, please..." I whispered.

"Please? Please, what? Have mercy on you? You've been like a damn tornado rippin' through everyone's life since the day you were born. Now that you're facin' the truth of what you've done, you think someone should have pity on you? Ain't gonna be me."

I lost control over my tears and cried out when he pushed my arm out of his grip. It wasn't just me stumbling backward. The thread that tethered me to my daddy broke with my fall. When I hit the floor, my head cracked on the wood. As I sat up, rubbing the back of my skull, I dared to ask, "Why are you being so cruel?"

He quit moving, put his hands on his hips, and glared at me from his towering view. I'd never felt so small and insignificant. "You ever stopped to ask yourself why your mama left? Just picked up and walked away without so much as a word...on your birthday?"

Every day for years. Until one day, I refused to think about her at all. She'd been gone as long as she'd been around at this point.

Either Daddy didn't believe I had an answer or he didn't care to hear it. "You." He pulled on his hair and kept ranting. He spoke at me, but no longer to me. "You tried her patience. Pushed her to her breakin' point. Never could sit still, always yappin' 'bout somethin', smart-mouthed. Just too much sass for your own good. You drove her away."

I shook my head. "That's not true. I was just a kid," I cried, but it fell on deaf ears. Sarah and I had both asked Daddy over and over why she'd left, and he'd never given us anything other than she wasn't happy. "If she wasn't happy, that was your job, not mine!" I wailed.

He continued as though I hadn't even opened my mouth. "No one could control you. I should have tanned your hide that morning when you came in after roamin' the town all night. Maybe if I'd done more disciplinin', takin' the strap to you a few times, then you woulda learned 'bout consequences."

I hadn't done anything that every other senior hadn't done, most of them more frequently. Teenagers in ranching communities had bonfires and field parties. We spent time at the lake. They drove trucks with big tires and played loud music. There wasn't anything malicious about any of it, and no one thought anything of it, including my sister...until she found out that I hadn't played matchmaker for her with Charlie Burin.

"Your sister almost died 'cause a you. Yet, she ain't seen hide nor hair of you since."

That was it. I'd never be able to prove him wrong when it came to Mama. If he wanted me to shoulder that burden, fine. And I'd be the first to admit that I should've listened to Sarah that day. If I could go back in time, I'd change everything about it. But I'd agonized over that accident since the day it happened. He should be able to look at me and tell I hadn't taken it well. Somehow, he had missed my clothes hanging off me from the weight I'd lost, the bags under my eyes from lack of sleep, and the weight of the world that pressed on my rounded shoulders.

I scrambled to my feet, unsure whether facing off with a man this angry was in my best interest, but there was little more he could say or do to hurt me. There would most certainly be a handprint on my face tomorrow and bruises on my arm. Unless he planned to throw me out of the window, I'd weathered the worst of it.

"Do you have any idea where I've been for weeks?" My calm voice appeared to surprise him into sudden silence. "You don't have a clue. And you know why?" I inched closer to him. "Because you weren't concerned about it. Not once did you worry about how I'd eat, what I was doing, or how I handled the situation." One step closer and I noticed his fists clenched at his sides. "But since you missed it, I'll tell you exactly where I've been." I could smell the coffee on his breath as he huffed. "Every day I've sat on a bench in the parking lot, waiting for you to go home. Then I sat next to Sarah's bed, holding her hand until the nurses made me leave." I poked him in the chest. "Every. Dang. Day. So, while you thought I was out whoring around or had my legs spread for any man willing to take a stab at me simply because I wasn't at the house when you got here, doesn't make it true. I sat at my sister's side begging her not to die."

"You've done enough damage. You need to stay away from Sarah." A switch flipped. The emotion drained from his weathered skin. "You're poison, Miranda." He dropped his head. "Any chance Sarah had at a normal and happy life was lost the day she ran after you." He'd hardened his heart. In trying to protect Sarah, he'd turned his back on me.

"I didn't make Sarah get in that car and chase me, Daddy. She did that all on her own. And I wasn't the one driving that semi." I softened my tone in hopes of reaching the part of my father that had always doted on me despite my mistakes. "Yes, I screwed up. And I will pay for that for the rest of my life, but—"

He laughed, yet he still didn't lift his head. "You don't get it. This ain't 'bout you, Miranda. Sarah will never walk again. She's an invalid in a ranchin' town. What kinda life she gonna have? No man's gonna take a wife who can't help out or give him young'uns." Daddy finally met my gaze. "*That* is on you."

I had carried that guilt with me every day, and I would for eternity. But it didn't matter in Daddy's eyes that I hadn't been driving that truck or that I hadn't pushed Sarah into the car and forced her to race down the street. His mind had been made up before he ever set foot in the house. None of that had anything to do with Austin; he'd just been at the wrong place at the wrong time.

"What do you want me to do?" My voice cracked, even though it was nothing more than a whisper.

He reached into his back pocket and produced his wallet. I tracked his fingers when he pulled every bill from inside and then shoved them at me. "You love Sarah?"

"Of course, I do." Just because we fought didn't mean she wasn't family.

My dad's hand shook in front of me. "What about Austin? You love him?"

I nodded when words failed.

"Do them both a favor." His pitch didn't rise or fall. His hand continued to tremble while his voice stayed strong. "Give them a chance at happiness."

"I-I don't understand."

"Long as you're around, neither one's got a fightin' chance." He couldn't be saying what I thought I heard. His eyes went soft, but it only took a second to realize it wasn't for me. "The sun rises and sets in you for that boy. He ain't never gonna look twice at another girl long as you're 'round. Austin's got big shoes to fill, and you ain't doin' nothin' but holdin' him back. He needs a good woman..."

I stared at my father. "A woman like Sarah?"

"There's nothing about cattle ranches you like. Think about it, Miranda. You gonna make him choose between you and the life he was born into? Lord knows you wouldn't make it a day as a rancher's wife. Where does that leave him?" To add insult to injury, he lobbed another grenade. "His parents don't want him to see you anymore."

My jaw hurt from grinding my teeth, and my head began to throb with the intensity of all that had taken place—or maybe it was the slap to the face. "And Sarah?" I pried.

"She don't want you around." He couldn't even look me in the eye when he said it. "And right now, I gotta do what's best for her recovery."

My mind swam with all he'd said, but it locked on my sister. "She told you that?"

His head bobbed, and he dropped his hand from in front of me, still holding the wad of cash. "She's got every right to be angry."

"Did she tell you she doesn't want me here?"

He ignored my question. "You'd be mad, too."

Maybe I needed to be clearer. "Did. She. Tell. You. That?"

He puffed his cheeks out, took a deep breath, and then blew it all out through his mouth. "She did."

"And you think I should go?" I could barely muster the words, much less the idea.

My dad leaned toward the dresser he'd cleared in his rage and set down the money he'd held in his hand. "There's a couple hundred dollars there."

He was a coward. The man had burst in here with an agenda, sent Austin away, and then pounced on me when I was vulnerable. I hadn't seen it coming, and I didn't have a clue what to do with it. But by God, if he wanted me to leave his house, he was going to have to tell me to do so. "Is that for a trip? Or a new life?"

"Whichever you decide to make it...as long as it doesn't bring you back to Mason Belle."

I stared at the bills he'd offered. I didn't even have a car or a job. That wouldn't get me anywhere. Questions dangled from the tip of my tongue, but my mind had shut down. I could see; I just no longer felt—I stood there, empty.

"There's a couple suitcases in the hall closet." His voice gathered my attention, but I found myself staring at his back. He didn't have the guts to face me. "I'll take you to Laredo when you're ready."

I listened for him to start down the stairs, and once I was certain he wasn't coming back, I sat on my mattress. The destruction around me represented everything I'd done to the people I loved. I didn't know if Mama had left because of me; although, I didn't find it hard to believe. It had never been a secret that I was a "surprise," I just never realized that might have been a codeword for an accident.

I bent over and picked up the frame that had broken in the storm. My finger started to bleed when I moved the shards of glass from Austin's face. The shot had been taken at his parents' Christmas party. His arms were wound around my waist, and his chin rested on my shoulder. It was my favorite image of the two of us. My dad was right. I was *it* for Austin Burin; he was *it* for me. And it might as well have been written on a banner in front of us; it was that obvious.

I pulled the paper from the back. The glass had scratched the image, but I still loved it. And after today, it would be the only thing I had to cling to. Maybe his parents knew better than we did. They lived the ranching life, and I hated it. I loved the land, but I wasn't cut out for the work. I'd never be in the kitchen before the rooster crowed, making meals for ranch hands. If I could have gotten out of it, I wouldn't have done any of the chores Daddy deemed my responsibility.

Austin and his brother would inherit their parents' farm. And while I'd always seen myself married to Austin and believed that, one day, my last name would be Burin, my vision never involved cattle ranching. Austin would tear himself in two trying to make me happy and please his parents, and that wasn't fair to anyone involved.

Between him and Sarah, I loved them both enough to go. It terrified me to think of braving the world alone. The two of them hating me scared me even more, and in the end, that was exactly what would happen if I stayed. Sarah wanted me gone, and Austin needed me gone.

I set the picture on the bed, gathered my clothes and stuff from the bathroom, and retrieved the suitcases from the hall. Daddy had managed to destroy any memento that I might have wanted to pack. There wasn't much left. I put the picture on top of my clothes and closed the lid. I stared at the blue plastic, wondering how my life had come to this when only a handful of weeks ago, I'd been on top of the world after graduation. The crack in the cheap case ran right up the middle. One hard whack and the plastic would split in two, just like me.

When I pulled it off the mattress, I noticed Austin's hat on the floor in the rubble. I picked it up and held it close to my nose. I'd miss that smell—him. I should have left it. Instead, I pulled my long hair through the hole in the back and put it on my head, bringing the bill low to shield my face. I stuffed my bank book and wallet into a purse. The money still sat where Daddy left it when I exited my bedroom.

My dad waited by the door with his keys in hand. He didn't look at me or offer to take the luggage. He simply walked out of the house and assumed I'd follow. I kept thinking he'd come to his senses, that he'd realize he had two children and kicking one out wouldn't fix the other. But he didn't say a word. I didn't know where he planned to drop me off or how he could just dump me in another city like a stray dog. Maybe the only way he could go through with it was to pretend I didn't exist.

An hour later, he stopped in front of the bus station in Laredo. There, at the curb, I wrapped my fingers around the handle and took one final look at the man who'd given me life, and now so cruelly took it away. "Daddy?" It was as much a prayer for forgiveness as it was his name.

His jaw ticced, and he held his stare out the windshield. I bit my bottom lip and nodded. No sooner had I closed the truck door than he pulled off. I stood there long after he had disappeared. My father had dumped me on a street corner and driven away.

Sweat trickled down my spine, and the humidity made it hard to breathe. I refused to admit that my lungs not working properly might have to do with the crushing blow I'd just been dealt. I didn't have a cell phone, but even if I had, I didn't know anyone who didn't live in Mason Belle.

There were no lifelines. No mulligans. No do-overs.

I'd picked a location as far away from Texas as I could get, and one that I thought would be the opposite from anything I'd ever known. Ultimately, I had narrowed it down to Los Angeles or New York City. In the end, I picked the one that took the longest to reach. It gave me more time to figure out a plan and more days on a bus, which saved money on hotels.

By the time I got into my seat, the day had exhausted me, and I couldn't keep my eyes open. I slept through the night and woke to a guy leaned on my shoulder, drooling. My effort to get him off gently proved fruitless, and I finally shook his arm. He woke slowly and, eventually, wiped the saliva from his mouth.

I offered him a polite smile, even though we hadn't exchanged any words. It was too much to ask to have an empty seat next to me. There was still hope that he wouldn't travel all the way to New York, though.

He extended his hand—the one he'd used to clean his lips—for me to shake. "I'm Garrett."

To avoid touching his germy palm, I tried to fidget with my hair. "Miranda. Nice to meet you." I still had on Austin's hat. I pulled it from my head, set it in my lap, and then took the tie out of my ponytail.

Garrett's eyes went wide. "You okay?" There was a lot of concern marring his green irises and perfect nose for someone who'd just met me.

Working my hair into a knot on top of my head, I secured the elastic to hold it in place and dropped my hands to the hat. "Yes. Are you?" My thumb would go numb if I didn't stop rubbing it in circles on the rough material.

"That's quite the shiner you got there." He pointed to my cheek, and then he glanced at my arm.

I followed him until I saw what he gaped at. My bicep was

clearly marked with purple fingerprints and what looked like rope burn. I couldn't imagine what my face must look like. I swallowed and covered the tender skin under my eye with my hand. All the while, Garrett continued to study me. I couldn't figure out if he believed I was a criminal or a flight risk. Although, I had no idea where he thought I'd escape to. I certainly couldn't get far on a bus, and hiding in the bathroom held little appeal.

Garrett reached toward my cheek, and when I flinched, he slowed his approach and purposefully kept his eyes on mine. Every instinct told me to bat him away. But not doing what I should was what had landed me on this bus, and I apparently had yet to learn that lesson. I searched his face for any indication that he might hurt me and found none. I lowered my hand, and he used the back of his fingers to softly caress what I had to assume was a large bruise that started above my eye socket and ran well beneath my cheekbone.

It was still early, and dawn had barely begun to break. The bus remained quiet with most of the passengers still asleep. I wanted to scream to bust up the silence. I needed noise, but my entire world had gone quiet with one argument. It wasn't possible to be more alone than I was at the moment, and it ate at me like a leech the longer Garrett observed me.

"Do you need help?" he whispered.

I appreciated the discretion. I shook my head, and he dropped his hand. I'd never been shy, yet suddenly, vulnerability snapped my mouth shut. I couldn't do anything other than wait for him to speak.

He angled his body toward me and leaned into the seat. I mirrored his movement as though we were close friends about to share secrets. "Are you going all the way to New York?"

I'd never done this. New people didn't come to Mason Belle, and I had never left. But Garrett forced out the silence that ate at me, so I went with it. "Yes. You?" For someone who never shut up, I wasn't much of a conversationalist this early.

"Yeah. I go to school in the city. NYU."

I could tell by the way he said it that I should know what NYU stood for and maybe even be impressed by his attendance. "What are you studying?" I assumed it was a safe question since it was a college.

"Law." Even I picked up on the displeasure in that response.

"Do you not like it?"

He shrugged against the seat. "I like the people and the city. I'm just not all that interested in the law program."

I didn't know anyone who'd gone to college or even planned to go. There were plenty of kids in Mason Belle smart enough; it just wasn't in our cards. Life in Southern Texas included cows and horses, not fancy universities and degrees. The closest we got to college was football on TV. "So why not do something else?"

"My parents don't think acting is a career."

I didn't follow, and I couldn't respond without admitting that.

Thankfully, he changed the subject. "What's waiting for you in the Big Apple? School? Modeling? Boyfriend?"

The last one stung more than the others. "Nothing. I don't know a soul there."

He chuckled. "Did you throw a dart at a map and decide to get on a bus?" He must have assumed my departure was related to the marks on my body. "Shit. I'm sorry. That was insensitive as hell."

"It's okay. It wasn't a planned move," I admitted.

He leaned forward and pulled a backpack from under the seat in front of him. I couldn't see what he was doing, but when he offered me a banana, I took it. I couldn't remember the last time I'd eaten, and my stomach growled at the sight of the bright-yellow peel.

"Thank you," I said as I pulled down the side.

He ate half of his piece of fruit in one bite, while I nibbled on mine. "Do you have a place to stay, a job, anything?"

It probably wasn't smart to admit. "No." For all I knew, he might be a serial killer, and I'd given him the go-ahead to maim me since no one would be waiting for me to arrive. I shrugged. "I'll figure it out."

Garrett's green eyes lit up. "I've got a buddy who needs a roommate. If you're interested, I could call him." He burst into unexplainable laughter and woke up everyone I could see from my spot by the window. "He's a good guy. I go to school with him."

"Why don't *you* live with him then?" My voice carried farther than intended, and a cranky man across the aisle shushed us both.

"I live on campus. He has an apartment. Eason's a class act. What do you say?"

I wasn't sure what to say. I didn't know the man making the proposition, much less the one he talked about. Living with a guy didn't hold a lot of appeal, yet neither did living on the street. I had some money my grandma had left me when she passed away, but I'd blow through it in no time if I weren't careful.

Garrett wasn't giving up on the idea. "He doesn't live far from the bus station. We can walk down there. I'll introduce you, and you can check the place out. If you're not interested, no hard feelings."

I nodded quickly before I chickened out. "Okay. That sounds fair."

Over the next forty-eight hours, Garrett told me every story he could recall where Eason McNabb made an appearance. By the time we had reached New York, I felt like I'd been friends with the guy—Eason, not Garrett—most of my life. So, when we got off the bus, I stopped in the restroom to freshen up as best I could. The bruises on my cheek had a halo of yellow around the blue and purple, but the swelling had subsided. I braided my hair down both sides and put Austin's Longhorns ballcap on. Ready or not, things were about to get real.

Garrett made good on his promise. We didn't walk. Instead, he hailed a taxi in the downpour that greeted us in the city. It might have only been a couple of blocks, although it seemed more like a few miles based on how long we sat in the back seat of the cab. I couldn't see anything we passed through the rain, and when we got out, Garrett tossed cash at the driver, and we raced to the entrance. We could be in New Jersey for all I knew.

Wide-eyed, I trailed behind Garrett. He stopped in front of a door and knocked. A deep yet mellow, masculine voice called out from the other side. My stomach flip-flopped in my belly while we waited for Eason to answer. It might have been nerves or possibly fear. All I could say for certain was that my breath caught when he appeared.

Austin had my heart, hands down. He was perfect in every way. This man—and he *was* a man—was the most beautiful thing I'd ever laid eyes on. From his stone-colored irises to his inky hair and all the way down to his bare feet, not a single flaw existed. This was a bad idea. A very bad idea.

Garrett stepped in front of me, and I expected he would go inside. He did not. He grabbed Eason's neck—or who I assumed to be Eason, since we hadn't been introduced—and laid a rather passionate kiss on his supple, pink lips. My jaw still hung slack when they broke apart.

Eason's mouth turned up into a smile too perfect not to have been painted on. "I missed you, too."

Garrett leaned in for one more peck, and then he popped me on the behind as he walked backward away from the door. "You two get to know each other," he said to me. Then he winked at Eason. "I'll call you about dinner."

Eason nodded. "I'm Eason McNabb. You must be Miranda."

Shock and awe. Those were the only words that came to mind, and I looked like an idiot.

"Garrett can be a little overwhelming. I'm definitely the more conservative one in the relationship." The affection in his tone slowed my erratic heartbeat. "Come on in."

16

AUSTIN

I'd expected her to call. After the things Miranda had admitted, I thought she'd use my number when she got up. The minutes and hours barely moved on the clock. Exhausted wasn't a good way to spend a day on a ranch. The work was physical, the sun was brutal, and I needed it to end. Hearing from Miranda would have broken up the monotony, and I'd hoped the two of us could sit down to talk.

The few hours of rest I'd had last night were spent mulling over every word she'd said. The things she had confessed brought on more questions than answers. I doubted I wanted the answers, but in the end, I'd need them. Since she hadn't called, it was clear, I would have to force the conversation. She needed to get her rental car from The Hut which gave me an excuse to be alone with her without making an issue out of it.

But when I got back to the barn, the only vehicles there were mine and Brock's. I'd successfully avoided him all day, and if I played my cards right, I'd get out unnoticed. I didn't have any information to give him about last night, since I didn't have a clue what was going on myself.

I knocked on the front door of the farmhouse and turned to

see if anyone was around. No one answered after I had knocked twice, so I let myself in. Miranda had consumed a lot of alcohol last night, so it was within the realm of possibility that she hadn't gotten out of bed—not even to answer the door.

"Hello?" I called out. Scaring the crap out of her or Jack wouldn't benefit anyone. "Hello?" I peeked into the kitchen. The lights were all off, and the house was quiet aside from my boots on the hardwoods. "Jack?" The stair creaked under the weight of my foot. "Miranda?" The hall on the second floor remained dim, the bedroom windows providing light that escaped through all the open doors.

The house was empty. I stood in the doorway with my fingers wrapped around the frame. The room appeared the way it had for years. Bereft—as if the space had mourned her loss like the rest of us. She'd taken all her belongings when she left Mason Belle. Not a single picture or trophy remained, just the furniture, curtains, and bedding. If I hadn't known she'd picked them out herself, they would be as anonymous as the room itself.

The bed was made. The room was clean. My heart pounded, and my breathing became shallow. Both were indications Miranda wasn't here. I raced in and threw open the closet door. Empty.

She'd left.

I'd been around all day. I had intentionally stayed close to the house in case she called. If I saw her, I had planned to offer to take her to get her car, even if it meant I had to work later into the afternoon. Yet somehow, she'd slipped by. Someone had to have seen her leave with a suitcase, and no one bothered to tell me.

I ran down the hall, then the steps, and out the front door. "Did you see her leave?" I half growled and half yelled at my best friend as I stormed toward my dually.

Brock leaned against his truck, and I could tell by the look on his face, he had something to say. "She left with Sarah." He crossed his arms, but his relaxed stance didn't change.

"It didn't dawn on you to tell me? Did you miss the suitcase in her hand?" I needed to reel this in.

"I saw them pull off. I didn't see her actually leave the house. What's the big deal?" He'd gone from casual to irritated in a couple of sentences. "You've wanted her gone since she got here." He pushed off the truck and stalked in my direction. "Your wish was granted."

My fingers were wrapped around the door handle that I was on the verge of yanking open when he grabbed my shoulder and spun me toward him.

"You've treated her like manure since she strolled into town. Did you expect any different?" Brock barked.

I took a step back to put some space between us. His current stance posed a physical threat that didn't sit well with me. "I didn't expect her to leave." Not after last night...although, I didn't tell him that part.

"What *did* you expect? You had every opportunity to convince her to stay. Instead of making her feel welcome, you fought with her and pushed her out of town."

"Where's this coming from? Why am I the bad guy?"

He huffed out a laugh and shook his head. "You're not. Everything you did was justifiable. I understand why you've been angry since she left. I get that she destroyed you. I was here for all that, remember? I've watched you suffer every day for years."

"Then you get it."

"Oh, I get *that* part. What I don't get is how you thought things would be any different. Most people don't bid a fond farewell to people who hate them."

But I didn't hate her. I hated what she did. I hated that she left me. I never hated *her*. "How long ago did they leave?" I didn't have time to debate any of this with Brock.

"A few hours ago, I guess."

I reached for the door handle, and the grip of his fingers digging into my shoulder again stopped me.

"Don't do something stupid, Austin."

I jerked away from him at the same time I opened the truck. I cranked the ignition, rolled down the window, and then glanced over my shoulder to make sure Brock wasn't in the way when I backed out. Every rock I passed over sent a jarring memory before my eyes. Randi turning up the radio. Randi singing any song that came through the speakers. Randi's Southern drawl. Her hair whipping around her face with the wind that came into the cab. The way her throat danced when she tossed her head back in laughter. Her lips. Her nose. The way her eyelids fluttered just before I made her come. It was all as real as if it were happening.

I pulled my cell out of my pocket and searched for my sister-in-law's name in my contacts. When I glanced up, I'd swerved into the other lane and jerked the wheel to get out of the path of an oncoming SUV. I hadn't heard his horn until I passed, and he shook his fist at me.

The phone connected on the second ring, but I didn't wait for her to acknowledge me. "Where is she?"

Sarah sighed on the other end. "Hey, Austin."

I didn't have time for formalities. "Did she leave?" My questions sounded as desperate as I felt.

"Yes." That was it. One word.

I slammed my fist onto the steering wheel. "Why'd you let her go?"

"Austin, you're scaring the kids. They're in the car, and they can hear everything you're saying. Can you calm down, please?"

If she'd answer my question, I would. I took a deep breath and started again in a less aggressive tone. "Why didn't you convince her to stay, Sarah?" If I had a third hand, I'd pull my hair.

"For what?"

It seemed everyone I knew was either stupid or didn't care. "Because this is her home."

Sarah ignored me and scolded the kids in the back seat. "She doesn't think so."

I couldn't understand Sarah's indifferent attitude. The topic of Miranda might not have been discussed with me directly, but that didn't mean I was oblivious to what went on. Sarah was married to my brother. Brothers talk, even when it's in circles and indirect. Our parents were friends. I worked for her dad. So just because Miranda's name hadn't been said to my face didn't mean I'd missed the implications. I'd simply chosen to ignore them instead of engaging.

"And you just let her go?"

"We talked first."

Jesus, this was like pulling teeth. I waited, thinking the silence would indicate that I wanted more information. When she didn't fill it, I did. "And?"

"Tell your daddy I'll be back in a little while. I'm going to run to Piggly Wiggly." The kids each told her goodbye in the background, and when the door shut, Sarah returned to our conversation. "And we're good."

She had to be kidding. "You're good?"

"Yeah."

"Then why did she leave?"

"Because her friends and her job are in New York."

This took me back to my childhood. Anytime Charlie and I had a secret and our parents questioned us, we'd only answer the question they asked. Neither of us would elaborate or provide any details. I'd thought it was funny then, but now it infuriated me to have it returned.

I'd always believed when the time came, when I got to face Miranda, that there'd be a line in the sand. She'd be on one side, and my friends, my family, and I would all be on the other. Yet, here I was, and one by one, each of those people had switched teams. "When does her flight leave?"

"Why are you doing this?" she asked.

Doing *this*. That was rather vague. I could give her the same short responses she'd given me, but it wouldn't help in the long run. I pulled into my driveway and sat there with the truck idling. "Did she tell you about last night?"

"No. She said she told you how she felt, that she and Eason aren't a couple, and that you weren't interested."

With the truck in park, I was able to remove my ballcap and pull my hair in frustration. "That's not true," I said through gritted teeth.

"She didn't tell you how she felt?"

I shook my head, not that Sarah could see me. "Yes, she did. I didn't tell her I wasn't interested. She was drunk. I took her home. She said a lot of things, and I didn't want to take advantage of her."

"And *that* led you to tell her you weren't interested?" Her confusion told me Miranda hadn't given her specifics, just a rough overview, if that much.

"No. I never said I wasn't interested. I took her home, tucked her in bed, and kissed her forehead. I left my number so she'd call me today. That wasn't a conversation to have when she'd been mainlining whiskey. I *tried* to do the right thing."

"I don't know what time her flight left. She wasn't in a hurry to get to the airport, but that was a couple of hours ago. Why don't you call her?"

That would be a great idea, except for one thing. "I don't have her number."

Sarah giggled, and I pulled my hair again. "Luckily for you, I do."

I jumped out of the truck and ran inside to find something to write it down with. It didn't dawn on me until after I'd hung up that I could have put Sarah on speaker and added it to my phone while she rattled it off. Not that it mattered. I had it, and I used it.

And it went straight to voicemail. Twice.

I debated driving to Laredo, hoping I reached her before her flight left. For all I knew, she was already thirty thousand feet in the air. Not to mention, I couldn't get past the security gate without a ticket.

Miranda had managed another escape.

But this time, I refused to let her run.

J'd made it this far without nerves taking over or second-guessing my trip, not even on the flight from hell where I swore the masks were going to fall out of the overhead compartment at any given moment. Oddly, I'd been most apprehensive over leaving my truck in an uncovered parking lot at the airport. Now, standing on Miranda and Eason's doorstep, I hesitated to lift my fist to knock.

For two days, I'd tried to reach Miranda, and for two days her phone went to voicemail, even after I assumed she'd gone back to work. That same lost feeling I'd experienced when she left the first time had returned, except this time, I wasn't willing to accept her decision as my fate. I didn't ask Sarah where she lived. I didn't talk to Jack about where I was going when I told him I needed a couple of days off. Not even my parents were aware I'd left the state. I made the choice to chase her, and no outside influence would alter my plans, so there was no point in discussing it.

It proved a tad difficult when I tried to find Miranda Adams in New York City...when I looked for her. Eason McNabb, on the other hand, had been quite easy to locate. He was a partner at what appeared to be a huge law practice in Manhattan, and the website for his firm listed all the employees, along with their cell phone numbers and email addresses. Miranda's number proved a dud in a reverse search on Google. Eason McNabb's was a gold mine. For the low price of nineteen ninety-five, I had access to his home address, date of birth, and family tree. Most importantly, I had found Miranda.

The element of surprise should work in my favor. If Miranda didn't know I was coming, then she couldn't hide or avoid me. I hadn't thought about the role Eason might play in my arrival. I wasn't dumb enough to believe that man couldn't throw his weight into a hearty punch that would pack a nasty blow. So, with my knuckles hovered in front of the wood, it occurred to me that while this whole thing might prove to be romantic, it wasn't terribly realistic. In the South, someone unexpectedly shows up at your door at night, you could anticipate being greeted by the barrel of a shotgun.

This didn't appear to be that type of neighborhood. In fact, if I didn't knock soon, I ran the risk of having the cops called on me for loitering. The more I looked around, the more suspicious I felt. So, I did what I came here to do.

I knocked.

And waited.

Maybe coming without an invitation wasn't the brightest move I'd ever made. I rapped one more time and finally heard a voice call out from the other side. The door swung open, and a groggy, sleepy-eyed Miranda leaned against the jamb. I tried to take in all of her at one time from her messy hair to her matching tank top and sleep shorts and down her toned legs to her bare feet, but she yawned and pulled my attention back to her face. I could stand here all day and bask in the sight of her, and that might be precisely what happened since she hadn't invited me in.

She reached up and tucked her hair behind her ear and then rubbed her eyes with her fingers, all while I waited. "Austin?" Gone was the haze of exhaustion, and in its place came startled recognition. *"What* are you doing here?" Miranda leaned out the door and glanced down the sidewalk, as if she expected someone else.

I took off my baseball hat with one hand and raked the other through my hair. I didn't claim to be poetic or even to have the right words at the appropriate times, and it had never been more obvious than it was at this second. I bent the bill back and forth in an attempt to expend some of the anxiety that coursed through my veins. It didn't work, and I'd likely destroyed my favorite hat in the process. "I came to see you." *Obviously.*

"From Texas?"

At this point, I wasn't sure where else she thought I might have been. "Yeah." I should write love songs as eloquent as I'd become in the last thirty seconds.

"Why?" That was never the reception a man wanted to receive from a woman when he showed up at her door, much less when he'd flown across the country to do so.

All the rehearsal on the plane had gone straight out the window the moment her door opened. "Because you left."

She rolled her eyes. "If you came all this way to fight, you could have saved yourself a trip. I don't have it in me to argue with you." I didn't miss her fingers curling into a ball at her side, or the way they seemed to clench and release.

"Can I come in?" It was a beautiful neighborhood, although seeing it from the front stoop wasn't ideal, and this conversation wasn't going to happen with her door half open.

Miranda sighed, contorted her lips into something akin to resignation, and she stepped back to wave me in. I almost asked her if I should take off my shoes when I saw the massive rug in the foyer, but when she started moving, I was afraid I'd get lost if I didn't follow. Their house was nothing like anything that existed in Mason Belle. From the colors on the walls to the drapes and rugs, every inch screamed wealth. Surprisingly, it was also warm and comfortable.

Miranda led me into the living room where she tossed her body onto the couch and pulled a worn blanket over her lap. The television and visible sound equipment were every man's dream, but since I wasn't here to ogle Eason's electronics, I took a seat on the sofa next to her.

"Did I wake you?" I already knew the answer. I was just trying to ease into a conversation.

She stared at me blankly then blinked and said, "Yes." She had no intention of making this easy.

"Is Eason here?"

"No."

If I continued to ask yes or no questions, I would continue to get one-word responses. I wanted to dive in and tell her why I'd shown up unannounced. But my eyes flicked to hers, and her lids had narrowed a hint, and her jaw tensed as she ground her teeth. The fight I'd expected to experience back home and hadn't seen, now marked her features. The tides had turned. Her confidence shone through in full force since she was comfortable here, at ease.

Miranda had decided to take control in the midst of my assessing the situation. "Why are you here?"

"Because we need to talk."

She folded her arms and kept her expression clear. I couldn't read anything in her eyes, her posture, or her words. "I said what I had to say."

"Then I guess you need to listen." There was no malice in my tone, and I remained as relaxed as I could under the circumstances. I situated myself on the sofa. The velvety feel of the material under my palm and the softness of the cushions under my ass and thighs almost stole my focus, so I regrouped as I leaned against the arm. "You dumped a lot of emotion at my feet on Friday—"

"And you ignored all of it."

"That's not fair." I bit the inside of my cheek. Fighting wouldn't get us any closer to resolution. "I heard every word you said. I wanted to respond. I wanted to react. What I didn't want was for you to wake up the next morning with regret."

Her eyes left mine and drifted off to something across the room. "Ironic."

We weren't going to get anywhere if there were walls between us. I'd torn mine down between Friday night and now. It was time for Miranda to expose herself, too. "Maybe." My voice was almost a whisper when I leaned toward her. Taking her chin between my thumb and finger, I encouraged her not to just see me, but I needed her heart to hear me. "I wanted to be certain that when I told you that I still loved you, there wouldn't be a second of it you couldn't remember because the whiskey blocked it out."

Her jaw went slack, and her eyes widened. Neither of those gave me what I needed to proceed. When her bottom lip trembled, I felt it in my fingers, and when her pupils dilated, that was the moment I had her on my side of her defenses. She was vulnerable, and I struck with a thunderous roar.

"And Randi, I *do* still love you." I gave that a second to sink in. "There hasn't been a day that's passed since you left Texas that I haven't wanted you back, regardless of how angry I was." *Then and now.* Although, I left that part off. I figure it was implied.

She shook her head, and I dropped my hand to my lap. "Then why were you so mean?"

It was time to play my hand, and I hoped like hell I still held my queen of hearts. "You want brutal honesty?"

"Seems kind of silly to have come all this way and give me anything else."

"Because part of me wanted you to hurt the way I had." It was immature but truthful. I closed my eyes for a moment and took a deep breath. Admitting what I had experienced after she left would be almost as painful as the reality of living it. "When you ran off, I had no idea what happened. Your dad wouldn't say anything. Sarah didn't know anything. And all I could do was wonder if you were safe, coming back, dead, upset. You disappearing blindsided me, and it nearly destroyed me."

She cocked her head to the side like she wanted to say something, so I paused to let her. "My dad didn't tell you what happened?" It wasn't surprise that lined her face. She appeared completely dumbfounded when I shook my head. "What about Sarah? He never told her?"

"If he did, Sarah never told me." It didn't take a lot of effort to recall those times. They haunted me with vigor. "I went to the ranch every day, hoping you'd come home. I spent hours there. For weeks, which turned into months and eventually years."

Randi pulled her knees to her chest under the thin blanket and squeezed her shins. "Why?"

It wasn't rational, and looking back, it now seemed stupid. "If you showed up, I wanted to be there. I needed to make certain you saw that I'd been faithful. I'd been loyal. I'd taken care of the things you loved when you couldn't." It sounded even more ludicrous when I said it out loud than it did in my head. "Because if you ever came home, I needed you to see I'd done my best to keep my promise to you, and that I'd waited for you."

"And I never came." She murmured the sentiment more to herself than for me to hear.

"Six years is a long time to be faithful to someone who's absent and chose to leave. But I was, one hundred percent. My heart has belonged to you since we were kids, and it will until the day I die, regardless of whether we're together."

"I didn't choose to leave, Austin." Her pitch rose, as did the decibel level of her voice. Color tinged her cheeks, and it hit me that her truth might be as painful as my own. "All these years, you thought I left Mason Belle because I *wanted* to?" She stretched her legs out and tossed the blanket aside. In no time, she stood and began pacing the room. "He's let everyone in town believe I walked away? Not that he sent me away?"

I shrugged, but she had her back to me and missed it. It was probably for the best because she didn't actually want an answer, Randi needed to unload. Tears hung from her jaw when she faced me. "He attacked me after you left that morning."

Jack had been on edge after the accident. Finding his daughter in bed with her boyfriend wouldn't please any father, much less one dealing with all he had been going through.

"I don't mean he yelled at me. He destroyed my room and everything I owned. He grabbed me. Hit me. Called me names—"

I saw red. That was the last day I had seen Randi, and I had all but refused to leave her. I'd seen it in his eyes, even though I couldn't identify it at the time. "Why didn't you call me?" I wondered if the pain of reliving these events would ever go away, if there would ever be a day where we forgot them.

She sat on the edge of the coffee table close to me. The temptation to reach out and take her hands nearly took over. If she needed a tether, she'd grab one. I shifted on the couch to face her. With my legs spread and my elbows on my knees, my hands dangled within her reach. Randi didn't take them. Her shoulders slumped, she bowed her head, and her body shook when she began to sob.

I couldn't take it. Every tear that fell, every shuttered breath she took, they each hit me with the force of a train. "Randi." I whispered her name, trying to bring her back to me.

The sight of her bloodshot eyes and soaked cheeks when she lifted her chin were nothing compared to the agony that ripped through her chest and out of her mouth. For the second time in her life, I bared witness to the betrayal of one of her parents, and it was like we were ten again. Except there wasn't a pasture to hide in, and we weren't kids.

At the point she spoke, I'd forgotten the question I'd asked. And with each word that came out of her mouth, I understood a little more of the guilt Jack had carried over the years. His affection for me, giving me the ranch, it all made more sense. He knew I could bring her home because he knew she had never wanted to leave. My parents had adored Randi. My mom had daydreamed about our wedding like Miranda was her daughter. I didn't know where Jack had gotten his information from, but it wasn't Jessica Burin.

Randi cupped my jaw and waited for the rage to simmer. And my heart broke when she conceded to her father's deception. "Don't you see? He was right."

I sprung up from where I sat on the couch, towering over her. "No. I don't see. What about any of that trash holds any validity?" I realized my stance intimidated her when she bit her lip. I had too much adrenaline racing through me to sit, but I didn't want her to shut down, either.

"You needed a spouse, one like Sarah or your mom, not one like me. I wasn't built to be a farmer's wife."

She was dead serious, and I couldn't stop the rumble that started in my chest. The laughter that exploded from my mouth scared her. "Then I wasn't built to be a farmer. Because, sweetheart, no one else will ever meet me at the end of an aisle, much less carry my last name."

We'd lost six years because her father made choices for us, and then we hadn't bothered to communicate. Then I'd spent the last three weeks making her life miserable because I didn't know the truth. As much as I wanted to place the blame on her over the years, after hearing what she had gone through that day after I left, I had to admit it was as much my fault as hers. I hadn't chased her, I didn't try to locate her, and even when Sarah had found her, I did nothing.

I sat on the couch and pulled her with me as I went. She

didn't put up much of a fight, not that she would have won, anyhow. Randi landed in my lap, and I wrapped myself around her. Her arms were chilly, but her breath was warm. She shook like a leaf until she relented and put her head on my shoulder. Emotionally, she was spent, and I,wasn't in much better shape. I needed to give her some space; unfortunately, I didn't come here to let her go. Even with the stress of everything I'd learned since I walked through her front door, holding her had never been as right as it was in that moment.

There was nothing we could do to change the past; I just needed to grasp the future. I reached for the blanket on the opposite side of the couch to cover her and leaned back with her safely pressed against my chest. The scent of mint filled my nostrils when I pressed a kiss to her forehead. I hadn't expected her to peer up at me or for her to say anything.

"When do you have to go back?"

Regret stained her eyes where I longed to see hope. She still hadn't figured out why I'd come. "How long will it take you to pack?" We had a lot to figure out, and I didn't know where Jack stood on all this. I'd been allowed to believe lies for years by a man I trusted, but maybe he needed to find a way to make his own amends and believed I would be the catalyst. I didn't know.

Cold air seeped between us when she pulled away, and the blanket fell from her arms. "Austin, I can't go back." She believed that. "There's nothing for me in Texas." That was where she was wrong.

"There's me."

*W*e had talked late into the night. I didn't know where her roommate was, but I was glad he hadn't interrupted. Eason would throw a monkey wrench into any progress I made once she realized she hadn't factored him into the equation. By the time she had convinced me to spend the night, I didn't have a commitment from her to come home with me. She had, however, admitted that she wanted to be together. If that meant I needed to sell my house in Mason Belle and relocate to New York, then I'd do what I had to do. Life without Randi was no longer an option.

She held my hand and led me down a dark hallway and up a flight of stairs. Randi didn't bother flicking on a light until we stepped into her room. Her life had changed drastically while she'd been in New York. Her family had money by Mason Belle standards—at least they had while she lived there—but she lived in luxury here. Her bedroom was the size of my den and kitchen combined, her king-sized bed overflowed with pillows, and while I didn't know much about fabric, I was fairly certain her drapes were some sort of silk. Her open closet door revealed racks of shoes and clothes, and from where I stood, she had enough purses to open her own boutique.

I continued to browse the space—it felt like window shopping in a department store. The few pictures on her dresser were of Eason, Miranda—Randi didn't make an appearance in any of them—and a guy I didn't know and she hadn't mentioned. It was easy to see that both men cared deeply for her just by the way they looked at her and held her close in each shot. I didn't want to be jealous that they'd had her for years, although the emotion still pricked at my heart...until I reached her nightstand.

The frame had changed, and there were random scratches and creases on the picture itself. I picked it up and stared at it. I'd never seen a woman as beautiful as Randi. When I'd picked her up that night, I'd choked on my own saliva as she came down the stairs. I loved seeing her in red, and she'd gone all out for my parents' Christmas party. That picture captured *us*.

"My dad broke the frame you gave me." It—the photo

included—had been a gift on New Year's. My mom had taken it, and as soon as I saw it in the stack of pictures, I had insisted on a copy to give to Randi. "It was one of the only things I took with me the day he kicked me out. Well, other than my clothes." She stood next to me as she talked.

I didn't have to see her face to hear the fondness in her voice. She'd kept a crummy picture on her nightstand, and I had to assume it had been there as long as she'd been in the city. "I can't believe you kept it."

She peered up at me, and her eyes sparkled. It might have been the light that reflected in them, but I chose to believe it was Randi coming back to life. "If you think that's bad, wait 'til you see this."

Randi's shorts had ridden up on her waist, exposing the crease between her butt and thighs. With each step she took across the room, I remembered the feel of her legs wrapped around me and that perfect ass in my hands. My dick twitched, and I realized Randi wasn't the only one coming back to life. She disappeared into her closet and took my fantasy with her.

She reemerged with a dingy, orange ballcap on. The same one I'd lost around the time she'd left. "Remember this?" Her smile was radiant, and if I hadn't been thinking about her naked before she put my hat on, I would have been now.

I closed the distance between us and stopped once I could put my hands on her hips. "Where did you get that?" It hadn't weathered the storm well. I didn't remember it being so beaten up. I'd gotten it for Christmas that year.

"You left it in my room that day. When I packed, the picture and the hat were all I took." She pulled it off her head and turned it over to look at it. "It's seen better days. I wear it a lot."

"You wear it a lot." My girl was still in there. It might take me a while to find her Southern drawl, and her hair would grow in time, but the grit I loved about her hadn't disappeared, she'd just hidden it.

I hadn't let go of her when she twisted at the waist and tossed it Frisbee style into the closet. "Yep. It's my favorite."

"It's your favorite."

She giggled, a sound so pure I imagined angels sang. "Are you going to repeat everything I say?"

"I'm at a loss for words."

Her eyes fluttered, and a blush crept across her cheeks. "Good, I wasn't interested in talking."

Randi didn't give me time to ask another question. She kicked her door shut and reached for the hem of my shirt. I helped her remove it and dropped it to the floor. The same smirk that seized her lips any time she got me naked in high school made an unexpected appearance, coupled with what I presumed to be shock.

"What?" I asked.

Her gaze traveled from my shoulders to my jeans and back. "You've just... You've grown up."

I'd put on weight since we graduated, and I spent a lot of time in the sun, working. I never thought much about having filled out, but I guess I had. "I do a good bit of physical labor."

She held my eyes while her fingers worked the button on my jeans. "It shows." Clearly, she wasn't disappointed in the changes. After Randi released my zipper, she traced the muscles in my stomach, sending a chill up my spine. For someone who hadn't been with anyone else, she'd mastered the art of anticipation.

I moaned when the warmth of her palms spread over my chest and her hands rounded my shoulders. Her lips shined and begged to be kissed, and every part of me ached to take them—and her. Bent at the waist, I tilted my head to capture her mouth, and her nails dug into my flesh. I didn't know which of us had deepened the kiss, nor did I care. Her tongue massaged mine, and she tasted like honey. A sin so sweet I could dine on it for eternity.

My hands slipped under her tank top and eased up the curves of her sides and over each rib until the swell of her breasts and the intoxication of her touch nearly had me undone. I ran my thumbs over her taut nipples and cupped her mounds. She was as soft as a rose petal, and I wanted to bathe in the sensation—skin on skin. Six years was a long time, but our bodies remembered everything our brains had tried to forget.

She didn't resist when I took her shirt over her head, and she didn't pull away when I hooked my fingers in her shorts and panties to ease them down her thighs. As much as I wanted to drown in the sight of having Randi Adams naked in front of me, I wanted to lose myself *in* her even more. And she knew it.

I stifled my complaint when she broke away and moved toward the door. I'd been too enthralled in the sway of her bare hips and the lean lines of her spine and legs to move. But when she turned off the light, I didn't wait for her to come back. I took it upon myself to push the twelve tons of pillows onto the floor on the opposite side of the bed and pulled the blankets back. By the time she'd joined me on the mattress, my eyes had adjusted to the dark, and the moon peeked through the gap in the curtains.

Her head rested on her bent arm. She was on her side, and I was on mine, facing her.

This would change everything between us.

I wasn't foolish enough to believe it would solve anything, but it didn't stop my desperate need for us to connect. Our fate had been sealed years ago; tonight, we got to remind ourselves of just how sweet that destiny could be.

It wasn't until we became one that I finally understood that our journey was more important than our destination.

17

MIRANDA

*I*t took me a moment to recognize the arms wrapped around me and realize the heat behind me wasn't a blazing inferno I needed to escape before the house burned to the ground. In the haze of waking, last night was more like a dream than reality, and his embrace reminded me that life didn't always follow an expected path.

I wiggled free without rousing him and rolled to my side. As soon as I did, I regretted losing the comfort that being close to him provided. Although, the view made up for the loss of contact. Austin's disheveled hair gave him a boyish appeal in direct contrast to the maturity that age had given his body. My heart swelled, knowing I could think about him and not feel like a dagger had pierced my chest. He had the capacity to forgive, and despite the unknowns, that trait had the power to heal. Couple it with devotion and love, and somehow, we would get through this together.

Austin stirred in front of me, and my picture of perfection came to life when he moved. His biceps strained under his skin as he stretched, and every well-defined ab made an appearance when his stomach constricted. I hadn't meant to groan, but when a dry spell had gone on as long as mine had, it was hard to stare at the only person I ever cared to have scratch that itch without acting.

His warm-brown eyes peered through tiny slits, and a lazy smile turned up his lips. "Mornin'." That lazy Southern drawl sent heat between my legs, and I pressed my thighs together to relieve the pressure.

"Good morning," I cooed.

God, he was beautiful. I'd made it without him for six years, and yet lying here next to him, I couldn't imagine enduring another day. The idea of him going back to Texas left a weight pressed against my ribs that made it difficult to breathe if I thought about it too long. And that led into the logistics of how we could ever make this work. And the high I'd started the morning with faded when Austin smiled.

He propped his head in his hand. "What just happened?"

The tears started before I could stop them, and I'd become a bumbling mess of incoherent thoughts and words.

Austin propped himself against the pillows on the headboard and pulled me between his thighs. With my back to his, he dipped his face next to my ear and draped his arms around me. "What are the tears for?" The words were a whisper of concern and sentiment of love. The tips of his fingers ran the length of my forearms, calming my anxiety. "Talk to me." Austin had always had a gentle soul, and that hadn't changed.

I sniffled and composed myself enough to be able to communicate everything that ran through my head. "I don't know how this will work, and I can't bring myself to say goodbye."

"Goodbye isn't an option." He paused, and the soft strokes of his hands kept me from getting irrational. "Do you remember the day your dad told you that your mom wasn't coming back?" It was an odd thing to bring up given the topic at hand, but I nodded.

"Do you remember the promise I made to you that day in the pasture?"

Of course, I did. I hadn't comprehended the weight of that commitment as a child, but I certainly did once we got older. "Yeah." He'd held fast to that every day until I got on that bus.

"Give me the chance to prove to you that I won't let you down. Let me protect you." There was no sign of the frustration I expected to hear. "Randi"—the sound of that nickname parting his lips in love healed a broken part of me—"sweetheart, it's time to come home."

I needed to believe that. Everything in me told me to trust him. But my rational side doubted his ability to heal relationships he hadn't broken. He couldn't control the way I would be received in Mason Belle or how my father kept me at arm's length. I could deal with the Charitys of the world; I couldn't handle the distance that remained between Daddy and me. Sarah would welcome me, Rand had my back in the best way a three-year-old could. Brock might not have thought I picked up on his emotional struggle at The Hut when he faced defending me to his wife, but even drunk, I'd seen the sorrow in his eyes. He'd come around. And while I hadn't seen Charlie when I was home, I had no doubt that he would follow Austin and Sarah's lead. That only left Austin's parents and Daddy. And all three were deal breakers.

His chest was firm behind me when I leaned back and lay my head on his shoulder. Austin's hands hadn't stopped tracing patterns on my skin, and his touch held a magical power to calm my deepest fears. The only problem was, this didn't affect just me. He had relationships with those three people as well, relationships he cherished and depended on.

I hadn't given him the chance to provide me with options six years ago, and if I wanted this to work, that meant I had to give him that opportunity now. The only way to do that was brutal honesty. "I want to, Austin..."

"But?"

"I can't come between your parents and you, and I don't think my dad will ever forgive me for my role in what happened to Sarah." I shook my head. I hated to remember the look on his face when he tore apart my room or the rage and disgust that poured from him as he screamed at me. "He didn't even hug me when I left last weekend. His feelings for me haven't changed."

Austin pressed his lips below my ear and nibbled at my skin. The heat of his breath broke my focus, and I melted into him. He played me like a fiddle until I was putty in his hands. "My parents are not an issue. And Jack wants you home." He teased my stomach with feather-like touches and peppered my neck with kisses.

"You sure are confident for a man who hadn't mentioned my name in six years."

He pulled back and stared at me with confusion, and I angled my face so he'd see my raised brow.

"Sarah might have mentioned it," I confessed with a shrug.

He grinned. "We can talk about Sarah's big mouth later."

I chuckled and relaxed against him.

"The issue at hand is your dad. And I can tell you with absolute certainty that while he might not have a clue how to go about mending fences, he wants to."

I shuffled between his thighs to face him. There was no real room for me to sit cross-legged, so I put my feet over his legs and rested them on the mattress at his sides. To my knowledge, Austin had never lied to me, but I had seen him twist the truth with other people. His nose would scrunch, and he'd scratch his ear. I'd only be able to see his tells if I could see him. I didn't prepare myself for his naked chest or how badly my body ached to touch his.

Austin laughed, and it came from his belly. Each chortle caused his muscles to flex and me to inwardly groan. Sexual frustration was a bitch. "You have a horrible poker face, Randi."

I rolled my eyes and ignored that comment. "Tell me how you can be so sure Daddy wants me home."

The laughter died, although his smile did not. "That's why he gave me the ranch."

"What?" He was close enough that I didn't need to raise my voice; it was just my natural response to shock.

He cupped my jaw and stole the air from my lungs with one kiss. "It didn't make any sense to me at the time, and honestly, I thought the smoke had done damage to his brain that the doctors had missed." I loved when he winked. "Now, I get it. You love Cross Acres, and I love you. Jack knew you'd never come back as long as it was his, but if it were mine, he was convinced I'd make it your home."

Someone needed to have Daddy's mental faculties checked out. That was farfetched, even for a dreamer who loved romance. He wasn't old enough to be senile, but Austin might be onto something with the smoke damage.

He lifted my fingers to his mouth and kissed my knuckles while holding my gaze. "Please trust me."

Austin had never been able to tell me no, and it seemed the tides had turned. Despite my hesitation, the idea of a day without him hurt worse than facing the demons of my past. Daddy included. "Okay," I whispered.

"Okay?" He appeared more surprised by my answer than I was.

I nodded and shrugged. "I trust you. But...you have to be the one to tell Eason." I couldn't keep a straight face.

My head fell back when I laughed. Thinking about Austin asking Eason for permission tickled me until I was giddy.

He poked his fingers into my ribs and trapped me between his legs, preventing any movement on my part. "You think that's funny?"

I did, but my joy didn't just come from Austin messing with

me or me kidding with him. It was that coupled with love, hope, forgiveness, and healing. My past, my present, and my future all had the chance at converging into a place that I'd be more than just content. It would be the best life could offer.

Austin grabbed my hips, and he lifted me into his lap. With my knees at his sides, straddling his waist, he cradled my butt in his hands. "I promise, I'll take care of you."

*E*very inch of my body coiled, and each step I took required more effort than the last. I'd left Austin to explore New York—well, the bagel shop at the corner—while I went to have a conversation with my best friend and boss. My stiletto-clad foot slipped on the marble floors in the lobby, and an older gentleman kindly prevented my fall. Heat rose in my cheeks, and embarrassment gripped what little hold I had on reality.

"Don't worry, sweetheart. Happens to me all the time." He lifted his hand, and a nervous giggle passed my lips. Even at his age, he was spry, and I found humor in the cane he showed off with pride. I wondered if women found that attractive later in life, although I didn't ask.

Instead, I patted his hand and thanked him.

He then shooed off my apology. "A girl as pretty as you, the pleasure was all mine." Yeah, this guy definitely played the geriatric field.

The man straightened his suit jacket, tipped his cane to the up arrow, and then pressed the button to call the car. I half expected him to bow before he excused himself. I imagined Eason at his age and giggled at how he'd work the ladies and the men.

The ride to my floor ended as quickly as it had started. It left me no time to collect myself when the doors parted. Rachel greeted me with her usual exuberance and welcomed me back.

The phones ringing, the murmur of voices, and the shuffle of paper reminded me that life here wouldn't stop without my presence. It hadn't in the weeks I'd been gone, and it wouldn't in the future. Eason could replace me as a paralegal, and moving to Texas didn't mean our friendship had to end.

I'd miss the people I'd worked with, but there was nothing to keep me from visiting. And while I didn't have a contingency plan if things didn't work out with Austin, I was confident Eason would always have a place for me. Even still, I dreaded the conversation about to take place. My focus remained on the door at the end of the hall. I passed my own without so much as a sideways glance. The click of my heels matched the thump of my heart, and when I crossed into his office, it went from a steady rhythm to a thunderous roll.

His secretary's desk sat empty. I'd hoped for a distraction or even a deterrent. This was silly; Eason was my best friend. There was no need to be nervous, so I squared my shoulders and lifted my chin with confidence. My knock brought his answer, and I entered. I hadn't planned to talk to two partners, but now I wouldn't have to track Garrett down to rehash the same story.

Eason stood from behind his ornate desk, and a blistering smile lit up his masculine features. "Hey, gorgeous. Glad to have you back." He rounded the corner and met me in the middle of his office where he rocked me back and forth in a mammoth hug.

"Let her go before you cut off her air supply."

I wiggled to lean around Eason and let my tongue hang out of the side of my mouth as if I were being squeezed to death in my confinement. "Help me," I mouthed.

He turned his back to me, adjusted himself in the chair, and said, "You're on your own." Garrett's laid-back personality hadn't changed with age or his relationship with Eason. They were the yin to each other's yang.

"I'll remember that the next time you need a tie-breaking vote and I'm the decisionmaker," I teased.

My palms landed on Eason's chest. I'd never figured out what his dress shirts were made of. They looked like linen and felt like satin under my fingertips when I pushed him back. "Isn't this sexual harassment in the workplace? Let me go."

Garrett ignored my plea for freedom, still focused on losing the majority vote in our next family squabble. "Your loyalty should be to me." He stared out the window, and while I couldn't see his face, I could tell by his tone he was on the verge of pouting. "I've known you the longest."

"You're also the biggest pain in her ass." Eason motioned for me to take the seat next to Garrett, and he returned to his own. "I don't think that tips the chips in your favor."

Garrett dropped his foot to the floor with a thud and leaned forward with his forearms on his knees. "Come to think of it, you both owe me. Without my charm and wit, and ability to spot a damsel in distress, neither of you would have met. So, by my estimation, you"—he glanced at Eason and then me—"and you have me to thank for years of beautiful friendship."

When it came to Garrett and his rationale, there was little I could do other than smile. He could argue with a lamp post and have a judge uphold the verdict when he took the inanimate object to court. It made him an incredible lawyer. It also made him an entertaining friend.

"I'm sorry I wasn't home when your plane got in." Eason made no attempt at a subtle shift in the conversation.

Garrett laced his fingers behind his head and relaxed next to me. "I'm not. The Hamptons were fabulous."

If I'd had anything other than my purse to throw at him, I would have launched it at his head. The weight of my handbag might do actual damage. "You're such a jerk." He wasn't; I just liked that he played the part. That trait made my fictional, office romance with Eason easy to believe, and it distracted from the fact that two of the partners were partners in more ways than one—a well-kept secret they'd both shared for as long as I'd known them.

In a city like New York where people were free to be whomever they were designed to be, I hated admitting there were still those who could twist love—regardless of the couples' gender —into a reason for hate. Unfortunately, Eason's parents were old school and narrowminded, and Garrett's were Southern and ignorant, leaving both men to hide their relationship. I worried what my departure would do to them without me as a buffer with their families and here at work.

"Miranda?" Garrett waved his hand in front of my face. "Where'd you go?"

I hadn't realized I'd gotten lost in thought and missed whatever they'd said. "Sorry." Sitting here and dragging this out wouldn't change the outcome. "I need to talk to you."

Garrett perked up, excited to be included in what he presumed to be a proverbial "you." "Me too?"

"Sure, why not? I'm going to have to tell you, anyhow."

Garrett scowled, and Eason grinned. I narrowed my eyes at Eason. He wasn't making this any easier by keeping Garrett riled up. Eason raised his hands, pulled an invisible zipper across his lips, and tossed away the key.

Garrett crossed his legs, angled his body toward me, and gave me his undivided attention. His bare ankles peeked out from under the hem on his slacks. For someone who'd been in the Hamptons, his legs hadn't gotten any color. "Did you not do your laundry?"

Eason leaned over his desk and shook his head, although he didn't seem the least bit surprised.

"I'm not a fan of socks." He bounced his foot, drawing more attention to his blinding-white legs. "So, what did you want to talk about?"

My palms were wet with sweat, and my mouth was dry. No matter how many times I adjusted my position in the chair, I couldn't get comfortable. "I-I, umm..." I needed to spit it out. "Austin..." Nothing came together in a coherent thought or intelligible sentence. "When I was in Texas..." I had started and stopped so many times I wasn't sure what I even came here to say.

Thick lines of concern marred Eason's brow. "Did something happen after I left?" His normal baritone dropped into a deep bass, and the smooth tone turned dark.

The incident at The Hut didn't bear repeating, and he'd witnessed Austin's interaction with me, so there was no need to regurgitate that information for Garrett. Eason had likely already filled him in, anyhow. "Austin flew into town last night."

"Okay..." Eason let that word hang in the air, and Garrett looked like he wanted a bucket of popcorn for the show he anticipated.

I stared into a sea of stormy grey and prayed the next sentence out of my mouth didn't hurt the one friend who'd been there when life had given me nothing other than lemons. It was hard to make lemonade without sugar. "I need to put in my notice."

Garrett's jaw dropped; unfortunately, he hadn't been stunned into silence. Quite the opposite. "You're resigning? Do you plan to move back to Texas? You haven't even seen these people in years, and now you're going to uproot your life to go back to the sticks? Are you insane?"

"Garrett!" Eason's voice boomed. The open door didn't lend any privacy, and I was certain that Eason didn't care for the entire office to get a play by play. Once he'd successfully quieted his boyfriend, he returned his attention to me, and his expression softened. "Are you sure this is what you want to do?"

I bit into my bottom lip and nodded. "Yes."

"I'm proud of you." Not the reaction I had expected. "When are you leaving?"

I hadn't wanted to hurt him, but I hadn't thought he'd push me out the door, either. I expelled a bit of nervous laughter. "Sounds like you've already got my position filled and my bedroom rented."

"Nah, Garrett hasn't been allowed to take any more solo road trips since he returned with you. And I've banned him from all travel by bus. I'm too old for more strays."

My feelings shouldn't be hurt. Nevertheless, they were. It didn't matter that he wasn't *my* man, he was *a* man, and every woman needed the men in her life to fight for her, not open the door and push her out. And his attempt at being cute didn't soften the blow.

"Miranda, I'm kidding." He got up and came around the desk. Eason leaned against the wood and crossed his ankles. When he gripped the edge so tightly that his knuckles lost their color, I recognized that this wasn't any easier for him than it was for me. He simply attempted not to make it harder. "I've been trying for years to get you to reconcile with your family. I didn't expect that Austin would be part of that, but really, I'm not surprised. I've got motormouth over there to keep me company"—Garrett's attempt at an objection was overruled—"and I want you to be happy. New York was never a permanent gig for you." He'd tried to tell me that for years.

"You're not mad?"

The corners of Eason's mouth turned down when he shook his head. "Of course not. I've always wanted to buy a house in south Texas." He winked, yet I wasn't certain he was kidding.

Garrett interjected, "You're on your own, McNabb. I'm not interested in mosquitos and the smell of manure. I got enough of that growing up." It was easy to forget that Garrett had grown up an hour down the road from Mason Belle since he never went back, either.

Eason ignored him. "Miles between friends just mean more

phone calls and vacation time. I'm good with both." He appeared to be finished, and then he added in one final point. "But if you need me—here or there—don't hesitate. I'll be at your side without question."

The four-day drive back to Mason Belle turned into seven. Austin and I used the time to catch up; although, not a lot had gone on in either of our lives. Our greatest sticking point had been my relationship with Eason. It took a FaceTime call to him and Garrett to get Austin to relax about the security of our friendships. By the time we'd hung up, Garrett had Austin howling with laughter and Eason shaking his head in the background. Austin and Eason would need to get to know each other, and that could happen over time. For now, they seemed to appreciate what the other brought to my life and left the mutual understanding at that.

After stopping at the airport to pick up his truck, we arrived at Austin's house before lunch, and he'd insisted we go inside to eat before he went to Cross Acres. Unable to convince him that food and a nervous stomach didn't make a happy union, I gave in. It dawned on me that it wasn't his refrigerator he wanted to show off. Austin was proud of the two-story ranch that he'd made a home. As hard as I tried to give him my undivided attention, I simply couldn't focus on bedrooms and bathrooms.

I stared out the window in the kitchen to the pasture behind his house, trying to calm my anxious heart. Deep breaths did little to ease the nervous tension being in Mason Belle brought, but there was peace in acres of pastures. The fields went on for miles, and I wondered if our children would grow up here. My entire body stiffened when Austin rested his chin on my shoulder, and then I relaxed when he pulled me against his chest.

He kissed my cheek and whispered into my ear. "What are you thinking about?"

The puffs of white clouds floated across the blue, Texas sky, and I grinned. Not all my memories were tainted, and I couldn't wait to make new ones. "I was just thinking about our kids running in those fields."

He'd asked, so I was honest. It might have been too soon, but I'd known Austin my entire life. Starting over still had history.

"Mmm. Three or four of them. You might talk me into five if you play your cards right."

I couldn't tell by his tone if he was joking, and when I tried to spin in his arms, he held me in place. It took a bit of effort to crane my neck into a position where I could see his face, but it was always worth the reward. "For real?"

Now Austin chose to turn me around. He grasped my waist and lifted me onto the kitchen counter. My legs spread to allow room for his hips between my thighs, and he leaned onto the counter, caging me in with coiled muscles.

"I want as many as you'll give me." The intensity and sincerity of his statement hit me hard.

I wrapped my legs around his waist and draped my arms over his shoulders, drawing him impossibly close. "We'd make beautiful babies." And somehow, that notion pushed out all the fears I'd had over coming back. Maybe because it was permanent.

"Give me the green light, and I'll do my best to make it happen." If it were possible for a man to impregnate a woman with a look, my ovaries would have just exploded, and Austin Burin would have a child on the way.

While I wasn't in a hurry to be barefoot and pregnant, I did have an issue that had to be dealt with before Austin and I could start our lives with any semblance of peace. I kissed the tip of his nose. "How about when I get back, we can start practicing?"

He helped me off the counter and walked me to the door. I held out my hand and waited.

"What?"

I wiggled my fingers. "Keys. I'm not going to walk to Cross Acres."

Austin dug into his pocket and pulled out the set to the rental car. He had to be kidding. I'd spent the better part of seven days in that thing. "What?" he asked.

"The other ones."

He adjusted the baseball hat on his head. Bless his heart, he didn't want me to drive it, yet he wouldn't tell me no. "You want to take the truck?"

"Yep. Hand 'em over."

Austin produced the other set from a hook by the door. "Please be careful." The man acted like I'd never driven a dually before.

I lifted onto my tiptoes and pecked his lips with far more levity than I currently felt. "Promise." I turned to walk out the door, and he grabbed my wrist.

His fingers slid to mine, and once again, he brought me flush with him. "I love you, Randi."

"I love you, too. I'll be back soon."

For all his bravado and certainty regarding Daddy wanting me to come home, he didn't seem quite as confident when I pulled onto the county road. I waved out the open window and enjoyed the drive. It wasn't more than a few miles from Austin's to the ranch, and when I made the left-hand turn through the iron gates, I listened to the sound of the truck tires on the gravel. Peace washed over me, and I felt lighter than I had in years. It didn't matter what happened after I knocked on Daddy's door. I'd know I tried, and from there, Austin and I would figure it out.

There wouldn't be a need for me to knock. Daddy appeared to have expected me. My eyes went wide seeing my dad sitting in one of two rocking chairs that now adorned the porch. He had two empty glasses and a pitcher of sweet tea on an end table next to him. I pulled into the space Austin always parked and killed the ignition.

Daddy didn't get up when I crossed the driveway, and I wondered how he was holding up. So much had happened here in the last month, and his health had taken quite a beating.

I stuck my hands into my pockets and raised my shoulders. "Hey, Daddy." Each stair proved to be harder than the last. It took a lot of encouragement from Austin to get me here; being rejected by the first man I'd ever loved would be crushing.

"Hey, sugar." The term of endearment flowed from his mouth to my heart. "You and Austin have fun on your trip?" It took him longer to gain his balance when he stood. It was hard to see the toll the years and wildfire had taken.

My gaze found a spot on the ground near my father's feet, and I kicked my foot out and made contact with a pebble from the driveway that had hitched a ride on someone's boot to the porch. "Yes, sir." I felt like a child, uncertain of what to say or do.

For the first time in so long, I couldn't recall just how many years it had been, Daddy stepped up. His chin quivered before he gave me a long-overdue hug. Old Spice and hay were like coming home.

I took the second chair and the glass of tea Daddy poured. Under the shade of the porch, the sun didn't burn quite as hot, but the heat was still unbearable. It would take time to get used to it again. I figured I'd have to start this discussion, and I would, right after I enjoyed the solitude country living provided. I'd never appreciated it as a kid; now I wondered how I'd survived the bustle of the city.

"I'm glad you're home." The sudden conversation and the topic at hand weren't what I'd anticipated hearing.

Daddy was set in his ways. I'd never witnessed him apologizing; although, prior to the exchange in my room after Sarah's accident, I couldn't recall a time he'd ever needed to. It would be optimistic to think I might be the recipient of the first one Jack Adams ever uttered.

I didn't meet his eyes and continued to stare off into the distance. "It's good to be back." I had other emotions vying for top billing on my list. As much as I'd love to rock until the sun set and talk to my dad the way I had when Mama was here, today wasn't the day. "I quit my job in New York."

"I know." He sounded pleased with that decision, but if I weren't willing to look at him, there was no way to verify it.

There wasn't any point in tiptoeing around the elephant on the porch. "Are things going to be hard for you if I'm around?"

"No."

I sighed and set my glass on the table. I'd faced Austin Burin—nothing could be as terrifying as that. And honestly, my frustration with my dad had reached a point where it had to be addressed. "We've got to talk about what happened."

"No, *we* don't."

The bubbling anger served no purpose. If Daddy didn't think we needed to iron things out, I wouldn't force it. Mason Belle was a small town, but I didn't have to step foot on Cross Acres if that was how he chose for things to be.

"*I* do," he said.

I whipped my head so fast, my hair slapped my cheek. Unsure of what I'd heard, for once in my life, I shut my mouth and listened.

"I ain't gonna make excuses for what happened, Randi. I ain't got none." Daddy stared at a blank spot in the sky that had kept my attention since I sat down. "All I can tell ya is that fear changes people. My anger shoulda been taken out on the only person there was to blame. Me."

Daddy did everything at a pace that would drive a nun to

drink. He walked slow, talked slow, and thought slow. It was why the argument we'd had in my room had blindsided me. I'd never heard him say anything he regretted because he'd always milled it over a hundred times before it ever left his mouth.

He placed his cowboy hat on his knee and ran his hand through what was left of his sweaty hair. I hadn't noticed how much of it he'd lost in the time I'd been gone. "Sarah shouldn't have been dolin' out punishment; she ain't your mama. But I didn't know how to be that and your father." Daddy rolled his neck and rested his cheek on the back of the chair. "You both deserved better."

We had, but Daddy had tried to do right by us and give us a loving home. He couldn't help that his wife left him alone with two girls he didn't know how to raise.

"Your mama didn't leave 'cause of you. She hated ranchin', and I never shoulda married her."

That wasn't new information. "Then why'd you tell me she had?"

"You remind me so mucha her when she was your age. I didn't think you'd ever be happy livin' this life for the long haul." He shook his head as if he still couldn't believe the things he'd said years ago. "But truth is, I lashed out. The older you got, the more you became just like her. And at the time, I needed to believe if she'd been here, Sarah wouldn't have been laid up like that. Anger toward her spilled over to you."

It might have made sense in his mind; it didn't in mine.

Daddy reached out and covered my hand with his. I stared at his weathered and wrinkled skin, resting on top of mine, and a chill ran up my spine. I'd never been afraid of my father, and now, I wasn't comfortable with even a simple touch.

He must have recognized my discomfort since he didn't read minds. "Never shoulda led to you, touched you, or called you names. And, sugar, I'll carry the weight of that guilt to the grave."

Sitting on this porch managed to suck the serenity I'd clung to for seven days right out of me. If Austin weren't down the road, I couldn't promise that I wouldn't climb into his truck and drive until I ran out of gas.

"But, I gotta come clean. Your sister never wanted you gone. That fell on me. I was mad as fire, and I couldn't fix nothin', so I broke everything. It don't make no sense. I know that. All I can tell ya is I messed up. And I kept messin' up not callin'. I shoulda dragged you home. Then each sun that set made doin' it harder."

It wasn't much of an explanation, but I doubted I'd get anything different. "So, why now?"

He met my eyes, and I held my breath, waiting for his answer. "When I needed you, nothin' stopped ya from gettin' on a plane, not even six stubborn years of silence on my part. And once I saw you again, I had to figure out how to get ya to stay." That was the most honest thing I'd ever have to reconcile my emotions and my past with.

"So, you gave Austin the ranch." It was a statement of confirmation, not a question that required an answer.

"He's a good man, Randi. And he deserves a good woman. Ain't a day gone by that boy hasn't loved you. I saw it in his eyes when y'all were kids. Ain't nothin' changed, and it ain't gonna. All it took was one crack in his wall for your light to shine through, and I knew you'd win him back all on your own. The ranch was for you. I just needed Austin to give it to you."

A lump had long since formed in my throat, and my eyes burned with the threat of tears. I wasn't dumb enough to believe one conversation fixed everything that was wrong between Daddy and me, but it was enough to be certain that I'd be welcome at home. If Jack Adams stood at my side, Mason Belle would open its arms...eventually.

It wouldn't be flowers and chocolate, but I could count on cows and manure.

18

AUSTIN

*T*here'd never been a day in all the years I'd been coming to Cross Acres that I'd dreaded it. Even when Randi had shown up unexpectedly, it was never the ranch I didn't want to be near. For years, this place had been my solace. Today, however, I had to have a conversation I wasn't keen on having with a man I'd respected my entire life. Not even the sound of the gravel under my tires soothed the ache in my chest.

I'd debated on whether or not to go straight to the farmhouse or get the guys out working before I pulled Jack aside. I'd opted for the second. If there were a scene, no one needed to be around to witness it. I didn't care if Jack had deeded the ranch over to me; this was still his home, and these men respected him.

It had taken me a little over an hour to get everyone out of earshot, and once I had, I climbed the steps to the front porch. At a little after six, there was no doubt in my mind Jack was awake—it was in his blood. He'd get up when the rooster crowed for the rest of his life. It helped that the kitchen light lit up the front window. I knocked before I turned the handle and walked inside. Jack wasn't into formalities, and we were too close to need them.

"Jack?"

He coughed, and the sounds of smoke damage rattled his lungs. "In here."

My heart pounded beneath my sternum, and my hands shook so badly I had to stuff them into my pockets. I wasn't certain whether my body was reacting to fear or adrenaline, but either way, I couldn't let this go.

With only a few feet between the foyer and the kitchen, it didn't take long for me to come face to face with Jack. He pointed to the percolator on the stove, and I took him up on the offer. If nothing else, the mug would occupy my jittery hands. I'd done this more times than I could count, but it was different today. And when I turned around, I realized Jack knew it, too.

I didn't take the stool next to him. I opted to lean against the counter next to the stove. Distance was safer for both of us.

Jack sipped his coffee as steam wafted from the cup. When he set it down, he met my stare. "I'm surprised you didn't come with Randi yesterday."

I set my untouched mug on the counter and crossed my arms over my chest. Taking a defensive posture didn't help the situation, but it made me feel better. My biceps flexed, and my jaw ticced while I counted to ten to quiet the cadence in my chest. "The two of you needed to do that on your own."

He slowly nodded. Jack took his time formulating words. "We did." His tired eyes searched my face, and he swallowed hard. His Adam's apple took a slow trip down his neck and back up before he spoke again. "Thank you."

It was hard to be mad at a man who appeared so downtrodden. It seemed every day brought a new wrinkle to his weathered skin, and he moved a bit slower when he walked. But I was angry. I was irate. "You stole her from me, Jack."

He held my eyes and bobbed his head in acknowledgment.

"And as much as that pisses me off, it's not even the worst of what I learned."

"I don't have an excuse, Austin."

My chest rose with the deep breath I inhaled and fell when I released it. "You had no right to touch her. I don't care if she's your daughter. Never, in a million years, would I have believed you'd lay a hand on her."

His eyes painted a picture of regret and heartache. Jack didn't have to spell it out with words. He'd been punished for six years for that mistake. Unfortunately, the rest of us had too, and Randi paid the biggest price.

There wasn't any point in dragging this out. I came here to say one thing. "I'm only going to say this once, Jack. This isn't a warning. It is absolutely the promise of a threat. If you ever so much as raise a finger to Randi again, there won't be anything left of you for police to find. I never should have left her alone with you that day, but I can't take that back. What I can do is assure you I'll never make that mistake again. I will protect her with my life... even against you."

Not once did Jack look away. He didn't flinch or even so much as bat an eyelash. "Understood."

I rolled my lips between my teeth and released them to utter my final thought. "You've got a mess to clean up in Mason Belle. This town believes she left on her own not knowing what would happen with Sarah. People think she abandoned her family when they needed her most. And because of that, there haven't been many arms opening in her direction."

"I'll make it right, son."

I believed him. It calmed me a little, but I wouldn't be able to breathe easy around him until Randi could walk the sidewalks of Mason Belle and be greeted with warm smiles. Once Jack started to make amends, word would travel fast. The women in this little town loved gossip more than biscuits, and this would be juicy. I just hoped they forgave Randi as quickly as I knew they would Jack.

*M*y phone rang for the fourth time since I'd left for work this morning. I couldn't stop the smile that spread across my face seeing Randi's name flash across my screen. Her calls came at inconvenient times, but damn if it didn't make my day.

I slid my hand from the glove I was wearing to swipe my finger across the screen. "Hey, sweetheart."

"What are you doing?" The boredom in her voice was palpable, and it caused me to snicker when I responded.

"I'm working. The same thing I was doing the other three times you called."

"Oh... I'm sorry. I'll let you go."

I tucked the phone between my shoulder and my ear so I could talk to her and at least make it appear like I was working to anyone who might see me. "Everything okay?"

"Yeah, I'm just bored."

We'd had this conversation several times in the last few days. "Why don't you get out of the house? Go into town. If nothing else, go grocery shopping."

She was afraid of the reactions she'd get without me, Sarah, or Jack at her side. No one could quiet those fears. Randi would have to take the plunge at some point. "I'll wait for you to get home."

"Sweetheart, it's only noon. I won't be home for several hours." I knew she hated ranching—or manual labor—but it was all I had to offer her that was under the umbrella of my safety. The safety she believed she had to have to face Mason Belle. "Wanna come out to the ranch and help me? I'm trying to round up cattle to take to auction in a couple days. You could get some time in with Nugget." It was low to use her horse against her.

"You'd let me ride him?"

A rumble started in my chest, and my shoulders shook as it

erupted from my mouth. "Of course. He's your horse. I've just been keeping him company." We hadn't talked about the palomino since she'd first arrived back in Mason Belle, but he'd always been hers.

Hesitation held the other end of the line. The only thing indicating she was still there was the shallow breaths I heard whispered across the speaker. "Daddy won't mind?"

It tore me up to see Randi this way. There was no doubt it would take some time for her to feel confident in this town again, but each time I saw a hint of her insecurity it shredded me. "Nah. We're going to disguise it as work. So I'll see you in a bit?"

"Okay." Her tone had changed. Happiness carried that one word across space and time to my ear—I'd do anything to keep her this way. "I'll be there soon."

I probably should have been concerned when Randi showed up approximately three minutes later. Seeing her pull in, driving my old Ford, caused excitement I didn't need to experience at work. There was nothing sexier than Miranda Adams behind the wheel of a truck that made her appear tiny. That was, until she stepped out. I stood corrected. There was nothing sexier than Miranda Adams in a tight, white tank top, jeans that fit like a second skin, and cowboy boots that added three extra inches to her petite frame.

Jesus.

She was gorgeous.

My heart sputtered, my breath hitched, and when Brock clapped me on the back—hard—I nearly choked on my own saliva. God, I needed to make her legally mine before anyone else tried to steal her away.

Brock's voice was not what I wanted to hear, interrupting my perverse thoughts of what I could do to Randi out in a field or hidden away in the barn. "Your girl's here."

"No shit? I didn't see her pull up." I rolled my eyes, but with him behind me, it was in vain.

"Really? Dude, you're staring right at her."

I glanced over my shoulder, uncertain how he could possibly be so daft, only to find him grinning like a jackass. "Don't you have something to do?"

"Yeah. Corey and I are riding the perimeter. Just wanted to see if you needed anything before we took off."

It was going to take a lot of work to fix the damage the fires had done and time for the land to regenerate vegetation. Selling off part of the herd would eliminate some of the immediate burden; unfortunately, Jack and I had decided to sell off more than we'd originally discussed. Without any real cash flow, we couldn't fix fences, we couldn't get the insurance back in place, and we couldn't continue the medical care for the herd. Not to mention, regardless of who now owned the ranch, Jack still had to be taken care of.

With my sights set on the woman I'd loved since I was ten, I answered Brock. "Nah. Randi and I are going to head out to pull cattle in." I didn't have to tell him we were going in search of those that would bring the highest bids; he knew.

If Brock had said anything else, I didn't hear it. The sight of Randi waltzing in my direction blinded me, and the sound of gravel under her feet muted all other noise. The sway of her hips, the bounce of her hair, and the swell of her breasts had me para-lyzed. I'd waited years to hear the grit of the rocks accompanied by the girl who'd always made them music to my ears. My heart was so full, I wondered if it might explode. And just as she reached me, it nearly did.

Randi leaned in, pressing her lips to mine. It wasn't deep or passionate, but it was familiar and intimate. Casual and confident. "Hey," she cooed against my mouth.

I tilted my forehead to hers briefly. "Hey yourself." With

another quick peck, I pulled back and took her hand. I'd waited six years for this, and having her with me now made every painful day worthwhile.

She followed me without question or hesitation as I led her to the barn. Most of the horses were either working or turned out in the fields to graze, but there were always a few kept in the stables. Thankfully, Nugget was nearby, as was Midnight.

With her hand still tucked in mine, we stopped at the tack, and I turned to her. She was so freaking beautiful. There was innocence and wonder twinkling in her eyes, and her pouty lips deepened into a crimson hue that Cover Girl should market. "You remember how to saddle a horse?"

Her brows arched, creating subtle lines on her forehead. It took her less than a second to roll her eyes and drop my hand. "Really?"

Randi's question was rhetorical, so I didn't bother to answer, and instead, I just winked. Time had changed a lot, but it hadn't touched my effect on Randi. If I had to guess, I'd bet she was just as worked up as I was. When I reached for a bit, I took the opportunity to adjust myself, so I didn't end up embarrassed in front of the guys who worked under me. They could imagine what I did with Randi at home if they wanted to, but I'd be damned if I'd give them proof of it.

We worked quietly, saddling both horses. Randi finished before I did, and as much as I wanted to check her work, I refrained. She'd find it insulting, and if there were nothing wrong, then I would have upset her for nothing. The second she put her foot in the stirrup and tried to hoist herself up would be the only proof I'd need. If the saddle didn't spin, she hadn't lost her touch. If it did, at worst, she'd end up on her butt.

I kept a close eye on her, taking longer than I actually needed to mount Midnight. Thankfully, Randi didn't notice that I lingered, and as soon as she'd swung her leg over Nugget's back successfully, I did the same with Midnight. Neither Randi nor I made a sound. We fell back into a rhythm that had existed between us as kids—each knowing, anticipating the other's moves.

Together, we trotted out at a relaxed pace that wouldn't tire the horses, and it gave me a chance to toss out something I hoped she'd consider. "Have you thought about what you want to do with your time? I know you're bored sitting at home."

Randi and I hadn't thought about what she would do in Mason Belle when I uprooted her from New York. She was so concerned with the reception she'd receive that it never crossed her mind that a paralegal didn't have many career options in Tiny Town, Texas. And I'd been so intent on getting her home, that it never occurred to me she'd be bored. I made decent money. Even with the ranch in a bit of turmoil, my salary wasn't in jeopardy. So, she didn't need to work, but I couldn't chance what had happened with her mom repeating itself in Randi.

"Not much I *can* do. You know as well as I do that jobs don't open up in Mason Belle." She kept her line of sight straight ahead, though I would have had to be deaf to miss the air of disappointment in her voice.

Randi held the reins in one hand and tucked a stray strand of hair behind her ear. I'd always loved watching her delicate fingers try to tame her unruly locks. I admired the way she almost became one with the horse. It was hard to believe it had been so many years since she'd been in a saddle.

"What if I had a job for you?"

She pulled back on the reins, bringing Nugget to a halt as Midnight and I strolled by her. "Austin!" Randi called after me when I didn't stop. "What are you talking about?" She clicked her tongue and was by my side seconds later, in line with Midnight.

"You could work with me...at Cross Acres." I turned my head just in time to see her shoulders slump and her spine round.

"I can't escape it, can I?" She shook her head. It was as if she were talking to herself more than to me. "It's what I'm destined to do here. Get up at four thirty. Shovel crap. Feed horses. Bake in the sun." Randi was always so quick to jump the gun, assuming the worst-case scenario.

I chuckled beside her and got her attention. The scowl she offered me was cute, although I was certain she hadn't meant it to be. "I don't mean *with me*, with me." I took a deep breath. I needed her help with this, but I worried she'd shut it down just because it was attached to the ranch. "I have no idea what kind of shape the books and the paperwork are in. We need to get the insurance reinstated, sooner rather than later. I need help with the business side of the auctions. Someone needs to keep up with and pay the bills and payroll. Jack has always kept meticulous logs on the herd—those haven't been maintained since the fires, although I do have the records. It's a lot of work, and no one on staff has the time to do it."

I'd rambled while she hadn't said a word. There was no indication by her facial expression whether she thought I was a loon or that there might be some possibility this could work.

It seemed best to keep talking. "It wouldn't pay much, at least not until we get back into the black, but we don't need the money at home. And you could set your own hours—work from home or at the ranch. We could set up an office in the house. If you wanted—"

"Okay." Randi's brown eyes met mine and tears shimmered, threatening to fall.

I wanted to grab her, to pull her to my chest. "Sweetheart, if you don't want to work here, you don't have to. It was just a suggestion." Being on top of a horse didn't make consoling her terribly easy.

She blinked, and the tears streamed down her cheeks just before a hint of a smile tugged on the corners of her mouth. "It's perfect. I don't know how you managed to come up with something I might actually enjoy that would contribute to the well-being of Cross Acres, but I love you for it."

It had been a long road, and mostly unpaved...but somehow, the dust that gravel had kicked up hadn't managed to blind us to the truth of where our destiny lay.

And it would always be with each other.

EPILOGUE

Jack—Five years later

I threw the truck in park, glanced at the clock, and then jumped out, slamming the door behind me. It had been over an hour since I'd gotten the call, and I hadn't been able to reach Austin since. My feet refused to carry me as fast as I wanted them to move, and the second I made it inside the emergency room, I came to a halt. A flood of memories hit me, and they weren't the good kind.

The last time I'd stood in this room, I was blind with rage. It was also the day Austin became a man, and I lost my little girl to the person who owned her heart. It took guts for him to step in front of her that day. Almost as much as it took for him to confront me when he got back from New York. I'd hoped that day would never come, but I prayed for it all the same. In order to atone for a sin, I had to confess it...and then deal with the punishment. Austin had made damn certain I understood that if I ever raised a hand to Randi again, there wouldn't be a hound in the world who'd sniff out my remains. I believed it. Thankfully, time healed most wounds.

I cut loose the memories to focus on the present and found the nurses' station unoccupied. There wasn't a bell to ring to get anyone's attention, and I didn't want to be rude by screaming over the counter, hoping someone heard my call. It wasn't likely Randi was in the emergency room anyhow; I just didn't know where the maternity ward was located since none of Sarah's kids had been born here. The elevators to my right caught my eye, and I decided it was a better option than waiting.

It didn't take long for me to get directions from a nurse on the second floor. When I made it to the sixth, I expected far greater fanfare than what I walked into. No one other than me appeared to be in much of a hurry.

The nurse was quite pretty and older than most. The silver in her hair hinted at her age, as did the crow's feet caused by years of smiles. "How can I help you, sir?" Her warm voice instantly calmed my hurried fear.

"I...um." I cleared the frog from my throat and started again. "I'm lookin' for my daughter, Miranda Burin."

The lady's eyes sparkled at the sound of Randi's name, and a subtle smile rose on her pink lips. "She's got her hands full. I'm sure she'll be glad to see you."

It hadn't occurred to me when Sarah called that they had all four kids with them. At ten, the twins could either be a tornado or a huge help. Rand worshipped the ground Randi walked on, but he and Wyatt butted heads. Nine-year-old boys didn't want to play with three-year-olds. Add to that that Wyatt stole Randi's attention from Rand and it often caused a ruckus only Austin and Randi were able to manage. I had no idea how either boy would take the newest addition to the family. "Can you tell me what room she's in?"

"I'll do you one better. How about I walk you down there? I'm going in that direction anyhow."

Another time and another place, I might have been swayed to

try to catch the nurse's attention. Not that I had any idea how to court a lady at my age. "Thank you."

Turned out we didn't have far to go, and had I just listened for the sounds of bickering, I could have found the Burin clan all on my own. I didn't bother knocking since I was certain no one would hear me.

Randi occupied the bed with Wyatt curled up on her side with his thumb in his mouth, the twins were arguing with Rand, although I couldn't tell what about. And the wrinkles across Sarah's brow indicated her frustration.

"Hey, Daddy." Sarah's shoulders relaxed the second she saw me, and the kids all stopped talking long enough to turn around.

Thankfully, hugging me was more important than whatever debate they'd been involved in. The only grandchild who hadn't wrapped themselves around me was Wyatt. He was a mama's boy through and through.

"Where's Austin?" Randi wasn't panicked yet, which meant we still had time to find him.

I scratched my head and scrunched the side of my face. "I'm not sure."

My youngest daughter sat straight up, jostling the little boy at her side. "What do you mean?" Randi hadn't freaked out, but it would come quickly. She didn't do anything without Austin at her side, and I was quite certain she wouldn't want to welcome their second child into the world alone.

"I tried to reach him, but you know how signals are out in the fields, Randi—"

"You left without telling my husband I'm in labor?" When she put it that way, it sounded kind of selfish.

I tried to keep my tone level. "Corey rode out to get him. He'll be here, Miranda. Calm down." I didn't mention that I'd continued to call the entire drive here and kept getting his voice-mail. I trusted Corey to get Austin here. "How far along are ya?"

Both of my daughters stared at me like I'd sprouted a second head. They seemed to have forgotten I was around when both of them entered the world, along with four grandchildren, and countless numbers of livestock. This wasn't my first rodeo, and I doubted with the way Austin and Randi couldn't keep their hands off each other that it would be my last.

Randi leaned against the pillows and welcomed Wyatt back into her embrace. "Six centimeters the last time the nurse checked. But that was over an hour ago."

"The contractions bad?" It was hard to talk over the noise Sarah's kids made.

Randi shrugged and glanced down at her son. The grimace on her lips told me it was worse than she let on, but I didn't think she wanted to scare Wyatt. "I'm okay. I just wish Austin was here."

As if her mentioning his name conjured him up out of thin air, the hospital room door burst open with such force I worried it would slam into the wall. "I'm here." He was out of breath, but he'd made it just the same.

He bypassed his nieces, nephew, sister-in-law, and me to go straight to his wife. Austin always made sure Randi got his attention first—that would never change. Regardless of how many children she gave him, he simply couldn't exist without her. No sooner had he kissed her forehead than he scooped Wyatt up and requested an update.

Austin was a good man. Far better one than I'd ever been. Over the years, he'd accomplished more with Cross Acres than I'd ever been able to. He'd done what had to be done to get the ranch healthy after the fires, he'd wooed and tamed Randi, he'd given me a home with a complete family, but most of all, he'd shown me grace and forgiveness. Watching him with Randi—Wyatt perched on his shoulders—I realized just how blessed I was. With the exception of Charlie, every person I loved in life now stood in this room. And as rowdy as they were, they were mine. I wouldn't trade a one of them.

"All right, everybody." Austin broke through my thoughts as he tried to rally the herd. "Y'all need to find something else to do until the baby gets here." He lifted Wyatt and set him on the floor. "You go with Sarah. Next time I see you, you'll be a big brother." His voice was as singsong as he could make it.

Wyatt wasn't buying any of it. Crocodile tears welled in his big, brown eyes. He kept his thumb in his mouth, and before he could refuse, I grabbed him. He was the only one I could still pick up, and I loved to tickle him. His laugh was just as infectious as his mama's. It was music to an old man's ears.

"I'll take ya down to the cafeteria to see if we can find some ice cream. How's that sound, Wyatt?"

He giggled, unable to do anything more with my fingers dancing on his sides. Sarah and her kids exited the room first. Sarah promised her sister she'd be just down the hall if she needed anything.

With my free hand, I gave Wyatt a reprieve from the tickle monster and clapped Austin on the shoulder. "Take care of my little girl."

"Always." Austin responded the same way every time I said it. There wasn't a fiber in my being that didn't believe him, either.

It was hard to let the door close behind us, but I followed after Sarah. Unable to carry Wyatt for any great length of time, I set him down and took his hand. "You hoping for a brother or a sister?" I asked him.

Wyatt pulled his thumb out of his mouth long enough to answer. "Neither. I don't want one."

"Nonsense. You'll be a great big brother."

With his thumb back in his mouth, he glared up at me. A smile erupted on my lips. I didn't envy Austin and Randi having to deal with this. This kid was severely unhappy about an addition to their family.

When we reached the cafeteria, our choices were limited. I did manage to find him a cup of chocolate ice cream, and together with Sarah and her kids, we waited it out. I wasn't sure which one of us checked our phone more often, but when the text we were waiting on came through, it took monumental effort not to run through the hospital, back to Randi's room.

The newest member of the Burin family had arrived, and none of us could wait to meet the baby—except Wyatt. And of course, he was the one who would get the honor first. I knocked on the door to her room. Austin opened it enough to come out, but not enough for any of us to get a glimpse or even a hint at whether it was a boy or a girl.

Austin squatted in front of Wyatt, meeting his son at eye level. "You ready, buddy?"

Wyatt bounced from foot to foot. He wanted his mama, but to get her, he had to get a sibling, too. I chuckled to myself when he finally reached out to take his daddy's hand. The two of them disappeared, and the door closed again.

I leaned against the wall. Sarah and her kids hung out in the hall with me. They'd quieted down, but I think it was the crash after a sugar rush and not that they'd actually mellowed out.

"Daddy, how long do you think it's going to be before they let us in?" Sarah was more excited about this baby than Randi, and that said a lot. "This is so silly. Wyatt doesn't even care about meeting his brother or sister. And what's with them not finding out the sex of their children before they're born? It's like torture for the rest of us."

My chest rumbled with the laugh that formed. "Sugar, they do things their way. They always have. Ain't nothing you say gonna change that."

Sarah crossed her arms and let out a little humph. "I'm going to go call Charlie."

"Why don't you call Austin and Randi's friends, too? Brock and Charity first. I'm sure they'd like them to know." Thank God Randi had managed to mend the fences I'd torn down in her life. Charity had been the hardest and the longest one to heal, but once she came around, those two had been thick as thieves, just like in high school.

"And tell them what?" she scoffed. Her hands moved wildly as she spoke. "There's a baby here, but I can't say whether it's a boy or girl. Do I know how much it weighs? Oh no, don't have that information, either. How long was the child? Not a clue. I can't even tell you if it has all its fingers or toes because my sister won't let anyone else in the room." She threw her arms in the air, exasperated.

I raised my brows and stared at her.

She shooed me off with the wave of her hand. "Fine... I'll go call them." Sarah looked down at her three kids sitting on the floor. "Come on, guys."

And then it was just me. Alone in the hallway. Nurses passed by. Doctors appeared randomly. But all in all, the floor was rather quiet. When the door to Randi's room finally opened, it wasn't Austin who invited me in...it was Wyatt.

"Hey, Papa." His smile was bright, and his eyes danced with excitement. They glittered the way Randi's did as a little girl. "Wanna meet my sister?" Gone was the unhappy child who didn't want to share his home or his parents.

A lump formed in my throat that I struggled to swallow around. Tears threatened to fall. Joy was one of the strangest emotions. "You have a little sister?"

He puffed his tiny chest out with pride. "Yep. Her name's Winnie."

OPERATION BUILD A BAG

WWW.OPERATIONBUILDABAG.COM

In the midst of writing *Gravel Road,* a guy I'd followed on Instagram for quite some time posted a picture of himself that screamed "Austin."

On a whim, I reached out to him and asked if he'd be interested in doing a shoot for my cover, and the rest of that is history. But there's more to Steve Kalfman than just a pretty face. He's a First Lieutenant in the United States Army, a devoted father to a beautiful little girl, and has a heart for the homeless.

He, along with other veterans, founded a non-profit organization dedicated to combating one of our nation's biggest problems, homelessness. Operation Build A Bag is in its early stages, but together, this group of veterans has committed to delivering bags of necessities to homeless men, women, and children, and eventually, they hope to spread their project nationwide.

You can make a donation and see what they're all about at www.operationbuildabag.com. Each bag is filled with basic necessities to get people through some of the toughest elements out there. I ask you to consider making a donation of *ANY* amount to help further their cause.

322 | *Operation Build A Bag*

Operation Build A Bag Donations
Operation Build A Bag on Instagram
Steve Kalfman on Instagram

ACKNOWLEDGMENTS

On my way to the Asheville airport at o-dark-thirty, a Lee Brice song, "That Don't Sound Like You" came on the radio. The moment I heard the chorus, I had to pull over and download the song. I listened to it on repeat the remainder of the drive, and as soon as I got to my gate, I pulled out my computer. Austin and Randi's story began to pour onto the screen, and the more I wrote, the more I loved them. So while I'm quite certain Lee Brice will never see this note of thanks, his song inspired this story. Thanks Lee!

As with every story an author puts out, there are countless people who help make it happen. *Gravel Road* is no different.

Leddy. Good Day. #GFY. For reals though, you're the bestest wobbie a girl could ever have. Thank God for you, otherwise 2018 would have completely sucked donkey balls.

Linda—I've lost count of how many releases you've been through with me, but I'm fairly certain this makes ten. Double digits and all that jazz. Your endless support and countless hours of work behind the scenes are priceless. Thank you for all you do!

Angela—You keep me entertained and one step away from the edge of the cliff.

Kristie—without entire conversations in GIFs my world would be bleak. #bestie

Carina—My cheerleader.

Steve Kalfman—Thank you for being open to a new idea. You made this process so easy and seamless. It's been a pleasure working with you.

And finally, M. Your pride in me makes me want to be the best I can be. I love your sensitive heart and your gentle spirit. I couldn't have asked for a better daughter. I love you more.

ABOUT THE AUTHOR

Stephie is a forty-year-old mother to one of the feistiest preteens to ever walk. They live on the outskirts of Greenville, South Carolina, where they house three cats and two dogs in their veritable zoo.

She has a serious addiction to anything Coach and would live on Starbucks if she could get away with it. She's slightly enamored with Charlie Hunnam and Sons of Anarchy and is a self-proclaimed foodie.

facebook.com/stephiewalls2014

twitter.com/stephiewalls

instagram.com/stephiewalls

amazon.com/author/stephiewalls

bookbub.com/authors/stephie-walls

goodreads.com/StephieWalls

ALSO BY STEPHIE WALLS

Bound

Freed

Redemption

Metamorphosis

Compass

Strangers

chimera

Beauty Mark

Fallen Woman

Girl Crush

Unexpected Arrivals

Label Me Proud

Family Ties

CO-WRITTEN AS STELLA WITH LEDDY HARPER

Third Base

Home Run King

Dr. Fellatio

Made in the USA
San Bernardino, CA
18 October 2018